LARGE PRINT

Fic

Jen   Jennings

             Caught in The Middle
             34981

FEB 03 2015

FEB 26 2015

NOV 22 2016

CAUGHT IN THE MIDDLE

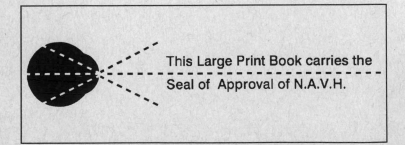

This Large Print Book carries the
Seal of Approval of N.A.V.H.

CAUGHT IN THE MIDDLE

REGINA JENNINGS

THORNDIKE PRESS
A part of Gale, Cengage Learning

GALE
CENGAGE Learning·

Farmington Hills, Mich • San Francisco • New York • Waterville, Maine
Meriden, Conn • Mason, Ohio • Chicago

GALE
CENGAGE Learning®

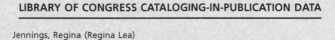

LIBRARY OF CONGRESS CATALOGING-IN-PUBLICATION DATA

Jennings, Regina (Regina Lea)
    Caught in the middle / by Regina Jennings. — Large print edition.
      pages ; cm. — (Thorndike Press large print Christian historical fiction)
    ISBN 978-1-4104-7031-7 (hardcover) — ISBN 1-4104-7031-8 (hardcover)
    1. Abandoned children—Fiction. 2. Texas—History—19th century—Fiction.
    3. Large type books. I. Title.
    PS3610.E5614C38 2014b
    813'.6—dc23   2014010295

Published in 2014 by arrangement with Bethany House Publishers, a division of Baker Publishing Group

Printed in Mexico
1 2 3 4 5 6 7 18 17 16 15 14

To my husband Coy

Brave enough to buy a Harley without
permission . . .
Charming enough to get away with it.

1

Pushmataha, Indian Territory
September 1883

The serving line hadn't moved an inch, and the mood of the men in the depot diner was growing ugly. Nicholas Lovelace rapped the flimsy tin plate against his knuckles and took a deep breath. No warm scents of meat and potatoes. No bread baking that he could detect. If dinner wasn't simmering, he might as well get back on the train. No point in crowding around the kitchen door with the lumberjacks, the Indians, and the hunters voicing their complaints.

The plate clattered on the roughhewn table as Nick abandoned the depot. His stomach gnawed at his ribs, telling him that the roll and coffee from the last station had burned away hours ago. Could he wait for supper at the hotel in Garber where he was staying?

He'd rather not. His only hope for nourishment this side of the Red River was the ramshackle general store. Otherwise he wouldn't live long enough to prepare Mr. Stanford's report, which would be a pity. He'd so anticipated the praise it would bring.

Nicholas's crew was performing ahead of schedule — clearing the timber from the railroad's future path, shipping it to the mill, processing it into ties and trestles, and shipping it back to the railhead. He had ridden the train as far as the track would carry him, and his men toiled a good three miles further still — a nice lead, but no more than he expected.

And no more than Ian Stanford expected. Mr. Stanford had contributed more to the success of Lovelace Transportation Specialists than anyone outside of Nick himself. In fact, every merchant, every trapper, hunter, and farmer along the twin rails owed Mr. Stanford — and Nicholas was blessed to call him his mentor. Stanford had taught him much, but now Nick wanted to expand. Upon his return to Garber, Texas, Nicholas would begin seeking contracts with other railroads. It was time to grow.

Even with eyes closed, he could tell by the hot fumes that he was standing on the train platform. The black engine shimmered under the relentless sun, but it didn't shirk. It would continue its quest, plowing through the prairies, unstoppable, proving that God-approved ambition could conquer any obstacle.

"Nicholas" — Miss Susan Walcher's head emerged from a train window — "when will we leave this dreadful place? I'm nearly asphyxiated."

"I heard your father warn you." As an investor of the NTT Railroad, her father handed out warnings aplenty, but only his connection with Ian Stanford could've forced Nick to endure hours of her complaining. "The Indian Territory line isn't luxurious. There are no Pullman cars here."

"But I'm famished. Didn't the station house offer any refreshments?"

"I stood in line for a quarter of an hour and saw nary a one. Perhaps you'd like to serve up something?"

She crinkled her nose at him to the delight of her companions. With shrieks they pulled her inside the suffocating car amid a flurry of fans.

Rather than being stuck inside an airless car with the daughters of railroad investors, Nicholas would see what Pushmataha had to offer. Besides the piles of buffalo hides awaiting the eastbound train and the hastily constructed depot, the dusty general store was his only hope for finding something to eat. He needed nourishment if he was to entertain the girls all the way back to Garber.

Rounding the corner of the depot, Nick was struck afresh by the beauty of the vista. The trees still held their summer hues, patches of green spotting the golden prairie. He never tired of surveying the landscape, picking out the smoothest route for the parallel ebony lines to stretch to the unseen population beyond. Even though the tiny water stop of Pushmataha had its connections, Nicholas's fortune was tied to the forests on the hills just east of the railroad. Mr. Stanford's railroad couldn't pass until the trees had been felled and shipped to Nick's sawmill, which, located a convenient distance from town, was the nearest to the new construction. As long as his crew stayed ahead of the railroad, clearing the path and providing the lumber needed, his future was set.

Angry voices reached him as he neared the store — most notably a woman's voice, strong and insistent. Never one to miss out on a spectacle, Nicholas edged his way toward the far side of the building.

"I won't cook. I refuse. You're making a

big mistake."

"Now, Annie," a man said, "simmer down. We're not talking permanent, only until Anoli can get another cook in. You heard how irate those men are. If we want the railroad to stop here and pick up our hides, we have to keep the depot open."

Nicholas stopped at the edge of the building and peeked around the corner. What appeared to be a company of hunters — buffalo, judging from their Sharps rifles — was gathered around the back door of the kitchen. But where was the lady he'd heard?

"I have an idea." The woman, dressed like a man, rapped the butt of her rifle against a filthy boot. "We'll shoot for it. Whoever misses the knothole on the fence over there will stay behind to cook."

When the men turned to squint, Nicholas caught a better glimpse of the speaker. Slight, bristling, and wrapped from her bandanna to her boots in a faded green duster, her rifle was already at her shoulder before the older Indian man could intervene.

"Arguments aren't settled by the skill of a shooter." The leader swatted at the muzzle, throwing her aim off.

"Why not? My skills are more valuable hunting than they are in the kitchen."

11

"But you're a woman," one of the men protested. "It's only natural —"

Nicholas stepped closer, curious what she'd done to silence the hapless man. He'd only known one woman in his life who'd dared to dress like that. Surely his mind was playing tricks on him. Anne Tillerton had been odd, no doubt, but a buffalo hunter in Indian Territory? He could be mistaken, but the soft brown curls peeking out from beneath the hat said otherwise.

The shuffling hunters obscured his view of her face, but the set of her shoulders, visible even beneath the loose duster, further confirmed his suspicions. Anne's name had come up occasionally in conversation with his sister — Molly speculating on whether Anne had found a nice man and raised a family like women ought. From the looks of things, Anne had shunned domesticity since her husband's death.

"What if I find Tessa and bring her back?" She squinted up at the Indian man. "Anything but staying in this crummy depot feeding the rabble while you hunt."

The Indian man nodded. "A reasonable suggestion if you can get your gear together before the train pulls out. And if you can't get Tessa to cook again, hire someone else, but don't be long. We don't want to be poisoned by Fred's cooking while you're in Garber."

"My cooking?" A man threw his hat to the ground. "Why's it gotta be me? I swear you always . . ."

With a silent chuckle Nicholas backed away from the gathering. So the Garber train had picked up a new passenger? Interesting. Now if he could find some jerky in the general store, the ride home might not be so tedious after all.

By the time the whistle blew, Anne Tillerton had stashed her drawstring knapsack in the luggage compartment and found an empty seat in which to spend the next few hours, hopefully undisturbed. She'd left her rifle in Pushmataha in favor of a pistol, hidden beneath her duster. If Tessa had gone in search of that no-account Finn Cravens, she could be staying in a true snake hole. Anne slouched against the bench and pulled her duster together over her curvier parts. If only the buttons would've held. Her vest and bandanna covered her chest, and her smelly boots kept the other passengers from sharing the alcove with her. Usually her disguise effectively protected her from unwarranted attention, but when it failed, misery was sure to follow.

From beneath the brim of her hat Anne watched the performance of a passel of girls seated near the front of the car. With bobbing feathers and squeals of laughter, they were making more noise than a rabbit caught in a trap. One in particular, perched at the edge of her bench, rocked like a canary on a swing, her frequent chirps and flapping hands attesting that a man was no doubt sitting across from her. Anne looked away. Didn't those foolish ladies have any idea the dangerous attention they were attracting?

She removed her hat and laid her head against the glass window. She'd tried to warn Tessa about getting mixed up with Finn, but the stubborn girl wouldn't listen. His intentions were as unhealthy as Tessa's deep-dish cobblers, and for the cook, just as irresistible. They'd all hoped that Finn would do the honorable thing and marry her, but he grew bored of Tessa the same way he grew bored of buffalo hunting and disappeared one night without even a note.

Anne could still picture Tessa's tear-watered face and Anoli's stoic glare. The camp leader had been generous in letting Tessa stay on with an illegitimate child, but his mercy didn't extend to Finn.

"The man had no family to shame," he'd

said, "and can feel no shame for himself."

Anne wormed her finger through the empty buttonhole of her duster. She hadn't any family to shame, either, but she had a code she lived by, even if no one else understood it. She didn't seek rewards for her good deeds from some distant deity. No. That deity had meted out more punishment than anyone should have to bear. However distant He was, it wasn't far enough.

The birdie girl's companion stood. He pushed a final bite of jerky into his mouth and waited for the lady to excuse him. Anne crammed her hat on her head and pulled it down over her thick curls. She shouldn't have sat by the water cooler. If he was looking to stretch his legs, it'd be his logical destination. She flexed her fingers. He had no reason to bother her, but if he did, she'd be ready for him. Before he could turn to face her, her sharpshooter's eyes took in details not important to anyone else, but knowing them gave her a feeling of control.

His height wasn't noteworthy, but his well-tailored suit hugged broad shoulders. The hair brushing his starched collar wasn't quite blond. In the right light it probably showed some red. His manicured hands hung easily at his sides. He was obviously unconcerned that a sudden lurch might

15

shove him into the benches. Although the feathers in the ladies' hats before him bobbed, he stood erect, his posture correct even with the swaying of the train. He probably hadn't spent much time on a horse, but judging from his balance, he could learn.

With a playful bow he ended their conversation and turned in Anne's direction.

Her heart stopped. She knew him. Before she could look away their eyes locked. This was bad. No, this was disastrous.

Anne pulled her hat lower until the band dug into her forehead. She slunk into the seat and tried to disappear into her duster as the man approached. She rolled her shoulder toward the window, giving him only her back. She knew him, but he didn't know her. Surely not. No way in God's green earth he'd remember.

"Excuse me." His tone was friendly, curious. "Have we met before? There's something about you . . ."

Anne forced her face into its fiercest scowl and remembered to gruff her voice. "You're wrong, sir. I'm a stranger here." She turned again to the window, dismayed when the large bulk barely visible from the corner of her eye made no departure.

"Oh?" He stepped into the alcove, took

the seat across from hers and stretched his legs. "You can understand my confusion. I thought my sister's friend, Anne Tillerton, was the only woman in North Texas who dressed like a man."

The courage Anne had mustered fled like field mice when the barn door opened. He must think her a fool. She dared a peek, and met such keen blue eyes that she regretted it immediately.

"We're not in Texas, Mr. Lovelace," she said.

"But we will be shortly." He smiled. "It's kind of you to acknowledge our acquaintance. I wasn't quite sure that we'd ever been properly introduced back in Prairie Lea."

"We most definitely weren't." Anne had enjoyed only a few days of proper society in her life, and those had ended long before she'd been carted to Caldwell County.

"Then allow me to rectify the situation. Nicholas Lovelace, at your service."

Anne narrowed one eye like she was sighting down her rifle, but he didn't appear the least bit discomforted and continued unabashed.

"Now that all the niceties have been observed, what has brought you to Indian Territory, Mrs. Tillerton?"

Anne tugged on the leather thong that laced up the neck of her loose shirt. Her business was her business. Besides, she had her pistol if he made a nuisance of himself. No reason to fear him. "I've been here for a while. What about you?"

"Me? My company provides the lumberjacks and the wooden ties for the railroad. We stay ahead of the line and use the resources from the railroad's own land allotment."

He acted as if she should be impressed. He'd get used to disappointment.

"How's Molly?" she asked.

His head tilted. Those blues twinkled. "My sister is well. She and Bailey are keeping the old sawmill rolling, taking care of Mother and Father, and raising a couple of mischievous progeny. She'll be thrilled when I tell her that you are . . . what exactly did you say you were doing here?"

Anne pursed her lips. Her heart raced at the memories Nicholas Lovelace resurrected. The Lovelaces. The Garners. Prairie Lea. She'd tried to forget that town, but the pain wouldn't fade. She couldn't change the past, but she could avoid rehashing it. Anne straightened her shoulders. How to deal with the prying Mr. Lovelace?

"I'm a buffalo hunter. I hunt with an

outfit in Indian Territory." From the concern on his face, she realized that her bluster wasn't convincing. She hardened her jaw. "It pays well. The freedom is . . . it's important to me."

"A buffalo hunter, you say?" Mr. Lovelace clasped his hands together. "Quite a profitable occupation, so I hear. Our trains carry the hides out by the carload."

Anne unclenched her fist. He hadn't laughed at her. He hadn't tried to persuade her to find a more ladylike pursuit. Perhaps he, like his sister, could be trusted. At least for the duration of the train ride.

"And I bet you bring down your share of the beasts," he continued. "From what I remember, you're a dead aim."

A look of abject horror crossed Mr. Lovelace's face when he realized what he'd said, but it was too late.

The memories burst forward like the bloom of crimson that had stained her husband's vest. Anne sprang to her feet even as Mr. Lovelace reached to detain her. Twisting, she pushed her way past his knees and into the aisle. She made her way blindly to the back, not caring where she was going, not concerned where she'd end up. She only wanted away from him and his awful knowledge.

"Please wait."

But she wasn't listening. She entered a narrow corridor flanked on one side by luggage stacked to the roof. The paneling on her left blurred as she hurried away from the quick footsteps behind her.

"Mrs. Tillerton, please." He grasped her elbow and turned her.

Anne flattened herself against the wall, jerking her arm away in the process. "Don't touch me."

He lifted his hands in the air. "I'm sorry. I just wanted —"

The train lurched. The wheels screeched like a mountain lion as the car teetered.

Anne's head bumped the wall as Mr. Lovelace was flung toward her. He braced himself with outstretched arms on either side of her.

The violent rocking stopped. The screams of the passengers quieted, and Anne was face-to-face with the man. His breath fanned her cheek. His disconcerting eyes were just inches from hers.

"The remark was completely innocent. If you —"

"Step away," Anne ground out between clenched teeth. "You don't know what you're doing."

His eyes held hers as if willing her to calm,

willing her to trust. "You're right about that. I made a dreadful mistake." He pushed away from the wall, another foot or so. "But I'm afraid I have nowhere to go. I can't move."

Anne followed his gaze to the crates that had fallen against the back of his legs. He was holding back a tide of luggage that could crush her.

"If someone would give me a hand," he called out.

But the passengers ignored Mr. Lovelace's request. And then Anne saw why. Their attention was riveted on the masked man with the gun at the front of the car.

2

His train was being robbed? *His* train?

Well, technically it wasn't his train, but as a contractor for the railroad Nick felt responsible for the safety of the passengers and the quality of their transport. The engines ran over track he'd provided, after all.

"Go on," he whispered.

Only after Mrs. Tillerton ducked beneath his arm and filed out amid the crying children and angry men did Nick extract himself from the crates. A train robbery and he'd been tied down when it occurred. Didn't see the horsemen approach. Didn't hear the brakeman's signal. Too diverted by a lady. Ian Stanford wouldn't approve.

The last to depart the car, he had to fight the urge to clobber the outlaw as he walked past him. Nick's thoughtless remark to Anne Tillerton had embarrassed him, and that embarrassment could easily turn to anger given the right target. Nick hopped the last giant step from the train to the packed ground beneath and heard the thud of boots as the man descended behind him.

Through the waves of heat shimmering from the engine he made out three masked men, one mounted. A skinny kid holding a rusty six-shooter waved him toward the group of men and Mrs. Tillerton. She hid among them, her dusty buckskin pants and floppy slouch hat blending perfectly.

From the passengers' nervous glances toward the front of the train, Nick assumed more men were in the express car. One bandit remained on his horse, which pranced nervously, dancing sideways as the man kept his gun trained on the small gathering. The other two outlaws had trouble keeping their eyes off the tight cluster of ladies huddled in the midst of the vast prairie.

"Should we see what these ladies would like to contribute, Boss?" a stocky man asked.

The leader looked to the express car. His neckerchief stretched as he opened his mouth to answer. "Might as well. I don't know how they're faring with the safe."

Sliding his pistol into his belt, the scrawny one ambled to the women. He took his hat off, revealing hair plastered to his head by sweat. "Pull those earbobs off. Drop your rings. Don't make me come looking for them."

Nick's jaw clenched. Spoiled Miss Walcher and her friends could be pigheaded, but surely they knew to take these men seriously. Or not. His heart sank at the amount of tucking and arranging going on in direct defiance of the outlaw's order. In seconds they had hidden most of their jewelry between the folds and flounces of their gowns.

Evidently the kid wasn't as ignorant as he appeared. He stopped before Miss Walcher, recognizing her as the instigator. "Now, don't you give me no trouble, miss. I saw that gold locket on my first pass. Where'd it go to?"

Miss Walcher's eyes grew wide. "I don't know what you're talking about. I don't have a locket."

"You sure about that?" Nick didn't like the gleam in his eye, nor did he like the chuckle of the other man. Didn't appear they had any compulsion against harassing their victims. "Why don't I have a little look-see?"

The robber shoved his pistol into his waistband and lunged for her. Her scream rent the peaceful prairie like Gabriel's trumpet, definitely more painful than her weak swats at the robber, but neither slowed the man down. He grabbed her by the collar and forced her to her knees.

Nick had seen enough. He knew he shouldn't get involved, but he wouldn't stand by and allow a lady to be molested on the NTT line. Hollering at the outlaw would've only warned him, and Nick wanted a chance at him unprepared. His toes dug into the hard ground, propelling him forward. Blood pumping, he hit the man at a run, knowing the satisfaction of laying him flat before the fear of the consequences reached him.

The kid was no match for him. Pinning the outlaw beneath him, Nicholas punched him once in the jaw and took the fight right out of him. But the click of a hammer had the same effect on Nick.

The man on the horse sent a stream of tobacco flying to the dust. "Shoot him," he ordered.

At first Nicholas thought the stout man refused to obey, then he realized he was merely dragging him off of his accomplice for a clean shot. Well, Nick wouldn't go down without a fight. He might not live on the range like these hardened outlaws, but he'd been loading lumber wagons since he was tall enough to see over the bed.

When the man grabbed him by the shoulder, Nick pulled his knees under him, but before he could spring, a cloud of dust exploded in his face. He blinked and fell as the other robber scrambled out from beneath him. His hand covered his chest. He wasn't shot. At least he didn't think so. Now the leader's gun was out, as well, and it was trained on their hostages.

The passengers scattered, leaving one lone gunman peering down her six-shooter. "You shoot him, you'll die," Anne said. "I took the toe off your boot, mister, and that wasn't a miss. The next shot knocks your leader off his horse, and if you're not one hundred percent certain that you'll hit me, the second will drop you like a fly."

"You talk awfully tough, son," the leader said. "Don't know that you've got the nerve."

"She's got nerve." Nick needed them to be afraid. Terrified preferably. "She's already shot her husband. She'll plug you without blinking."

"She?" The leader's gun lowered, and his eyes turned cold as he studied Anne.

"Let's go!" The cry came out of the express car. Two men loaded their saddlebags and climbed on their mounts.

"Take the money," Anne said. "You got what you want."

Take the money? Was she crazy? Nicholas started to protest, but the gun aimed at his cheek increased his intelligence.

Their leader spat again. "Come on, boys. Payout on corpses is mighty poor."

"You owe her your life." The gunman kicked Nick with his toeless boot. "You better do right by her, or I'll come looking for you."

"I appreciate your concern —" But before Nick could point out the irony of an etiquette lesson from a bandit, the kid shoved past him and jumped on his horse.

The whistle of the steam engine blocked out the sound of their thundering hooves, and in seconds they had raced out of range. Families rushed into each other's arms and the ladies' voices pitched higher and higher as each told her version of the events. Nicholas stretched his skinned knuckles. He hadn't punched anyone since grammar school, and it stung more than he remembered.

"Mr. Lovelace, you are my hero." Miss Walcher grasped his hand with both of hers and pulled it against her bosom. "You were magnificent."

No, he wasn't. He'd lost Mr. Stanford's safe and nearly got himself killed. Even worse, his valiant attempt to be a hero had put Mrs. Tillerton in danger. Not the outcome he'd imagined.

Miss Walcher still held his hand. Her eyes filled with tears. Pretty thing, but no challenge. Extracting himself as gracefully as possible, he took his leave of Miss Walcher and searched among the animated throng for the britches-clad woman who'd stood down a whole gang of train robbers. He should express his gratitude no matter how bad he wished he hadn't needed her help.

No one back in his hometown of Prairie Lea would be surprised to hear that Anne Tillerton had rescued him. Hadn't she saved the life of their neighbor Rosa when Mr. Tillerton attacked her? Everyone knew she was capable of pulling the trigger, but what intrigued Nick was the flash of fear he'd seen in her eyes when he recognized her. Could she be more afraid of him than an armed outlaw? He would relive the harrowing moment when he thought his life was over, but he would lose sleep wondering at the way she trembled when he fell against her on the train.

Where was she, anyway? Almost everyone had re-boarded. Had she slipped into the car without his seeing her?

With his back to the train, he made one last scan of the area. When the bandits rode off, everyone had rushed toward the passenger car, but she hadn't joined them. If she'd headed in the opposite direction . . .

Nicholas jogged only a few steps and found her. She hadn't made it far. Sitting half-hidden in the tall grass, knees pulled to her chest, the coolheaded warrior had been replaced by a shaken young woman in ill-fitting clothing.

She was the hero, but perhaps he still had a chance to help a lady in distress. "The train's leaving. You don't want to be left behind."

"Go on. I'm fine." Her shoulders quivered like it was frigid December. She didn't raise her eyes. She didn't raise her voice. And if she was in trouble, it was because he'd put her there.

"But if that train leaves, then I'm honor bound to stay with you, and that might get a bit uncomfortable. Just the two of us . . . alone . . . in the middle of nowhere."

Now she looked at him. Her gray eyes reflected no emotion. Their gentle lift at the corners belied the solemnity they held. No response.

He shifted his oxford shoes on the hard

sandstone. "It doesn't look like a comfortable place to pass the time, but if you insist. Scoot over."

Her mouth tensed. Rocking forward, she scrambled to her feet, ignoring his offered hand. She swayed and he was at her side in a heartbeat, but once again she refused his help.

Her first few steps were shaky, so she paused, hands on her hips, facing the horizon . . . and no telling what other terrors. Her chin lifted. Her brow wrinkled. A spasm ricocheted through her, yet she didn't blink.

He wouldn't intrude, not yet. If she needed a moment to master her demons, well, she'd given him the rest of his life. He could give her some time.

"I never wanted to do that again, but what choice — ?" She couldn't finish but continued to gaze across the prairie.

He waited until finally he had no option. They had to get on the train, and he wasn't sure she was steady enough to make it on her own.

She seemed ready this time when he took her arm. Her posture didn't sway, but he doubted she'd remember boarding the train. Nick frowned. He couldn't question her bravery, but did it stem from a reckless disregard for her safety or from genuine concern for others? Not that he'd judge her. Especially after the nightmare she'd lived through — or at least what he knew of it. Rumors, mostly.

Every few steps she paused before mustering the will to continue. He didn't wait for her permission but lifted her onto the step, quite a distance without the help of a depot platform, and followed her as she made her way to a solitary bench.

"There she is," a woman said.

"Are you sure it's a girl?" a man asked.

"Of course. Did you see the way he was gazing at her?"

Nick had to smile at the wistful tone. Leave it to the ladies to turn a disaster into a love story.

Garber, Texas

Flashes of wood-planked buildings streaked past the window. Anne could make out barking dogs and impatient coach drivers waiting to cross the tracks as they sped by. They would be at the station soon, and she could finally be rid of the nosy man. Dressed so fine with his city manners — he reminded her of another man who'd impressed her foolish heart. She knew now that charm was more dangerous than fierceness.

"Do you have anyone meeting you at the station?" Mr. Lovelace asked.

Why hadn't he humored the quibbling girls and joined them, as they'd begged? Anne lowered her eyes, refusing to remember the hour she'd spent listless as he'd sat guarding her. She should've insisted he leave. What a ninny she was.

"Once I find the cook I should be back in Pushmataha by tomorrow." Anne leaned forward with the train's deceleration. "Don't fret over me —"

"You saved my life. I'd be singing with the angels if you hadn't intervened."

She grunted. "Even angels know not to jump into a gunfight without a gun."

He rubbed his forehead. "I owe you. Besides, my sister would expect me to accompany you while in town. I'll cancel my evening plans and help you find this cook of yours. Garber isn't large —"

The train whistle interrupted him. Anne pulled her hat over her head. She would've been quit of the man much sooner if she'd let those yahoos have their way. Instead, he'd spent the whole trip watching her. She adjusted her gun belt. Why did he have to do that — really see her? Most people broke eye contact when she caught them looking. Either he couldn't hide his curiosity, or he had no desire to.

"Stop staring." She stood with the rest of the passengers. "I'm beginning to regret saving your hide."

His neck tensed against his collar. Evidently he didn't appreciate the reminder. Still, it didn't dissuade him from following her off the train. "Too late for regrets. You're in my town and I can't have you going around unprotected."

"You're going to protect me? You weren't much help during the holdup."

Now he was annoyed. He crossed his arms. "But you certainly appreciated my company afterward."

Anne's throat closed at the memory of her weakness. Shame on her for having one.

She swung her knapsack over her shoulder to exit the platform. He was dangerous, mostly because he didn't believe she was. She hadn't made it two steps when he once again grasped her arm. This time she expected it.

Whirling, she flung his hand away. "You have no right to detain me, Mr. Lovelace. You do not intimidate me."

A couple of men stepped closer. Whether looking for entertainment or to be of assistance, Anne couldn't tell, but Mr. Lovelace eyed them warily. The all clear was called as the train left the station. He grimaced.

"I've made a mess of things, Mrs. Tillerton. I'll let you depart, but first, please promise me that should you ever find yourself in a bind, you'll call on me — Nicholas Lovelace, Lovelace Transportation Specialist, supplier to NTT Railroad. Anyone at the train station can direct you. Will you remember that?"

He was doing it again — looking past her battered clothing and wind-burned complexion, past his own inconvenience — at what she was trying to disguise. Vulnerability.

Everyone watched for her next move. Well, she'd got what she was after. She'd chased the annoying puppy away.

"My word." She held out her hand to shake on it like her brothers had taught her, minus the spit in the palm, of course.

His hand engulfed hers, a broad, powerful hand with scraped knuckles that had pummeled a man earlier. The vitality that sprang from his clasp frightened her. What could he do to a woman her size? Anne pulled away quickly. She squinted up at him one last time. How odd that their paths should cross now. All that time in Prairie Lea and he'd never spoken a word to her. Of course, she hadn't been allowed to speak. Not to anyone.

But no one controlled her now.

She ambled past the station house and studied the river unfurling outside of town. She'd grab some grub and slip away to the outskirts for the night. Better to sleep beneath the stars than at an inn where every creak or footfall would have her checking the lock on the door. And she'd need a good night's sleep, for tomorrow she'd begin her search.

3

Feet propped up on his desk, pencil between his teeth, Nicholas could no more concentrate on the bid before him than he could endure the fit of a ready-made suit. During the holdup, he'd had the best intentions. Instead of shaking in his boots like a dandy, he'd charged into the fray. He hadn't flinched when death seemed certain, but his salvation at Anne's hands embarrassed him. His friend Joel would want to hear every last detail, and he'd howl when he heard that Nick owed his life to a buffalo-hunting lass.

Well, if his good friend couldn't laugh at him, he needed to be taken down a peg — and that's exactly what this Anne Tillerton had done.

Nick's assistant rushed into the room, pen still between his fingers, ink smudged on his high forehead. "I'm finished with the monthly report. I can look over the bid now if you want me to."

"Thanks, Harold." Nick swung his scuffless shoes off the polished desk and grasped the half-blank paper. Where had the hour gone? He'd accomplished nothing since the last time Harold had checked on him.

Turning the paper facedown, he threaded his fingers together and adopted a pensive expression. "The main difficulty I foresee in the Karber bid is the transportation of the ties. If we don't build another sawmill at the base of the Karber railroad, we'll be paying Mr. Stanford to ship the wooden ties to his competitor."

"Probably not a viable option."

"I wouldn't think so, but we don't have the capital available to construct another mill. Either Karber would need to advance us some funds, or we'll have to request a loan at the bank."

Harold cupped the nib of his pen, saving the Oriental rug from an inky droplet. "Ask for the advance. You don't want to pay interest."

Nicholas smiled. "I thought that once the business was established, I'd never be as excited as I was in the beginning, but every expansion thrills me just the same."

"Because each contains greater risks . . . and greater rewards."

"If Karber's railroad is as profitable as Stanford's, we'll be well rewarded indeed."

Harold tapped the stack of envelopes on the corner of his desk. "You haven't gone through your mail yet? I thought you'd wonder what the letter from the courthouse is about."

Another task forgotten during his day-dreaming. He slid the stack into his hand and rifled through them. The letter opener sliced through the heavy envelope. Nick's brows lowered as he read. "Who would've thought?"

"Not bad news, I hope." Harold had given up on his pen and deposited it nib up into his shirt pocket.

Nick flipped the letter over as if the message were written more clearly on the back. "I'd heard that the county commissioner had died."

"Richard Garrard?" Harold nodded. "Gored by his bull."

Nick barely heard him, his mind whirling to make sense of the contents. "According to this it's the judge's duty to appoint another commissioner to serve until the next election. He requested that I step in."

"You? A county commissioner?" Harold's eyes rolled heavenward. "How can we expand the business if you're busy scampering around for the county?"

Nick tossed the letter onto his desk. "Which is why I'll decline. This bid could double our income. We can't afford to be distracted while stalking the elusive Mr. Karber."

A door in the front office opened. Harold's eyes widened. Nicholas took a quick inventory of his office — ferns green and healthy, spittoon hidden behind the velvet drapes, lamps trimmed. The room appeared to be in order for their guest, which was fortunate because Ophelia Stanford noticed everything. Generally this caused Nick no hardship beyond the fact that she expected to be noticed, too.

"Mrs. Stanford," he bellowed, as if announcing her arrival at the Cotton Festival cotillion.

Her entry was just as grand. Hands clasped gently in front of her, elbows floating a distance from herself as though escorted by a gallant on each side, Mrs. Stanford crossed the Persian rug she'd chosen for his office and presented a cheek for his customary greeting.

He smacked the air, remembering to breathe through his nose so as to avoid the taste of the lilac-scented powder swirling around her.

Harold quietly returned to his office.

"I haven't finished the report for your husband, but progress looks to be ahead of schedule." Nicholas ushered her to the leather chair sitting before his desk.

"That's pleasing news. Is there ample timber for ties, or will we need to purchase lumber?"

Nicholas took the chair opposite her, remembering that she didn't like to speak to him over his desk. "That depends. Most of the trees along this portion of the route are pine. Some cottonwood grows that could be useful, but even it will need to be replaced in a couple of years. If you use hardwood the expense will be considerably more. On an unproven route, it would be a gamble."

With precision, Ophelia adjusted the lace at her wrist. "We could build an inferior track of cottonwood and pine and then see if the proceeds merit a larger investment. If this line turns a profit, we build a stronger track parallel and then with switches we'd be able to run both directions, even if the outlet was in bad repair."

No wonder Mr. Stanford didn't mind his wife interfering in business. Given the chance, she would've been a success without him.

"My thoughts exactly. And once we break through the forest, I'll have my men go back to the more wooded areas. They won't be needed to clear the trees, but you'll need the ties at a faster rate."

"Sounds like your report is nearly complete, and that's good because I didn't come here to discuss business. I came to get a scintillating firsthand report of the train holdup. You can imagine how overcome by curiosity I've been since I learned of your adventure."

Nicholas rested his elbow atop the chair arm. "I suppose you talked to the conductor and the engineer?"

"I haven't seen their reports yet, but I have heard from some ladies who mentioned a passenger who displayed uncommon heroism. Imagine my surprise when I reconciled the dashing account with my mild-mannered lumber supplier."

Nicholas snorted. "Mild-mannered? Of all the things I've been called —"

"Now, don't misdirect me. I want a full account. How did the attack start? When were you first aware?"

When was it? Mrs. Tillerton had bolted and he was chasing her. Next thing he knew he was thrown against her so closely he could see the flecks of blue in her gray eyes.

41

He could distinguish each eyelash that curled beneath her brows.

"Who was she?"

Nicholas blinked, bringing Ophelia's image into sharp focus. "I beg your pardon. I was trying to remember —"

"She must have been beautiful. I don't think I've ever caught you in a reverie before." Ophelia's narrow lips were pursed. Her head tilted sympathetically. "Straight from the schoolroom, pure white skin plump with youth, dress flounced with more petticoats than she's seen years. Experience hasn't taught her to guard her laugh. No depth to prevent her from instant familiarity. I know her well."

He filled his lungs in a long breath of the lilac cloud. *You don't know her at all,* he wanted to protest. But prudence restrained him.

"How could I not be distracted with Garber's fairest aboard?" He swung his foot easily. "Mr. Walcher's daughter Susan had secured tickets for herself and some companions, little realizing that their lark would encounter violence. Yes, they required my full attention, and regretfully I didn't foresee the trouble in time to be of assistance."

"But you assisted Miss Walcher, I understand, and at great peril."

His foot swung a little faster at the memory, grateful that Miss Walcher preferred the version where he was the rescuer instead of the rescued. "Oh that." He shrugged. "Instinctual, I suppose. Didn't realize what I'd done until I felt that pistol barrel against my head."

Ophelia leaned forward and grasped Nick's arm. "Don't ever do that again. To risk your life . . . You must take better care of yourself, Nicholas. Especially now with so much on the horizon."

Her smile hinted at a great surprise. Nick shifted in his seat. Maybe he should have been more grateful to Mrs. Tillerton for saving his neck, especially when life promised so much.

"Now that you mention it, I did have a surprise awaiting me. It seems that Judge Calloway has appointed me as a county commissioner. Can you imagine? Naturally, I have to turn it down."

"Turn it down?" Fine lines appeared around Ophelia's frowning lips. "Whatever for?"

Why had he mentioned it? Oh well. Too late to reverse course. If he signed a contract with Mr. Karber, the Stanfords would know it sooner or later.

"I'm considering an expansion. Mr. Karber mentioned that he was extending his southeast line and could use another crew. I'm meeting with him tomorrow, and I wouldn't want to take on additional duties that could interfere with my plans."

Mrs. Stanford rose. She glided to the window behind his desk and gazed upon the street below. "I shouldn't be surprised that you want to grow. Your ambition was the first quality that attracted us to you, along with your honesty — a trait desperately needed in government. Perhaps we could find an alternative."

"I don't understand."

"Don't refuse so hastily. Being appointed to a political office is an honor that could lead to astonishing opportunities. And what if Mr. Karber doesn't accept your bid and you've thrown away this chance for naught?"

"But I intend to expand eventually. The flaws have been worked out of my operation. Why would I stop with only one crew?"

Her lashes quivered as she came to a decision. "Then get another crew, but forget about finding new partners. Ian is planning another line even now. We could use your services there. Without having the trouble of hammering out new terms and expectations, you'll have plenty of time for your

44

county duties."

Nick's eyes narrowed. He didn't like being pushed toward a decision. Besides the increased profit that diversification would bring, he also wanted to lessen his dependence on the NTT Railroad. The Stanfords, Ophelia in particular, could be difficult to please, and Nick could foresee the day when he'd tire of the dance. Still, wasn't the sure promise of more business better than the gamble of securing new clients? New commissioners would be elected in a few months. Surely he could coast until then, or if he got in over his head, he could always resign before any harm came to his business.

"Another line, you say? When do we break ground?"

Every good hunter knows that the trick to finding game involves predicting where their prey feels most at home. Buffalo, rabbits, foxes — they all skedaddle to their lair when pursued. Errant cooks would be no different. And Anne was an excellent hunter.

From the moment she spotted the Velvet Palace, Anne knew with disgusted certainty that Tessa called it home. As soon as the bartender finished with his noon customers, she had her question answered, then jaunted up a painted staircase to stand in Tessa's doorway.

Finding her had been the easy part. Convincing her to return would take patience, and patience wasn't Anne's strong suit. If Tessa would only stand still long enough to hear her plea, but she obviously didn't have time for Anne or for the infant who pulled on her skirt as she preened in the mirror.

Anne watched the child with fascinated horror. The baby. His presence threatened to undo her, especially in the cramped bedroom, so similar to one she'd learned to loathe, but Tessa couldn't know how her stomach churned at the sight of him.

"I'm so glad you found me, Anne. This baby is bound and determined to ruin my life. Eddie said that he won't step out with me if I bring Sammy again." Tessa licked her finger and then pressed it to her eyelashes, curling them upward.

"Eddie? I thought you came to town to find Finn." Anne tried to open the window to dilute the dank air, but it was nailed shut.

Tessa snorted. "Finn Cravens better hope I don't find him, that scoundrel. If I ever lay eyes on him, I'm handing him his son and running for the hills. How dare he leave me with a baby —"

Anne frowned. "Go back to Pushmataha.

46

Anoli needs a cook and the men enjoy having Sammy around. A room above a saloon is no place to raise a whelp."

Tessa turned away from the mirror. "You're right about that. Eddie's asked me to go with him out west. It'll be tough at first —"

"— but better Sammy be on the frontier than here."

With a hand to her hip, Tessa stared at the child. Savoring his mother's attention — which Anne feared was rarely awarded — Sammy babbled "Ma-ma-ma" as he bounced vigorously on his haunches. His soiled diaper gapped around his chubby legs.

"Fix him for me, will you, Anne?"

"Fix him? You mean change his . . . his . . ." Anne twisted her mouth to the side. "I'm a buffalo hunter. I might take the hide right off him."

Tessa tossed her a slightly damp diaper and flipped Sammy onto his back. "Nonsense. I've seen you covered in filth. You won't mind nearly as much as I do." She pushed him toward Anne, whose hands hovered above him, not sure where to start . . . not sure if she could start.

"I don't know what to do," Tessa continued. "If Finn had any family I'd send

47

Sammy to them, but he's an orphan. My own family is out of the question. I'd rather he be raised by coyotes than endure what I went through."

Gingerly, Anne laid a hand on his stomach and unclasped the safety pins. She had no sympathy for the whining woman, not while trying to keep two kicking legs from landing in the mess. Using the front of the diaper she wiped him off the best she could before rolling up the soggy cloth and replacing it.

"How do you pin this? I could do it up tight, but he'd have saddle sores by morning."

Leaning against her bureau, Tessa didn't answer at first, but feeling Anne's disapproval she snapped to. "Oh, he'll be fine. It's time for his nap. Just give him a spoonful of Godfrey's Cordial, and he won't move until this evening."

Anne straightened. "Give him a sleeping draught? He's an infant. Besides, I'm not watching him."

"You don't have anywhere else to stay, do you?"

With a glare Anne bent to clasp the second pin and then lifted the child to his feet. Holding onto the bed for support, Sammy squealed at her and then laughed delightedly when the diaper slid to his

48

ankles. Anne wasn't amused.

"Listen to me, Tessa Drumright. Sammy is your responsibility. You can't put him in a stupor while you go out. It isn't right."

Tessa wrung her hands. "You're right, of course. Sammy needs a better home. He needs a better mother. I'm not good for him. Surely you agree."

"But you could be. You decide what kind of person you're going to be, and you be that person. If you want to be friendly, you talk to people. If you want to be strong, you keep your distance. If you want to be a good mother, you stop chasing after men like a lovesick polecat and take care of the kit you already have."

"Easy for you to say." Tessa picked up a powder puff and dusted her bosom. "You don't mind being lonely, but I need a companion. I want attention."

There were worse ills than loneliness. The child swatted at Anne's knee and grinned impishly. His white-blond hair fell in long wisps across his forehead, just like his father's. Finn's devil-may-care attitude had been frustrating to work with when running alongside a stampeding herd of buffalo, but back at the depot he'd had the gift of spinning windies. Tessa in particular had found him charming. Two years and a child later,

49

she wasn't as impressed.

Sammy plopped onto the floor and began to explore on all fours. No matter what Tessa thought, Anne didn't enjoy the prospect of going through life alone. The choice had been made only when all other options had proven too dangerous.

"Well, you aren't going to find a cook sitting in the room." Tessa clasped a string of beads around her neck. "Why don't you go downstairs and ask around the kitchen? There are a few establishments on the other side of the square that might know of someone looking for work."

"You won't come back to Pushmataha?"

"No. My heart belongs to Eddie. I'm going with him."

Silence fell. Tessa lifted a pick to her hair and jabbed at a tangle. Anne winced. Better to be attached to a job than a man.

"I guess I have no choice if I want to go back on the hunt."

"But you are coming back?" Tessa asked. "You're staying here tonight, right?"

Ugh. But once you found your target you stayed with them until they were bagged. "I'll stay here and hope I can talk some sense into you before I leave tomorrow."

Some of the tension that Anne had carried

beneath her duster had faded away. Her mission had been successful. Took most of the afternoon, but she'd finally found a cook and purchased the widow-woman's ticket to Pushmataha. Tomorrow they'd board the train together and head back to the depot. By the next evening she'd be on her bedroll, gazing up at the stars sprinkled generously across the sky, away from the curious stares of strangers. Back to the life she'd created for herself.

Speaking of strangers . . .

Footsteps sounded behind her as she marched across the squares of light thrown through the saloon windows onto the board-walk. She paused at the batwing doors, and the steps halted. In a motion that was universally understood, she slid her right hand inside her duster to her hip, where the smooth handle of her six-shooter met her fingers.

"I wouldn't do that if I was you," the voice behind her called.

Anne remembered to deepen her voice. "Are you going to shoot me in the back?"

"The lawmen of Garber don't shoot citizens unprovoked. Turn around slow."

Anne extended her arms to her sides and turned to face a scowling young deputy.

"Evidently Garber lawmen don't mind

harassing visitors."

He didn't answer until he'd looked her over. His dark beard wasn't quite grown in but accomplished what he no doubt wished by covering his youthful face.

"Visitors are invited and last time I checked the guest list it didn't include a woman masquerading as a man. I'm only looking for a chance to become better acquainted with a new face in my town."

Anne stiffened. His words could be misinterpreted by a woman. What were his intentions?

His face reddened and he stammered. "Just tell me your business and I'll leave you to it."

"I'm a buffalo hunter out of Pushmataha. Anoli Parker, our outfit leader, sent me here to find a cook for the depot. First train north, I'm headed out."

"A buffalo hunter?" He nodded. "Then welcome to Garber. I hope your stay is pleasant and your journey home uneventful." He tipped his hat and reversed course.

"A train ride without the holdup would be nice," she muttered and continued on to Tessa's apartment.

A thin scrap of the sun's disk hung behind the row of buildings. No possibility of watching it all the way to the horizon. Out

52

on the plain, it was Anne's favorite time of day. Physically exhausted, Anne would toss her saddle on the ground away from the fellas, rest her head in the seat, and wait for the sky to fade. She'd catch snippets of their ribald stories, a song on the harmonica, low laughter, and she was at peace. Under Anoli's protection, none of them dared mess with her. She was safe from everything — except her memories.

If the stars were bright enough, the music lively enough, and it'd been a good day, Anne could almost imagine that she'd come to buffalo hunting straight from her home in Ohio. Bull's-Eye Annie leaving school to chase down the stampeding herds and clear the land for the settlers.

But most days her few years of bondage as Jay Tillerton's wife erased anything that came before and overshadowed everything that came afterwards. No relationship was untainted from her fear of once again falling under the influence of an evil man. No exchange escaped assessment.

She'd do whatever was required to remain free, and her best defense involved her disappearance from society. The sooner she could get out of town and back to the isolated outpost, the better.

Certain that Tessa wouldn't have any plans

to feed her, Anne walked into the saloon on the ground floor of Tessa's apartment. The bartender stood behind a row of glasses, drying them one by one with a wadded cotton rag. Without looking up he asked, "What'll it be?"

"What grub do you have for supper?"

His head popped up. "A woman in britches? That would make you Tessa's friend. Well, you're late and I don't appreciate it." He set the glass down with a thump before picking up the next. "It's not my place to play nursemaid."

"Listen, mister. Tessa is not my problem and her son even less so. If she left him with you, I had nothing to do with it. I tried telling her she shouldn't be leaving him at all."

"Well, that's what she's done. Her and that drifter Eddie Starkley have pulled up stakes and skipped town. If the stagecoach driver hadn't come in to wet his whistle, I wouldn't have got the room lease out of the two of them."

"Stagecoach?" Anne placed both hands flat against the bar and leaned forward. "You don't mean —"

"Gone. They hightailed it out and told me you were the child's new ma. Poor kid never stood a chance with that flighty woman." The bartender paused to scrutinize her thoroughly. "Can't say you'll do any better."

Anne sputtered. "She left without the kid? She can't do that. I've got to go back to Pushmataha tomorrow." Her eyes went so dry she couldn't blink. Her fingernails dug into the bar. "Where is he?"

The man turned the glass around the rag until it squeaked. "Maude is upstairs with him. Cute little pup. Congratulations."

Anne couldn't respond. Who gets congratulated for a disaster? These people didn't think she wanted him, did they? She ran up the steps, swung around the finial, raced down the hall, and burst into Tessa's room. The sleeping baby jolted awake and sat upright. His face screwed into a wrinkled mess and opened to emit a monstrous howl.

"*Shh . . .*" The woman glared at her. "I just got him down." Sighing, she gathered her knitting. "He's your problem now."

"Wait! I don't know —"

But the woman didn't give her a chance to continue. Anne stood in the doorway, watched the tears pool in the boy's eyes, and almost shed a few of her own. She spun around the room, taking in the empty wardrobe, the bare vanity; even the pillowcase had been removed. All she could do was sit and watch him howl.

"Go on and cry. Your momma left you. You have every right." Should she track down Tessa? It wouldn't be difficult. Even once they left civilization, Anne could strap the cub on her back like a papoose and follow Tessa anywhere.

But then what would his prospects be?

His round little face grew redder as he worked himself into a fit. Tessa didn't want him. Her new beau resented him. What would happen to Sammy out on the frontier with no one watching? What had Anne suffered as an adult when people should have noticed? At least Tessa had given him a chance of having a family that wanted him.

Hadn't Anne survived growing up without a mother? Her pa had seen that she had a roof over her head. He didn't offer much by way of guidance or affection, but she'd learned to take care of herself. If she could, couldn't a boy?

She would find his pa. If Finn Cravens wanted to put his child in an orphanage, that was his business, but he deserved the opportunity to do better by the boy. Who knew? He might change his ways when he realized that he was solely responsible for a baby. Stranger things had happened.

Anne knew nothing about caring for

babies, but surely she could keep him alive until his father could be tracked.

4

The next morning Anne practically exploded out of the saloon with one arm tucked around Sammy's chest, holding him against her, and the other bearing the weight of two knapsacks, a food parcel, and a baby blanket. Sammy flailed his arms upward and squirmed until his chin was hung in the elbow of her thick duster, his gown pulled up beneath his armpits.

"Stop it, Sammy, or I'm going to drop you."

A woman gasped and stopped on the boardwalk to glare.

Anne wished she didn't feel the need to defend herself, but she did. "It's a prediction, not a threat. I wouldn't purposely drop him."

"What a relief," the woman sneered. "It'll be a comfort knowing when he hits the ground it was an accident. I only wonder how the poor babe survived this long under your care."

Anne wrinkled her nose at the snooty bat, and with a bounce of her hip repositioned Sammy into a more manageable hold. She'd stayed ahead of a stampeding buffalo herd. She'd survived a spring storm with hail the size of tomatoes, but nothing had exhausted her like getting Sammy ready for an outing.

This baby required more gear than a whole troop of buffalo hunters.

She hoped the new cook would relay her message to Anoli and that he'd waste no time finding Finn. Until then she had to locate a safe place where they could stay while she waited, preferably with someone who didn't mind lending a hand with the boy. Surely there was a widow woman with a boardinghouse nearby.

Papers waved from a notice board tacked up across the way. Anne looked up and down the street before trudging across. The writhing child against her bosom hampered her usually acute perception. A horse could barrel down the road right on top of them, and she'd never hear it coming. Not over the kid's grunts.

Her glance skittered over the various advertisements and legal proclamations until she spotted what she'd been looking for. She recognized the street as one she'd crossed when leaving the train depot. Not a far distance she hoped.

Sammy fussed. He crammed his fist in his mouth. There'd be no place to get him food between the main street and the neighborhood, but once at the boardinghouse she could get him some milk or even figure out the strange powder Tessa had left behind with the glass bottles and rubber nipples. As long as he didn't see the bottles again. When she'd pulled them out of his knapsack, he'd started fussing. When she put them back without feeding him, he'd gone berserk.

By the time she knocked on the door of the tidy house, Sammy was throwing a royal tantrum. The peephole slid open, Anne was inspected, and then the door moved cautiously.

"How might I help you?"

Anne bounced Sammy on her hip, hoping he'd shush and she could be heard.

"I'd like to let a room."

One eyebrow rose on a humorless face. "Excuse me . . . er, ma'am?"

Anne shifted Sammy to her opposite side and let her knapsacks slide down to her boots. "It'd only be for a day or two while I find the kid's father. I don't plan to stay long —"

The woman's chin lifted. "My boarding-house serves only the finest clientele. Women dressed in men's clothing, toting around illegitimate children, are not welcome."

"He's not illegitimate." Anne stopped. "Well, actually he is, but he's not mine, and I had nothing to do with this mess. His mother left him —"

"Your appearance would distress my boarders. I'm sorry, but I'm unable to help you."

With that the door slammed firmly in her face.

Sammy slurped on his fist, still hungry. Anne drew a long breath, picked up the bag, and trudged back toward town. She'd have to buy them a meal after all, which meant that more than likely Sammy was headed back to the Velvet Palace.

Wednesday afternoons mustn't be a busy time for county government, because the halls of the courthouse were nearly vacant. Nicholas gave his name to the judge's assistant. "I was told to report to Judge Calloway. Is he busy?"

"Of course he's busy." The assistant rubbed his eyes beneath smudged glasses and then motioned to a chair.

Nick sat and flicked a speck of sawdust off his trousers. He'd thought he'd sent all his traveling clothes to the washwoman, but he must have missed some. Had Ophelia not noticed? She always expected perfection from those in her circle of society. Not that the Stanfords were what his mother would call society. No, they'd climbed the ranks on wooden ties like those he provided, but in the meantime he was riding along in their wake, following the path they'd blazed.

A bell hanging on the wall suddenly dipped, its mellow chime disturbing the office. The assistant sat a bit straighter. "Mr. Lovelace, Judge Calloway will see you now."

Nick straightened his cravat and strode to the massive door with heavy brass trimmings just beyond the assistant's desk. Taking the curved knob in his hand, he opened the door.

There was a flurry of activity at a second door behind the judge's desk. The judge pushed it closed and turned with fire in his eyes.

"You didn't knock."

Nick's mouth went dry. "I'm sorry, Your Honor. You rang for me. I thought —"

But Judge Calloway strode to his desk without further comment. He picked up a pen and began scribbling furiously, ignoring

Nick's contrition.

Even without the robe that hung on the hook behind him, everyone recognized the judge. He had more hair than a wigmaker, combed in golden swoops over his temples and forehead.

Nick eyed the chairs positioned before him. Better not risk it. Instead he studied the wall hangings, various documents with thick gold seals declaring that the man before him was entitled to make you wait. Latin. Not his best subject in school.

"Sit," the judge finally said.

"Yes, sir." In two strides he reached the chair. "It's a pleasure to meet you. I didn't know —"

"There are times when I must trust my instinct. I believe I've found the right man for the job, and I solemnly hope you won't disappoint me."

Nicholas clasped his hands together and sat as proper as a choirboy. "We share that hope, sir. I couldn't imagine why you'd think to honor me —"

"As you know, Commissioner Garrard died unexpectedly. Ghastly. And so despite my numerous contacts I decided to turn to someone untested. This situation could use fresh insights. Under normal circumstances I'd wait until after the election when the new commissioners are installed, but there's a vote that we are anxious to get settled. It's about a bridge."

"The Choctaw River Bridge?" Nicholas leaned forward. "I've heard talk over it."

"It's been debated by this commission for the better part of a year, and the vote is scheduled for next month. Everyone wants it settled before a new slate of county commissioners comes in and decides to revisit all the findings. I've been a judge for twenty-two years and can't remember any committee vote that's seen more controversy. I hope you'll see the issue through."

"Me? I'm going to vote on the bridge? Are you saying —"

"You are reported to be an intelligent man. Your experience with the construction of the railroads and your knowledge of the various forms of transportation to and from Garber make your appointment as county commissioner a logical choice."

"I don't know how much time I have to research —"

"Commissioner Garrard's office is already empty. Considering the brief span that we will require your services, you might want to minimize any changes to the décor."

Nick wouldn't change the décor. He might not have time to check the mail. "There could be a conflict. This is a busy month for me. Mr. Stanford is expanding his business, and I don't have much time to spare."

"You should find Mr. Stanford willing to wait." The judge studied him through sparse eyelashes. "Now, learn what you need to know about this bridge, so this issue can be put to rest. The vote is at the end of October."

"Yes, sir." What did he know about building bridges or commissioners' meetings or county government? Still, it was a simple vote. Yes or no. His vote might not even make a difference.

The judge cleared his throat, reminding Nicholas that he hadn't left.

"Sorry, sir." He hurried out of the room, unsettled by the thought that he may have committed to more than he'd expected. And yet, a vote on a bridge couldn't affect his ability to process lumber into railroad ties. As long as his crews and machinery were working, what happened at the courthouse couldn't touch him.

The smell of spilt liquor oozed out of the dirty floors. Anne sat in the Velvet Palace, her back against the wall, and cradled Sammy. After downing two bottles of milk the baby was slowing, getting drowsy as he lolled the nipple around his mouth. The day was half gone and she'd accomplished nothing besides spending many of her precious coins and attracting attention from a table of poker players.

She couldn't make out what they were saying exactly, but every now and then play would halt, jeers would fly her way, and the table would roar with laughter. Best to ignore them. Or ignore them while taking inventory of their features and whatever arms they carried. She'd want to recognize them should they cross paths again.

With a sigh, Sammy gave in to sleep. His warmth made Anne's eyelids heavy, too. She leaned her head against the wall. If only she had somewhere to close her eyes for an hour. Babies didn't sleep much at night, at least this one hadn't, and neither had she.

"Can I help you?"

Anne bolted awake. She hugged Sammy to her as the table erupted into hoots of laughter. Before her stood who could only be the saloon manager. He was a wide man, soft with a thick beard reaching to his chest.

"No, sir. I'll be on my way."

"Is this Tessa's boy?"

Anne took the bottle from Sammy's hands. "I don't reckon that's any of your business."

He shrugged. "I'd heard she'd left him with you. Where are you staying?"

"I don't know yet."

"We have rooms."

Anne's eyes flickered to the men at the table. They were awfully quiet. Too quiet to be doing anything besides eavesdropping.

"I don't want to stay here. Not with a baby."

"A few of our ladies have children. In fact, they don't mind helping each other out when necessary."

By intoxicating their babies with cordial? But where else would she and Sammy sleep that night?

"How much for a room?"

He gathered her dirty dishes. "Let's see what we've got first. Follow me."

Anne hefted Sammy's weight into her left arm so her right was free if she needed it, but once in the kitchen the man dropped the dishes into the sink and escorted her to the staircase leading up to where Tessa's room had been. "Where'd you get that outfit?"

"I'm a buffalo hunter."

"Unconventional but not unattractive."

The sleeve garters dimpled into his soft arms. He pulled a key ring out of his pocket and unlocked a door just down the hall from where she'd found Tessa.

"How much?" The nightstand and wardrobe wouldn't be of any use, but the bed looked inviting.

"Free if you could help downstairs. We're shorthanded tonight."

"If I wanted to cook I would've never left my buffalo outfit."

"How about waiting tables? We'll be busy in a few hours."

"I didn't see any women serving."

"The ladies don't come in until evening. By then you'll be ready to have someone else entertain the child." He grasped the brass ring on the wardrobe and swung open the heavily varnished door. "If you work in front of the customers you will need to wear a dress." He tossed a bouquet of bright colors and gathers onto the bed.

Anne nestled Sammy in the thin mattress and lifted the dress gingerly. Not much to it — one piece, buttoned up the front with a loose cut, but it was a dress. She didn't wear dresses anymore. Not since her husband had died.

"No, thank you," she said.

"And why not?"

"I prefer my clothes." Although the velvet felt much finer beneath her fingers than her old canvas duster. She dropped it on the bed.

"Try it on. You'd be surprised how comfortable it is. We don't expect our ladies to work all trussed up like a roasting pig."

Every bone in her body rebelled against the thought. Dressing up, looking pretty, only led to trouble. Still, she needed a place to stay for a few days. If the rest of the women wore similar gowns there'd be no reason for her to stand out.

"I'll try it on." She held it before her and bit her lip. "I suppose you'd want me to get started immediately."

The man nodded. "We'll show you around until the supper crowd drags in."

The boy was sleeping, and if she didn't get a place to stay, she'd go another night without rest.

As soon as he stepped out of the room, she turned the lock on the door and unbuckled her gun belt. She sat on the bed and unlaced her high boots, dropped her drawers, and shrugged out of her duster and buckskin shirt. Her underthings were in sad disrepair. They'd never do beneath a fine dress, but this looked more like a bright, festive sack. Another reason she could wear it.

She pulled the frilly gown over her head.

It fell easily around her shoulders. Impressive. Anne didn't have much experience with ladies' clothing, but she'd never imagined anything as simple to put on or remove as this dress. Five buttons up the front and a sash around the waist. She didn't like the capped sleeves that left most of her arms exposed. And this dress was too short by far. The hem barely reached the tops of her slouchy socks. No, that wouldn't do.

The man knocked at the door. "Let's see how you look."

Anne's heart skipped. "It doesn't fit." She stepped in front of the mirror and her mouth dropped. The gown's loose fit left the scooping neckline gapping. If it weren't for her chemise, she would've been totally exposed. Did their help really dress like this?

The doorknob rattled. "Let me judge. Open up."

Anne snatched her trousers. She'd inserted one leg when she heard the key ring jangle and the lock click. She swept her gun and duster into her arms and held the bundle before her exposed chest.

He cracked the door open, slid inside, and shut it behind him. His nose flared at the trousers around her ankles and the crumpled duster hiding her.

"Don't be embarrassed. It's nothing I

haven't seen before."

"Get out." In many social situations Anne was uncertain how to behave. This was not one of them. "Leave this room immediately, or I'll raise such a ruckus the whole town will wonder what you're about."

"A woman's screams won't attract any attention here."

Anne lifted her pistol above the folded duster. "What about a man's?"

His protruding stomach sucked in flat. "You're not welcome here. Get your things and get out."

"I'll even leave the dress, but you're going out while I change," said Anne, "and drop your keys on the table."

He tossed his keys and stomped out the door. Anne rushed forward to latch and lock it once again. She holstered the pistol and moved the belt away from the sleeping child.

Once again she'd been denied a safe haven.

She'd give Anoli one more day to contact her. After that she'd head to Pushmataha with the kid. She didn't know what else to do besides flee to the only safety she'd ever known.

Once dressed, Anne eased the door open and carried the sleeping child into the hallway. Up the stairs came an unlikely couple, the woman wearing a dress similar to the one she'd left behind. Her cold eyes looked Anne over from head to toe.

"I'm just leaving." Anne leaned against the wall to let them pass, but the man stopped.

His expensive suit didn't belong in the cheap establishment. His finely groomed appearance spoke of money in an intangible way Anne couldn't pinpoint. Or maybe it was his confidence and his silver-streaked hair.

"I hope you'll be back. I think I'd enjoy the novelty of a frontier lass."

"Come on." The woman tugged his arm and with a laugh he followed, allowing Anne to escape.

Even the streets didn't feel safe. Too many people to watch. No refuge from curious stares or prying questions. After stopping at the store to buy provisions for the night, Anne trekked out of town to the thickest stand of trees she could spot. She'd wait the night out there and check with the telegraph office the next morning. She placed Sammy on the ground and tore off a piece of bread. His chubby, eager fingers pinched for it in a way that was almost endearing.

She tossed her knapsack to the ground, eased his bag with the glass bottle to a safe place, and settled in to wait.

The lightning tore across the sky. Anne
didn't breathe until the thunder rumbled,
shaking the ground. With the next strike she
saw that the baby was still asleep, but he
wouldn't be for long. Rain was on the way.

She pulled her hat over her curls and put
on her duster. If she were alone she'd
hunker down and ride it out, but she
couldn't do that with a baby. Could she?
Stomach-down he slept with his seat
bumped up in the air. Finn wouldn't know
what to do with him if he caught cold, so
she'd better keep him healthy, if possible.

Anne had him bundled in his blanket
about the time the first drops fell. Her hat
and duster protected her from the growing
onslaught, but the splashes on Sammy's
head made him squirm. With him stowed
inside her coat, she couldn't get along very
quickly.

They were drenched by the time they
reached town. The only lights shining
belonged to the saloons. Anne's arms tightened around Sammy. They'd be better off
on the street.

The next flash of lightning illuminated the
deserted city. Shutters latched. Wet, shiny
doors locked. Sammy's struggling became

urgent. He got a handful of her wet hair and pulled. Anne almost dropped their bags in her attempt to get free.

"No, no!" she scolded, but Sammy howled back at her.

No wonder he screamed. She was out of sorts, too.

Without another lightning flash she couldn't read the sign on the building, but a large covered porch beckoned to her. She ducked beneath the roof. Her foot slid on the slick wooden platform, but she caught her balance before her knee hit the ground.

"Listen, kid. You need to be still," she said. "Swinging all over like this is going to get us both hurt."

He cried even louder. Anne paced the porch wishing someone, anyone, could alleviate his suffering. And hers. Naturally she was worried about the kid, but if there'd been a safe dry barrel to stash him in, she'd do it in a blink.

At least his lungs were as strong as bellows.

She found herself bouncing him and it seemed to work. He rubbed his eyes and voiced a few angry complaints but soon lost his enthusiasm. His forehead dropped against her chest, and he drifted back to sleep.

Anne stood at the edge of the porch. He'd quieted. How did she know to do that? In gusts, the rain reached beneath the roof to splash her face. She headed back toward the dry center of the porch, hoping to sit and doze until morning, but when she stopped walking, Sammy stirred.

"I guess I don't have it all figured out, then." And she never would. She'd do what she could to make it through this miserable night, but she couldn't take anymore. She needed help.

5

Skipping every other step on his way up, Nicholas reached his second-story office quickly. True, the façade wasn't as fine as the storefront of the collateral broker's beneath it, and the outdoor staircase gave his acquaintances fodder for harassment, but once inside the doors, no one could fault his taste. Someday when he moved to a better location, the oak desk, Persian rugs, and glass-enclosed bookshelves would go with him, but he wouldn't waste money on high rent until he was ready to announce to the world he'd arrived.

Nick stepped inside and dropped the newspaper, messing Harold's organized desk. Even though Harold's hairline was retreating prematurely, it didn't prevent him from keeping a dapper, trim moustache. Harold squared his notepad and continued his perusal.

"You're looking over my notes, I see,"

Nick said. "What's your assessment?"

"I agree with you. A steam engine would be the best option for our second mill. We'd have more flexibility on where we locate the mill, because we wouldn't be tied to a waterway." Harold bent over a sheet of paper, bringing into sharp relief the shoreline of his forehead. "And when we're finished with Stanford's line, the equipment would be easier to relocate."

Nick slapped Harold on the back, forgetting to rein in his enthusiasm. "I'm glad we're in agreement. I'll look over the different sizes of engines and see what will work for us. In the meantime we could start putting a crew together. Perhaps run an ad in the paper."

Nick closed the office door behind him and within minutes was lost somewhere between the paper before him and the figures crowding his head. The speed with which Ian Stanford wanted to lay out the new NTT line was hard to fathom. He might need to work weeks ahead of the graders. He'd need to have his crew getting the mill together soon if they were going to stay ahead. He scratched his forehead. Was Vernon Springs big enough to hire locals, or would they need to ship in some lumberjacks? How many railroad ties an hour could they produce working with a new crew?

When the door swung open, Nick didn't even look up.

"Someone to see you," Harold said.

"Send him in."

He tallied the numbers in the column, getting a preliminary figure on the bid. The dark blur in the doorway alerted him that he was not alone, but the man would just have to wait. Nicholas couldn't be interrupted —

A gurgle. A happy gurgle like his nephew made. Nick lifted his head. No, his ears hadn't deceived him. A man with a baby stood in his doorway.

"You said to find you if I needed help."

Nicholas rose when he heard her voice. Her appearance hadn't changed since the train — if he didn't take into account the fact that she was drenched. But somehow here in his plush office she didn't look as quaint. Instead of intriguing, Mrs. Tillerton looked a little . . . well, dangerous. Maybe it was the way she held the child as though she feared becoming contaminated by it.

"Come in. Here, have a seat." He motioned to the chair. With long strides made uneven by the weight of the child on her hip, she crossed the room and seated herself. The baby squirmed. Without hesitating she deposited him on the rug and fell back into the chair like a prisoner released from the stocks.

At least the leather chair wouldn't be hurt by the moisture.

"I need a place to stay," she said.

He blinked. Their parting hadn't exactly been cordial, at least from her end. "As a bachelor there's not much by way of —"

Anne sank further into the seat and pulled the drawstring on her collar tight. "A boardinghouse. Do you know of one that accepts children?"

The infant pulled up to his feet but stood about as steady as a drunk on a barge during a hurricane. A child? Mrs. Tillerton was a widow, but Nicholas didn't remember any children from her marriage. How long ago had Mr. Tillerton died, and where had the child been while she was in Pushmataha? He cocked an eyebrow and tried his hand at guessing the baby's age. Less than a year. Not nearly old enough. Maybe he needed to change his impression of Mrs. Tillerton. Perhaps she was friendly to some men, just not him.

He didn't realize he was staring until she pulled her coat around herself. He felt his ears burning.

"Last I heard you were looking for a cook.

I'm no expert on infants, but I don't think he'll be much help in the kitchen." Falling into conversation came so naturally to him, his discomfort faded. Especially as he watched hers grow.

"I found the cook I was looking for . . . and her son." Anne lowered her eyes. "Not only did she refuse to come to Pushmataha with me, she also skipped town and left Sammy in my care."

"Sammy?" Nicholas stepped around his desk to smile at the child. "So now you're a mother?"

Her stare could turn boiling water into ice. Or it could amuse him.

"I can't hunt buffalo with a baby. There's no point in going back to Pushmataha until I find his father. In the meantime, he needs to be somewhere safer. Last night we had to sleep in the rain . . . or he did at least. I didn't sleep a wink. And I don't know how much I can afford. If Finn is hard to track down, I might need a paying job to make ends meet."

A house, a nursemaid, and a job? At least she wasn't asking for much.

"What exactly can you do?"

"I can shoot, skin, and tan. And although I won't admit it to Anoli, I'm a decent cook — nothing fancy, but I work hard. I've worked with horses a fair bit — can groom them, trim their hooves. I'm not above working for my keep. I don't know of any other skills that are worth paying for, but I'll try about any kind of work."

Her soft gray eyes held a challenge, daring him to laugh at her skills. Just how well did he know Mrs. Tillerton? Not at all, actually. He knew his sister held her in high regard, but everyone else from home thought her odd.

Nicholas sat on the edge of his desk. Introducing Mrs. Tillerton into his society would cause a sensation, but she wouldn't appreciate the attention. Come to think of it, her presence in Garber could be awkward for him, as well. Better find somewhere for her out of the way — not one of the boardinghouses, definitely not one of the hotels that the socially mobile haunted. A private residence would be ideal. He had just the place.

"I recommend the Pucketts. Their son is a friend of mine, and they have room in their house. I'm not sure about the baby, but my guess is they'll be delighted."

A sudden movement over Anne's shoulder caught his attention. The Boston fern waved wildly, and then with a crash it disappeared. Both he and Anne scrambled toward the howling baby. Anne pulled him upright and brushed the soil off him — right onto the Persian rug.

Nick wrinkled his nose. "Please . . . let's carry him to the window and dust him off there."

"You're not going to hold a baby out a window, are you?" Her reproachful eyes made him squirm, but his property had to be protected.

"The more you clean him the more dirt you're getting on the rug. Let's take him out to the landing." But the rug was already buried under a thick layer of black loam. The clumps falling out of the child's thin blond hair weren't enough to do any more damage. "Oh, never mind. I'll get Harold. Harold!"

Harold peered around the corner. His chin dropped at the sight of the disaster on the carpet. "Mrs. Stanford is coming today. She could be here any moment."

"Then help me sweep this up. We have a broom, don't we?"

Harold's eyes widened. "Of course not. You pay to have the office cleaned."

"Stars and bars!" Anne thrust the crying child into Nick's hands, almost releasing him too soon. "You surely have a clothes brush for your coat. Bring me that and a

82

newspaper. We can tidy this up."

"And then who'll tidy me?" Nick walked to his desk with outstretched arms, keeping the slobbering child well away from his satin vest. He sat the baby in the middle of his desk and bent to retrieve his clothes brush from the bottom drawer. "Wonderful! Now he's smearing my figures." The tears and spittle had mixed with the dirt, creating a thin mud that must have been delightful to spread over columns of numbers. At least the brat was acting like it.

Giving up on his clothing, Nick cradled the baby in the crook of his arm, igniting new screams when he was removed from his muddy masterpiece. What a disaster. She had no idea how much time he'd spent on that spreadsheet — a lot less than she'd spent saving his life. Maybe he owed her no further. Put a bullet in his head before ransacking his office.

"Thanks." Anne took the brush without looking at him. She had stuffed the fern back into its pot with the majority of the soil. Besides sitting cockeyed, it looked like it would survive.

Harold dropped the newspaper next to her as she knelt on the ground. "I just saw Mrs. Stanford out the window. She's turning the corner off Oak Street."

Heaven help him. Nick picked up the fern, barely able to palm the heavy pot with one hand. "Delay her. Tell her I'm busy."

Harold wagged his head. "And let her gnaw on me? No thanks."

When had Mrs. Stanford got her bluff in on Harold? Nick set the potted plant on the narrow stand and surveyed Mrs. Tillerton's progress. Not bad. Maybe Ophelia wouldn't notice the rug, although the baby in his arms would make for an interesting conversation. Nick turned toward the desk, and as he did, the little boy grabbed a handful of fern again.

"Watch out!" he said.

This time it didn't fall on the rug. It fell on Anne, smashing the ceramic pot into shards.

With a hand on her head, she turned horrified eyes on him.

"Why did you hit me?" she asked. And then fainted dead away.

For crying aloud. "Take the kid." Nick thrust the child into Harold's arms and rolled her over, the dirt sticking to her wet coat. He patted her cheek urgently. "Come on. Be a dear and wake up. We have to get you out of here."

"Before what?" a chilling voice intoned. "Before your employer catches you in a prickly situation?"

Anne tasted dirt. She slid her jaw from side to side, testing the pain and the grit between her teeth. She turned her head and knew immediately when she'd rolled onto a tender spot. Why had Jay hit her this time? She tried to remember what had precipitated the encounter, but her memories were too foggy. Nothing came to mind.

She forced her eyes open, expecting the next blow, but instead she saw three concerned faces bending over her.

Pushing off the ground, she raised enough to send sharp pulses through her skull and into her eyes.

"Don't get up." Nicholas Lovelace pressed against her shoulder, preventing her from rising any higher.

"You have yet to explain to me this person's identity," the woman was saying.

"I barely know myself," he answered.

"Yet you are caring for her child? If I weren't so generous, I might suspect a closer relationship than you're acknowledging."

Between the two of them? If her head didn't hurt so, Anne would've snorted. She covered her eyes, blocking out the light. She had to get her wits about her. Remaining supine in a man's office wasn't an option. What had happened?

Determined to fight through the throbbing, she managed to sit up, dirt tumbling into her eyes, her hair falling until it brushed her shoulders. The rug beneath her hands felt silky but soiled. Her fingers searched it until they found her wet hat. She wouldn't breathe easy until her disguise was in place again. A moan escaped as the hat touched her sensitive skull.

"I wish you'd rest, Mrs. Tillerton."

She bristled at Mr. Lovelace's voice. A memory stirred. There was a baby. She'd come with a child who had made this man mad, and then when she wasn't looking he'd clobbered her. Her stomach lurched. If he was that angry, what had he done to the baby?

"Where's Sammy?" Anne tried to roll onto her knees, but fell back on her seat when dizziness erupted. "What have you done with him? Did you hurt him, too?" Her voice rose over the shocked room.

"I say, Nicholas, this young woman doesn't appear to be in her right mind. Is she some relation of yours?"

"The ceramic pot fell and landed on your head. I didn't hit you." Mr. Lovelace sounded patient, but she couldn't get her eyes to focus and see if he meant it or not. "Sammy's all right. He's over there shredding my business files, happy as a lark."

On cue Sammy squealed and peeked around the desk, waving crumpled papers. Mr. Lovelace took her arm, helped her to her feet, and guided her to a chair. At least he seemed unconcerned with the cache of dirt falling from each wrinkle of her clothing. She'd made a mess and then accused him of violence. What a fool she was. "Are you sure you don't want to hold me out the window and shake me off?"

The twinkle in his eye was worth the effort.

"What is the meaning of this?" The dirty rug muffled the sound of the woman's stomp. "I demand an explanation."

"I apologize for my inattention. How reckless of me to neglect you when you came all this way to call," Mr. Lovelace said.

Anne almost grinned at his sarcasm, but the icy glare from the woman made her think better of it.

"Mrs. Stanford, allow me to present to you Mrs. Tillerton. She's an acquaintance from home — a friend of my sister's."

One severe eyebrow rose higher the longer she evaluated Anne's choice of garments. "Your sister? I'm astonished."

Poor Mr. Lovelace. Anne had come asking for a favor — never intending to leave his office in shambles and his employer in a tizzy. She hadn't meant to cause him trouble. Sammy crawled to her and tugged on her pant leg. She helped him scramble into her lap.

"I'll leave . . . just as soon as my head stops spinning enough to make it down the staircase."

"Stay where you are. Mrs. Stanford won't mind conducting her business while you recover and Harold cleans up."

But she obviously did. The woods of Ohio had heightened Anne's powers of observation. A broken twig, droppings, scraped bark — little signs had meanings, and Mrs. Stanford's reaction was based on something more than impatience and a busy schedule. Perhaps she had a daughter hoping for a marriage to Mr. Lovelace. He could be engaged already, for all she knew.

Mrs. Stanford refused to take a seat. "I merely wanted to leave this report with you, as promised, and to discuss your recent appointment to the commissioner's court, but Mrs. Tillerton's needs are more pressing. I suppose I don't need your attention until they are met."

But she wouldn't leave his office until

Anne did.

Mr. Lovelace bowed. "Then if you'll allow me to escort Mrs. Tillerton to her lodgings, we can meet again tomorrow." He dropped his Derby hat on his head and took Sammy from Anne. "You're coming with me, mister. We must give Mother some time to recover before she attempts to carry you again."

Mother? He knew better, but Mrs. Stanford didn't.

She got to her feet and exited the office with Mrs. Stanford and Mr. Lovelace. What did it matter? As soon as Anne found Finn Cravens, she'd leave Garber behind and never come back. Until then, Sammy was her responsibility. Unmarried mother sounded better than husband killer. What harm was another mark on her already soiled reputation?

6

Anne followed Nicholas down the walkway of finely chopped gravel. He stopped and turned to her once again. "I wish you'd let me carry Sammy. He must be heavy."

"You have our bags, and I'm getting used to him." Anne flicked a bug off of the child's shoulder as they brushed by rosebushes lining the walk. She wasn't getting used to him, but dealing with the boy gave her an excuse to keep mum. After demolishing his office and accusing him of striking a woman, Anne was ready to call it quits. Once she found a place for her and the child to stay, she would do her best to avoid the unlucky Mr. Lovelace.

The houses they had passed occupied the back half of spacious lots, giving the owners a cool distance from which to judge the pedestrians. The manicured lawns intimidated her. Too perfect. Obviously, she'd never belong in a place like this.

"Do you ever think of living in town?" Nicholas asked.

Anne shrugged. She'd had a house once — perfect from the outside, but what happened on the inside was nothing like she'd imagined. Maybe that was why she didn't want one now.

"The Pucketts are my closest friend's parents," he continued, "my surrogate family. Joel acts gruff but only because his mother refuses to cut the apron strings. She won't forgive him for getting a place of his own." Nicholas bounced his hand over the top of the pickets as they passed.

"Are you sure these people want lodgers? This doesn't look like a neighborhood for boarders."

"I'm not sure, but Mr. and Mrs. Puckett are very hospitable. It won't hurt to ask."

Sammy pulled at her hair, sticking his wet fingers in her ear. She grimaced.

"You might want to keep ahold of him." Nicholas stared at the child. "If he repeats his earlier performance you'll be on the street."

How could she know whether the situation she was bringing him into was any better than the one Tessa had provided? Would these people be any safer than the crowd at the saloon? Anne squeezed Sammy against her. If he got loose he might destroy the Pucketts' house, along with their chance, and although she didn't want to stay with strangers, neither could she camp with an infant. The unforgiving perfection of the lot worried her. It evidenced a meticulous, exacting personality that Anne was only too familiar with.

Growing up, she thought nothing was worse than her father's neglect. He didn't notice her. He didn't care. And then she married someone who noticed every movement, every expression that crossed her face, and nothing he noticed pleased him. Were these people the same?

Nicholas halted at an iron gate and turned toward Anne.

"What?" She was surprised to find herself shielding Sammy.

"I'm holding the gate open for you. Nothing sinister."

The brick path from the street led to a wide verandah, complete with porch swing and potted pansies.

"Funny these customs," she said. "You treat the ladies by making them walk into unknown territory first?"

He pulled the gate "closed" with a bang. "You don't have to go first. We'll go together." Taking her arm he dragged her down the walk without waiting for her consent.

Anne was more comfortable with the looks Nicholas was giving her now, as they waited before the brass door knocker. He seemed frustrated, impatient, and ready to wash his hands of her. Good. They'd part ways soon. Let him leave with no fond memories or curiosity — no reason to follow up on her progress.

The woman who opened the door didn't appear exacting. Her mobcap slanted over gray hair and above merry blue eyes . . . until Anne's appearance turned her joy into confusion.

"Hello, Mrs. Puckett," Nicholas said. "I apologize for not sending word that I'd be calling."

"No apologies necessary, Nicholas. You are welcome anytime." Her doughy face creased into pleasing lines. "And who have you brought to see me?"

"These are some friends of mine from back home — Mrs. Anne Tillerton and Master Sammy. They are new to Garber."

Friends? If he was calling her a friend then how well did he really know these people?

"Won't you please come in? I'd offer refreshments, but supper is on the stove. You might as well stay."

He really should be going. The Stanfords were waiting on his report from his trip and his bid on the new project. If he stayed with the prickly lady any longer, he was bound to agitate her again, and he'd already caused her enough grief.

Then he thought of his wrecked office and took a seat.

Nick passed the bowl of mashed potatoes to Mr. Puckett, who still sat in shocked silence. He'd probably never thought he'd have a wild she-cat sitting at his table. Nick's eyes flickered down her grungy getup for the last time. Her appearance begged him to slap her on the back and provide her with a spittoon, but the manners embedded into him by his exacting mother wouldn't allow him to do so, even if Mrs. Tillerton would prefer it.

So the best he knew to do with her was to hand her off to someone else. Mrs. Puckett and her Esther Circle at church could think of some way to help the vagabond. As much as he'd like to further their acquaintance, to do so would risk the displeasure of his largest . . . and only . . . contractor. This was for the best.

"So tell me about yourself, Mrs. Tillerton. When did your husband pass away?" Using her fork, Mrs. Puckett smashed some carrots in a saucer and handed it to Anne.

Anne took them but looked confused. Good grief. What was she going to do with that baby?

"He died four years ago." Anne bent over the carrots and missed the significant look that passed between Mr. and Mrs. Puckett. The lady placed her hand on her husband's arm and with a slight twitch of her head dissuaded him from the words on the tip of his lips.

"How awful — to be widowed so young. Was it an illness? Accident?"

Anne paused with the spoonful of carrots midair. Sammy grunted, mouth opened, trying to reach it.

"No, ma'am. Neither." She gave the boy the bite and kept her head lowered.

Nicholas spread a generous amount of butter on his roll. She'd drawn the short straw when it came to conversation skills. If she wasn't careful, she'd ruin her chances of getting to stay. Intervention was needed.

"Mrs. Tillerton and my sister Molly grew close after her husband's passing, and then she left Prairie Lea. We lost track of her until

95

recently, when she intervened in a train robbery."

Mr. Puckett leaned forward. His white moustache twitched. "Now, there's a story I'd like to hear."

Anne looked like she'd just found half a worm in her apple, but why wouldn't she want her heroic story told? Much better than waiting for them to ask more questions about her late husband. Well, if she wouldn't tell it, he would.

"I was coming home on the NTT line after scouting out the lumber sources around the Antlers area. Mrs. Tillerton and I had only just renewed our acquaintance and were having a word in the luggage —"

Anne's eyes widened. Nicholas raised his glass and gulped a mouthful of tea. "We were talking when the train stopped, and an armed man got on board. Next thing I knew, they were harassing some of the ladies. I couldn't endure to see a lady in distress, but as usual I was unarmed —"

Sammy blew raspberries unceremoniously, bringing laughter from around the table. Nick grinned. "You're right, Sammy. I'm turning this into a fish story, aren't I? The short of it is that I jumped in over my head, and if it wasn't for Mrs. Tillerton and her quick draw, my last breath would've

96

been filled with train soot and the dust of Indian Territory."

Mrs. Puckett pressed her napkin to her lips. Her blue eyes fell on Anne. "You carry a gun on you?"

Anne wiped the carrots from Sammy's chin. "Yes, ma'am. Usually there's one in my knapsack when I travel."

The gun hadn't been in the knapsack on the train, and he'd felt hers beneath her duster when he'd knelt at her side after the accident with the fern. A crafty reply that avoided an outright lie. He'd have to remember that in dealing with her. No, he wasn't going to deal with her again. As soon as she found Sammy's father —

"Where are you lodging, Mrs. Tillerton? Do you have family in town?" asked Mrs. Puckett.

"No, ma'am. I don't know where I'm going to put up." She held a little tin cup for the boy to sip from.

"I see."

It was Nick's turn to focus all his attention on his plate. Now they understood why he'd brought Anne to them. How would they respond?

"I hate to think of that little fellow in a boardinghouse," Mr. Puckett said.

"And we have an empty room," Mrs.

Puckett added.

Anne had stopped feeding Sammy, as his grunt reminded them.

"How long do you plan to stay in town?" Mr. Puckett cleaned his fork and reached for the pumpkin pie on the sideboard behind him.

"Just until I find his father." The room went silent. Anne looked up. "This isn't my baby." Her lips went firm. "His mother left him with me."

Mrs. Puckett exhaled. She turned to her husband and waited for a silent verification to pass between them before speaking again. "Perhaps this is where God wants you to stay. You know the Good Book says to entertain strangers. You just might be an angel in disguise. We'd be honored for you to stay with us."

"I intend to pay." Anne set down her spoon. "Once I find Finn, Sammy's father, I'll return to Pushmataha and will send you the money. I didn't bring enough with me. I really thought I'd be headed back by now."

The pumpkin pie was passed to Nicholas. He took a thick slice. The most beneficial negotiations occurred when the other party came to your conclusions without any directing.

"You know," Mrs. Puckett said, leaning

forward, "Joel is being downright stubborn about providing us with grandchildren. I think it'd do me some good to have Sammy to play with during the day. If I took him on my rounds, calling on my friends, why he'd be the life of the party. He'd have more grandmothers than any child —"

He was just inhaling the warm spiciness of the pie when Anne shot to her feet.

"I'm going."

Anne swooped Sammy up from his chair and plopped him on her hip. Pulling Sammy's napkin out from his collar, she tossed it on the table.

"Thank you for the food. It was right nice of you." And without another word she strode out of the room toward the front door.

With a groan Nick dropped his forkful of pie on his plate and chased after her, only catching her before she reached the gate.

"What are you doing?"

"I'm leaving. I'll find somewhere else."

He stepped in front of her, blocking her way. "No you don't. You're staying here."

"I can't. Those people are crazy."

"Who's calling whom crazy?"

Anne winced as Sammy tugged on a handful of her hair. "They are too eager. The room — it's not right. Everything seems so nice. So safe. It isn't real. Why would they let me, a stranger of questionable reputation, stay in their home? Did you hear that talk about angels? And can anyone honestly think that watching an infant all day would be fun?"

"They are compassionate, God-fearing folk. They know you don't have any other choice, and they are trying to help you. And many women Mrs. Puckett's age enjoy young ones — especially since she doesn't know what a mess he is."

"Then let him stay. I'll come back and get him when I find Finn."

"No, ma'am. What's to keep you from doing the same as his mother and disappearing?"

Her face grew fierce. "As tempting as that is, I'm made of sterner stuff. But these people . . . they have some other motivation, probably sinister, that I haven't detected yet."

"You think the Pucketts are deviants?"

"You don't know. Your pa, your ma, they'd never hurt you. You don't know how people are."

Her impenetrable mask was slipping again. Her tough act cracking. He reached to smooth Sammy's tousled blond hair, and she shied away from him. Did Jay Tillerton still haunt her? Nick knew she had a past darker than his shoe blacking, and while he was sympathetic, he couldn't lose this chance to leave her in competent hands. It was the best he could do for her.

"You're right, Mrs. Tillerton. My experience with evil is limited. I don't know people like that, but I know these people. You and Sammy will be safe with them. You came to me for help, and this is the best help I can offer. Please give them a chance."

The slant in her eyes made him want to smile, even now. "I can't go back. What will they think?"

"They'll understand."

"What if they've already changed their mind?"

"We won't know unless we ask."

Absently she bounced Sammy on her hip as she considered — her rough-worn duster out of place in the tidy neighborhood. And to think she was afraid of them.

"I'll leave if they act suspicious. And if they hurt him . . . so help me . . ."

"For being unprepared to care for the boy, you sound like a regular Momma bear." Nicholas smiled. "Now, let's get you and the cub settled in your den."

7

The next day Anne heaved a sigh of relief as she left to find employment. Although she questioned if leaving the baby with Mrs. Puckett was wise, she couldn't deny the relief of being alone. The baby had snuffled and whined all night, although it was still the best night's sleep she'd had since coming to town. He probably missed his momma. Nothing she could do to help him there.

On the street, Anne stepped aside to defer to a stylishly dressed lady and thought of the flimsy dress the saloon owner had offered. Not again. Anne was done with dressing to please men. She had donned dresses for only a few years at the encouragement of her schoolteacher, Mr. Tillerton. He challenged her to better herself and not hide her talents. Too late she realized which talents interested him the most, and by that time her father had an opportunity to rid himself of his daughter. Jay Tillerton had been forced to marry her and leave the state, carting her to live among total strangers — where no one felt obligated to speak up for her.

Anne scanned the various shops and businesses up and down the street. Finding work for the day would solve two of her problems — she could recompense the Pucketts for her board, and she'd escape from Sammy. But who would hire her?

She slowed as she passed the bank. While she could figure and write in a clear hand, she'd never seen a woman dressed like herself working in an office. Maybe a tanner or a farrier would need an extra hand.

The livery stable bustled with carriages lined up and men waiting for their mounts. Anne stuck her head inside the office, not surprised to find it empty. She cut through the crowd and found the boss.

"You look busy. I could lend a hand for a few hours."

"Do you know how to unhitch a horse from a carriage?" He didn't even look her way as he buckled a bridle.

"Sure do."

"Then get out there and move those carriages."

Anne marched toward a fine buggy. The

man holding the reins didn't act accustomed to waiting, but he lit up when he saw her. "Well, now. What do we have here? Mackie is hiring fancy women to work the stables?"

Anne raised her eyes warily. His hat hid the silver streaks in his hair, but he was definitely the same man she'd seen in the upstairs of the saloon. She took the reins from him. "I've got it. You can go."

"It's not your place to dismiss me, young lady. I know everything that happens in this town, so why haven't I heard of you?"

"Maybe because I don't plan to be in this town much longer. Now, if you'll excuse me, I have work to do."

"Wait." Commands came easily for him. "I have heard of you. You rode in on the train from Pushmataha, didn't you? The one that got held up?"

Anne clicked her tongue. The horses followed. The man reached up and threw the brake on the carriage.

"You are the woman from the train. Well, well. And I'm someone you'd benefit from knowing. Meet me at my . . . well, let's meet at the hotel. I want —"

"No." Anne put her hands on her hips and glared. "If you don't release the brake, I'll move on to the other carriage."

"You don't know to whom you are speaking. You should reconsider —"

"Ian?"

Anne sighted the woman immediately. Although not clad in the same gown that she'd worn in Mr. Lovelace's office, Mrs. Stanford's dress was just as extravagant. She approached purposefully, and the expression on the man's face made the whole encounter almost worth it. Mister Powerful-Influential-Romeo glowered at the lady in the expensive fitted gown, but his interest in Anne had vanished.

"Why did you come back?" he asked.

"I left my portfolio in the carriage." Her eyes, sharp as knives, picked Anne apart feature by feature. And her words cut even cleaner. "I thought you would've left town by now."

Her husband stepped up and retrieved the portfolio for her.

"I'll leave as soon as I'm able," Anne said.

"Are you employed here?" The lady stood with perfect posture, her skirts fluttering where they flared from her knees downward, her hands folded together before her.

"Temporarily."

The woman's face remained impassive. She rotated slowly, took her husband's arm, and led him away.

Seeing her opportunity, Anne pulled the

brake free and led the horses to the back of the barn, where the carriages would be stored. She found an empty stall and unharnessed the horses. She'd just led them out of the traces when the yard boss waved her down.

"Here's a half-dollar — a generous wage for the little time you spent, I'd say."

Anne looked at the men waiting for their horses. "That's all you need? It looks like —"

"That's all. I've already had a complaint from one of my best customers. I can't have you enticing the men here."

"Enticing? Listen, mister. You can string me up if I as much as smiled at one of your customers."

He looked as aggravated as she felt, but he didn't change his mind. "Get on, now. No point causing a scene."

Anne shoved the coin into her pocket. She knew where the charge had come from, but there was nothing to do besides accept her money and leave behind another place where she was unwelcome. At least she'd made enough to pay Mrs. Puckett something for supper without tapping into her train-ticket money.

She headed back to her temporary lodging. She couldn't say that she missed the child — not when she was counting the hours before he'd be removed from her care — but she didn't want her absence to trouble him. The boy needed someone who could love him. Everyone deserved that much.

Nicholas hadn't had much reason to go to the courthouse since settling in Garber. Occasional permits and taxes had to be filed, but neither increased his desire to visit the white marble structure, bland and devoid of ornamentation. If he had county work that needed to be done, he took the papers with him, which was exactly what he was doing as he left the courthouse. He much preferred to labor in his more comfortable space than in the utilitarian building. Persian rugs and potted ferns gave his office an air of luxury that the government found unnecessary.

As did Commissioner David Anderson. Gaunt, bespectacled, and careful with his words, his only concession to fashion was a handlebar moustache that the town barber trimmed every Saturday morning. Meeting him in the vicinity of the courthouse wasn't unusual, which was precisely where Nick saw him today.

"Good morning, Nick." The other man

stood in front of the dry goods store located directly across the street. "Are you finding your way around the courthouse?"

Nick joined him under the awning and out of the sun. "I have to count doors in that hallway to keep from walking into the wrong office, but I think I can remember now. Considering the short duration of my service, there's not much to worry about besides the bridge project."

David peered over the rims of his spectacles. "The bridge project has provided enough worry, as it is."

"Tell me why. The only reason I'm given is that the river is too wide and not easily spanned, but if the railroads can bridge it, why couldn't we?"

"Your vote is yes?"

"I haven't had time to delve into the numbers yet, but if I vote no, it won't be because of construction fears."

"Interesting." David rubbed his chin. "Do you have any desire to run for election in November?"

The white of the courthouse loomed like a palace across the street. "No. I mean, I hadn't considered it. This was just an appointment."

"Someone will be elected to fill your spot. Maybe you could get an extension on the filing, considering the circumstances. We could use another honest man."

His tone caused Nicholas to look over his shoulder, but the potato barrel on the store's porch was the only witness. "Are you trying to tell me something?"

"Only that things aren't always what they seem — you, for instance."

But before Nicholas could puzzle out his meaning, Anderson stepped off the porch.

"Good day, Mr. Lovelace."

Election? Nicholas shook his head as he made his way to his office. Every minute spent worrying over the bridge was a minute lost overseeing his own interests. He'd accepted this post, but he wasn't looking to extend his stay.

When he reached the rickety outside staircase to Lovelace Transportation Specialists, the door above him opened. Out stepped Harold, his arms full of files and ledgers.

"Is it quitting time already?" Nick met him halfway up the staircase.

"It's Saturday," Harold said. "I shouldn't be here at all, but I came back to take another look at the figures we're presenting to Mr. Stanford on the second line."

Nicholas slapped his back. "Don't bury yourself in the books, Harold. Your wife will be mad at me."

"I'm charging you overtime, so she approves."

Harold turned sideways as Nicholas squeezed past him on the staircase. Nick hugged as close to the building as he could manage.

"Don't lean against that rail," Nick warned. But it was too late.

With a sickening crack the rail gave way, and Harold teetered at the edge. Nicholas made a grab for him but came up with only ripped paper.

"Harold!" He leaned over the gaping hole to see his employee lying on the ground. "Are you all right?"

Harold rolled to his back, exposing his right arm bent in places that arms shouldn't bend. "Does it look as bad as it hurts?"

Racing down the stairs, Nick's heart hammered. "It looks bad. Can you move your legs?"

"I think I'm going to be sick."

"Just stay put and I'll get a doctor." Nicholas wasn't feeling too healthy, either. The sight of the disjointed arm turned his stomach inside out.

"Help me up."

Nick supported him the best he could without putting any pressure on his shoulder. Harold's face turned white and his lips tightened, but he was on his feet, and they were on their way.

The next hour Nick spent agonizing over each of Harold's whimpers as the doctor set his arm. He should've insisted that his landlord fix that staircase. Harold's injuries could've been much worse. By the time the doctor broke out the bandages, Nick's teeth had ground themselves smooth.

Joel's voice carried into the office. "I know you're here, Nick. You might as well speak up."

"Come on back." Nick winced as the doctor wrapped another layer of bandages around the splint while Harold tightly gripped the bed frame.

Deputy Joel Puckett stepped into the room, his wide-set eyes still carrying the innocence of youth despite six years as a Texas deputy. "When I spied that broken bannister, I was afraid something like this had happened."

"I'll be fine." Harold licked his lips. "But I won't be doing any pencil pushing for a while."

"Well, I don't imagine that Nick will put you out to pasture just yet."

Nick scratched his head. "Don't know what we'll do. Just pray that Harold's arm miraculously heals."

"I don't think God owes you that big of a favor," Joel said.

The doctor raised his head only enough to catch them above the wire frame of his glasses. "I'm trying to work here."

"Go on home." Sweat beaded on Harold's face. "I don't want anyone seeing me like this. Besides, Doc sent for my wife. She'll be here soon."

Nick lifted his hand to pat Harold on the back but then thought better of it and followed Joel outside to the well on the back of the property.

Joel took a seat on the stone wall and fiddled with the bucket rope. "I came to get your version of the train story. Sounds like you nearly got yourself killed."

Nick shrugged. "What's a man's life worth if he allows a woman to be harassed in his presence?"

"So you put a stop to it?"

"Well, yes. Miss Walcher was left alone after I attacked the offender."

Joel didn't hide his skepticism. "Those must be the slowest drawing group of bandits to ever ride the range. I can't believe not a one of them got a shot off on you. But it would've been a pity to lose two county commissioners to the Grim Reaper

112

in a month."

"I'm more worried about Harold. The ink's not yet dry on my oath, and now I'm shorthanded at the office."

"I foresee long boring hours with your beloved ledger and maps."

"I foresee extra expense for kerosene and coffee." Nick leaned into the well and let his voice echo back at him.

"Come on over to my parents' place," said Joel. "No use in starting this marathon on an empty stomach."

"I've eaten with your parents since you have. And just to prepare you, your mother wants to know —"

"When I'm going to settle down and give her grandchildren." Joel bounced a pebble down the shaft. "Thanks for the warning, but if I couldn't predict that question, I'd have no business trying to track down outlaws."

8

Another fruitless day. No work, no word from Anoli. Anne traveled the tidy walkway to the Pucketts' home, glad that Mrs. Puckett had told some of the neighbors about her. At least a few braved tentative waves, but by the time they got used to her, she'd be gone.

The crunch of gravel alerted her that someone was behind her. She didn't change her pace. She didn't look over her shoulder, but she read what signs she could. At long intervals she heard rustling. A man — not in a hurry but covering ground just the same. He carried more than the usual amount of hardware — two six-shooters at least. Her path led into the setting sun, so there was no shadow visible. Her gun belt was hidden by her coat, but if he was trouble he'd assume she had one. If an animal were stalking her, she would stop and face it. Men were more complicated.

You couldn't take a shot at one just because they threatened your territory.

Especially when you didn't own any territory.

Three houses to pass before she'd reach the Pucketts', but did she want to go there? A stalked mountain lion didn't lead hunters back to her cubs. Better to see what he wanted.

She stopped. His footsteps slowed and then resumed their pace until he'd reached her.

The same young deputy who'd harassed her before stepped forward. Once again, he'd put her on trial when all she was doing was minding her own business.

"I thought you were leaving last week. What are you doing in this neighborhood?"

Anne tensed. Lawmen usually assumed she was guilty of something.

"My plans have changed. I found a cook and sent her on to Pushmataha, but I'm staying here, boarding with the Pucketts."

Her answer displeased him. "How did that come about?"

She matched his wary expression. "Are all the sheriffs of Garber as concerned about the boarding arrangements of women as you are?"

"I'm a deputy, and yes, it does concern

me when people claim to be living at my parents' home."

Parents? Anne swallowed. If only a giant eagle would swoop down and carry her away. She pulled her hat low and nearly ran to the house. She'd heard about their son, Joel. No one had mentioned he was a deputy. He didn't stop her but followed right on her heels. The previously friendly neighbors stopped to watch.

She didn't even pause in front of the house but walked around to the back, where she generally entered. The door didn't close behind her before he caught it and whooshed into the kitchen.

Mrs. Puckett wasn't there. He watched her, waiting for her to act. If it weren't for Sammy, she would've turned and fled, clear to New Mexico Territory.

"Mrs. Puckett?"

"Ma?"

They hollered in unison. Quick clicks in the hall, then the door swung open.

"Joel!" Mrs. Puckett handed Sammy to Anne and wrapped her arms around the relentless man. His arms returned the sentiment, but his face remained dark.

"Is that her baby?" he asked.

"Do you know Mrs. Tillerton? Why are you scowling like that, Joel? You have such a lovely smile. Haven't I told you it's unbecoming to frown?"

Anne bounced Sammy on her hip. Must be difficult to act tough with a mother like Mrs. Puckett in town. She could almost feel sorry for the man.

"She told me she was staying here. Sounded like a fabrication to me."

"Well, I never! Why would you doubt a lady's word?"

One eyebrow rose, letting Anne know what he thought of her claims to ladydom.

"How exactly did this come about?"

Before Anne could answer, Mrs. Puckett bustled to the stove and slid an apple pie inside. "Nicholas brought her to us. She's from Pushmataha. Her husband died, and she's here looking for work. We're letting her lease a room, and I'm sitting with the baby."

"Pushmataha, you say?" His eyes narrowed. "I don't remember any deaths reported in Pushmataha. How did your husband die?"

Anne tried to freeze her face. No emotion. No response. "Your mother has the events a little confused. My husband died years ago. I came to Garber to find a cook for the depot in Pushmataha, and the cook I came after gave me the slip . . . and her son. Now I'm waiting to hear from the child's father before I can return to the hunt."

"Where is he?"

Anne could only shrug.

"But she's a decent, hardworking young lady," Mrs. Puckett said. "I've told her she's welcome to stay as long as she needs, but she insists on finding employment."

He raised an eyebrow. "And did you find any?"

"It's harder than I expected."

"But you know Nick . . ." He nodded slowly, and gradually that smile that made his mother proud began to emerge — a smile that made Anne mighty suspicious. "I might know of a position for you. Be ready first thing in the morning."

Despite his glowering demeanor, Deputy Puckett seemed to have plenty of friends in town. In their walk from his parents' house to the business district they were never alone, always at the mercy of some man wanting to hear the latest town news or to report what he suspected. Others trailed along to hear what their neighbors had uncovered. Deputy Puckett listened much, spoke little, and never acknowledged the woman briskly striding next to him, proud that she was keeping up.

He sped as he neared the fancy hotel and burst through the doors. Anne stayed at his heels with no time to take in the elaborate foyer or the startled guests as they rushed into a dining room that wafted with laughter and the clinking of dishes — all of which went silent when she and Deputy Puckett entered.

"Where's Nick?"

All the wide eyes in the room turned to the far corner where Nicholas Lovelace was sipping his coffee.

Perfectly attired from his jaunty Derby to his spotless shoes, his face lit up when he saw the deputy, then his brows lowered when he saw her.

"Mrs. Tillerton, I see you met the elusive Deputy Puckett."

Elusive? Seemed like the deputy followed her everywhere.

Anne marched to his chair. "You could've told me the Pucketts' son was a lawman."

Someone by the buffet twittered. Nick stood, crumpling his napkin in his hand. "So you've made the acquaintance of your parents' new boarder, Joel. Glad to see you're getting along."

"I could hardly credit that Mrs. Tillerton is a friend of yours."

Anne could almost hear Joel's tanned skin crackling as his face scrunched into a grin.

"She doesn't resemble your usual companions."

Nick's eyes traveled the dining room. Every young lady present was in danger of slipping from her chair while leaning closer to catch their conversation. With a jerk of his head he motioned them into an unoccupied corner. "It's a long story. Have you found Sammy's father?" he asked Anne.

"Not yet."

"That's too bad." Nicholas glanced wistfully at the room past them. "Well, if there were some way I could help —"

"There is," Joel said. "You're shorthanded at the office, aren't you?"

"Yes and I'm running late this morning. My vest had a grease spot on it. Had to completely reconsider my wardrobe —"

"Mrs. Tillerton needs a job."

In the silence that followed, Anne could've tracked a fox to its den. Nick's blue eyes flickered once to her.

"I don't think so." He started past them again, but Deputy Puckett restrained him with a hand on his chest.

"You thought she was good enough to live with my parents. Is there a reason you wouldn't allow her in your office?"

Anne's face burned when Nicholas didn't answer. "I'm not working for him," she blurted. "I couldn't stand to be cramped all day in that tiny office. I'll find somewhere else."

"But you haven't. Mr. Lovelace was kind enough to introduce you to my parents' charity, so surely he'll be generous enough to give you a chance to pay them back."

"I will pay," Anne said. "I insist on paying. As soon I hear from Anoli, I'll have the funds wired here. Your parents won't be out anything."

She kept her chin up, daring them to communicate over her head. Why had she come to Nicholas for help in the first place? Her position was insufferable. She wouldn't allow him to fulfill his promise so begrudgingly.

"Come on," Nicholas said.

She wished she hadn't seen the glare he threw at the now beaming lawman. "You've trapped Mr. Lovelace. He feels like he owes me for saving his life."

Joel cocked his head. "You saved his life? When?"

Nicholas turned his back to Joel. "It's not that I mind your company, Mrs. Tillerton, but if you need money, I'll give you some and we'll see that Joel's parents are recom-

121

pensed. Joel, thank you for bringing Mrs. Tillerton. I'll see her home."

"Not yet. Is she talking about the train robbery? If I find that a witness misled me, then he could face criminal charges."

"That deputy badge must be agitating you," Nick said. "I didn't give you an official statement. We were just visiting."

"Maybe, but I'd rather hear Mrs. Tillerton's story of how she saved your worthless hide."

The morning light coming through the window illuminated Nicholas's weary face. He knew enough about her past to get her kicked out of town, much less out of Joel's parents' house. If she painted him gray, he'd do her black in the end.

"He was the hero," she said. "One of the bandits grabbed ahold of a woman, and Mr. Lovelace clobbered him. In a fair fight I think he could've taken him."

Joel's eyebrows inched higher. "But it wasn't a fair fight. What happened?"

She opened her mouth, and then turned to Nicholas.

"Go on." He waved his hand at her. "You're quite the storyteller. Why stop now?"

The diners had resumed their chatter, having given up on hearing the conversation.

"One of the robbers pulled a gun on Mr. Lovelace — put it right against his head. The leader told him to shoot. He didn't stand a chance . . ." She swallowed, remembering the comfortable feel of the gun in her hand and the disgust that it felt so soothing.

Nick's feet shifted toward her. She looked up. No longer did he look irritated. That same sad understanding etched his face. That same response that threatened to be her undoing. She squared her shoulders, determined not to let him see her weakness again.

"She shot a warning that made them reconsider their plan — right through the toe of his boot." He tossed his napkin onto a table. "Mrs. Tillerton keeps her head in a fix. You might think about deputizing her. She'd make a better marshal than a clerk."

"Nice try, Lovelace." Joel wiped his sleeve against his bearded chin. "How well could you describe the robbers, Mrs. Tillerton?"

"If you need someone identified, you can call on me," Nicholas said. "I was a lot closer to them than she was."

"But you couldn't see anyone well enough to put a bullet in their shoe." Joel smiled.

"Everyone's face was covered," Anne said, "but I'd do the best I could."

"Are you finished?" Nicholas asked. "I really must be going."

"I'm finished. I'll leave it to you to get Mrs. Tillerton safely to Mother's tonight . . . or maybe I should ask Mrs. Tillerton to escort you —"

"Come on." Nicholas waited to hold the door open for her. She skittered through, certain she didn't want to go anywhere with the frustrated man.

"It's only temporary." Her buckskin britches looked thick and heavy next to Nicholas's fine trousers. "As soon as I get Sammy with his father, I'll be gone."

"Can you read?" He strode into the busy street.

"Of course."

"Write? Do sums?"

"I was a decent student." Especially when the handsome schoolmaster kept her after class for tutoring. "I went to school only a couple of years, but I have a clear hand, know basic sums, and can make sense of most writing."

"Nicely played, Joel Puckett, nicely played," he muttered. "Well, as soon as Harold is able, he can sit at his desk and dictate to you what needs to be written. He can figure the wording and the accounts — you just write. Until then, we'll muck along

124

as well as we're able."

They turned the corner of the collateral broker's shop to the back, where Nicholas's office was located, and nearly ran into a lumber wagon. Tools and planks lay scattered around. The only thing missing was the staircase.

Nicholas pushed back his hat. "For the love of Pete, how am I supposed to get to my office?"

Clad in a pair of dungarees, a stained shirt, and a straw hat, a man dropped boards from off his shoulder. "The building owner ordered a new staircase. Can't build it with the old one standing."

"But I have to work. I must get in there."

The man chuckled. "I'll have a frame up by the end of the day. Tomorrow I'll start filling in the steps. Unless you got wings . . ."

Nicholas stood, hands on hips, and surveyed the door that posed like a victim at the edge of a pirate's gangplank. Anne half expected him to start flapping his arms, but instead he turned and rummaged through the pile of lumber the man was unloading from his wagon. Locating his prize, Nicholas grasped the ends of two long planks and walked backwards until they fell free of the wagon.

"I didn't grow up at a lumber mill for

nothing. I suppose you have a saw?" He slid out of his coat and handed it to Anne while the man went to fetch one. Anne laid the coat across her arm, surprised by the supple cloth. It looked so firm stretched across his shoulders, but really it was —

"Good grief, woman. Are you rubbing my coat?" He paused with a vest button halfway through the buttonhole.

"It . . . it feels soft."

"Compared to canvas, I suppose it is."

He was insulting her ugly duster. Let him. No one would daydream about running their hands over that ugly material. Or the woman beneath.

He tossed her the vest. "It's satin. Do try to control yourself."

She let her lip rise in a near snarl but then wished she hadn't when a whiff of his cologne reached her nose. Woodsy and warm. Knowledge about her employer's clothing that did her no good.

By the time the carpenter returned, Nicholas had his sleeves rolled up and the long boards lying parallel to each other. He laid a third board across the top of a barrel and sawed off a three-foot piece. The sound of it falling to the ground echoed off the building on the other side of the alley.

Nicholas tossed it to the carpenter. "Get

126

busy and I'll let you keep the ladder when we're through."

Anne stepped into the shade and leaned against the building, surprised at this unexpected side of the dandy. The blond hair on his forearms seemed out of place. It was almost . . . well, masculine. She hadn't thought he'd get his hands dirty, but here he was plying a saw, forcing it through the honey-colored wood. She threaded her pinky through the buttonhole on his vest, thinking again how he'd risked his life to protect the woman on the train — a woman with whom, as far as Anne could tell, he had no serious ties.

He was a complicated man, she'd give him that.

Had he relinquished his life before he rushed the man, or had he assumed that he would live? Four years ago Anne had hidden in the bushes on the riverbank, fleeing her abusive husband, when he'd attacked another woman. She and Mr. Lovelace might not have anything else in common, but that one moment was an experience that few others shared. The rare decision to give up your safety for a near stranger could've bound them together, but Nick gave no sign of being changed by his dangerous act.

Then again, what had changed Anne? The

danger she'd faced or the fact that she'd been victorious? Challenge the evil and die, or challenge the evil and live with the consequences of killing a man who'd once owned your heart?

Before she was ready, a dubious ladder was propped against the wall. Nicholas sprang up the first board and bounced.

"It'll do." He hopped down. "Ladies first."

Anne handed him his coat and vest and planted her foot on the first step. Her hands were too small to get a strong grip on the cross boards, but she'd take what she could. The ladder shuddered. What was he doing?

"Can't you wait until I'm off?"

"No, ma'am. I'm behind you in case you slip."

"And then what?"

"I'll cushion your fall."

What a view he must have. Another good reason to wear her ugly clothes.

She reached the top, but the ladder only touched the floor of the second story. Summoning her courage, she had to release her hold on the ladder and lunge for the floor, but she made it.

"That wasn't so bad, was it?" Nick's eyes sparkled as if he'd enjoyed climbing like a possum to his office. He leaned out the door, and with a call down, his portfolio was tossed up into his arms.

"Now, let's get to work."

He couldn't concentrate. Nick tapped his pen on the blotter and watched the wet ink absorb into the green felt. Of the thousands of tasks to be accomplished today, he couldn't stop gloating over the one already completed — he'd surprised her. She probably thought he didn't know the business end of a hammer from the hand grip. She probably thought he'd pull out a wallet and hire the carpenter to build the ladder. Well, what Anne Tillerton didn't know about him was that he had poked around a sawmill since he was a little turnip. He'd watched his father's business grow from axes and saws to a waterwheel, pulleys, millstones, and outbuildings. And with each building that went up, little Nick was there watching and learning. Manual labor wasn't the fastest path to accumulated wealth, so he favored the managing side, but that didn't mean he couldn't jump in and lend a hand when his crew needed it.

And for a moment he'd thought he'd seen admiration in her eyes.

Dropping his pen on the desk, Nicholas leaned back in his chair and laced his fingers behind his head. Too bad she couldn't see him out at the railhead, directing the lumberjacks or at the sawmill, testing the machinery. There was more to him than this office. In fact, he'd much rather take her on a survey of his work at the railhead than have her inappropriate self gracing his front room.

At least it wouldn't be for long.

She might be able to copy the contracts as she had claimed, but Nicholas's productivity had grounded to a halt. He couldn't stop thinking about her in there. Who would've thought her hair would be so curly? Every time she removed her hat, he was shocked by the caramel ringlets that sprang out. She kept it cut, so it didn't hang long, but even then, if stretched out it'd probably touch her shoulders — if they weren't covered by that hideous coat. The image of white shoulders in a sapphire evening gown teased him.

Women. They had no business in his office.

"Excuse me." Anne stepped into the doorway.

Nicholas dropped his feet off the desk and fumbled with his pen in a vain attempt to look busy.

"That woman is coming up the alley."

"Mrs. Stanford?" He bounded to his feet.

"What did she say?"

Anne blinked. "She didn't see me."

"Yoo-hoo, Nicholas. Are you up there?"

He strode across the room and grasped Anne's shoulders, unable to avoid the thought of an evening gown to replace the duster. "Don't go near the door."

Her forehead wrinkled, but she nodded as he made his way to the entrance in Harold's office.

He pulled open the door, startled by the sheer drop below. "Hello, Mrs. Stanford. Fine day we're having, is it not?"

Ophelia's head tilted until she was in danger of toppling over from the weight of her enormous hat. "Yes, of course, but what on earth happened to your stairs?"

"The rail collapsed under Harold. Terribly dangerous. We're fortunate it didn't fall while you were on it."

"Impossible. I wouldn't be so . . ." She frowned at the carpenter, who didn't have the grace to hide his appreciation of her charms. "Please, come down. I wanted to discuss our plans for your expansion."

But Nick recognized an advantage when he saw one. "Why don't you come up here?"

"You jest. Ladies don't ascend ladders."

"Quite so. Well, I'm afraid I'm unable to make the trip down. With Harold's injury, I have no time to spare if I want to keep my most important client satisfied."

Ophelia grasped a rung and leaned into the ladder, frightening him with the threat that she might ascend after all. But instead she only smiled. "Keeping your client satisfied is very important. I suppose our plans can wait until tomorrow."

"Marvelous."

With a smile, she sped away like a warship with full sails. When the last fluttering ribbon disappeared behind the corner of the building, Nick flagged down the carpenter.

"Hey, Charlie, do you have another job you could work on tomorrow?"

"Yes, sir, but Mr. Butler told me that if I finished the staircase in two days, he'd give me a bonus."

"Leave it off for four days, and I'll double that bonus."

He could hear Anne's soft breath behind him as he tried to get the carpenter's understanding without being explicit. He couldn't ban Ophelia, but he couldn't have her waltzing into his office at will. Not with Anne there. She'd already been quite clear on her opinion of Mrs. Tillerton. Four days. Surely Anne would have her business settled and be headed back to Indian Territory by then.

"You got it, Boss."

As the carpenter began gathering his tools, Nick turned to Anne.

"I hope you're willing to climb for a few more days. She won't approve of my new assistant, so the longer I can keep her out of here, the better."

"So instead of telling her it's not her concern, you're hiding from her?" Anne's gray eyes pierced through him.

Nicholas shut the door with more force than he'd planned. "I don't like your insinuation. What right do you have to judge me when you shun society altogether?"

"Why do you think I'm no fan of the public? I don't need soirees to learn herd behavior. I've watched the buffalo."

"You learned your manners from buffalo? That explains a lot." Imagine! Anne Tillerton criticizing his methods. Didn't his success speak for itself?

"Does Mrs. Stanford tell you who you can hire? Befriend? Court? I saw you at the robbery. You're capable of courage. How has this woman gained mastery over you?"

Nick's jaw grew taut. "It's not that simple, Mrs. Tillerton. I'd rather risk my life at the end of a pistol than risk my financial success. And what do you suggest? Should I break contract with my sole customer in hopes of getting smaller, less reliable contracts? I know to be cautious, but I face my fears. Now, if you'll excuse me, I'll finish this loan paper work, and you can take it to the bank on your way to the Pucketts'. That is, if you're not afraid to walk that far by yourself."

Irritating. That's what he got for getting involved with a pariah. He cut a straight path to his desk and shuffled through papers to find the form — the one he'd been working on when daydreams of the unsuitable woman before him got him distracted.

His pen made sure scratches across the page, listing his assets and debts for the loan officer. The sooner he could finish it, the sooner she would leave him to his work.

"Here you go." He dipped his pen for the last final scratches, pleased that she stood waiting on him. "The bank will be closed already, but you can drop it in the slot on the main door."

He folded the application into thirds and extended it toward her without looking up.

She didn't take the paper. "Look, I shouldn't have said all that. I only meant it to warn you." She nibbled on her bottom lip, waiting for his response. Well, she wasn't the only one who could deliver a warning.

"Your honesty is refreshing — as long as

you can accept the same from me." Her eyes lowered and Nicholas felt vindication was near. "Why don't we always tell each other the truth? It'll be a fun experiment."

"Well, then . . . truthfully, I'd like to leave now. Who knows what kind of trouble Sammy's been for Mrs. Puckett."

She reached for the paper, but Nicholas swung it to his chest. "But first it's my turn. Truthfully . . . I think you and Ophelia have more in common than you might think."

Anne frowned. "Impossible."

"While I haven't studied buffalo, I have studied women, and I agree with your assessment of Ophelia. She enjoys her power, and her expensive wardrobe announces to all society that she isn't to be trifled with."

"I want nothing to do with society."

"Precisely. For you to participate in society would mean giving up control. Your power comes from your rejection of the customs and niceties that everyone else is forced to play. You can be a hermit on the prairie and feel superior to everyone here who has to cooperate and compromise to build relationships. And by your dress you announce that you aren't to be trifled with, either. Instead of intimidating them with your riches, you keep them at arm's length by looking untamed and frightening. Unfortunately, where you are concerned, I feel no fear."

His smile widened when her eyes turned stormy. So now she knew what scrutiny felt like. She spun on her boot heel and stalked out of his office. He followed just to see her fling the outer door open. Anne stood, the autumn sun outlining her bulky clothing.

She didn't bend and scurry down the ladder. Was she formulating a reply? Poising for another attack? Or was she thinking through his statements? Nick felt a twinge of guilt. Perhaps he'd been too hard on her. Perhaps it was time to call a truce.

"Neither of us was at our best back there, Mrs. Tillerton, and I appreciate your not leaving in anger. If we're going to get along for the next few days, we do need to be honest with each other but without rancor."

She continued to look down through the failing late-afternoon sun at the ground below them.

"Like right now," Nick continued. "I have no idea what you're thinking, but obviously something is weighing heavily on your mind. Can you tell me? Can you tell me what has stopped you from running?"

Anne put her hands on her hips and widened her stance in the doorway.

"I'll tell you what kept me from leaving." She pointed. "The ladder is gone."

9

Anne squatted to peer at the ground growing dimmer in the waning light. The carpenter's wagon and his tools had vanished. Nicholas had told him to skedaddle on to his next job, which must have been on a tall building, for he took the ladder with him.

"There's no way on earth I'll spend the night with you here," she said. "I'll jump first."

He didn't protest.

She studied the wall that the staircase would be built into. Just siding. Nothing to hold on to. The frame the carpenter had built for the staircase was lying on its side, unattached.

"Do you have any rope?" Anne asked.

Nicholas leaned against the wall, crossing his leg at the ankle. "This is an office, not a toolshed."

"If you held my wrists and let me dangle, I might be able to drop the rest of the way."

"But I won't. I'm already responsible for one employee's injuries. I'll have nothing to do with yours." He straightened and yawned. "Feel free to gather attention using any means at your disposal. I have work to do." And he left her to her office on the back of the building.

The alley beneath her window contained no traffic. The only people Anne had seen all day were those coming specifically to Nicholas's office — the carpenter and Mrs. Stanford. Anne leaned her arms on the sill and watched as a cat slunk from shadow to shadow, careful lest it get trapped by a stray dog. Night was falling and she was hungry.

The thought of Sammy's sitting next to her empty seat at the dinner table caused a pang of regret. Did Sammy miss his mother? Did he realize Tessa wasn't coming back? Even though it'd be impossible for him to be attached to Anne already, would he realize she was gone and miss her? She wouldn't have him long, but until his father came, she wanted him to have a measure of security.

If only she could be sure that Mrs. Puckett would send someone to check on her, but she probably wouldn't, trusting that she was in Nicholas's safe hands.

Again she could see him swinging the

hammer, driving nails flush into the boards with one strike. And she could see his fist smashing into the train robber's face, his nose flattening before his feet flew up and he was laid out. Nicholas did not have safe hands. Not for her. Not for anyone.

She straightened. No one would wander down that alley. Nicholas's window was street side. She'd have more luck there.

The door was closed. Anne took a deep breath. He was surly today, but she preferred that over prying. She needed to get out before he was struck by a better mood.

She knocked. He didn't answer. She knocked again.

"I'm working."

She cracked the door open. "You said for me to get attention. It'd be easier from the front window than the alley."

He rubbed his eyes. "All right, then. Go ahead. Just keep in mind, I really do need to finish this paper work. If I can't eat supper, I might as well —"

"I know. I know."

Anne walked behind him, sliding between the back of his chair and the window. She unlatched the frame and slid open the pane. The collateral broker below them had already closed his doors with the rest of the businesses on the block. The tinny music of a saloon wafted over the streets. Voices, low and guttural, could be heard from the building that shone brighter the darker the street became.

Anne spotted two men on the boardwalk across the street making their way toward the den of iniquity.

"Excuse me," she yelled. "Hey, up here." They didn't respond. She whistled.

Nicholas spun his chair around. "Must you bellow in my ears?"

"Can you hear me?" she wailed. But it was no use. The men continued their trek toward cheap entertainment and rich drink. In vain she searched the road. This part of town didn't have any eating establishments or hotels. After hours it was pretty much deserted.

"You couldn't get an office with a better location?" She craned her neck as far out the small opening as prudence allowed.

"I think my office shows refined taste, unlike your wardrobe."

Suddenly aware of her posterior, Anne straightened. "I thought we'd kicked that topic until it'd given out."

But Nicholas wasn't dissuaded. "Not at all. You wore dresses back in Prairie Lea. I saw you only a time or two, but I think you looked nice enough."

"Mind your own business."

"You are my business if you are representing Lovelace Transportation Specialists."

"But I'm not. I represent myself."

"I don't know if I can stomach seeing those same ratty clothes every day. It's a blight on the atmosphere I've cultivated here."

His desk reflected the gaslights above them like a mirror. The rugs were thick enough to be luxurious and short enough to be practical. Even the deep colors of the walls and curtains complemented each other so that no random hue could be introduced without upsetting the balance. Like she did.

"You have work to do," she said.

"You're raising such a racket as to make it impossible."

Anne looked out the window one last time and, seeing no one, returned to her office.

With a clatter, Nick rose out of his chair and followed. "Why don't you buy a new dress? I'll give you the money if it means I don't have to look at this dreary ensemble every morning."

Retreating behind her desk, she buried her head in a file. He was no better than the saloon owner, wanting to deck her out to amuse his clients.

"Doesn't that interest you?" He rested both hands on her desk and leaned forward. "What woman doesn't want to look beautiful?"

Anne slammed the file down, sending loose papers flying. "Me. I don't. It's not that I don't know how to dress. It's not that I'm lazy. It's that I do not want attention from you or any other man. Do you understand?"

Nicholas stepped back, mouth slightly open. Well, good. He needed to believe her. He needed to go back in his office and leave her be. If they were stuck until the Pucketts came looking for them, she wanted him as far away as possible.

When he left, she was relieved. When he returned, wrestling the leather armchair through the doorway, she was horrified. With a thud he set it opposite her desk and planted himself squarely in front of her.

"The waiting-room benches aren't comfortable, and I plan to sit here awhile. I can't concentrate with you flouncing around."

"I've never flounced in my life." Her pen nib dug a hole in the balance sheet.

"Since we have the time, how about you explain your objection to dressing like every other woman in Texas?"

Anne dropped her pen and ducked her

head behind the paper she held before her. "Why? To satisfy your curiosity?"

She could feel his eyes burning through her paper shield.

"For reasons I can hardly fathom, I do find myself curious."

Anne lifted the paper higher until she could no longer see him, but neither could she make out the words printed before her, her thoughts too jumbled to string the characters together.

"Let me tell the story and see if I get it right," Nicholas said. "After you dissected me to the marrow, it's only fair. Let's see . . . you grew up playing with the boys, never thought you were any different. Maybe you even made fun of the girls from town. They weren't tough; they weren't fun. But then you grew up."

The mocking tone disappeared. He spoke with a kindness that was unwelcome.

"What made you grow up? Was it a country boy — best shot in the woods — and you were trying to catch his eye? Or maybe the parson's son? You had to dress up for church —"

The paper that shielded her face shook. "Why are you doing this? You, with your storybook childhood, the favored son, you wouldn't understand."

143

He slowly pushed her paper lower. "But I want to."

The concern in his eyes surprised her. Ever since their parting on the train he'd seemed like the fickle man she remembered from home. This intuitive, perceptive man was hidden behind social prattle and economic maneuvering, but when he made an appearance, she wanted him to stay.

Warily, she watched for the first sign of ridicule or annoyance. She would regret it, but she couldn't help herself. No one had ever asked so sincerely. Besides Mrs. Puckett no one else had asked . . . period.

"It wasn't a boy," she said. "It was a man."

"Jay Tillerton?"

She nodded and buttoned her duster up a notch against the evening chill seeping into the room. "My teacher. He said I was a good student, had a lot of promise. He told me stories of fine ladies and opportunities. Talked sweet. None of it was true. The only opportunities he gave me . . ." Why was she telling him? It sure didn't do her any favors. "I was just a stupid girl."

Her heart pounded, whether from the memories of the horror she'd lived through or from Nicholas's gentleness, she didn't know.

"Do you feel like your beauty made you

vulnerable?"

Beauty? Anne wouldn't go that far, but neither could she deny that she was vulnerable. Even now, knowing how fickle Nicholas was, knowing how he regretted ever seeing her and fought against hiring her, even now she could see how he could win her trust if she wasn't vigilant. Nice enough to get close, strong enough to hurt her.

"I learned that I can take care of myself. I could've all along, but escaping Jay proved it. I see no reason to pretend I'm the helpless girl he wanted."

Nicholas placed his hand palm down on the desk. "Heaven help the person who thinks you're helpless."

She met his eyes, drinking in the understanding she read in them. Could it be that he disguised even more than she did?

She looked away. What was behind this mask of compassion? What was he trying to get from her? How could he understand her when she didn't understand herself?

"Nick! Are you up there?"

Nicholas slapped the desk, bounded to his feet, and pulled open the door.

"Joel! Am I glad to see you!"

"How did you manage to get caught high and dry?"

"It's a long story, but Anne and I are

hungry. Can you find a ladder?"

Anne. She stiffened at the sound of her name on his lips.

"Roberts has one," Joel said. "Sit tight."

His horse backed up the narrow alley and turned when it reached the corner of the building.

Nicholas winked, rushed to his desk, and hurriedly gathered papers into his portfolio. "There's something about knowing I can't leave that makes me impatient. If we had stairs, I'd probably work all night, but now I can't wait to get back on the ground."

Anne leaned against the doorframe. He didn't seem the least uncomfortable with her. Not embarrassed by her story or faking an affectation of sorrow on her behalf. Maybe he'd already forgotten all about it.

"Nights are pretty quiet at the Pucketts'. I could take some work home if you'd like, Mr. Lovelace."

He looked up. "I called you Anne, didn't I? In front of Joel." He rubbed his forehead. "I'm sorry, Mrs. Tillerton. I hope I didn't embarrass you. Molly always called you Anne, and since then, when I've thought of you, that's how I imagined you. You're Anne to me." He placed the portfolio in a larger case and snapped it closed. "If it offends you, I won't say it again."

"It's fine," she said and then wondered what bothered her more — that she wasn't offended or that he'd been thinking of her at all.

"I knew I shouldn't worry." Mrs. Puckett's knitting needles clicked cheerily. "Nicholas wouldn't let anything happen to you."

Rebuttal was on the tip of Anne's tongue, but then she remembered the birdie lady from the train. At least one incident that spoke in his favor. Anne sat on the floor and didn't resist when Sammy climbed into her lap. He babbled at her, swinging his arms, so she handed him two empty spools to beat together.

Mrs. Puckett continued in her singsong voice. "I prayed for you today. Every time I wondered how you were doing, I'd send a quick request to the Lord to watch out for you, help you learn what Nick was teaching you, help you feel safe. I also prayed for Sammy's father, that he'd be reunited with his son soon."

Anne absently combed Sammy's thin blond hair with her fingers. She didn't like someone talking to God about her. Shouldn't Mrs. Puckett have asked her permission first? Maybe Anne didn't want her plight brought to His attention. Whenever God looked her way, it seemed that trouble followed hard behind.

"You are certainly quiet," Mrs. Puckett said. "Probably worn out. If you'd like to go on up, I can bring Sammy in later. He took a late nap."

"I'm not tired, just run out of things to say."

"I can imagine. You worked all day long, and I feel awful about it. We don't need any money. That Joel should tend his own affairs and leave us be." The needles paused as she let out more yarn. "Having you and Sammy here has been a joy to my heart. My own daughters have carted my sweet grandchildren plumb out of reach, leaving only Joel, and he's been nothing but a disappointment."

The pronouncement dripped with indulgence. Clearly, Mrs. Puckett would forgive her son anything.

A luxury Anne couldn't imagine.

"So tell me about your own family," Mrs. Puckett urged. "Robert goes to bed so early that my evenings have been quite dull of late. I hope you don't mind a tête-à-tête."

"My family . . ." What to say? There was her father, who dragged home from the stone quarry to cradle his jug and sit on the porch. Many nights, long after her brothers had come in from their adventures in the woods and gone to bed, Anne lingered, hoping that her pa would notice the black-eyed Susans she'd arranged by the washbasin, or that he'd have a kind word for the dinner she'd cooked. But he didn't. And asking him if he noticed felt too needy, too pathetic.

"My mother died when I was born," Anne said, "so my father and brothers had to put up with me."

"You poor thing. I bet you were the apple of your father's eye."

Anne wedged her finger into Sammy's grasp alongside the spool. "You could say that . . ." *Because you weren't there.*

"So you married and moved to Texas? I can't seem to recall exactly how your husband passed away."

Anne's mouth went dry. Mrs. Puckett was tying off her knitting, not even looking her way, but she couldn't fib, not even to keep a roof over her and Sammy's head.

"I shot him."

Mrs. Puckett dropped the yarn, sending it rolling to Anne's feet with a trailing line. She gave a nervous chuckle. "I'm sorry. I thought you said that *you* shot him."

"Yes, ma'am. I did."

Mrs. Puckett's mouth trembled. She set

her needles down firmly on the side table with a clatter. "Well, I'm sure he had it coming."

Without thinking, Anne pulled Sammy against her and buried her nose in his sweet-smelling hair. "I had reason enough for two years, but when he attacked my neighbor lady, I knew I couldn't stand by and watch. You can tell your son if you need to. The judge cleared me."

"I won't tell him if you'd rather me not, although he would be interested."

"It doesn't matter too much. Mr. Lovelace has surely spilled the beans by now."

Mrs. Puckett's eyebrows rose. "Nicholas knows? You were acquaintances then?"

"Not really. His sister befriended me after Jay died."

Anne looked over her shoulder. Speaking his name aloud couldn't summon him from the grave, but it did resurrect a hopelessness that had nearly destroyed her. While in his grasp she never knew whose hand would take her life — his or her own.

"What you must have gone through." Mrs. Puckett continued her words of comfort, but they fell unheard as she gathered the ball of yarn.

Jay had stolen everything from her, and he was still destroying. She had no peace, she had no relationships, she had no safety. Everyone was suspect, and if she didn't learn from her mistakes, it could happen again.

"I apologize for bringing up painful memories. Is there anything I can do?" Mrs. Puckett's sweet face was furrowed with concern.

"I'm fine." Anne didn't lift her eyes from Sammy, and from the pause, she guessed Mrs. Puckett didn't believe her.

"If you aren't busy Sunday, we'd be honored to have you accompany us to church. My friends dote on Sammy, and they'd love to meet you, too."

Anne grunted her approval. Anything to speed the coming of the night. She wanted to know what nightmares she'd be fighting. Mrs. Puckett was only delaying the inevitable.

"And, Anne, I want you to be assured that you are safe. At least here in my house you are. Mr. Puckett won't lay a hand on you — he doesn't even speak harshly. Joel acts gruff, but he'd never hurt a woman. And Nicholas . . . well, how could anyone be afraid of him? He is courtesy and charm personified."

Anne wished she could believe her. The charming ones worked the hardest to hide what they really wanted. Nicholas might not even know what he was capable of — but she did.

There'd be no sleep tonight. Not for Anne.

The rock building with the sweeping arches and honey-colored pews was the finest structure in town, much nicer than the simple wooden church Nicholas had attended in his childhood. Sundays were his favorite day of the week. Fine manners, spiffy suits, languid lunches at the hotel — everyone gracing the church lawn was on their best behavior and at their most presentable.

At least that's what he thought until he saw Anne.

"Is that the woman from the train?" Miss Walcher spread her fan over her lips while exchanging significant glances with her companions. "I don't think she's changed clothes since."

"She has," Nick said. "Those trousers are canvas, not buckskin." And she wore them to church.

"Must be her Sunday best." Miss Walcher's fan fluttered under her eyes.

"Well, I'm glad she's here." Nick's back straightened. "Don't forget, she saved my life . . . while I was saving yours."

Chastened, Miss Walcher clasped the gold locket at her neck, hopefully thinking of how her attempt to save it had put them all in danger. "You're right. I must insist on an introduction. Would you do the honors?"

"Susan, you don't mean it," her friend gasped.

"She's showing off," another said.

"I'll introduce any and all of you. Mrs. Tillerton won't be in town long, but while she's here it'd be nice to show her some hospitality." He didn't wait to see their stunned expressions, but took Miss Walcher by the arm.

Anne was standing by a concrete bench in the shade, watching Mrs. Puckett pass Sammy around like he was the county fair's prize pumpkin. Her determined perusal told Nick that she saw him coming and was doing everything in her power to ignore his approach, but he wouldn't be discouraged.

"Mrs. Tillerton?" Her sharp eyes pierced through the curls that had blown across her face. "I'd like to introduce you to Miss Susan Walcher. You might remember her from the train robbery."

"I certainly do. You still have your locket? It must be priceless to you seeing how you were willing to risk your life."

Susan blushed but didn't waver. "That

was foolish of me. I never considered the consequences. If it weren't for you, I'd have Mr. Lovelace's blood on my hands, and I could never forgive myself."

Anne watched her patiently and then seemed to make up her mind. "I appreciate your thanks." She looked away.

Miss Walcher fidgeted, drumming her fingers on Nick's arm. "Well, that's all I had to say. I hope your visit in Garber is pleasant." She nodded to Nick, disengaged her hand from his arm, and walked back to her twittering friends.

Nick sighed. "You have no idea how difficult that was for Susan. You could've made an effort at small talk."

"I have nothing small to talk about." Anne refused to meet his gaze. "What do Miss Walcher and I have in common?"

"I bet you thought the same about my sister. Until recently Molly's never been concerned with anything important. Now she's reaching out, leading the women of her church to minister to the outcasts."

"That's awfully nice of her, but how does she know God's going to behave like He ought?" Anne asked.

"God behave?" Her question took him aback. "We have to worry about our behavior, not God's." What was she talking about?

Heresy in front of the most expensive church in North Texas.

"You might do something good, but you have no guarantee that God's going to return the favor. And if God is as powerful as you believe, He could ruin you without lifting a finger."

Nick wanted to laugh at her simplistic statements, but she was deadly serious. He motioned her to the bench. "God wants what's best for me. He wants me to be successful and to achieve great things."

"So God's not allowed to do anything to you that you don't like? That doesn't sound like you're following Jesus. That sounds like Jesus is following you."

His eyes widened. "That's not what I mean at all. It's just that we're in agreement. God wants to prosper me and to bless me. That's what I want, too. It's simple enough."

"If you're only talking about prospering, where's the pain? What if God wishes you ill and wants something bad to happen to you? You're saying that's fine?"

"He loves me. He loves everyone. He would never do that."

Her eyes narrowed. "He wouldn't? Hasn't anything bad ever happened to you, Mr. Lovelace?"

His mind skipped across event after event, year after year. "My father had a bad spell a couple of years ago, but he's recovered. Then there's what Molly went through with that cad Edward Pierrepont, but it all worked out."

"I'm talking about you. No wonder it's easy for you. You've never had to make a choice between your own comfort and living what you believe." She was agitated, but about what he couldn't guess. "No wonder you find Christianity an easy stroll down a flower-lined path. You only obey if God asks you to do something you want. It does make sense now that you've explained it."

Before he had to answer, Mrs. Puckett arrived, leading Sammy by the hand. The child pulled free and staggered to Anne. She gathered him in her arms, much more comfortable with the boy than the last time he'd seen them together.

And while he couldn't help but smile at their interactions, her questions bothered him. He shouldn't be surprised that she would question his faith — she questioned everything else from women's wardrobes to the honesty of law enforcement, but the manner she used made him feel as much of a heathen as she.

No, he didn't expect God to always do

what he wanted Him to do, but was it his fault that most of the time it'd worked out that way? Sammy pulled on Anne's hat, trying to remove it in a game that had obviously been played before. Nick admired his exuberance. Why not try to win? Why not chase your dream? What did life mean without achievements? And wasn't it God's plan to help him succeed?

Nick believed that. Then why did Anne's questions seem to distort his beliefs into something incredibly shallow and self-serving?

10

October 1883

Her answer had finally come.

Anne gripped the telegram in cold fingers and nearly ran to Nick's office. A quick good-bye and then she could leave, not a moment too soon. This Nicholas Lovelace with his questions and arrogance was best kept at a safe distance, but he'd been worming his way closer ever since she'd arrived in Garber. Finally, she could flee.

She burst into the office, forgetting to marvel at his new staircase. His door stood open. He lifted his head. "You're late."

"I'm leaving. Anoli telegraphed. Finn is in Allyton."

Nick laid his pen aside. "You're leaving? When?"

"Now. I just came to tell you before I get Sammy."

He didn't say anything. He spun his chair toward the window, his fingers steepled together. "It's going to rain."

"It's just water."

"Do you know how to get to Allyton?"

"Just across the river, right? The telegraph man said the road would take me to the ferry and Allyton is on the other side."

Nick continued to gaze out the window. "I'm really too busy for this. The bank has asked for last year's records before they approve the loan, and with Harold gone — but I need to look the river over anyway. The bridge vote is a responsibility of mine, as well." He clapped his hands together. "It won't take long. I can get the records together tonight if needed."

Anne blinked. "I didn't ask you to go with me."

"It's a trip I need to make."

"Then you better hurry," Anne said. "I'm not taking any chance on Finn flying the coop."

Nick grabbed his umbrella and in seconds was following her to the Pucketts' house, where Mrs. Puckett gave Sammy a series of kisses and slipped her address into Anne's knapsack, begging for a letter once she got settled. Sammy chewed on a hard biscuit, oblivious to the hustle around him even after Anne scooped him up and followed Nick to the ferry just outside of town.

"Ma-ma-ma," Sammy chanted as he bounced against her.

"Your momma is gone," Anne replied. "You'd better learn to say *Papa*. We'll be seeing him soon."

"Hopefully," Nick said.

"We won't take any more of your time, Mr. Lovelace. Once Sammy is safely with his pa, I'm boarding the first train to Pushmataha."

"I'm not complaining on my behalf," he said. "I'm happy if you're happy."

Of course he was. He'd be rid of her and she'd be rid of Sammy. When they reached the ferry, Nick stashed her belongings and his umbrella inside the locker. The wooden barge glistened darkly. Anne grasped the rail and widened her stance just as the ferry dipped. The ferryman eased his pole into the water and pushed off, causing the ferry to lurch away from the levee.

The current fought against the guide cable above their heads. Heavy drops of rain began to pock the river like a slow boil. The deck tilted. Nick wrapped his arm around her and anchored himself to the rail.

"I didn't think the river would be this rough."

Anne couldn't answer but focused on the opposite shore, willing it closer.

"Can you swim?" Nick asked.

She shook her head.

His jaw worked as he looked at the baby and then her. "We'll be fine. Don't worry."

Advice he couldn't follow himself.

By the time the ferry bounced against the north levee, the ferryman couldn't hide his nervousness.

"We made it." He tossed the thick rope over the post to anchor the boat to the riverbank. "It must've rained a heap up-river."

"Thank you for getting us here safely." Nicholas pulled out two bits, even though the fare had already been paid. "Not an easy crossing."

The ferryman removed his hat and swiped his handkerchief across his forehead. "I've seen worse but barely."

The town of Allyton began only a few yards away, the street reaching the shore. The sprinkling rain hadn't ceased. Anne wasn't concerned, yet Nick stretched to keep the umbrella over Sammy and her.

"Don't bother," she said. "Your coat won't wear the weather as well as mine."

"No matter. I won't have it said in Allyton that their councilman left a lady in the rain."

They ducked into a small store and shook off.

161

"You didn't just cross the river, did you?" The man behind the counter polished an apple and set it back on his display.

"Yes, sir, and it was nasty." Nick took two apples, handed one to Anne, and sunk his teeth into his. "How often is the crossing bad?"

The shopkeeper rubbed his chin. "If you're talking about flooding, only a few times a year. More often it's the sandbars that keep us from crossing. When the water gets low, the ferry hits them before it can reach the levee. Cross on foot and you might have quicksand to contend with."

Sammy watched Anne take every bite of her apple, but she didn't think he should eat it. Mrs. Puckett had said something about smashing food for him to keep him from choking. She looked around the store as Nick kept talking. Maybe they had something she could get for him. Finn wouldn't have anything for a baby. The voices faded. Anne realized they were both looking at her.

"Excuse me?" she asked.

The shopkeeper leaned against the counter. "He said you're looking for Finn Cravens."

"Yes, sir. Do you know where he is?"

"If you're asking after the man with white

hair, hair the same color as that boy's there, he was here yesterday. Last I heard he was squiring Miss Turnbull around. You could inquire at the Turnbull place if you're ready to face the truth."

"Can you give me directions?" Anne kept up her tough attitude. Otherwise she'd turn beet red at the storekeeper's insinuation. He probably couldn't wait to see her confront Finn in front of Miss Turnbull.

"Actually, now that I think about it, Cliff Turnbull is coming to town today. He's got a load of pecans he's bringing in, if this shower don't stop him. This fellow might be with him, but if not, Turnbull will know where he is."

Anne looked to Nick. "And what will you do?"

"I'm going to take a survey of local opinion of the bridge — wander a bit, visit with the townsfolk. You don't need to worry about me."

"We might be gone before you return."

He smiled at Sammy. "Then I wish this little fellow the best. And you, too. Take care of yourself."

A deep satisfaction spread through her chest. Nick was letting her go. He wasn't tracking her down, threatening her, promising her that she could never hide from him.

Maybe he could be trusted.

"Thank you, Nick." Her cheeks warmed at the familiarity, but she was proud that she'd dared. "Thank you for watching out for us in Garber."

Nick held out his hand. Anne met his grasp with a firm handshake. He chuckled.

"It was my pleasure."

Nick headed to the first home the storekeeper had directed him to. Life would be easier without Anne underfoot, but he'd miss her. How dull the ladies of his acquaintance seemed in comparison. Now that he knew she frequented Pushmataha, he'd be sure to inquire after her when passing through. No longer were they strangers.

The man of the house answered Nick's knock on the door. He was a leatherworker, and he knew to the penny how much it cost for him to ship his handiwork to Garber. "What's more, when I break a tool or need materials, I pay extra charges for them, too."

"How much a year would a bridge be worth to you?" Nick asked.

"I don't know. A hundred dollars? One and a quarter? And if people think a businessman should just take his loss, they need to consider that I pass that expense on in the price of my goods. Eventually, everyone pays for the difference."

At the next stop, the man of the house wasn't home. He worked just south of Garber and didn't come home every night because of the fare.

"So if there were a bridge, your husband would be home more often?" Nick asked.

"He'd better be." The woman laughed, but her façade was fragile. "People were already talking before he took that position."

Upon reflection, Nick had to admit that building a bridge may or may not help her marriage, but he tipped his hat and thanked her for her time. The people of Allyton certainly didn't mind visiting with him. They probably thought he was insane, wandering through town while a storm was threatening, but he couldn't afford to lose another day of work. As long as he was in Allyton, he'd make the best of it.

As he exited the post office, he saw Anne trudging through the rain, which had finally arrived in its full strength. Her head was bowed against the gusts until he could see only the top of her hat. Sammy squirmed, trying to get down, and by her posture she looked about ready to let him go his own way.

Unfurling his umbrella, Nick jogged to her.

"Are you looking for me?" he asked.

Anne raised tired eyes. "Finn's gone."

Nicholas held the umbrella over her and took the baby from her exhausted arms.

"Do you know where he went?"

"No. He had a falling out with Miss Turnbull and rode off, swearing he'd never return. So unless you have a better idea, I'll go back to Garber — although I'd rather step barefoot into a rattler's pit. Maybe Finn will show up there."

Anne was returning? He'd already looked forward to locating her on his next journey north. Somehow he'd had time to imagine crossing paths in the wilds of Indian Territory.

"I'm sorry you didn't get what you wanted," Nick said as they started toward the levee, "but word will get to him. You won't have this boy much longer."

"What if he doesn't want him?"

"He has no choice. It's his son. Even the shopkeeper recognized it."

Anne kept her head ducked and dragged her bags behind her.

The river roared viciously, even more loudly than when they'd crossed earlier. And when Nick saw the ferry anchored on the bank, he knew they were in trouble.

With his hands full, he jerked his head

toward the small shelter. Anne lifted the sign hung on the door.

"No Ferry Service Due to Weather," she read. She let it drop and swing by its string. The door was unlocked. They entered to find the potbelly stove still warm, but no ferryman inside.

Anne held her hands out to the fire. "Now what? Can we catch the train?"

"Not until evening." Nick lowered Sammy to the floor and consulted his pocket watch. "Six hours from now — six hours I don't have to waste."

With a gasp Anne snatched Sammy. "He was going to touch the stove. You can't just let him loose in here."

"What am I supposed to do with him? He wanted down."

"He always wants down. He would've crawled right into the river if I would've let him." She sat and latched her arms around his waist, even as he tried to wiggle away.

Nick stowed his umbrella beneath the bench and sat next to her. "With a child that busy, when are you supposed to rest?"

"When I'm working for you."

His laugh almost teased a smile from her lips. Almost, so he laughed again. Those gray eyes sparkled before her dark lashes lowered and hid them from his view. With her boot Anne nudged Sammy's bag toward Nick. "Do you know how to make a bottle?"

"Of course. Doesn't every bachelor?" He pulled the bottle out of the bag. "Now, I just find a cow . . ."

"There's a canister of infant food in there. You mix a spoonful of it with water. One of the women at the saloon showed me how after Tessa left."

Nicholas juggled the bottle and the tin can to the water jug. "How long is he going to need this type of food? Finn Cravens won't know anything more than I do about tending a baby."

"Sammy can drink cow's milk, but it can be hard to come by away from town."

Sammy bucked against Anne's hold as Nick shook up the bottle. Nick smiled at his eagerness. The boy knew what he wanted.

Anne set him down. Nick stood between him and the stove, but the child was only interested in draining the gray formula from the bottle.

The shack creaked in the wind. The stove sizzled rhythmically as rain dripped in from the leaky roof. He wished he had brought along his paper work to pass the time, although judging by the gales outside it would've been drenched by now. Still, the day wasn't a complete loss. He better understood how a bridge to Allyton would help the residents, although there were questions of whether the expense could be justified. Beneficial did not equal feasible.

Sammy's eyes drooped. Anne retrieved the bottle before he could drop it and lifted him from the floor. Nick couldn't help but compare how she held the child now to when he first saw them in his office. She wasn't doing too badly after all.

"Did you hear that?" Anne asked.

Nick straightened. "What?" Then he heard a shout. As he turned the doorknob, a gust of wind caught the door and it flew open. In the gray light stood a horse and rider, the young man leaning down to be heard as he shouted his request.

"I need the ferry." His eyes darted from Nick to Anne and Sammy, then back to Nick. "Where's Pikey? I have to cross."

"He's not here, but the ferry isn't running. Have you seen the river?"

The man shook his head. The rain streamed off his hat and dripped from his moustache. "But my wife. She's in labor. I have to get a doctor."

Nick's throat tightened at the pain in his face. Anne stepped closer.

"Isn't there anyone here that can help?"

she asked.

"The midwife sent me. She wouldn't have if she didn't think . . ." He looked away and swallowed. "I have to cross the river. That's all there is to it."

Still sheltered by the roof, Nick consulted his watch. Hours still before the train would come through. "I'm sorry. There's nothing we can do. We crossed this morning, and it was treacherous. It's even worse now."

The man stared straight ahead at the churning water. Like a sickness growing in his belly, Nick felt disaster barreling down on them as the man's resolve grew. The man opened and closed his gloved hands around the reins. "I'll ride across. It's my only option."

"You can't," Nick blurted. "What's it going to accomplish? Even if you make it across — which you won't — the doctor isn't going to come back with you. You're sacrificing your life for nothing —"

"For nothing?" the man roared. "My wife and my child are in danger and you think I'm going home to tell her I failed before I even tried?" He nodded toward Anne and the baby. "Surely you understand. Kiss your woman when I'm gone and thank God that you still have her."

"Nick!" Anne cried. "Stop him!"

The man spurred his horse toward the bank. Nick ran behind, calling him, but he'd already determined his course. The horse sped down the embankment, shied at the first contact with the water but followed his master's urging into the fury.

In seconds the river reached the horse's chest. Their way slowed as each step now was a battle against an irresistible force. Crying filled Nick's ears as Sammy screamed against the rain, but Anne was riveted to the drama before them.

"Isn't there something we can do?" she shouted above Sammy's wails.

Now the water coursed over the horse's back. Its eyes flashed wild with terror. The man's arms wrapped around its neck. He spoke into its ear, but nothing he could say could compete with the anger of the water. Another step and the horse lost its footing. They both went under and when they re-appeared less than a second later, they were ten feet further downstream. Together, Nick and Anne rushed to the bank. The water swept the man off the horse, but he held on to the saddle. Both of them floundered as the dark water crashed over their heads, each time dragging them further off course. They swirled around. Were they trying to come back? Now hatless, the man was almost too far away to see. He dipped again. A swifter current caught him and he disappeared. The horse thrashed, water spraying as it crashed into him, but then it too was gone.

Nick waited, scanned down the river, waiting. Waiting. Again he heard Sammy's cries. He turned to find Anne dry-eyed but as white as bones. What was he thinking? He should've sent her inside. She shouldn't have witnessed that.

And neither should've he. His knees suddenly felt weak.

"Let's get you out of the rain," he muttered.

She didn't argue as they walked back to the cabin and both collapsed onto the bench. Hadn't they just been sitting there? Besides their dripping clothes, everything was exactly the same, but one family would never recover.

"We should go to town and tell someone." Anne melted into the wall. Her boots stretched before her, showing her exhaustion.

"I'll go," he said, but he couldn't. Not yet. He'd been sapped. Already in his mind's eye he'd imagined a bridge spanning this river, and he couldn't stop thinking that somehow he could get it built and help that man. Somehow, if he hurried, the rider wouldn't have to swim the raging river. He could ride across and come back with the doctor in a buggy. If only time would stop, if only he'd decided . . . or someone had decided two years ago that the bridge needed to be built, the man would be knocking on the doctor's door even now.

He'd always remember this day and the quiet woman who'd borne it with him.

"I'm sorry that happened," he said. "And I'm sorry you had to go through it. But at the same time I'm glad you're here with me. That's not nice, is it? To be glad someone else feels as awful as you do?"

Anne's eyes captured his, the gray as calm as he'd ever seen. "I've been through a lot on my own. I understand why you'd feel like that."

Something passed between them. Something . . . a message, a glimpse of herself she held close? Whatever it was, Nick felt privileged. "Thank you." He took her hand, barely visible at the end of her long loose coat sleeve, and pressed it to his lips, fulfilling the last request of a brave man.

11

Anne hadn't expected that sunrise would find her back at the office of Lovelace Transportation Specialists, but because of the tragedy the night before she didn't have the heart to complain.

The man's devotion to his family, the price he paid, towered above any inconvenience she felt at being delayed by Sammy. She only hoped Finn would grow to love his son with the same dedication.

The door opened. Nick's puffy eyes evidenced a night poorly spent, but he smiled just the same.

"*Mm,* the scent of sawdust reminds me of the sawmill back home." He slid his outer coat off. "How do you like that new staircase?"

Anne spun so she wasn't facing him head-on and watched through the corner of her eye.

"They're stairs. You can't mess them up."

"Sure you can. What if they didn't reach the top? What if they didn't reach the bottom?" With his hand still on the hook he turned to her. "What if the carpenter mistakenly created them to only go up, and not back down?"

"But now that the stairs are there, Harold can come back." Anne pushed her hair behind her ear.

"That doesn't mean I won't need you for another day or two. He still can't hold a pencil."

Having Harold there — having anybody else there — would make it easier. It seemed she couldn't be alone with Nick without something significant passing between them.

"I sent Anoli another telegram letting him know I missed Finn. Until I hear back, I can help."

"Anne, about yesterday" — he braced himself against her desktop — "are you all right?"

His concern rattled her. "I'm fine."

"I talked to the doctor today." He lowered his head, studying the papers scattered before him. "Our man made it across after all and lived long enough to send someone with his message to the doctor."

She swallowed. "And his wife?"

"She delivered a baby girl. The doctor

crossed on the train last night. The baby had already arrived, but the mother probably wouldn't have survived without his help. Might not, even now."

The little family had fought so hard for each other. What made them willing to give their lives? Anne didn't know anyone capable of loving like that.

"And I saw the postmaster this morning," Nick said. "Molly sent a letter. It seems that she, Bailey, and their youngest are planning to come up for a visit."

Anne picked at her fingernail. The last time she'd seen Nick's sister, Molly was shouldering the disappointment of a socially optimistic family and a scandal that almost cost her her longtime beau. "I'd like to see Molly. Sammy would like to have another child to play with."

Nick straightened, his brow wrinkled. "I didn't think about Sammy. Do you think he'll still be here?"

"If Sammy leaves, so do I."

His mouth turned down. His eyes didn't leave her face, then as he blinked his neck turned red.

"Bring him. When she comes, I'll reserve one of the parlors at the hotel for supper. Maybe a dining room so we can have a place to visit."

A dining room. Anne looked again at Nicholas's fine striped suit. Knowing Molly, she'd be dressed like a princess. Would she be irritated to find that Anne's wardrobe hadn't improved over the years? The thought almost brought a smile to her lips.

After a week with no stairway, Anne jumped at the unaccustomed sound of the office door swinging open, and when Ophelia Stanford entered, she probably more resembled a fox caught in the hen-house than a confident clerk.

"Mrs. Stanford, come in. Have a seat." Nicholas waved expansively but failed to draw her attention from Anne. "I was just telling Mrs. Tillerton that my sister and her husband are coming to town. I'd love for you to meet them, if you and Mr. Stanford have an evening free."

The icy chill that entered the room wasn't a result of the October weather, and the lemon-yellow dress did nothing to lessen the sour look on Ophelia's face. She ignored his remark and pinned Anne with a glare. "What is she doing here? You said she was only passing through."

Oh brother.

Nicholas escorted Ophelia into his office and pulled a chair to her, since she refused to walk any further.

"Mrs. Tillerton is helping me while Harold recovers."

"Nicholas." She drew a long breath while sinking into the chair. "I understand the compassion you must feel for her, but her presence here —"

"Ophelia, I have a decision I'd like to discuss with you." Nick stepped between them, giving Anne a chance to slip out of sight.

Anne pulled her coat around her and lowered herself into the chair behind Harold's desk. She ripped a long strip of paper off the back of the ledger, tore it width-wise to about the size of a .45 cartridge, crushed it tightly, and put it in her mouth.

"After looking over the work that could be done in the county office," Nick said, "I've concluded that a month isn't enough time to see anything through. Do you think it's too late to register for the election?"

Anne sat up straight and launched the spitball at the spittoon.

Bing!

"What a splendid idea! I don't know when the deadline for candidates is, but since Garrard was the forerunner and he died, it could possibly be extended."

Anne rolled another one.

"So you think it's a good idea? Will I have Mr. Stanford's approval?"

"Mr. Stanford?"

Anne recognized the sarcasm from a room over.

"We aren't currently on speaking terms. He's run afoul of me, and he knows what he must do to rectify the situation."

Good for Nicholas. He didn't ask, but Ophelia told him anyway.

"The emporium has an adorable beaded reticule that perfectly matches my red boots. I've made it very plain that when Ian decides to repent of his vile behavior, he can signal his repentance to me with that purchase. So far, he's unremorseful, claiming the bag is too expensive — as if I haven't earned it many times over."

Nicholas hesitated. "But your spat — it's not going to affect our contract, is it?"

"Of course not. Nothing must get in the way of our partnership."

Bing! Another hit.

Ophelia cleared her throat. Anne froze.

"And speaking of impediments to our future —" She turned in her chair to stare through the doorway directly at Anne. "How do you suppose you can win an election while associating with the likes of her? Her appearance detracts from the profes-

179

sional image you've worked to present. With the election —"

"But you are the only customer who ventures up these stairs," Nick said. "It isn't as if she's working in my office at the court-house."

Ophelia rose. Anne's chewing halted when they walked in the room. Ophelia didn't look her way, but she did startle when the spittoon at her feet rang out. She pulled her skirt away from the spittoon and shot Nicholas a look full of meaning.

"Whilst I strive for perfection in my appearance, sparing no expense, this young woman doesn't know the first thing about fashion."

Anne quirked her mouth. "I like your boots. They look like fine workmanship. Good brain-tanned Indian leather."

Rose and ivory blended perfectly on Ophelia's powdered face. "Brain-tanned? Because they look so smart?" Her haughty expression implied that nothing Anne could do or say would affect her.

Anne was willing to test her assumption.

"No, it's called brain-tanning because the tanners put the animal's brain in hot water and mush it between their fingers until it makes a nice soup."

Ophelia make a strangled sound, but Anne

kept right on.

"Then they rub it into the animal skin. The incredible thing is that every animal has enough brains for its own hide. To cover every inch, they have to scrape brain soup out of the bottom of the kettle —"

"Thank you, Anne," Nick interrupted. "Mrs. Stanford doesn't need any more information."

"No, but she might need more powder. Look at her face. I've never seen such a sickly green color."

"Think about what I said," Ophelia gritted out between her teeth. "We don't want to waste our time supporting you in the election if you're going to throw it all away."

Anne fell back into her chair as Ophelia stalked out. She missed riding, shooting, and traveling the prairie, but being in town offered its own entertainment.

Anne spent every Saturday helping Mrs. Puckett, doing her best to make up for the tasks she missed during the week. At first the household chores made her uneasy. She kept glancing over her shoulder, waiting for Mrs. Puckett to explode if she did something wrong, but once she realized that no punishment was forthcoming, she began to relax and enjoy the tasks, glad to contribute to the family that had given Sammy and her a place to stay.

And their stay was about to end.

The smooth handle of the dasher stilled in her hands, the butter churn between her knees sharing its coolness. For the tenth time that morning Anne reached into her pocket and pulled the telegram out to stare at the words.

Finn Cravens informed. STOP. Coming to Garber. STOP.

Wordlessly she stuffed the telegram into her pocket. It was for the best. She wiped her palms on her trousers, found dry purchase on the agitator, and jerked upward with a force that rattled the ceramic lid.

She would miss the little fellow. Every time Sammy looked up at her with his big sweet eyes, every time he clapped his hands and laughed, a piece of her stone heart warmed to living flesh again.

And now it was over.

Sammy had a father who was willing to take him. Who knew what kind of family Finn could provide, but she needed to return to Pushmataha. Anoli, Tracker, Fred, and the other hunters needed her. She had a knack for choosing the bison with the best coats, even from a distance.

The thick buttermilk sloshed in the crock.

The longer she'd stayed at the Pucketts', the more chores she'd turned her hand to. At first, every domestic activity chilled her, accompanied as they were by the ghosts of her brief married life. But as she persevered through the bad memories, she made new memories — Mrs. Puckett's laughter filling the kitchen, Sammy tugging on her britches as she stood at the worktable, the crisp scent of the laundry she pinned to the line.

Nicholas had been right. Gradually she realized that she could crack the fragile eggshell and stretch out her neck a bit further. She hadn't lost her heart to Sammy. She'd held back enough that his departure wouldn't shatter her. Her defenses weren't quite as vulnerable as she'd feared.

The kitchen door swung open. Mrs. Puckett entered with Sammy on her hip.

"He was fussing upstairs. Naptime is over."

Anne slid away from the churn and held out her hands. Parallel tracks from the seersucker coverlet wrinkled his face, and he almost leaped out of Mrs. Puckett's arms to her.

"Momma." Sammy buried his face into her neck.

"Isn't that the sweetest thing?" Mrs. Puckett rested her fists on her hips and swayed. "He's taken to you. That's for sure."

Anne cupped his head, stroking the innocent silkiness. "I just got word that Finn Cravens is on his way into town. He'll be anxious to see his son."

The smile slid off Mrs. Puckett's face as she sank into a chair. She wagged her head from side to side. "I guess we knew this day was coming. His folks will sure be proud of the little fellow."

"Finn doesn't have any family to speak of, but I guess he can't be any worse than Sammy's mother."

Mrs. Puckett peered at her from over her spectacles. "This Finn, I don't suppose he's mended his ways, has he? Maybe he'd be willing to marry so his precious son would have a mother."

"I wouldn't be surprised." Anne scooted back from the churn. "And if he chooses to, he won't have any trouble finding volunteers. He could sweet-talk a frog into a boiling pot of water."

Mrs. Puckett straightened. "That sounds promising. I hate for you to leave us, but if I thought that you'd found a family of your own —"

Anne spun in her chair, her knee nearly knocking over the butter churn. "I'm not marrying Finn. I'm not marrying anyone.

I'll go back to what I know best — hunting, trapping, and living without . . . without all these people staring and talking."

"Oh dear. I'm sorry that's been your experience."

"I didn't mean it like that." Sammy squirmed out of Anne's arms and crawled toward a bag of potatoes propped in the corner. She paused, trying to find words of gratitude from a rarely used supply. "You've given me friendship when I had nothing to give in return. I won't forget your goodness."

Sammy beamed at them with a toothy grin.

"Just knowing you has been gift enough. And I'm afraid you're going to have trouble forgetting that little guy, too."

"Yes, ma'am." Anne's throat felt unusually raspy. "I don't know how, but he's become the best thing that ever happened to me."

12

The rose-colored draperies reflected on the gilded gas sconces and mirrors until the whole room showed pink, even tinting the white in the lapel pins scattered across Ophelia's desk.

"Red, pink, and blue?" Nick held up a ribbon. "Not very patriotic."

She slapped his hand. "Behave. Ian thinks my extravagance knows no limits, so I need you at least to be on my side."

In the week since Ophelia had committed to Nick's campaign, she'd immersed herself in local politics, gaining a remarkable understanding of who the influencers were and how to win their favor. Her relentlessness embarrassed him at times, but he couldn't complain when she was acting on his behalf.

"Yes, ma'am. You just tell me what to do."

"Naturally." Holding a pamphlet out at arm's length, she tried not to squint. "Sterling character, transportation expert, successful entrepreneur." She lowered the bill and smiled. "Sound like anyone you know?"

"I hope you don't print much of that nonsense, or my hat will get too tight."

"No time for modesty. Have these phrases on the tip of your tongue. You'll hear that you're too young, too inexperienced, too beholden to the railroads, so then you toss these answers like buckets of sand on a fire. Don't hesitate. I'm planning a dinner for you in two weeks, a fund-raiser, where you'll meet all the leaders of Garber enterprise."

"Dinner? That reminds me, are you and Mr. Stanford planning to join us for dinner when my sister arrives?"

Ophelia smiled. "Of course. Only I'd rather not eat at a public house. You must bring your guests here and allow me to hostess. I'd be honored. Now, about this political event, not all of these men are supporters of yours, but this will be your chance to win them over."

"Do I have any supporters?"

"Certainly. Some dislike your opponent, Philip Walton, but many of your friends and contacts have already begun to spread the word."

Nick pinned the ribbon onto his lapel. "Then we mustn't let them down."

She beamed. "That's what I wanted to talk to you about. Campaigning should come naturally to you, Nicholas. You possess charisma that can't be taught. Make use of that and give no cause for offense. Don't frequent any establishments that might tarnish your reputation. Plan *accidental* encounters with influential people. Consider whose company you're keeping . . ." One carefully painted eyebrow rose. "Need I go any further?"

He owed Anne his life — a debt that felt like less of a burden and more of an honor the longer he knew her, but the best he could do with his benefactress was to ignore the slight. "I understand. Be me but even more so."

She tilted her head in modest agreement. "And in the meantime, don't forget to keep up your work at the courthouse. If you fail to perform your duties, all the ribbons in the world won't secure you a position."

He had to look away before she caught him smirking at the ribbons that bedecked her ensemble. "Now that you mention it, I have some correspondence about the bridge that needs a reply. I'd better be going." But before he even reached his hat, he heard Mr. Stanford's pounding footsteps approaching.

"Nick! Good to see you, my boy. How are you? Have Ophelia's efforts scared you off yet?"

Ophelia touched her pearl necklace. "I'm a great help, Ian. You, of all people, should know that."

He ambled to her desk with a grim chuckle. "Without you I would miss out on scads of opportunities, live in a hovel, and have no social connections whatsoever. Listen to her, Nicholas. She can get you places." He lifted the lid on a jar of sweets and took a handful of chocolate-covered peanuts.

"One place I've yet to go is to the emporium to get my crimson reticule. With all my campaigning it's a particularly appropriate accessory for my navy gown."

Ian rolled his eyes before addressing Nick. "How's business at the courthouse?"

"Not much with everyone preparing for the election — only the bridge vote at the end of this month."

"Ah, yes. The bridge. Awfully ambitious for little Blackstone County."

"But possible," Nick said. "You can't imagine how desperately Allyton needs reliable transportation across to Garber."

"We can't ask the population to pay for something that benefits only a few." Ian shook his head. "It'd be unjust. Those people chose to live there despite the lack of transportation."

True. Nick agreed with Mr. Stanford in theory, but the memory of seeing the panicked man brave the river was hard to ignore. Yet, what if that family were the only family living in Allyton? Could they spend tens of thousands of dollars to build a bridge for one family? They had to draw a line somewhere, but Nick wasn't sure where that was. He'd learned how to handle his own money. Distributing the money of others should be considered even more carefully.

After Ophelia's dire predictions about hurting Nick's campaign, Anne almost felt guilty showing up at the office in her dingy hunting wear. She'd expected an argument or maybe even for him to send her home. Why did he have to come out with that giddy grin and ask if she'd had an enjoyable evening? Why did he have to spread on the charm like marmalade at a fancy tea? Didn't he know she wasn't Sunday company?

She stomped to her desk, trying to squelch the speculative glances he was giving her.

"This afternoon is my introduction to the chamber," he said. "I've practiced my lines a hundred times. Would you like to hear them?"

She wrinkled her nose. "I can't vote. You'd be wasting your time."

He threw his head back and laughed. "That's just as well. I need to show you the payroll. My foreman will be in this afternoon to pick up pay for the crew."

He allowed her to pass and get behind her desk — Harold's desk — before flipping open a portfolio.

"The figure in this column shows the workers' hours. Multiply it by this here, and deduct the amount in this column from their total pay to cover their purchases at the company store, broken tools . . . and fees for refusing to listen to my speeches."

Anne raised an eyebrow. She wouldn't laugh, especially when he was trying so hard to elicit that response.

"I got a telegraph from Anoli," she said.

Nick sobered. "About Sammy's father?"

Anne nodded. "He's on his way."

Nick ran his finger beneath his starched collar. "Maybe he'll make an appearance this time. I don't want you disappointed again."

Anne blurted, "I'm going to miss Sammy. I couldn't wait to be free of him at first, and now I'm going to miss him."

"Funny how that happens." But Nick didn't sound like it was funny at all. "So now you wait. No hopping on a train unless you've said good-bye."

"No." Anne traced the edge of the desk. "I won't run off."

"And I hope you can stay to see Molly. She'll want to visit before going to the Stanfords'."

Anne's mouth dropped open. "What? I don't know what you're talking about."

"I was going to reserve the dining room at the hotel, but Mrs. Stanford insisted on hosting a dinner. It'll be grand. I thought we might as well make an occasion of it, especially if you're leaving Garber."

Dinner at the Stanfords'? Anne felt ill. She could stare Mrs. Stanford down on the street, but she'd be turned away at the door if she showed up dressed as she was.

Nick stopped. "Please come. I'd love to present you to Molly. Ophelia will behave herself. She's a wonderful hostess."

"Mrs. Stanford doesn't serve me as large of a piece of approval pie as she does you. I can't go to her house."

"She's got no reason to dislike you. Dress up a mite and there'll be no rift. Here, take this." He pulled a clip of money out of his pocket, slid the top bill off, and dropped it

192

on her desk. "Once you're finished with payroll take the rest of the day to get yourself an outfit together. We'll quit Wednesday when their train gets in." He started for his office. "Oh, and don't forget to write that in the ledger."

"Write what?"

He pointed to the bill that lay untouched on her desk. "Business gift. Note it in the third column."

"I don't need your gifts, business or otherwise."

Nick's mouth opened to retort when steps sounded on the stairs outside. Anne almost laughed at how quietly they listened, both certain it was Ophelia, but the door swung open to reveal a grim deputy.

"Y'all got a minute? I could use your help."

Nick wasn't afraid of meeting the outlaws again. True, he'd almost died at the hands of one of these blackguards, but he would enjoy the satisfaction of facing them on more even footing. He and Anne trailed behind Joel, letting him part the crowds like Moses and the Red Sea. They'd only caught three of the train robbers on this holdup, but if there was any justice under the sun, they'd be the same ones that had accosted his train.

A murmur swelled through the crowd as ominous as the thunder of a stampede. Judgment day for someone.

"Step back," Joel ordered as they reached the jailhouse door, then he looked surprised when they obeyed.

The onlookers craned their necks over Nick's shoulder as he guided Anne in with a hand at her back and pulled the door closed behind them.

"You almost got a lynch mob." Nick's eyes took a moment to adjust to the darkened stone interior.

"Don't need one." Joel gestured to three bodies lying in an unlocked cell. "They're already dead. Do you recognize these men?"

Nick's stomach lurched. He reached to lay a comforting hand on Anne's shoulder, but she walked directly into the cell and looked down on the slack faces.

Nick forced himself closer and averted his eyes from the ragged hole torn in the vest of the man at his feet, but the vest he'd recognize anywhere. "That's the leader. He's the one who told the man to shoot me."

Joel looked to Anne. Her jaw lifted in dark affirmation.

Nick walked around his feet to get a better look at the one against the wall. "I think that's the kid I scuffled with. If he has dark eyes —"

"Let me open them for you," Joel said.

"I'd rather you not."

"That's him." Anne's shoulders looked like they could withstand a hurricane. "He has a piece of his ear missing. I remember now."

Joel bent to inspect and was satisfied. "How about the third one? Does he look familiar?"

Nick shrugged. "He could've been the one who held the pistol on me. If so, he got new boots, because Anne shot the old ones."

"How about you, Mrs. Tillerton? Does he look familiar?"

She nodded. Weary lines appeared around her mouth. "He had a bandanna and a hat at the holdup so I didn't recognize him then, but now I do. That's Finn Cravens."

If Nick and Deputy Puckett hadn't been watching, Anne would've marched over and kicked the dead man hard enough to make him cry, even now.

Moron.

So he was on his way to town to claim his son, but he thought he'd pull one last heist before he retired?

Fool.

He quit buffalo hunting because of a better opportunity?

Imbecile.

Not until she heard Nick clear his throat did Anne realize that the last word had been pronounced aloud. She closed her eyes, unwilling to consider the implications and decisions before her.

Nick's shoes scuffed the floor. "The boy's father?"

Anne nodded. She'd counted the days, haunted the telegraph office, and pestered the postmaster, waiting for her opportunity to flee the confines of Garber. Looking again, she prayed that she'd made a mistake, but it was Finn's nearly white hair filled with dirt and grass splayed on the brick floor.

"We'll find his family," Nick said.

"He's an orphan." She tilted her head up to find the lone square of sky through the high prison window. "He doesn't have any family. He told us stories of growing up on the streets of New Orleans and heading west as soon as he was big enough to work." Anne covered her eyes. "What am I going to do?"

Neither man offered an answer. Not surprising.

"I want to go to the house," she said. "Sammy may not have known his father, but I want to be with him, just the same."

With bowed heads they stepped out of her way. Their low voices still rumbled as she busted through the prison door and pushed through the crowd.

Poor, poor Sammy. Abandoned by his mother, orphaned by his criminal father. She hoped he'd never know what happened to his parents. Maybe by the time he was grown he'd have a family and would never feel the lack. Anne shoved her fists into her duster. Her mother died giving birth to her, and she'd never gotten over the lack. Her father hadn't paid her a lick of attention through her childhood, and she was his natural-born daughter. What chance did Sammy have for a loving family?

She'd reached the Pucketts' neighborhood with its fenced yards when she heard Nick behind her. He fell in step, hands in his pockets, for once having nothing to say.

Anne opened her mouth but then, with a shake of her head, closed it again. She had no plan. She could make no promises, but a quiet determination was forming. Sammy would not be placed in an orphanage. He would not piddle his years away in an institution, only to be released on the streets when half-grown without any skills, connections, or way to support himself. In Indian Territory they'd met a handful of men who'd grown up in orphanages, were looking for work, and didn't know the first thing about riding, shooting, or getting along in camp — Finn, for example. She could do better for the boy.

But how?

Could she find a family for him? The Pucketts might take him in. Joel would raise Cain about it and accuse her of further taking advantage of his parents, but it'd be good for the boy. Then she could come back and visit between hunts.

But her heart pounded as she thought about leaving him. He would cry. His chubby fingers would twine around her hair and lock on to her sleeve. Every morning Mrs. Puckett distracted him with toast and jelly so Anne could leave for work, but she couldn't justify sneaking away permanently. Not like Tessa. Prying Sammy off of her would be the lowest point of her fairly miserable life.

White wispy clouds raced high above a bright sky. Every day she'd waited for Finn, hoping to get back to hunting while winter delayed. Now she wondered if she would ever be free to ride Indian Territory again.

They reached the Pucketts' house, but she couldn't go inside. Not yet. Anne darted into the gazebo with Nick right behind her. First, she must choose.

The leaves of the peony bushes shuddered as she brushed against them.

"I can't do it," she said.

Nicholas stood at her side. "No one expects you to. You aren't prepared to raise a child."

She spun around. "Aren't you supposed to encourage me? Aren't you supposed to challenge me to sacrifice? What about doing my Christian duty?"

"I'm thinking of you, Anne. All I've heard since you arrived was how you couldn't stand being here, how you detested Garber and couldn't wait until you got back to Pushmataha. Isn't that your first priority?"

Anne dropped to the iron bench and clasped her hands between her knees. Finding Finn had been her focus for the last month, but it had become a reluctant goal. Every day she spent with the Pucketts she felt her love for the family growing. Every day with Nicholas weakened her distrust of men. Instinctively Anne knew that staying with these people would destroy her carefully built defenses. She had to leave before she was tempted to give up her independence, but could she now?

"I'm surprised at you. You're so quick to free me from guilt." Anne wasn't being fair, but she had to say it anyway. "Your desire to be rid of me overpowers any compassion for Sammy."

Her aim was true. Nick flinched, but he didn't flee. "You are my first priority. I want what's best for you. As much as I care about Sammy, no one could fault you for placing him in an institution. That's what those places are for. This child isn't your problem."

"Whose problem is he, then? You may turn away, but I can't. I've been there, Nick. I've had my face bruised and swollen with no advocate. People saw, but I wasn't their problem. I've been hungry and unkempt, but the only one responsible for me didn't care. I can't pretend like I don't see."

Nick knelt before her. He steadied himself with a hand on her knee. "I know you. I know you want to help, but please give yourself time to think it through. This would be a permanent decision, and it needs to be the right decision for both of you."

Anne stared at his hand resting on her britches' leg. Sammy already felt like part of her. She carried his smile close, using it as a reward for a hard day's work. Sitting in the cramped office, hunched over tiny figures in a ledger, and all she had to look forward to in the evenings was his delighted squeal when he saw her. She didn't know how she'd do it, but her decision was made.

"Thank you for walking me home." She gave her leg a shake, and he dutifully removed his hand.

"It's a shock. Not that this Finn Cravens would've been a good father —"

"Still, he was Sammy's father, and I wasn't willing to interfere. Now . . . well, now everything has changed." A clearing breeze danced through their sanctuary. Anne stood and turned her face into it.

Nick rose. "Would you like me to stay while you tell Mrs. Puckett?"

"I think it'd be better if I talked to her alone." Would Mrs. Puckett recommend the same course Nick had, or would her mother's heart yearn to help the boy?

Anne watched the quiet house as she silently buried her dreams of independence. She'd have to make new dreams. No longer could she withhold her heart. Her boy deserved her love no matter what it cost her.

"It's not the right time to bring it up, but I'll be with Molly and Bailey on Wednesday. Under the circumstances, I don't expect you to go." Nick looked hopeful, desperate for reciprocation, but she had nothing to give. He lowered his eyes. "I'd be proud to escort you if you're up to it."

"Considering all I'm facing, Ophelia doesn't seem that scary."

"And as far as Sammy goes, I'll stand by your decision. You'll make the best choice for both of you. I know you will."

If only she was as confident. Anne wished she could reassure him. She wished she had the words to ease his haggard countenance, but she could barely hold herself together. "I'll go with you to the Stanfords' dinner." What all that entailed, she couldn't fathom, but she wanted to promise him something. "If you don't mind, though, I'd like to be alone for now."

"Of course." He wriggled his hat down tight over his head, his mouth pulled into an uncharacteristically grim line. "Send for me if I can assist."

He waited, but she had nothing left to say. With hands thrust into his pockets and shoulders hunched he trudged away.

Anne started forward and felt his absence. She looked for Nick, but he had already jogged out of earshot. Probably for the best. She couldn't rely on him indefinitely. Yet, with all her misgivings over her future, she still wasn't convinced that gaining custody of Sammy was a disaster. With everything that had happened in her life, she'd kept hoping that somewhere it would all make sense. Somehow it would all match up and she could see that her suffering had a purpose. She wasn't there yet. She didn't see any divine justice, and the offenses had piled higher and higher, but Sammy might be the turning point. Would everything now fall into place, or would this be just another calamity God was forcing her to endure?

And she still didn't know how to respond to God's interference. The way these people talked, God required a heap of meekness, surrender, and sacrifice — but she rarely witnessed any. And she couldn't afford to be weak if she had Sammy. She needed to be ready to fight, not go belly up and surrender. She wouldn't lose this child. Not again.

She needed to carry on just as she'd been doing. Every time she felt herself settling into the Pucketts' household, she told herself that she hated Garber, that she would soon return to the countryside, where she would be free, unshackled by responsibility. But the gentle routines had molded her. Could it be that her earliest desires hadn't been misinformed? Were there really homes like the Pucketts' everywhere? Was her husband, Jay, the exception rather than the rule?

Her desire to stay meant forming attachments that could be broken. It'd mean giving part of herself to people who could betray her, but Sammy deserved her love. She would have to change for him, and loving the boy would affect her other relationships, too. Her cup already brimmed with feelings that she'd denied, and caring for Sammy could be the droplet that caused it to spill over.

Well, she'd take her fences one at a time. She had enough to sort through before complicating matters further.

13

The humid night air stifled Anne's cry when she rolled to her side. Her arm. She'd forgotten how badly it hurt when she lay on it. Gently she lowered herself onto her back. She mustn't wake Jay, especially whining over an arm he swore wasn't broken.

Sweat dampened the back of her neck and her forehead as she searched for something to look forward to with the sunrise. Some reason not to end her misery. Maybe Jay's chores would keep him away from the house. Maybe he would allow her to scrounge the thickets for blackberries and mulberries. They had to eat, after all. At least, he did. Whether there was enough left for her didn't matter.

Silently she slid her hand over her tattered nightgown. It did matter. She remembered now the reason she must survive. Why she must stay strong and healthy. She carried a child. His child. Perhaps becoming a father would change Jay. Perhaps he'd be pleased with her and would treat her like he had in the beginning. This child would be their fresh start.

Anne must have drowsed, for a movement startled her awake. She tensed, prepared for anything from a brutal caress to an outright strike, but instead, someone snuggled against her.

Her eyes darted around the room. Where was she? This wasn't her home. She turned her head to see an infant curled against her.

Her child? She touched her flat stomach and the memories returned. The brutal beating that led to her miscarriage. Jay's death. Buffalo hunting in Pushmataha. Tessa's desertion.

Anne rose on her elbow. The springs on the iron frame squeaked beneath her. The lemon scent from the sachet that Mrs. Puckett stored with her linens wafted off Anne's sheets. Calm. Safe. Sammy's blond locks were matted to his wet head. He'd left his trundle to find her sometime during the night. Anne untangled the blanket that was wrapped around him and fanned him with its corner, her present catching up with her.

With the death of Finn Cravens, no one else could lay a claim on Sammy. She'd wanted to be a mother, to know the maternal bonds that had been denied her in her childhood, but Jay had stolen her baby from her. And Sammy had lost his family, as well. But perhaps it accomplished a purpose. Anne wrapped a blond curl around her finger. Didn't she deserve something good after the shabby way she'd been treated?

She would start small, ease into this new role. Instead of ridiculing the sermons on Sunday, she would give the pastor a chance. Praying would be a good start, and she could learn the language of faith that everyone around her spoke so fluently. If it paid off, then maybe she'd trust God with a little more. Selling her buffalo equipment to Anoli would give her some funds, so it wasn't like she was expecting God to handle it all on His own. She wanted to be fair. They shouldn't expect too much from each other starting out.

So she and God were good. She hadn't foreseen being a mother in this way, but she was ready. Somehow she would manage to give Sammy everything he needed. He belonged to her and no one would take him away.

Anne's half day at the office had flown by. Nick had seemed relieved that she'd decided to stay in town with Sammy and even referred her to a solicitor who might have advice on taking custody of the boy. Now, in her bedroom mirror she watched her jaw harden. She'd do whatever it took to see that Sammy was a permanent part of her family, but her time at Nick's office was temporary. Harold's recovery would soon bring her employment to an end, and she'd need to find another way to support herself. Of course, neither Nick nor she broached the subject, and Anne was glad to save that conversation for a later date.

What she couldn't delay was dinner with the Stanfords that night and her absolute dread of getting into a dress again, but she'd given her word.

Mrs. Puckett bent over a trunk, flinging wads of fabric in every direction.

"Mary wore this dress at her coming out, so it wouldn't be appropriate for a widow. Caroline's dress here is bound to be too short. Here's one of Sadie's. You're about her size. It looks nice enough and the mice haven't been in it." Mrs. Puckett lifted the gown out of the trunk and shook it, letting the protective tissue paper float to the attic floor.

"No, no." Anne pried a sheet out of Sammy's hand before he could rip it further. She went to her knees to collect them and

208

give herself time to collect her own thoughts. She hadn't worn a dress since Jay died.

She closed her eyes. Not just died. That wasn't the whole story. Anne hadn't dressed like a lady since she'd killed him. She'd shot him dead. Even through all the beatings she'd endured, all the losses, she'd never considered shooting him before. He was her cross to bear. She deserved her punishment the way she'd dressed up to be alluring. She'd wanted a man's attention, and she'd gotten it. Vanity had earned its just reward.

Could this dress undo all the independence she'd won? Was she any stronger than when she'd stepped into a feminine role the first time? She watched as Mrs. Puckett held the dress against herself and smoothed the wrinkles. It wasn't a cursed gown that would carry her off to a dank underworld. It was just a dress, worn by the fearless Puckett girls who'd gone on to marry happily and give their mother grandchildren, albeit at an unsatisfactory distance.

Anne would wear it to a dinner to see her old friend Molly. Nothing could happen there, could it? And besides, if she was dressed nice, Mrs. Stanford would have to allow her in. The woman had probably been salivating all day — if the lady made spit —

waiting for the opportunity to turn Anne away at her doorstep, but she wouldn't get it.

Anne could do this. Mrs. Puckett cooed and awed as she held the navy wool dress against her. She had to take care of Sammy. No longer could she ignore etiquette and convention. What kind of life would her boy have if his mother was an outcast? Until she thought of something better, working for Nicholas and living with the Pucketts was the safest place for them. And if her attendance could improve Nick's relationship with his employer, then it wouldn't kill her to share a meal with them.

Sometimes it wasn't about winning or losing. Sometimes it was about living to fight another day.

"You knew I couldn't stay in Prairie Lea when there was so much drama taking place here in Garber. Besides, you were so good to send us business when Bailey and I were getting started at the sawmill that we wanted to come applaud your success."

In her usual fashion, Nick's sister insisted on having two escorts. Her husband had her left arm and carried their son on his other side. Nicholas had her right and hauled their bag — allowing Molly to

210

promenade down the big city streets with her new gown on full display. Garber might be more cosmopolitan than little Prairie Lea back in Caldwell County, but his sister could teach these women a thing or two about presentation. He couldn't wait to hear her opinion of Ophelia Stanford.

"And to see Anne," Bailey said. "Molly's just itching to hear the latest on the mysterious Mrs. Tillerton."

"I haven't mentioned your association to Mother. Can you imagine what Father and she would say if they knew you were socializing with Anne?"

"I don't think anyone would accuse Anne of socializing, but she's a special lady — definitely more interesting than anyone else I've met here. Besides, I thought our parents had finally learned not to meddle."

Molly laughed. "If they objected to Bailey . . . But please tell me Anne isn't wearing her hideous buckskins here in the city. It was one thing when she was hunting . . ." Molly shook her head. "I guess that's how she wants to present herself, but I wish she'd reconsider."

"She promised me that she'd come tonight." Nick tipped his hat to some ladies as they passed. "Believe me, if I knew the key to helping her ease back into polite society

I'd turn it."

"That's the problem, though," Molly said. "I don't think she's ever been in polite society. She went from the backwoods to being imprisoned, and then she was ostracized as a woman who had killed her husband. It'll take more than a new outfit to civilize her. But tell me about this baby she has. Is he the same age as Carter?"

They reached the hotel with plenty of daylight remaining. Their early arrival would give them time to talk before they had to guard their conversations with the Stanfords. Molly toured the lobby of the hotel admiring the décor while Bailey plopped in a chair and stretched his long legs.

"I got you a room on my floor," Nick said, "although those are usually reserved for long-term residents."

Bailey bounced his son on his knee. "I don't know that you'll want us close to you. Carter throws a fit at bedtime. If he gets going —"

"Hopefully, he'll be fine," Molly said. "Look, there's another infant. They're probably used to children."

Nick saw the lady with the little boy standing at her knee. He nodded a polite greeting and stepped up to the clerk's desk. "I reserved a room for —" He blinked.

"Yes, sir?"

Wait a minute. It couldn't be. Nick didn't want to turn around, for he was fairly certain what he'd just seen, and if it was her, then he'd snubbed —

The hair on the back of his neck rose, and he prayed Anne hadn't bolted for the door after his insensitivity. Nick turned to search the room, but she had fled. He ran to the heavy double doors and threw them wide, looking down the road in both directions.

There. No mistaking Sammy's blond head or Anne's curly hair, although it was twisted up, leaving only a few corkscrew tendrils dangling. Lengthening his strides, Nick caught up with her before she reached the first crossroad.

"Good of you to make an appearance." He fell into step next to her. "I don't wish to correct you, but you do realize that you're going away from the hotel?"

She arranged Sammy up higher on her waist — a waist he couldn't help but notice now that there was no canvas duster or bulky pants to cover it.

"This isn't going to work," she said. "I'm exposing myself for no reason. I surely don't want to go to the Stanfords', so if you and Molly are going to cut me in public —"

"Molly didn't see you, and I . . . I . . ."

213

He stepped in front of her. "Please come back. You look very nice." He kept his eyes on her face, completely ignoring the compulsion to step back and appreciate the changes the somber dress worked on her. No, he had to walk a fine line. If he made his true evaluation obvious, she'd feel uncomfortable and want to hide. He dispensed praise easily. It was hard to remember that she didn't know what to do with it.

"I did want to talk to Molly . . . and that was Bailey, wasn't it?"

Nick held out his arms to Sammy, who, with a lunge, fell against his chest. "That's a good boy. Maybe Uncle Nick needs to come visit more often. You'd be glad to see me, wouldn't you?"

Anne followed him toward the hotel, steps only dragging a bit. "Uncle Nick? When did that start?"

"My nephew is here, and I like the sound of it."

She shook her head. Nick smiled. Anne could grouse all she wanted. She was there and she was dressed respectfully. He wouldn't expect much more from her. Incremental change, gradually increasing the grade — that's how trains got from swamp to mountaintop. You couldn't go steep, especially carrying a load as big as the one Anne toted.

Nick ushered Anne to a private alcove in the hotel lobby and was met by Molly, who immediately embraced the reluctant runaway. "Anne, how beautiful you look. Buffalo hunting has been kind to you."

Bailey nodded. "Nice to see you again, Mrs. Tillerton. Been killing any rabbits lately?"

Anne's brow lowered with mock ire. "No, I haven't. Been confessing any fool nonsense in front of the whole church?"

Bailey threw back his head and laughed. "Should've known you'd set me straight. Molly sees that I behave myself, so no more fool nonsense. Did she ever tell you how you scared her with those rabbits you left on the porch?"

Nick set Sammy next to Carter, who was tugging at the fringe of the rug, eager to know every memory they shared. "I didn't hear about that."

"It was when Molly was living at the parsonage. She found dead rabbits on the front porch and thought someone was making a threat."

Anne put a hand to her hip. "Really, Molly? They were a gift."

Molly fiddled with her earbob. "It does seem silly, but it never occurred to me that dead animals could be a friendly gesture. I didn't have the first idea what to do with them. But how did you come to be in Garber? Nick says you were hunting buffalo in Indian Territory."

A wildness clung to Anne — even in a dress — delicate but untamed. She was a prairie flower that might wither the moment it was put in a vase. Her time indoors had lightened her naturally fair complexion, and the dark gown contrasted, making her skin glow. Had Nick not seen her shooting the toe out of a gunman's boot, he would've suspected her of concocting her hunting stories.

Nick directed her to a chair. Anne glanced nervously around the room as they took seats. "I came here to haul our cook back to Pushmataha, but she gave me the slip. Left her little boy behind, too. Then we found out that his father's dead and the boy has no one. Not where I expected to be."

Bailey's eyes held his for a long moment. Nick felt the weight of responsibility that Bailey was bestowing on him. Yes, back in Prairie Lea you didn't allow womenfolk to face challenges alone. He drew in a long breath. She was his responsibility. Even if she didn't have any kin to hold him accountable, his own family would. They were all the family she had left.

His family and Sammy.

Molly leaned forward to smile at Sammy. "Happy boy. It's hard to believe he'll never know his family."

"But he'll know me, and I can keep him safe as well as anyone." Anne crossed her arms.

Nick felt the shock of surprise. Where was her gun? No doubt she had one. Her skirt was draped too tightly over her hips for a holster under there. Probably had one hidden in her boot, but how quickly could she get to it? Knowing her . . .

Bailey cleared his throat and Nick realized that he'd been caught staring. Anne blushed, but she didn't run this time. She ducked her head to fuss with Sammy.

"Let me tell you about my current projects with the railroad," Nick diverted. If there was anything that Molly liked more than fashion, it was industry. She wouldn't leave town until she had a chance to look over all his paper work, which was fine with him. She had a good eye for business, as her and Bailey's successful handling of his father's sawmill proved.

By the time he'd answered all her questions, Anne and Bailey had about exhausted themselves entertaining the two young ruffians.

"It's almost time to go to the Stanfords'." Nick stood.

"Can we wait a little longer?" Anne asked. "Mr. and Mrs. Puckett were going to meet us and take Sammy home. He'll be ready for bed soon."

Before Nick could give his consent, Molly spoke up. "Do you think she'd mind watching Carter, too? He spent two days on a train. I hate to hold him still all evening."

Anne bit her lip, but Nick could answer with confidence. "The Pucketts will be thrilled. Their grandchildren don't live close — a lament I hear frequently."

Molly giggled. "Well, Mother and Father don't have that complaint. They watch Eva and Carter for a couple of hours every day while I go to the mill to help Bailey. And they begged for me to let Eva stay with them. You should see her, Nick. So much energy. I'm glad we didn't have to wrestle her the whole trip. One was enough."

But Anne planned to keep the boy and provide everything he needed — without a husband's assistance. She was capable, but at what cost? How many daily sacrifices would she have to make to meet his needs?

"We have to walk to the Stanfords'?" Molly asked. "Where do you keep your buggy?"

Anne perked up. "Nick's buggy? He doesn't have one."

Bailey snorted. "Crazy railroad man. Not having a horse is like walking around without kneecaps. I suppose it's possible, but what an inconvenience."

"You were afoot after you stopped cowboying," Molly said. "Had to borrow Father's surrey quite often."

Bailey's neck turned red, but he grinned just the same.

Anne's heart lightened. Molly and Bailey's presence worked like a tonic. Now certain that Sammy would be in her future, Anne could look ahead and wonder — would her life ever assume this easy normalcy? Would she ever be as comfortable around a man as Molly was with her husband?

"At least we are able to walk through a fashionable district," Molly said. "I'm noting the new paneled friezes on the architecture."

"Paneled friezes, yes. Very nice." Bailey patted her hand. "I'll be sure to have Mr. Mohle add some as soon as we get home."

"Listen to you, Bailey," Nick said. "Are you really going to make more changes to your house? You just built it."

"Naw. Once she sees what they cost, she'll decide against it. I'm just playing along." He winked at Anne.

Her eyes widened. He was Molly's husband — a churchgoing, God-fearing man. Then she caught herself. He hadn't meant any harm. Just a friend being friendly.

As Molly and Nicholas discussed the rising price of raw timber, Bailey nudged her. "So how do you like working for Nick?"

"He can act pretty full of himself, but he treats me fair."

Bailey grinned. "Sounds like an accurate assessment."

She studied the manicured path as they walked toward the house on the corner lot. Bailey was teasing her. She hadn't said anything wrong, had she? Well, if Nicholas hadn't sent her packing after one of their many arguments, he surely wouldn't over that statement.

The nearer they came to their destination, the more Anne's confidence vanished. She propelled herself up the brick footpath like a sailor walking the plank, then hid in their small ensemble and waited for their ringing entreaty to be answered — hoping vainly that Ophelia Stanford would let her be.

Might as well hope that Sunday would come three times a week.

From the moment they were escorted into the parlor, Mrs. Stanford focused the bulk of her attention on Anne. The woman studied her like a tracker studied scat. Ophelia must have already made up her mind to be offended by Anne's appearance, but it seemed she couldn't decide why. Anne took her seat, her palms sweating. She sat with back straight and both feet on the floor, knees together. She wouldn't make any mistakes if she didn't open her mouth. Besides, between her three companions, there was no silence that needed to be filled.

Molly and Nicholas were both talkers and obviously missed each other's company. Molly did her best to draw Mrs. Stanford into the conversation, which was no easy task when she was dead set on picking Anne apart from across the room. When Mr. Stanford made his appearance, Anne nearly fled. His eyes lingered like a fly on raw meat.

"Mrs. Tillerton, is it? You look familiar. You weren't working at the livery stable a few weeks ago, were you?"

Anne shot a frightened glance toward Nick. Nick nodded calmly, assuring her she had nothing to fear.

"Yes, sir, but I was at the Velvet Palace before that."

"You worked at the Velvet Palace?" Ophelia stood. Her skirt twitched like the tail of a mountain lion. "Honestly, Ian, this has gone on long enough. I will not sit across the table from a fancy lady."

"I did *not* work there," Anne protested. "I only ate there while trying to find lodging, but I thought Mr. Stanford's recollection might be of seeing me there as he was going up the stairs."

Ophelia closed her mouth and dropped to her chair. "I'm . . . I'm speechless."

"Oh, stop with your righteous outrage." Ian pulled a cigar from his pocket and jammed it between his teeth. "Now you have one more misdeed to harangue me over. Add another expensive bauble to your demands."

The dinner bell chimed and Anne sprang to her feet. Mrs. Stanford deliberately refused to budge until everyone had an opportunity to notice who alone had jumped the gun.

"Mrs. Garner, I believe it's my privilege to escort you to supper." Mr. Stanford rose to offer his arm to Molly.

Molly's cheerfulness rang false. "My, we are dining in high style tonight, aren't we?"

Without waiting for direction, Bailey took Mrs. Stanford's arm and nearly pulled it off in his eagerness to see what fine food would be served.

Nicholas offered his arm to Anne and paused long enough for the room to empty.

"I've ruined everything," she said.

"You didn't create the problems that exist between the two of them. Forget about it and try to enjoy yourself. I'm looking forward to dining with a beautiful woman at my side."

She must have tensed, for he laid his hand over hers. "Don't be afraid. Just because you put on a skirt doesn't turn me into a crazed, violent maniac."

His eyes were kind, reassuring, and even though she could acknowledge the truth of his words, they still made her skin crawl in remembrance of the way Ian had looked at her. She squeezed Nick's arm. At least he hadn't believed Ophelia's accusation about her employment.

They entered the dining room last, and Nicholas dragged her to her seat. Entering a room before you had a chance to note every portal and window was foolhardy, but they weren't waiting for her to take a full account of the elongated chamber. Nicholas intervened awkwardly with the chair before

Anne could pull it out for herself, but how was she supposed to know? She plopped into her chair. Why couldn't she get along as well as Molly?

So for the next half hour she mimicked Molly religiously. Napkin on her lap. Her own utensils didn't touch the food until it was on her plate. Her fork didn't spear the mutton. Her knife didn't cut the butter. When she wasn't using the knife, it rested on her plate. She wished Molly would eat more green beans. They smelled good, but Anne was afraid to venture out on her own.

Molly pinned her meat with her fork rotated toward herself. Then with her knife in her right hand . . .

From the corner of her eye, Anne saw movement. A man's arm reached around her face, close enough he could break her neck with one quick jerk. Anne dropped her fork and grasped him by the wrist. Throwing her body forward she was able to catch him off balance. He fell against her back, and before he could move she had her dinner knife against his exposed neck.

Horrified gasps erupted at the attack. So were his actions planned all along, or had Ophelia given the signal after Anne's embarrassing exposure of Mr. Stanford's activities?

"Please, ma'am. I was just reaching for your glass. Please . . . the knife." The man's eyes bulged. A vein in his temple throbbed.

"Release him at once!" Mrs. Stanford stood, her outraged face causing Anne to wonder if she wasn't the biggest threat at the table.

Nick's voice floated smoothly beneath the commotion. "He's the butler, Anne. You can let him go."

With effort, Anne released her hold. She watched as he took her glass with shaking hands and refilled it with tea. From the hacking noise across the table, she summarized that Bailey had choked. His wheezing and coughing were laced with laughter while Molly pounded on his back. Only Nicholas remained unfazed, calmly cutting another bite of mutton.

"Sit down, Ophelia." Mr. Stanford chewed on his mutton. "Theo isn't hurt. This'll teach him not to go sneaking around without announcing himself."

Anne's glass was returned, although Theo took pains not to lean over her again.

"I'm surprised at you, Nicholas," Mrs. Stanford said. "You didn't make a move to protect an innocent man from this Amazon."

Anne placed her hands in her lap. She

wouldn't eat another bite of food provided by this woman.

"I know it's no use. If Mrs. Tillerton wanted to do harm to Theo, I couldn't stop her. You'll remember she saved my life on that train — and those weren't unarmed serving staff she went up against, either." He chewed and washed his food down with a drink. "She's a remarkable woman."

She'd come here to bolster Nick's relationship with his biggest client. Instead, she'd certainly destroyed it. And now he was defending her. Anne sank even further into her chair.

Bailey wiped his mouth with his napkin. His dark eyes grew thoughtful. Was he thinking of what had happened along the banks of Plum Creek as she was? Bailey and his cousin Weston had heard her gunshot. Yes, he'd seen her work before. She didn't regret saving Rosa's life. How could she? But her heroism had cost him dearly. Wasn't that the whole idea behind being a hero — sacrifice? But no one realized that her sacrifice was a daily burden. Her pain hadn't ended with his life. As long as she felt her life was in danger at a dinner party, she was still paying.

14

The breeze had picked up during dinner. Nick considered offering Anne his jacket, but with her wool dress and the challenging pace at which she barreled down the road, he assumed she was warm enough and kept his excess clothing to himself. He tried to stroll, hands in his pockets, but had to give up the pretense of effortlessness in order to stay at her side.

"Thank you for going."

She nodded once.

"The dress was a nice touch. Do you think you could wear it tomorrow?"

"You're pushing your luck."

Of course he was. Would he be having any fun if he weren't? "I'm sorry you got caught up in the Stanfords' feud, but I don't think you did any harm. It's an ongoing dispute. And nice work on the butler, by the way. Servants are notoriously untrustworthy. Always be on guard —"

"I'm glad you're enjoying yourself, but it wasn't funny to me." She fumbled with the latch on the garden gate.

"Come now. Don't you see the humor?"

She turned. "I don't. He scared me. Why would you laugh when someone thinks their life is in danger?"

"But all he did was reach . . ." He passed his hand through the air to the right of her. Anne ducked, flinging her arm over her head.

Nicholas's stomach dropped. "Oh, sweetheart . . ." When would he learn? He stepped backwards, giving her room, what she most desired. He'd tried to tease her out of her worry. He'd poked fun at the defenses she wore, but many times he lost sight of the fact that those defenses were in place for a reason. They'd been stormed and breached before, and he needed to be clear on his intentions. Would he let her remain protected, or would he stay to defend her if she came out of her fortress?

Her hand shone white against the dark fabric of her bodice. She pressed it against her waist and closed the gate, allowing it to separate them.

"I wish there was something I could do for you." And in that moment, he reached his decision. He loved her. How that love would express itself, how she would allow him to proceed, he couldn't predict, but he would proceed. "I wish you didn't live in fear of the next blow."

"It's all right." She straightened and brushed a stray curl out of her face. "I'm used to it."

"But you don't need to live like this. Jay Tillerton was an evil man. No one else wants to hurt you."

Anne studied the gate. "But I can't be sure, can I? And now I'm not just protecting myself, but Sammy also. My task is to raise him so that he knows nothing but love. Sammy should be able to stand tall and not expect pain and betrayal at every turn."

"That sounds like a fine goal." Nick leaned over the fence that separated them, energized by his newly discovered resolve. He knew he'd spook her if he gazed too long, but when his eyes met hers, he was lost. Who would've thought that scary Anne Tillerton was really scared Anne? Who would've thought that the little banty rooster was as tender as a spring chick, and as quiet as a dove when she peeked out of her armor? "I have a goal, too," he said before he could think better of it. "Someday you will know what it is to be secure in a relationship and loved by a touch."

Her gray eyes met his and searched their depths — looking for what, he knew not. Her lips parted. She was so close, but he feared if he came any closer, daybreak would find her and Sammy with their backs to Garber, headed to goodness knows where.

Her fingertips brushed the back of his hand. "Carter is probably asleep."

"Who?" He blinked. Oh yeah. His nephew. "I'm glad you reminded me. Molly would kill me if I returned to the hotel without him."

"I'd forgotten, too." Anne held the gate open for him and stayed by his side as he walked forward, unsure of where this path would lead.

After seeing Molly and Bailey off at the train station the next morning, Nick didn't expect to find Harold when he walked into the office. True, Harold's splinted arm meant that he wouldn't be able to write, but with Anne to help him, they would make up lost ground quickly. Besides, Harold's presence might prevent Nick from acting impulsively and frightening Anne away.

Where was their relationship headed? Nick was ready to find out, but above all he wouldn't rush her.

After getting settled Nick and Harold caught up on the work that had been put together during his absence. Nick went over the new hires on the line and the new equipment ordered from the money borrowed at the bank.

"Looks like you have it lined out." Harold dug into his sling to scratch beneath his bandage.

"We should be ready by the time Mr. Stanford breaks ground on the new track. The loan payments will squeeze our budget until we meet our first objective on the contract, but it will be worth it when we get both teams rolling."

The outer door opened and Anne stepped inside. "Harold's back?"

Nick hadn't meant to sigh, but when Harold's questioning face turned his way, he knew it'd been audible. And yet how else could he have responded to the beautiful, demure woman standing in the doorway?

She wore the same dark dress she'd donned the night before. Once again her curly hair was gathered and twisted up, and while nothing about her ensemble would've been considered fashionable, it affected Nick like a kick in the chest.

"He's going to be in my office for most of

the day," Nick said, "but he still can't write."

She fidgeted. Nick forced his shoulders to relax. He knew to draw his gaze away before he embarrassed her. Lifting a paper before him, he continued, "We have paper work to talk over, so we'll stay out of your way."

"If there's any way I can help —"

But before she could complete her thought the outside door opened. Anne looked over her shoulder and then grew sullen.

"It must be Ophelia." Nick spoke, barely moving his mouth.

"You haven't taught her to lock the door behind her?" Harold moved his chair closer to Nick's.

Anne returned to her desk, clearing the way for Mrs. Stanford to enter.

"I'm surprised to see you with two employees, Nicholas. Surely we're not paying you that well." The rich rust of her gown shone like a copper penny. Using her parasol as a walking stick, she made her way to her customary chair and sank into it like a queen on her rival's throne.

"Good morning, Mrs. Stanford, and while I appreciate your concern over my staffing, I promise nothing that happens in this office will adversely affect your business."

"She affected my staff last night."

"Regretfully so, but she can hardly pull a

knife on Theo from here."

Harold's eyebrows lifted until they met his hairline, which was a distance, to be sure.

"You should worry about your own well-being. As you pointed out, you couldn't stop her should she try something against your person."

Nicholas allowed his face to harden. He leaned forward against his desk, enjoying the feel of his coat straining against his arms and spoke loudly enough for Anne to hear him in the next room. "I was merely jesting. Please don't presume that I'm threatened — or burdened — by her. A woman with your resources and interests surely has more important concerns."

Ophelia stood. Ever in control, she sauntered to the new fern, obviously aware that both men followed her every move. She traced the curve of the pedestal with a manicured finger. "No reason for you to get upset, Nicholas. The purpose of this visit was to offer you a new opportunity — one that I think might interest you."

She turned, spinning her parasol slowly. "We have two options for a track to Muskogee. One proposed route would go through Bakersville, the other through Vannatta. I recommended to Ian that you go with him tomorrow to scout the two locations and help make the decision about which route would be more profitable."

"What did Mr. Stanford say? Can I leave so close to the election?" Nicholas hated that the prospect excited him so. And he hated that his eagerness pleased Ophelia.

"I insist. It's not good for Ian to go on these trips alone. He's susceptible to diverse temptations, and I'd feel better if you went along." She trailed her fingers along the back of the chair. "There are times when business decisions are made that have nothing to do with contracts, but everything to do with appreciation. Favors, compromises, courtesies — they all play a part in the advancement of a career."

A doubt gnawed at Nick's gut — a fleeting regret that he hadn't gone after another client and diversified his business after all. But why should he worry when such a shining opportunity was laid before him?

"Not only do I have the election, but we vote on the bridge a week from tomorrow. I can't miss that."

"Ah yes. The bridge. Ian wished to speak to you on that subject. Perhaps you'll find time to visit while on your little excursion?" One eyebrow curved like the top of a question mark.

"I'll need to talk it over and make sure

the office can do without me, but exactly what will my duties entail on the trip?"

"Those two towns will wine and dine you — dinners, parades, samples of their wares. There will be offers of every kind made to the men who have the power to decide whether the town gets a railroad or not. Remember" — she walked around the chair to stand before him — "it's not just a hotel and restaurant that will prosper. Farmers can get more money for their crops, because shipping will cost less. The goods for sale in the mercantile will be cheaper in the town with the depot, because those items will be unloaded straight off the train. No wagon fees. Every merchant, craftsman, farmer, tanner, and rancher will give anything for you to choose their town."

"Is that legal?"

She waved away his scruples with a genteel gesture. "Certainly. Your choice will be based on which town has the most to offer. They are merely demonstrating their riches. And then there are the railroad easements. As a reward for your extra work, you'll be deeded fifty acres of prime real estate on either side of the track. It's a standard benefit."

Nicholas studied his clean shorn fingernails. How many years of scrimping could he leapfrog in this one trip? The experience alone was worth the extra work. The faint sheen of greed glistened on Harold's forehead. His index finger mimicked a woodpecker against Nicholas's desk. Now that Harold was back and with Anne to help . . .

Ophelia's cheeks pinked like a girl with her first beau.

"You mentioned compromises," Nick said. "I assume you'll expect something from me in return for your generous offer."

She tapped her chin. "Ian has a matter that he'll no doubt discuss with you on the trip, but I have my own agenda. If you think you'll win an election — or that I'd want to be known as your sponsor — when you employ an outcast who thumbs her nose at all that's right and decent, then you are mistaken."

Nicholas spun his pen between his fingers. "I'm sorry you feel that way."

"Harold is back. There's no excuse for her presence." She jabbed her parasol into the rug. "Now, shall I tell Ian to expect you on the ten o'clock train?"

From the syrupy tone of her voice, Ophelia was smiling, but Nick didn't look up.

"I'll let you know before the end of the night."

■ ■ ■ ■

"If you'll excuse us, Harold." Anne heard Nicholas's chair scrape the wood floor as it slid away from his desk. She rustled some papers to disguise her engrossment with their conversation.

"Mrs. Tillerton, I won't be gone long. Will you help Harold until I get back?"

So he didn't call her by her Christian name in front of Ophelia?

"Umm . . . yes." There was more to say — wear garlic around your neck, watch your scalp — but Anne would have to wait until he returned to laugh at Ophelia's ridiculous demands.

Harold entered just as the door closed, then extended papers to her with his good arm.

"If Nick's going to be gone a couple of days, we might have a chance to catch up with him."

She dipped her pen into the inkwell. "Show me what to do."

"First let's see what you've already done."

As Anne opened files and ledgers, Harold's approval grew. Her work might have been painstakingly slow, but it was neat and accurate, leaving him with nothing to rework as he had feared. By quitting time they'd recorded all of the expenses and made updates to the employee rolls.

Harold was banking the fire in the small potbelly stove and Anne was tidying her desk when Nicholas opened the door.

"I didn't know you were returning." Harold straightened.

"I'm not staying long." Nicholas unbuttoned his coat. "Do you think you can handle everything while I'm gone? You won't be able to contact me for a couple of days."

"We're awaiting the shipment of the saw before any progress at the work site can be made." Harold fastened his satchel. "As far as the paper work goes, with Mrs. Tillerton's help I should be back up to speed, if not a little faster — three arms instead of two."

"Do you have a key for tomorrow morning?"

Harold nodded. He opened the door and stepped aside to let Anne pass first.

"Anne, please stay." Nicholas fiddled with a pen from the desk. "If you don't mind."

Harold pulled the door closed behind him, but not before leaving with a significant waggle of his eyebrows over his spectacles.

Nicholas's chin lowered. He sighed. "I

suppose you know what I must say."

Anne dug her boot heel into the soft pine floor. "You're going to apologize for Mrs. Stanford's rudeness. You're going to beg me to continue working for you, even though it means putting up with a she-cat with no manners."

He cocked his head. "What would be your second guess?"

The smoke from the dying fire pricked her eyes. "Ophelia hates me because I won't lick her boots. I've dealt with bullies before — and that's all she is, demanding her way."

"Unfortunately, Ophelia earned that right when her husband became my sole account." Nicholas dropped the pen into the inkwell. "Not only can she wreck my campaign, but she could also bankrupt my company. Now, surely there's a solution. If you've decided to stay in town and raise Sammy, we need to find you a position that's more permanent."

"You're sending me away?"

"Never. But I don't know how to keep you. I want you here. I want to see you — I will see you — every day, but if my business folds then neither of us will have employment. Maybe if you wouldn't antagonize her so —"

"This isn't about me. It's about control.

Ophelia is threatened by anyone who isn't in her pocket. That's why she has to remove me . . . and why she's so smitten with you." Anne hated the crack in her voice. She cleared her throat. "It's because you don't have a backbone where she's concerned. You're at her beck and call."

"I don't need advice from you, Mrs. Tillerton. I choose to live in society, and that means getting along with people, even when they are difficult. And you should be thankful I'm patient with difficult women, else you would've never lasted this long." Nick's brow lowered. "I have to please my customer, and I can't believe you'd hold this two-bit position dearer than my career — than our relationship."

"We don't have a relationship."

"Well, maybe I want one."

Anne's hand dropped to her side. Was he serious? He seemed as surprised by his admission as she was. Slowly he unclenched his fists, but he watched her as though there was more at stake than he was ready to admit. Even more than his contract.

"Look, I don't want to fight, but this is important. We both knew you weren't working here permanently. Why not let Ophelia think she's won a battle? If I can't find you another position, I'll keep your name on the

240

payroll, and you can collect without lifting a finger. Will you do that? For me?" His blue eyes could melt butter, but Anne was made of sterner stuff. She opened her mouth, and he amended, "Not for me. For Sammy."

Anne's jaw clenched. She knew loving Sammy would make her vulnerable, but she hadn't expected to be attacked so soon, and by Nick, of all people. "Don't drag him into this. If you're so set on pleasing Ophelia, fine. But if you're too ashamed to be seen with me here, don't think I'll welcome your company anywhere else." With a swish of her skirt she hurried to the door and called over her shoulder, "Stay away from me and my son."

15

The stagecoach slid sideways on the sandy road that spanned the gentle rises. With a practiced eye, Nick assessed the grade. As flat as one could hope for in this area, but the ground felt unstable. Of course if the railroad strayed too far from water, they'd spend more on lumber. Best option was to encompass enough timber in the land allotment that none had to be purchased. Still, this route seemed to be superior to the Bakersville option.

Ian Stanford belched from the seat next to him. "We've covered more ground going side to side than forward progress." He loosened his necktie. "Just another reason that railroads will make coach travel obsolete."

No reply was necessary and the less he had to say, the better. Nicholas was in no mood for small talk. Once again he'd gotten crossways with Anne. Once again he felt the stunning discomfort that accompanied every spat with her. He hated that she couldn't stay on at the office, but didn't she understand what was at stake? He had to keep peace with Ophelia if he wanted to be successful. What help could he be to Anne and Sammy if he lost his business?

The town of Vannatta appeared as the coach crested a bald rise. As they crossed a bridge, Ian waved to the people gathering by the road while Nicholas shoved aside his worries of Anne and prepared to greet the dignitaries gathered before the post office.

He hadn't expected a brass band to meet them at Vannatta, which was fortunate. Nowhere else could a tuba player, an elderly woman with a cornet, and a boy with a triangle qualify as a band, but there they were, filling the crisp air with a stirring rendition of "She'll Be Coming 'Round the Mountain."

"Not quite as big as Bakersville's welcome," Stanford said. "Hopefully they'll be more desperate." He straightened his tie and tightened his gloves before climbing out of the stagecoach.

Nicholas didn't follow too closely. After being trapped inside a coach with a man suffering from perpetual indigestion, he wanted some space — and some fresh air.

He hopped down and stretched discreetly before the crowd realized they had two guests of honor.

At Bakersville, he'd been treated like the visiting Prince of Wales. They'd generously given a sample of all the fruits of their labors, but by this time of year many of their crops were dried or canned. Balancing the glass jars of beets and tomatoes as he'd looked inside the general store had put him in a foul mood. What did he care how many shelves of goods were available in town? Didn't they realize the railroad would bring business whether it was already there or not? The saddle was an extravagant gesture, but one which was useless to him. Most of the riches Ophelia had hinted at had yet to materialize. Of course, at the top of that list was the land grant, and that would be almost worthless until the railroad was completed, anyway.

As for his mentor, Stanford's activities involved hinting, criticizing, and looking disappointed. Once inside the coach Nicholas was concerned to learn that Stanford's disapproval did not stem from the unstable topsoil and deep river crossing, but from the lack of goods delivered up front. "They are holding out, waiting to see what we decide," he'd complained. "How are we to make our decision before we see what is offered?"

Not what Nick had expected. Before Nicholas could reach the patriotically sashed top-hat wearer, Stanford had already accepted an armful of fall foliage and a kiss on the cheek by one of the local lasses.

Feeling a bit foolish for having missed the ceremonial greeting, Nick edged his way onto the platform. The lovely hostess had positioned herself at the side of a burly pouting youth, who had no interest in seeing the ceremony performed again, but someone, feeling that Nick had been slighted, sought to remedy his loss. The cornet player stepped forward, wrenched Nick's ear while moistening her lips, and planted a firm smooch on his mouth.

The crowd — such as it was — erupted in laughter. What could he do? Warmth crept up his neck like he was a boy in short pants. He waggled his eyebrows at the crone and sent her a saucy wink. Her eyes danced as she swatted his arm and stepped off the platform.

Stanford turned a shoulder to the crowd. "I thought she really liked you."

"I thought cornet players had to have teeth," Nicholas shot back, still smiling at the happy assembly.

Compared to Bakersville's, the speech was brief. A few farmers stepped up to make suggestions on the lay of the land and the water sources for the boilers. Women produced baked goods kept warm in baskets as children stole peeks from behind their skirts. Once the official pitch had ended, Nicholas excused himself from the gathering in order to explore the land stretching beyond Main Street.

Gentle slopes covered in dried prairie grass ducked and tucked into each other. The Blue Woman Creek ran along the proposed route through Vannatta, its tree-lined banks offering lumber for the ties and water for the steam engine.

Nick sensed before he heard the quiet man approaching. Stopping next to him, the man rested his hands on his narrow hips, his eyes seeing far across the plain.

"When I first come in 1860, I got holed up at this spot by a buffalo herd. Had to hide out in the trees yonder for two days to keep from getting trampled. Thought there was no end to the beasts."

"I've been in a coach for two days and haven't seen a single bison," Nicholas said.

The man nodded. "This land could never have been settled with them trampling our crops and passing disease on to our livestock. Figured I'd make my money thinning them out before I tried my hand at ranching. Did well for myself selling the hides, and yet I'm kind of sorry to see them go."

"You hunted buffalo here?" The man was as thin as a rail but looked like he could carry one unaided.

"Yes, sir. Name's Buck Chambers."

"Nicholas Lovelace." He offered his hand. "You wouldn't happen to know a lady hunter? Anne Tillerton?"

A warm smile crossed his face. "Little Annie. Of course. One of the best shots around. She had trouble handling that big Sharps rifle, but she'd never let on. Just did her job — which wasn't easy with all the attention she caught."

"Attention?" Nick's eyebrows rose. "What do you mean?"

"Oh, there was always some idiot greenhorn who'd saunter up and think he was going to fix her. Think he could say some nice words and woo her. She wanted nothing to do with them, which was for the best." He sent a stream of tobacco shooting. "Old Anoli had his hands full chasing them away, but I guess she's somewhere safe now."

Nick's chest expanded with a painful breath. Was she safe? Was she safe from idiot

247

greenhorns? Now that she was staying in town, he needed to be clear on what the future held for them. He'd never imagined courting a woman like Anne, but neither could he imagine his day without her.

"She works for me . . . she used to anyway, but she's not happy living in town."

Buck nestled a fresh lump of snuff in his lip. "Then why don't she come back?"

"She's taken custody of an infant, can hardly hunt with a baby."

"Oh yeah . . . Finn's by-blow. I heard about that. She must be powerfully attached to stay there. We could barely get her to go into Pushmataha, much less Garber." The aging hunter rolled a rock beneath his shoe. "Well, you tell her I send my best. I'm glad she's found a place to settle down and call home."

Had she? Before he could answer, Ian appeared.

"There you are." Stanford paused midstep to stifle another belch. "I'm afraid we're wasting our time here. They don't have much to offer."

How Stanford could miss the quick indignation of Buck Chambers, Nicholas couldn't fathom. Perhaps the same way he'd missed the gentle terrain and the ready resources needed to lay track. Had the free food blinded him? But it was Stanford's company and Stanford's call. Besides, with troublesome thoughts of Anne at the forefront of his mind, Nicholas was in no mood to argue.

Their hired coach met them as they reached the main thoroughfare through town.

"There's an inn at Caddo where we'll stay tonight," Ian said. "Only decent place to take a meal in Indian Territory."

How could he think about eating after all that'd been offered them?

A river crossing lay ahead. The stagecoach paused. The horses allowed it to rock backwards before heaving it up the ramp.

"Can we stop here?" Nick asked. "I'd like to examine this bridge. The river appears to be similar in size to the Choctaw."

"We won't stop." The edge to Mr. Stanford's voice could cut a rail. "And enough with this bridge nonsense. I can't believe you're still considering it."

"It's my job to consider it."

"But there are already bridges across the Choctaw. People have several options to get to town — the train, the ferry, or the Finkle Road."

"Those options aren't always good enough. The Finkle Road is hours out of the way, and the ferry and the train are both expensive options — especially if they are traveling with a large family or driving livestock to market. Besides, they aren't always available." Nick grasped the leather loop above the window as the buggy bounced. "I saw a man die trying to cross the river —"

"You can't base a decision on an isolated incident," Stanford snorted.

"I agree, but it gave me the impetus to do my own research. Because a man died doesn't make the bridge right, but if it's justified, then waiting could be tragic. Why delay if building the bridge would benefit everyone?"

"But it won't benefit everyone. The ferryman will be out of business."

"I considered that, but the ferry isn't even privately owned. It belongs to Blackstone County, and the ferryman is a county employee."

"And that leaves the railroad —"

"Honestly, I don't think it'll bother you much," Nick said. "Your railroad covers nearly a thousand miles. How much could the small section between Garber and Allyton hurt you?"

"Let me be clear, son." Ian's sudden sarcasm made Nick's skin crawl. "Considering all I've done for you, I thought you'd be more receptive to my advice. My railroad will continue to thrive even if the vote on the bridge passes, but our success depends on the allegiance of our partners. NTT Railroad will not do business with any supplier who acts against our interest, however insignificant it might seem. This isn't about a single bridge — it's about loyalty."

Nick's grasp on the loop tightened. Was Mr. Stanford actually threatening him? His stomach squeezed into a painful ball of iron. The Stanfords had supported him, given him a lucrative contract before he'd proven himself. They'd introduced him into Garber society and now were spearheading his campaign. He couldn't believe Mr. Stanford would sever their relationship because of one county vote, but was there any other way to interpret his message?

Ian leaned forward. "Now, last I heard you have the new equipment already ordered, don't you? You're all set up for that second line. Probably have that money from the loan already paid out, too."

"Yes, sir. We couldn't have bought the saw without the bank's help."

He smiled. "I admire someone who takes a risk . . . like investing before a contract is signed. I'd like to see your optimism rewarded, but there are no guarantees, especially in this shaky economy. I never know when we might need to cut our losses and find another opportunity."

Nick's throat closed. He turned his face to the window. Perhaps he hadn't understood the situation before, but his eyes were fully opened now. What had started as a thrilling opportunity had turned into a dangerous responsibility. He'd promised the citizens of Blackstone County that he would act with their best interests in mind, but he hadn't expected their desires to so conflict with his.

Anne pulled the solicitor's door closed behind her and journeyed down the long corridor, her footsteps echoing through the courthouse. While she should rejoice that the man saw no obstacles to her taking custody of Sammy, the thought that no one else wanted the child sorrowed her. Not for her sake, of course. Sammy belonged to her and she had no desire to share him, but she longed for the day when he had friends who loved and appreciated him.

Now that her courthouse task was complete, Anne would search again for employment. She hoped her more traditional appearance would help the search. Truthfully,

Anne didn't mind the dress too much. She enjoyed looking feminine when no one was around. Even though the desire to look pretty and be treated special had endangered her, it hadn't entirely disappeared. Anne ran her hand down the row of pearly buttons on the bodice. Being leered at and manhandled she objected to. The dress she could keep.

Anne had nearly reached the lone exit at the end of the corridor when the narrow door opened.

Ophelia Stanford.

How did she open the door without ever looking like she'd touched it? Must be some sort of deviltry she possessed that caused it to fly at her approach. She glowered at Anne as though she'd found her smeared on the bottom of her boot. "Your dress looks nice . . . at least that's what I thought when you wore the same one last week."

As if the remark could hurt her feelings. What was Ophelia doing at the courthouse, anyway? Slipping in a back door didn't fit her character. Anne squared her shoulders. Was Nick back in town? Was she coming to see him?

Anne stared at Ophelia's handbag. "I see your husband still hasn't given you that red bag you've been after. You must not have expressed yourself clearly enough."

Ophelia's nostrils flared. She marched resolutely forward, barging ahead as if to trample Anne. Was there room for her to pass? It didn't matter. Anne wouldn't step out of her way.

Ophelia sped up as she neared. Anne squared her shoulders. She'd seen similar showdowns every time her brothers fought. Would this confrontation end with Ophelia and her rolling on the ground plummeling each other?

She sincerely hoped so.

Ophelia continued forward but at the last moment angled her shoulders and pulled her skirts hard against the wall. Despite her effort there was a moment they were locked together with skirts tangled, but Anne refused to budge.

"For crying aloud!" Ophelia huffed as she stumbled past.

Gratifying. Nick might let Ophelia push him around, but Anne's boots were nailed to the floor. She watched Ophelia stomp away and wondered exactly which of those offices was Nick's and how he was feeling about his decision to keep Ophelia close and push her away.

His calf-leather shoes had never felt heavier.

Nicholas trod the bare dirt path that cut through the empty lot on his way to the courthouse. He'd arrived in town late the night before, but instead of checking in at his own office this morning, he'd make good on his promise to Mr. Stanford that he'd look once again at the bridge proposal and see if there was reason to reconsider his vote. Nick would go over every detail again, praying that there'd be some missed consideration and he could agree with his patron and preserve his clear conscience.

He swept down the lonely hall toward the commissioners' offices with the full intent of ducking past the judge's chambers, fearing that old Judge Calloway, with his twenty-two years of experience, would recognize his troubled soul immediately for what it was — guilt.

His soft-soled shoes made no noise as he approached the door, left open a crack, but the woman's voice from within was too familiar for him to ignore. Definitely not Judge Calloway's crotchety assistant.

"Imagine, after all the trouble we've gone through to secure his position, he tells Ian that he's in favor of the bridge," Ophelia said.

Nicholas halted so quickly he had to place a hand on the wall to steady himself.

255

"That's not my concern," the judge said. "I appointed him as promised. I've kept my end of the bargain. No refunds coming from me."

Nick's pulse leapt. The odor of the waxed floors grew suffocating, the hall too narrow. He raised his hand, intending to swing open the door and clear up what must be a horrible misunderstanding, but instinct halted him.

"You aren't to blame," Ophelia purred, "but you should be advised. If he's foolish enough to cross us, then our election strategy will have to be reevaluated. What's the point of electing him if he's uncooperative?"

"Do what you must. I'm washing my hands of the affair." Calloway's voice receded as if he were turning toward his private office. "As far as I'm concerned . . ."

Recognizing that the conversation was nearing its end, Nicholas spun to go, but where? Ophelia would emerge before he had time to exit the long corridor. He couldn't confront her. Not until he had time to examine the implications of what he'd heard. He jogged past two closed doors, trying each handle as the seconds ticked away. Footsteps sounded behind him just as a knob turned in his palm and he let himself inside without a second to spare.

"Mr. Lovelace? Nice of you to visit." David Anderson dropped his pen into the inkwell. "May I help you?"

Nicholas pushed the door closed behind him too quickly to escape the other man's notice.

"Are you hiding?" David's moustache lifted as he smiled.

Nicholas leaned against the door to catch his breath. David was the one person who might know what to do with the information he'd uncovered, but was Nicholas prepared for the consequences? Could he proceed with his suspicions? He edged his way forward and slid into a chair. "The other day you hinted at something . . . something corrupt, but you didn't tell me everything. What do you know? What are you keeping from me?"

Anderson's smile fled. His eyes darted to the door. "Maybe I don't know anything for certain. My observations wouldn't hold up in court, not without collaboration. Not unless you have something to add."

Nick's breath ripped out of his lungs. So Anderson had no proof. Did that relieve him or make his decision even more troublesome? His mind reeling, he knew he had to count the cost. No reason to destroy his future when he could be mistaken. Perhaps his conclusion was premature.

He inhaled long and evenly, willing his heart to slow, but Anderson's gaze probed clear through him.

"Let me guess. You don't know anything, either," the man said.

"Nothing for certain." Nicholas twisted his mouth.

"Then why do you ask? Do you really want to know the truth?"

Nick closed his eyes. "If the truth costs me my business, my friendships, and my political career, should I welcome it?"

When there was no answer he opened his eyes to see David leaning forward, elbows on his desk, hands clasped under his chin. "You're a God-fearing young man, Nicholas. You can quote the verse as well as I can — 'The truth shall make you free.' "

"Free to do what? Be unemployed and hated?" Nick's voice dropped. "Don't get all preachy on me. What have you done besides drop hints?"

David's chair bumped across the wood floor as he scooted away from the desk. "There's very little I can do besides point out that before Richard Garrard died, he allotted county land for the very railroad you provide lumber to and shortly thereafter was able to pay off his farm loan that had been overdue."

"How'd you learn that?"

"He told me. For weeks he'd been concerned that it'd be foreclosed on, but then he came up with the funds, not only to pay off the overdue portion but the entire sum. I doubt it was a coincidence that he and Mr. Stanford began sharing company at precisely the same time."

"According to Garrard's ledger, he had ample reelection funds — just as I do, thanks to Ian Stanford." Nicholas strode to the east wall and stood face-to-face with the tintype of Governor Roberts. "I wondered why I was honored with this appointment. I thought perhaps it was through some capability of mine."

"I'm relieved to know you aren't involved. I just assumed you'd taken the job with the purpose of doing their bidding."

Everything in Nick wanted to protest his assessment, but how could he when he couldn't promise that he'd do the right thing now? And yet, as much as he wished he could banish his conscience, such a decision would change him. If he betrayed his convictions, he could no longer laugh at the challenges to come. Surely God would bless him, even in this, but how, Nick could not fathom.

16

Night fell on Nick standing at the riverbank — the same location where a man had run toward his death. Now calm, the river reminded him of the spot on the San Marcos where his father's sawmill churned the water. The green banks of the Choctaw River dropped at the perfect angle to provide a seat for a fisherman or a ramp for a frolicking diver. With its good rocky riverbed, this river wouldn't be as difficult to span as he'd been told. If only the consequences weren't so complex.

It'd been so long since Nick had willingly left the city streets to forage through unmolested nature. Sure, he journeyed to the campsites where his lumberjacks worked in remote locations, but he never lingered. Whether to a tent or a railcar, he didn't pause until he'd returned to the comforts of civilization.

Anne would scoff to hear him describe

this as wilderness. The gas streetlights threw their ghostly beams through the tree branches, reminding him that he hadn't made much progress in his trek away from town. The sound of running water had drawn him close, and he found no reason to go any further.

Nicholas had gambled before. He'd relocated to a bigger market, even though it meant giving up his smaller contracts. He'd purchased expensive equipment that could've bankrupted him had he lost a bid. That was part of the game. Success always involved risk, and God had faithfully smiled on his endeavors. And would continue to do so. He had to, right? As long as Nicholas followed the rules and obeyed the Bible, his fortunes would continue to rise, his domain would continue to expand. Wasn't that the bargain?

But he couldn't see a way out of this dilemma. What could he do about what he'd overheard in Judge Calloway's chambers? He knew what he couldn't do — he couldn't vote against that pernicious bridge. Not when he knew it was best for his neighbors.

Finding a rabbit trail that led toward the lights, Nick dropped his hands into his pockets and started forward. How eagerly he'd jumped at the chance to be a county commissioner. How foolishly he'd thought that he would be immune to the temptations that had toppled stronger men than he. No, he wouldn't accept a bribe. No, he didn't solicit funds, but could he vote the truth if it went against his best interests? Could he sacrifice years of striving when only his enemies would realize what it'd cost him?

God would know. A sigh, almost voiced, escaped. No one else would understand the temptation he faced. A better man would wonder that he even hesitated to expose the corruption. A weaker man would ridicule him for bringing about his own destruction. Only God witnessed his struggle and knew what ineffectual weapons Nick possessed to fight with.

But he would fight. He had to. Anne was right. Somewhere along the line he'd let Ian and Ophelia decide his course. His progress had been so swift he hadn't questioned if he was headed in the right direction.

Now on city streets, Nick wasn't surprised to find himself nearing the Pucketts' home. His friends in Garber, his acquaintances and peers, would only remind him of all he was giving up. Their excesses and frivolity would weaken his resolve at a time when he was vulnerable. He wanted Anne.

His knock at the door brought immediate results. Mrs. Puckett led him to the parlor, where Mr. Puckett was popping corn. Nick stood in the doorway and watched Mr. Puckett rattle the popper over the fire one last time before laying it on the hearth and opening the latch with a rag. Anne sat on the sofa with Sammy at her side, a napkin spread to catch a scoopful.

She straightened when she saw him, her smile disappeared.

"I made it back in one piece." Nick took a chair beside the window.

Mr. Puckett poured more kernels from a paper bag into the popper. "How was your trip? Profitable, I hope."

Nick couldn't take his eyes off Anne as she broke off the white fluff for Sammy to eat. The simple calico dress she wore softened her appearance. The fitted sleeves defined her slender arms. The crocheted collar framed her face, although she was doing her best to keep turned away from him.

"I suppose the trip was a success, but I wouldn't want to repeat the journey. I'd much rather stay here."

Anne remained engrossed with her handful of popcorn. Mrs. Puckett's chin swung from her to Nick and back again. Her brow creased with worry. "What's the matter? Did something happen at the office today?"

"I didn't go to the office," Anne said.

"You didn't?" Mrs. Puckett blinked. "Whyever not?"

"Please come back." Nick leaned forward. "You can work for me for as long as you'd like."

"But how will you keep that she-devil happy? What else will you have to sacrifice for her?" Sammy pulled on Anne's arm, probably confused by her low shaky voice. Her chin dropped and she smoothed the child's hair.

"You don't have to worry about Ophelia again," Nicholas said.

"I'd imagine not," Mrs. Puckett said. "Anne's worth a dozen of that woman."

The metal corn popper clanged against the hearth. Mr. Puckett released the wooden handle and wiped his hands on the rag. "Ophelia Stanford has bigger concerns than Anne's employment. According to Joel, Mr. Stanford's been keeping company with another woman."

"Robert! That's hearsay," Mrs. Puckett said.

"But from a trustworthy source."

Anne appeared unsurprised and ignored the revelation. Defiance stamped her features. Righteous indignation that was her due. "Are you certain you want to be here? You're risking the displeasure of the almighty Stanfords. We mustn't strain your relationship, especially before the election."

Sammy turned on her lap and reached for her shoulder. Cradling him, she stood. "It's his bedtime. If you'll excuse me —"

"Don't go." Nick was on his feet. He couldn't let their rift continue. "I need to talk to you."

"Then talk." She didn't even blink.

Mr. Puckett's head cocked as he cleared his throat. His wife wrung her hands. "Perhaps we'd better go upstairs. I'll take Sammy for you."

"If Mr. Lovelace has something to say, he can say it here. He's not shy."

He had nothing to promise her. Nothing to weigh in his favor. All he could hope was that she'd show him compassion. Without her support he might not be able follow through with his decision.

"Please, Anne. I-I need you."

The light from the fireplace flickered across her face as she studied him. He prayed she saw his desperation, saw how badly he didn't want to return to his room alone without sharing his burden. Her lips parted, she nodded once and Mrs. Puckett reached for Sammy. Handing him off, she strode past Nick and out through the kitchen door, not slowing until she reached the gazebo in the garden.

One wrong word from him and she'd go inside so quickly he'd see only a blur. Strung as tightly as a trip wire on a rabbit trap, Anne picked at the dead morning-glory vine still clinging to the lattice. She separated a dried bloom from its stalk and gently pried it open. While he was gone, she'd mustered up her anger daily but found it hard to sustain. As she planned for her future — hers and Sammy's — she wanted him to appreciate how well she was managing. Going about town like a real lady, leaving her pistol home, chatting with the young mothers about child-rearing. Soon you wouldn't be able to pick her out of the herd. She'd even had time to wonder if a pair of earbobs mightn't be useful, since she'd taken to wearing her hair up.

But he'd given up on her. He'd yielded to Ophelia's demands before Anne had a chance to adjust to her new situation.

Nick's neatly folded jacket dropped on the iron bench that stood beside her.

"You were right to distrust the Stanfords," he said at last.

She stared ahead through the tangled vine.

"I'm not afraid. I've faced worse."

"I know you have, and I hope I can face this with half your courage."

Anne turned. She'd never seen Nicholas like this before — not even when he was staring down a gun barrel. His untidy clothing and his careworn expression weren't merely the product of his recent journey. Normally, he'd look assured wearing a flour sack, but tonight he stood before her more rumpled than his detachable collar.

"You aren't talking about my job?"

"No, ma'am. I offended you and I was wrong, but that's only the beginning of my trouble." He ran his hand through his hair, now curly in the night's humidity. "Tomorrow we vote on the bridge — the day I finally perform my duties as commissioner — but Mr. Stanford introduced the topic on the way to Caddo, and he made it exceedingly clear that there would be consequences if I voted for the construction."

Anne could feel her hackles rise. "How dare he interfere? What if you turned him in? He could get in trouble for trying to sway your opinion."

"I couldn't understand why I was appointed commissioner. I had no experience, few connections. Now I know. I overheard Ophelia and Judge Calloway in his chambers. I don't want to believe it, because if what they said is true —"

"The judge is dirty." Anne's throat tightened. Trusting those whose duty it was to uphold the law did not come easy for her. "Please overlook my lack of surprise."

He closed his eyes. "I'm such a fool. I thought I was appointed to this office because of some talent I possessed, some quality that put me above my peers. Instead, they thought I'd be easily manipulated. They set the trap and I walked right into it."

"I know a thing or two about traps, Nicholas Lovelace. You aren't trapped." However much she might fight with him, she was even more willing to fight for him. "With your money and contacts —"

"Anne, that'll all be gone. I have a business, but my only customer is the NTT Railroad. My contacts come through the Stanfords' good recommendations. Even their competitors won't cross them. I'll be finished." Nick sank onto the bench, resting his elbows on his knees. "I know what I have to do, but it feels like I'm ripping my heart out and serving it to them on a silver platter. If there was some other way . . ."

Anne found herself at his side, her hand on his shoulder. "They'll try to tear you apart, Nick, but you have to be stronger, or at least strong enough to take it. But you won't be by yourself. If it's any comfort, I'll be here with you. You won't go through this alone."

With a swiftness that startled her, he turned to her. Nick wrapped his arms around her waist, pulled her between his knees and hid his face against her side. Anne stood with her arms raised above the rippling fabric of his white shirt. His strength had always frightened her, but this was different. His bowed head reminded her of Sammy when he looked for comfort. Could she care for Nick in the same way? Could she love him? The fierce protectiveness erupting in her heart told her that she already did.

Timidly, she lowered her arms, allowing her hands to rest on his shoulders, surprised by the tension bristling there. Working one hand to his neck, she threaded her fingers through his hair, cradling his head against her. Her heart welled with unfamiliar warmth, hardly believing this tenderness could be for the man she'd fought with every day since she arrived in Garber. When had she grown to care? Looking at the broken man before her she knew the answer — she'd been waiting for Nick to need her as badly as she needed him.

His back stretched as he took a long breath. His voice was muffled, but easily understood. "I don't want to let go, mostly because I'm afraid to see your face. No doubt you're laughing at me for being a weakling."

Allowing herself to appreciate the luxury of his thick hair, Anne paused before answering. "You were strong for me after the train robbery, and you'd do it again if I needed you."

Nicholas turned his face up to hers. "Can you forgive me for leaving you at Ophelia's mercy? You won't do her bidding again."

"I never did."

Nick released her. Anne stepped away, not sure what should happen next. After a hug like that she would've kissed Sammy, patted him on the backside, and sent him to his toys. Nicholas wasn't as easily dismissed.

"Tomorrow I vote." He stood, once again in control of his destiny — and a mite too close for comfort. "The consequences are in God's hands."

The masculine scent of his shaving lotion teased her, reminding her that Nick was no child. She stepped back. "Are you going to expose their plot?"

"Not without further proof. Confronting

a judge based on one incident of eavesdropping would be reckless, possibly dangerous, and you mustn't get involved."

"Don't worry about me. I can take care of myself." Until she looked into his eyes. No longer was he only her employer or another dandy on the street. He'd sought her. She was someone to him, and the thought pleased her.

He stepped toward her. Anne clasped her shaking hands. She'd promised to stay with him. She couldn't run now. Brushing against her collar, Nicholas lifted a curl and tugged it gently. "Thank you, Anne. I cherish your friendship all the more knowing how poorly I deserve it."

Anne's pulse raced. If he pressed his head against her chest now, he'd be pounded by her leaping heart. She gave him a cocky grin, hoping to exude a lightheartedness that was far from natural. "I'll be waiting to hear from you, and if you don't show by noon, I'll track you down."

"We'll hope you're the only one hunting for me, but it'll be after supper."

"Another business meeting?"

"No, it's a campaign dinner the Stanfords planned weeks ago to show their support."

Anne didn't think it was as humorous as he did. "And they are still going to have it?"

Nick shrugged. "After the vote tomorrow, it might be a lynching."

17

Judge Calloway entered the small meeting room and took his seat. Nick was surprised to see he hadn't gone through the formality of donning his robe. Perhaps he didn't consider the five commissioners worth the effort. He greeted them, his expression impassive, considering what was at stake. Then again, Nick, not the judge, stood to lose everything.

"Commissioner Prater, yea or nay?" Judge Calloway slid a paper before him and took his pen in hand.

If only the unadorned room felt more significant. Nick was sacrificing his career. Was it too much to wish for a suitable venue? A coliseum would be nice. Padded chairs at the least.

"Nay." Prater chomped at his cigar as if crushing the bridge between his teeth.

"Commissioner Anderson, yea or nay?" the judge asked.

David sat opposite of Nick at the square table. He folded his hands before him.

"Yea."

Two precincts to go before reaching Nick's. His head throbbed. Maybe Ian Stanford was throwing empty threats. Why would the man ostracize him when he was on the brink of winning the election? Wouldn't Ian have more to gain by working with Nicholas rather than opposing him? While he couldn't base his decisions on their wishes, it might happen that they'd agree on the next issue. But his arguments did nothing to slow his racing pulse.

"Commissioner Reynolds, yea or nay?"

"Yea."

Who was he fooling? He wouldn't place his fate on vain hopes. No, Nick would make this vote in full recognition of the consequences. From here on he would have a powerful enemy, but he wouldn't falter. Nicholas sat a bit taller and nodded when he met Anderson's gaze. The people of Blackstone County wouldn't be inconvenienced to serve his agenda.

"Commissioner Hill, yea or nay?"

"Yea."

"And finally . . . Commissioner Lovelace, yea or nay?"

Nick swallowed. One word and his life was

changed.

"Hold up a second." David Anderson leaned forward. "What's the vote?"

Judge Calloway consulted his paper. "Three votes yea. One vote nay. We only await Commissioner Lovelace's vote."

David rapped his knuckles on the table. "Then I make the motion to call it. There's no reason to cast any more votes. The bridge passes no matter what Commissioner Lovelace does."

The judge's eyes slid from David to Nicholas. A sly smile appeared. "If Commissioner Anderson would like to call the vote, I'd approve. No use in beating a dead horse. Is the board in agreement?"

Eyes shifted, feet shuffled, but eventually assent was mumbled. Nick's jaw dropped. Around the table papers were gathered and chairs were pushed away from the table.

What had happened? Had God spared him this test? Nicholas stood, not yet able to believe his good fortune. He'd been reprieved from crossing Ian and Ophelia. They would honor their contract and he could keep his conscience. Everything had worked out perfectly.

But then he thought of Anne.

Ophelia's demands. Ian's threat. How could he pretend to play their game any longer? Never again would he count himself blessed to share in their success. He had to destroy any path that might lead him back into their fold.

"Wait!"

Conversation ceased. Startled faces turned to him. Judge Calloway's knuckles turned white on his fountain pen.

Nick cleared his throat. "I'm a commissioner. It's my duty to cast my vote."

"It's not necessary," David said. "The bridge has been approved."

Judge Calloway shook his head. "I appreciate your enthusiasm, but why don't you save it for the next battle."

Nick met the judge's gaze. "Because the next battle will come, and I'll be too weak to fight if I cower at this one." From where had this strength come? His voice sounded firm even to his own ears. "I'm voting and my vote is yea. Please record it with the others."

The judge blinked once, and then with the same deliberation he used to sign a death warrant, his pen moved over the page. Nick watched as congratulations were shared by some and whispers by others, mostly as they looked his direction in wonderment. Commissioner Reynolds picked up his satchel and exited with Prater.

Judge Calloway shook hands, made arrangements for future dinner appointments, and left. Suddenly exhausted, Nick wanted to leave, but his legs refused to obey. Thankfully, David stayed behind.

"You didn't have to do that."

Nicholas pried his hand open and dropped his sweaty pen on the table. "Ian was right about one thing. The vote wasn't about the bridge. It was about loyalty. Whether or not the bridge would pass, I had to choose a side."

"So where do you go from here?"

Nick rubbed his brow. "I suppose first I need to let Harold know that his employment is tenuous, then I'll do my daily correspondence with my crews on the line, make sure I'm honoring my end of this partnership for as long as it's in effect. Then tonight . . . tonight is a fund-raising gala given in my honor by the Stanfords." He grunted. "I'm guaranteed a warm reception, don't you imagine?"

"Warm?" David whistled. "You might as well douse yourself in kerosene and carry a flint."

The needle jabbed into Anne's finger. She jerked her hand away, bouncing the striped material off her lap and onto the floor.

Mrs. Puckett peered over her own stitching as Anne waved her hand, trying to shake the sting off the much-abused finger. "Slow down, dear. Instead of stabbing the material, try easing the needle through."

Anne bent to pick up her dropped work. Sewing Sammy a new gown wasn't distracting her as much as she'd wished. She shouldn't have promised Nicholas she'd wait for him at the house after work. For the hundredth time, she searched the portion of the street visible from the window at her side. The Stanfords' dinner probably hadn't commenced yet. He could be gone for hours, but she couldn't keep herself from watching for him.

The afternoon had stretched like a tortoise's neck. She'd polished the brass and trimmed the wicks, but besides sharing a picture book with Sammy, she'd noted every second of her wait.

"Watching at the window isn't going to bring him home any faster," Mrs. Puckett said.

Anne felt her face grow hot, wondering what else Mrs. Puckett had surmised. "I can't help it. If only there was something I could do."

Sammy pulled up to the window and tapped at it, grinning at his reflection.

"Pray for him. He's in God's hands."

That's what they said, all these cherished women who lived in quiet houses with their decent men. But didn't she want it to be true? Hadn't she decided to believe there was a God who could handle all her hurts? Either there was one or there wasn't — her belief wouldn't change the facts. If He existed and she refused to acknowledge Him, then she'd be guilty of a terrible offense.

Sammy babbled to her, banging his fist against the glass. Of all the futures Sammy could've had — living with his mother over a saloon, being neglected by his outlaw father, being forgotten in a children's home — he'd been given the best possible option. Anne loved him and cared for him. Mr. and Mrs. Puckett had both expressed their desire to be a family for him. She might need to find work, but as far as she could tell, Sammy was safe.

And so was she. The more Anne saw of the stable relationship between the Pucketts and even Nick's gentle patience with her, the more she could believe there was a God who was responsible for this good. And maybe there was more good than she'd ever imagined. Maybe women gathered in houses everywhere and prayed for their families.

279

Maybe men worked gladly to provide for their kin. At least she could acknowledge that the evil she'd experienced wasn't a product of God's Kingdom, but of her enemy's. And if there was an enemy, well then, whose side would she take?

She lifted her stitching and began again with gentler movements. "I will pray and trust Him." She didn't lift her eyes, but she felt Mrs. Puckett watching her.

"That's right, honey. Be willing to listen and He'll let you know what to do."

Willing to listen? Willing to do what He wanted, even if she didn't know what that would be? If only she could keep a bullet in the chamber, an escape if this Jesus thing didn't work out the way she wanted.

The row of neat stitches on the seam lengthened with her efforts. She'd halfway expected the Stanfords would cancel his fund-raising event, or Nick would decide not to attend. She knew she'd have a hard time accepting the hospitality of people who'd vowed to ruin her.

Or had they? She tied a knot and bit off the thread. Nick had confessed that he might not be strong enough to go through with the vote. Had he changed his mind? What if in the end he'd compromised?

Sammy took a fistful of material out of

the scrap bag and waved it over his head. She gave him the smile he sought before pulling out another wad. She couldn't believe that Nick and Mr. Stanford would find common ground. Come to think of it, she couldn't believe he'd sit across a table from Ophelia Stanford and make small talk.

Had Anne once again misjudged a man?

The back of a tightly laced satin gown was all Nick had seen of Ophelia thus far. Although she was everywhere in her gilded salon, their paths never crossed, and she was too polished to cancel a social event and abandon her guests, even if she despised the guest of honor. Judge Calloway must have reported the vote to them immediately, and if there was any detail left in question, the judge was clarifying it now behind the oak doors of Ian Stanford's study, where a handful of influential men had disappeared more than half an hour ago.

Nicholas smiled warmly and shook the offered hand. But not everyone knew . . . or cared. Ian Stanford would get to vote once, just like the rest of the men. Ophelia, based on her sex, wouldn't even get that. His campaign would chug along with or without the Stanfords. He'd advertised. He'd canvassed. Four days — that's all the time they had to disparage his character. The weekly newspaper wouldn't even run before then.

Amid the introductions and the well-wishes, he spotted Joel and his freshly trimmed beard. Joel's quizzical expression rested on the entryway, where a couple was just arriving.

Philip Walton. Nick's opponent.

Philip helped his wife out of her coat and handed it to Theo, evidently on good terms with the Stanfords' butler.

Beaming, Ophelia weaved her way toward them. She slowed at the sight of the beautiful Mrs. Walton, a young lady whose poise rivaled her own, then with determined steps took both of them by the arms and escorted them into Ian's office.

Heads turned toward Nick, but his smile didn't waver. There was relief to be found when an adversary showed his hand. No more dreading the strike, no more wondering if you were truly at odds. The first shot had been fired, and he knew the enemy. While he wasn't prepared to expose the corruption, he was ready to fight it. Winning this election was a moral imperative. The issue had grown to encompass more than a bridge. It was about ruthless, self-serving men being at the helm, steering the populace for their own profit.

"What's he doing here?" Joel took a pastry from a silver tray that floated past. "I can't believe Walton would talk to Stanford, much less bring his wife to Ian's house."

"He's the new favorite son." Nicholas shrugged. "It's a long story, but I can't squander my time tonight talking to you."

Joel nodded, not the least bit offended. "Whatever you did wrong, you did it thoroughly."

"As if I know any other way," Nick grunted.

"Find me when you have the time." Joel tossed the pastry into his mouth. "I can't wait to hear."

But Joel's curiosity would have to wait.

Wanting to view the disaster firsthand, people gathered around Nick as though he were a tightrope walker, but he wouldn't stumble with an audience. He answered the concerns of the businessmen eager to facilitate transportation. He took suggestions from the local doctor about the proper setup for a lunatic asylum that was overdue for the county. With a local minister he discussed the amount allocated for pauper burial.

Then the office doors opened and the men spilled out.

"Good evening, gentlemen." Ian pulled

his coat back, exposing the chain of his gold watch. "I want to thank you for your attendance and your attention to your civic duty, and in the interest of providing balanced information and real alternatives, we decided to introduce you to both men running for the office."

First, Ian curtly acknowledged Nick, and then what followed was a litany of Philip Walton's experience and qualifications. Chin up, Nick scanned the room, gauging the effect of Ian's loss of favor toward him. Brows furrowed. Glances darted. No one knew quite what to make of it. And among the dark suits, like a rosebud in a pile of coal, stood Mrs. Walton, her face suffused with pride. But she was glowing at Ian Stanford, not her husband.

Ophelia claimed to be offended by Anne's eccentric appearance, but did she prefer Mrs. Walton's artful beauty? And what about Philip Walton? Was he a conspirator or merely another naïve puppet who wouldn't feel the strings until it was too late? All Nicholas knew was that he couldn't sulk around with his tail tucked. Ian might be able to destroy his business, but he couldn't touch Nick's character. Nick was clean and he intended to stay that way.

"It's not as if the ladies don't notice him," Mrs. Puckett said, "but Joel is impervious to their attention. Just last Sunday Miss Darrell stepped right in front of him — I feared that he'd certainly bowl her over going as fast as he's wont to — but he doglegged his path, missing her by a hair and not slowing an iota. I thought she would cry her eyes out."

The hank of yarn on Anne's outstretched hands was getting heavy, but the faster Mrs. Puckett talked, the faster her hands wound the wool into a ball.

"Are you certain you don't want me to wind for a bit?" Anne offered.

"Not at all. You just sit there and rest."

Supper was over. The dirty dishes were soaking in the wash pan, and Mr. Puckett had taken his pipe to the porch. Sammy nosed around the kitchen, exploring behind the curtained cabinets, looking for mischief.

"Joel says I should be satisfied with my grandchildren from his sisters, but they're scattered from here to Timbuktu. I don't see them much. Caroline tells me to simmer down or Joel's going to up and marry some girl from goodness knows where, and

I'll never see my grandchildren anyway."

Anne didn't think Nick wanted her to tell the Pucketts his business, but she wished she had some way of signaling to Mrs. Puckett that she had more weighty concerns than Joel's failure to produce progeny.

"And that is why I won't hear of you moving to your own place. Certainly it's your right, but don't do it on our account. We'd miss you and Sammy sorely."

The hank of yarn almost leapt off her hands when the door opened.

Mr. Puckett entered, chewing his pipe. "Nick, I swear I'm going to give you one of my watches. You have no consideration for the hour."

"Come on in." Mrs. Puckett rose. "Anne's been watching for you all evening."

Nick stepped into the circle of light thrown by the table lamp. His eyes sought Anne's. She had a pang of embarrassment at the admission, but it was quickly overcome with relief to see his smile.

"I apologize for my timing. The event ran late." Nick bent, picked up Sammy, and returned his greeting — raspberries for raspberries.

Mrs. Puckett lifted the hank off Anne's hands and carefully folded it into her basket. "It's no trouble. We still have dishes to tend."

Anne was on her feet. "I'll do them. There's no need for you to stay up."

Mrs. Puckett rested her basket on the table. "Well, well." Her eyes took a speculative gleam. "Now that you mention it, it is past the hour, and although Sammy seems very content with Nicholas . . . almost as if they were family . . . I'll put him down if you'd like."

Anne nodded her agreement. Nicholas handed Sammy into Mrs. Puckett's capable hands. Mr. Puckett took a seat and was promptly scolded into leaving the room for the evening.

"I should've warned you." Anne folded her hands before her, suddenly self-conscious. "The discourse tonight covered Joel's avoidance of marriageable ladies."

"Ah, then I walked into the crucible."

"Yes . . . well . . . that's not what I've been waiting to discuss. Tell me about today."

Nicholas pulled the red paper garter off his arm. "The bridge vote passed."

"You voted for it?"

His eyes sought hers with an earnestness she didn't expect. "I did."

Anne leaned against the kitchen cabinet. "May no one ever drown crossing that river again."

"Construction should start this spring."

She straightened. "But you went to the Stanfords' tonight? They didn't know?"

"They knew. The guest list was unchanged, but the guest of honor had been replaced. Philip Walton never left Ian's side and was hailed by him as the most capable candidate."

She nodded. Cruelty didn't surprise her. She was familiar with those who took pleasure from hurting people, especially when it benefited them. What was unfathomable to Anne was that good people saw it and did nothing.

Feeling an urge to act, Anne took the kettle off the stove and mixed the hot water with the water already in the dishpan, then sprinkled in soap flakes.

"So nothing has been said about your contract?"

"No. This section of track is nearly done. We were preparing to begin on the next, but tonight left little doubt that they'll do what they can to ruin me." Nick removed his coat and folded it over the chair back.

"What if you proved what they've been up to? Could you save your business?"

"If they have no qualms about interfering with elected officials, if we have a judge who will accept bribes, then something should be done. Still, whether Ian Stanford goes to jail or he pays fines and NTT Railroad is closed down, I won't have a contract with them."

"Then what will you do?"

"Start all over, I suppose. I'll serve my term as commissioner and find work as I can. My biggest concern is for you and Harold. Harold has been so faithful. I hate that my convictions have cost him his employment. And you . . . you haven't made any plans I need to know of, have you?"

Anne rolled up the sleeves of her blouse and plunged her hands into the water. "As far as employment, I've gotten nowhere."

Nicholas fiddled with his wrists, then set his cuff links on the table. He rolled his starched cuffs to his elbows and came to her side.

"We could wash dishes professionally," he said. "Do you think Pushmataha might have room for two in the kitchen?"

"You'll have to stay here and serve as commissioner, silly."

He picked up the iron skillet, it being the dirtiest dish. Anne handed him the wire brush. "Careful, you'll bend the bristles."

"Sorry for my enthusiasm. I'm just glad to find one situation I know how to correct."

They worked in silence for a long comfortable time. Nicholas scrubbed the worst of the pans and then handed them to Anne for a final round and inspection.

"At first," Nicholas said, "it was difficult for me to believe you were a buffalo hunter. It was so unlikely for a woman, even given your childhood."

Anne's hands stilled. "Why are you trying to imagine my childhood?"

He shrugged. "I'm trying to understand you, and now that I know you better, I have to admit that the hardest part of your story for me to comprehend is that you were a wife once, that you ran a household and practiced the domestic arts. You rarely reference it. It's as if it didn't happen at all."

Her chest tightened. "Some things are best forgotten."

"But you haven't forgotten, have you?" He bent over a baked-on crust and left her with the characters she'd tried to banish.

A young lady, scraping enough money together from selling pelts to purchase her first dress. The charming schoolmaster who'd suggested that she stay after school for private instruction so she wouldn't throw away her academic potential. Her naïveté — and its loss. Once his secret was out, Anne stayed in Ohio only long enough for her father and the school board to produce a shotgun and a minister.

"Were you afraid of him in the beginning?"

Anne's face reddened. "He was my teacher. I didn't know anything about the world — or relationships. Everything he told me, everything he showed me was new. Some part of my soul protested, but he was my only means for escaping. No one knew the cruelty Jay Tillerton was capable of."

She fished for silverware in the bottom of the basin and encountered Nick's hand. He grasped her fingers beneath the water.

"Tell me more. I want to know everything." He didn't let her pull away.

"Why?"

"You can't guess?" He lifted her hand from the water. "I've spoken of our friendship. I've told you how I respect you, how I care. I've said a lot, but there's one word I haven't used. One word I hesitate to speak."

Anne closed her eyes. A word that would bind her, that would mean a loss of her independence.

He'd taken a towel and was drying her fingers, one at a time. "I don't think you want to hear it from me yet, and I want to understand why. I want to know if you'll ever welcome my devotion."

It was a question Anne was afraid to ask herself. Was she capable of loving Nick? Would she ever be?

He led her to the kitchen table. Directing her to sit, he pulled a chair before her. "Was Prairie Lea your first stop?"

Pushing her turmoil aside she reported the facts, even though those were painful enough. "At first we traveled south, wanting to leave the scandal behind, but the further we traveled the more hostile people were. Kentucky, Tennessee, Alabama — none of them wanted to hire a Yankee schoolteacher when times were hard. Jay groveled and flattered, but they would have none of it. He blamed me. That's when he started —"

She stopped. Nicholas's head was bowed over her hands as he worked the towel around each finger. Side by side he inspected them. "Does Mrs. Puckett keep any hand cream in the kitchen?"

"There on the windowsill."

Nicholas reached for the glass jar and uncorked the lid. "You don't use hand cream often, I bet."

"And you do?"

A gentle smile tugged at his lips. "I'm a hopeless city boy, no denying it." Taking one of her hands in both of his, he began to apply the rose-scented balm. "So the abuse began before you came to Prairie Lea."

She breathed in the soothing scent before answering. "And then we lived in that little house, so far from town. Before Rosa and Louise came to reclaim their farm, I never saw anyone out there. Jay could do what he wanted to me, and did. I tried running away, but I was foolish. I'd gotten soft and thought my best chance was to navigate the trains back to Ohio. Of course, the train station was the first place he looked, and it wasn't pretty when he found me."

Nick grew stone still. His hands paused. He took a long breath and eased it out evenly.

"Is that when you decided to shoot him?" His thumbs kneaded into her palms, working deeper than the hand cream could reach.

"I didn't plan to shoot him. I only wanted to get away. The second time I ran, I was wiser. I took my gun and started across country. It'd be slower going because I didn't have my old clothes, but he couldn't track me. I know how to disappear. When he came down to the creek bank, I'd left no tracks and was tucked away in a blackberry bush. He came within a few feet of me and never knew it. If Rosa Garner hadn't stepped into his path, he'd still be alive today."

"But he attacked her."

Anne stood. "These dishes aren't going to clean themselves." She approached the basin and swished the silverware around, silently staring at the swirling water.

"Do you have regrets?" Nick asked from the table.

"Over shooting him? No. Never. Taking a life is an awful ordeal. I wouldn't want to do it again, but Rosa's danger gave me the courage to defeat him." She turned to face him. "And now, there's only one thing that terrifies me — my own poor judgment. I never dreamed that Jay was capable of abuse. All the students adored him. The girls fought for his attention. There was no sign that he'd misuse his power."

Nicholas glanced up, an eyebrow raised, but he allowed her to continue unchallenged.

"That's what terrifies me. I know how to handle a gun. After years in the wild I hear noises other people don't. I read signs. I can predict what's fixing to charge from the bushes, but I never imagined someone could go from acting so nice to enjoying hurting me. That's what scares me. What if I make the same mistake twice?"

"It is possible." Nick pressed the cork lid onto the jar of balm. "I can't make promises on behalf of every member of my sex."

Her laugh was bitter. "And I thought you'd try to reassure me."

"Like I said, I can't make promises for anyone else, only myself."

Anne didn't know where to look. Over the last two days a barrier had come down between them, but she wasn't sure if she could go forward. The way looked clear, but so did most traps.

"You're tired," he said. "I won't keep you any longer. Will I see you at church Sunday?" He stood and swept his cuff links off of the table and into his palm.

Anne nodded, but she had questions of her own. "How about you? Why is Garber's most eligible bachelor unattached? Or do you have a favorite waiting in the remuda?"

"There's no one else, if that's your worry." Nick rested a hand on the doorknob. "I've been waiting for the right lady to come along, and I'll keep waiting for her until she's ready."

18

November 1883

What would his life look like a year from now? A month from now? Ever since the train holdup, Nick's carefully laid plans had veered out of control. The commissioner appointment had promised to be another laurel on his brow but instead had proved to be his undoing. Would he win the election and expose the corruption, or had he gambled everything and lost?

Nick smiled. He hadn't lost everything. Not when he was gaining Anne's trust.

The morning sun pinked the eastern sky, melting last week's blues away. It was Monday, the day before the election, and no matter how badly his turbulent situation in business, politics, and society had buffeted him, he'd found sanctuary in an unexpected quarter. He hadn't expected to find an ally in Anne Tillerton, but she shone as the only bright spot in an otherwise dismal future.

Anne's question about his having a lady friend in the wings had made him smile all weekend. Just imagine the consternation his troubles would bring on one of the refined belles of his set. Their fathers would lecture, their mothers fret. At least God had spared him that. At least he hadn't taken on a needy, extravagant woman whose demands would run him into the poorhouse.

A buffalo hunter and a baby wouldn't be nearly the burden.

As Nicholas approached his building, he saw Joel coming from the opposite direction.

"Coming for me?" Nick asked.

Joel's feet dragged. "Where's Anne?"

"She's probably upstairs helping Harold balance the accounts. Why?"

Joel looked at the office window above their heads. "Let's step into the consignment broker's first. We can talk while I check for stolen goods."

Nick took the steps to the door of the seedy establishment and followed Joel inside. "How did you like that reception at the Stanfords' Friday?"

Joel touched the brim of his hat by way of greeting to the clerk behind the counter and then perused the gold watches beneath the glass. "So Ian Stanford changed candidates midstream?"

"There's much I haven't told you." He found it difficult to bite his tongue as the clerk set tray after tray of jewelry and coins before Joel. Joel's eyes flickered over each, but finding nothing suspicious he stepped away from the counter. They wandered away from the clerk, giving Nick a chance to continue. "Stanford vowed to ruin me if I didn't vote down the Choctaw River Bridge."

"It passed."

"And I voted for it, but it's not just Stanford's interfering. I overheard a conversation between Ophelia and Judge Calloway."

Joel's chin shot up. He cast a nervous glance toward the empty store front.

"Judge Calloway involved in corruption? You're turning an already rotten day into the worst."

"I wish I could give you more evidence. If you could get records from the bank, maybe we could go over them together —"

"But the election is tomorrow, and I'm going to be otherwise engaged."

"What's more important than a crooked judge?"

"The judge can wait. I'm more worried about Anne."

Nick blinked. "Is Ophelia causing trouble for her?"

"No, but the Reverend and Mrs. Holland just might be." Joel held the door open for him and followed him out onto the covered porch. "The Hollands are from Atoka, Indian Territory. Seems they had a prodigal son that they never gave up on. He turned his back on them, even changed his name so as not to give them more grief."

"And they think Anne has something to do with him?" Nick asked.

"In a way she does. Anne knew Finn Cravens Holland. His parents' wire was waiting on me this morning. They asked about claiming their son's body — and his child."

Nick's mouth went dry. "It's some kind of hoax."

"I'm afraid not. Anne hired a solicitor to check into the situation, and when the lawyer tracked down Finn's identity, he had to contact the family. Turns out they want the boy."

Nick's stomach turned sour. His jaw chilled until his teeth hurt. "They can't take Sammy away from Anne. Not now."

"Believe me, I can't stand the thought, either, but they're his grandparents. Legally, she has no right to him."

Nick braced himself against the pawnbroker's wall. No one would be surprised that Finn lied, but why couldn't these people accept that they'd lost their son? Did they have to get involved?

Sammy's adoration had changed Anne. He'd softened her, allowed her to love someone who was safe. But no, now even the child had proven a bad risk. She'd given her heart to this little boy, and he was going to leave her.

He couldn't let it happen, but Joel's grim face told him there was no alternative.

"Are you sure we can't challenge their custody? Are you sure there's no recourse?"

"I've been ordered to take the kid to Atoka tomorrow. If she wants to apply to a judge, she'll have her choice of Judge Calloway here or Judge Parker in Fort Smith."

Nick moistened his lips. Could he convince Anne to apply to the judge? He shook his head. No judge in the country would give a baby boy to a widow woman with a shady background — especially when she wasn't kin. Anne didn't trust the law already. She wouldn't entrust Sammy's future to a judge.

"She'll run." Nick straightened. "And you won't be able to track her once she gets out of town. She'll disappear."

300

"I'll overlook your low opinion of my tracking skills and ask for your advice. Should I take the child immediately? Would that be easier on everyone involved?"

Nick's heart wrung. Take the child from her — her child — and hand it over to strangers? The situation scared him more than a viper's den of Stanford's. It would either break her or she would determine to win at any cost. Devastating either way.

"I can't . . . I can't even consider it."

"We don't have a choice, Nick. It's not our decision."

He grabbed Joel's arm. "Let her go with you to Atoka. Perhaps meeting the grandparents will make it easier on her. At least that way, you wouldn't have to tend the child by yourself."

"But watching out for her will be that much more trouble. The only way I'd let her come was if you'd come, too."

Nick lowered his head. Leave town on Election Day? How would that look? If word got around that he'd fled while the polls were open, the consequences could be disastrous. Still, Anne's very existence was at stake here. She would be tempted to act rashly, and even if she submitted, losing Sammy would destroy her. He couldn't place his success above her survival.

"I'll come. She's more important to me than this election."

"Then we'll cast our votes in the morning and get Anne and Sammy before the train leaves. My only fear is that she'll get wind of our plans and run. We'd better keep this to ourselves."

Planning the details was beyond Nick. He couldn't get past the fact that the child Anne loved would be taken from her, perhaps never to be seen again. He cast about, looking for some reprieve. He churned the news, the process, the possibilities, knowing that he would have a sleepless night rehashing the same poor choices.

"Tonight we're getting the soapboxes out on the square." Nick rubbed his forehead. "How in the world am I going to say anything coherent?"

"I just hope Anne understands I take no pleasure in this duty." Joel shuffled his feet on the boards. "Now about Judge Calloway: There's not much I can do before we leave tomorrow."

"I don't expect there'll be a simple resolution. After the election, I'll be in a better position to do something. I can't worry about that just yet. Not when I know what lies ahead for Anne."

"Then you fulfill your commitments tonight, and I'll meet you in the morning."

Nick nodded, his heart breaking. "And I'll go upstairs and try to forget what you just told me."

Where was he? Usually Nick was in his office before she arrived, but this morning even Harold was growing concerned.

"Could he be with the Stanfords? Tomorrow is Election Day, after all."

The bandages around Harold's splint looked like they'd been dragged behind a six-horse stagecoach.

"He'd better not be." Was it wrong to wish Ophelia would come to the office? Was it wrong to wish she could see Anne back at work? Anne watched the dust motes sparkle in the morning light. She stood and shook out her skirt. "I'm going after him."

Harold cocked his head. "Where?"

"I'll walk toward the Stanfords' house and keep my eyes open along the way. Heaven help them if they did anything to him."

Going down the stairs in a dress was a hassle. Especially when she was mulling over possible excuses for her tardy boss. Anne snatched her skirt away from her boots before she tripped over it. Her boss? True, he was more than that, but exactly what he was to her she didn't want to define. Not just yet. Life in Garber took getting used to, and she wanted to ease along gently. She was pleased with their current situation — Nick at the office, Sammy waiting for her at home. No use in rushing on past.

She reached the foot of the fresh piney staircase and took a deep breath. No telling what kind of mischief had befallen Nick. She aimed to lead him out of it.

Rounding the corner of the collateral broker, she nearly crashed into him.

"Why are you hiding here?"

His face turned red and he snapped to attention. "I'm not. I was talking to Joel and I lost track of time."

"Harold and I were worried. You could've been waylaid in a ditch somewhere."

The red ribbon on his lapel rose and fell in a dramatic sigh. He took her hand. "Listen, I don't think there'll be much for you at the office today. You might as well go home and play with Sammy."

Something wasn't right. They'd shared much recently, but Nicholas was hiding something from her. Had he come to his senses? Did the spotless Mr. Lovelace finally realize what a messy woman he'd gotten tangled up with?

"There'll be too much today for Harold

304

to handle alone. He's not supposed to use his arm until —" She took a sharp breath with the enlightenment. "You don't want anyone to see me this near to the election. Is that it? You could lose votes if people link us together?"

He squeezed her hand. "We are already linked, Anne. I'm not ashamed of our relationship."

But neither did he offer a forthright excuse for sending her home. Now she was positive that he was holding something back.

"What aren't you telling me?"

He avoided her gaze. "I've got a lot on my mind."

For someone as forthcoming as he, the effort it took to not share whatever was on his mind must be eating through him like termites.

"I'll go home, then. I've been eyeing the river just past Comanche Street. Looks like a good place to start teaching Sammy to read tracks and signs. Who knows, we might catch us a rabbit or something."

"Don't go to the river."

"Why not? You don't think the Stanfords are coming after me, do you?"

"No, nothing like that. It's just that I'd be . . . worried . . . if you left town today."

There it was again — his not saying what

he meant. Anne put her hands on her hips. "Maybe you've got the jitters. I don't know how else to explain the way you're behaving."

"I've told you what I can. Tomorrow I can talk more freely."

Tomorrow after the election? What secret was he hiding? She was on the verge of protesting when she spotted Mr. Stanford headed their way.

"Here comes Mr. Stanford. Do you want to talk —"

But no sooner had she said his name than Nicholas took off to confront the man in the middle of the road.

"You haven't come to my office in months, Mr. Stanford. I hope this visit brings good news."

Anne knew better than to step too close. She recognized fighting roosters sizing each other up.

"Good news for me, but devastating for you." Satisfaction dripped off Mr. Stanford's smug face. "Your crew failed to deliver out on the Northern Line. I'm afraid we'll have to consider the contract null and void."

"My foreman didn't report any problems yesterday. Can you be more specific?"

"If it was necessary, but it's not."

Nick's face hardened. "Why not be honest? I've delivered what I promised, but you aren't satisfied because I won't play your games. You want a puppet who'll dance when you pull the strings, and I refuse."

Ian tugged on the wrist of his black gloves, stretching over grasping fingers. "That's a pity. I can't work with lads who refuse to cooperate. If you are unteachable, then I'd rather share my experience with someone who can benefit from it."

"The person who benefits most is you." Nick's heels left the ground with each thrust of his finger.

"We'll see, won't we? See how you do on your own?" Ian smiled but his eyes were hard. "Good day."

Anne approached Nicholas cautiously, never taking her eyes off Mr. Stanford as he passed.

"I knew this was coming." Nick paced a circle around her. "Why am I so mad now?"

"Just because you expect something doesn't make it any easier to bear."

Nick spun toward her, dust flying from beneath his feet. "Would you rather be blindsided? Would you prefer to have tragedy thrust suddenly upon you?"

Anne blinked. What was he talking about? "I'm not picking a fight with you, Nicholas.

Just saying you can never prepare yourself for some strikes."

He looked away. "Last night I thought losing my business was the worst that could happen to me. I was wrong." He kicked up another cloud of dirt. "I'd like to prepare you. I wish . . . but I *will* be there. We'll be together, Anne. Now, go on. Go home and play with Sammy. Nothing you could do today would please me more."

His shoulders sagged under exhaustion.

"If that's what you want, you'll get no argument from me." Anne squinted at him in the morning light, her compassion tinged with annoyance that he didn't trust her enough to share his secret. "You're going to survive this. You're a fighter and this isn't the end for you."

His eyes flickered up, naked and miserable. "It might be more than I can bear, but not for the reason you imagine."

Nothing else was said. Well, if he wanted to keep his fears to himself, Anne could understand. Nicholas had to carry on as if business were steady and the election secured. Hopefully, when the election was behind him, he'd tell her what had happened since last night that had so shaken him. She'd like to hear it from him, but if he wasn't willing to talk maybe she could find someone who was.

"I'd wondered if we were going to see you today," Harold said. "Anne went looking for you."

Nicholas dropped his hat onto the bench. "I sent her home. We need to talk."

Harold lifted his splinted arm off the ledger as Nick took a seat. "If I write slowly with my left hand, I don't blot too much."

"I wish that was my only concern. You've performed your tasks here exceptionally well — taught me a lot — and you deserve stable employment."

"You're letting me go?"

"Not until I have to — definitely not until you're out of your splint — but I'm afraid it's inevitable. Mr. Stanford has said he's going to stick us without a contract on the second line, and he's threatening to break our current contract."

"Why? Isn't he campaigning for you as commissioner?"

"Not anymore." Nicholas picked up the rubber ink stamp on Harold's desk. "As it turns out, my appointment to commissioner wasn't based on my merits. A certain railroad man saw an opportunity to place a stooge in office. When I refused to vote as he demanded, he made the consequences very clear to me."

"But he can't do that. It's illegal."

"Yes, well, I doubt Judge Calloway would have much interest in presiding over the case when he's the one who appointed me . . . at Stanford's rather persuasive request."

"He's in on it?" Harold covered his mouth. "Do you have proof?"

"Only what I overheard. It'd be my word against a judge and Ophelia. A disgruntled former business partner accusing the wife of one of our leading citizens. How would my testimony be received?"

Harold chewed the end of his pen. "Still, if money changed hands there's a trail somewhere. You already thought you saw evidence of it in Garrard's records."

Nicholas nodded. "I'm not giving up. I intend to chase down every bit of evidence I can, but making accusations before the election will smack of desperation. I have a strong lead. It's best to pretend nothing has happened until after the vote. Once I'm on the inside, we'll have more access. But I wanted you to have time to look for another job. Without a contract I won't be able to make payroll for long."

"Have you told Sheriff Green about the judge?"

"No, but Joel knows. I have to leave tomorrow on personal business and will be gone for most of the week —"

Harold tucked his chin. "Tomorrow is the election."

"I haven't forgotten, but there's nothing I can do once the vote is cast. As long as you're here to pay out the last payroll, then everything else can wait."

"I can handle it," Harold said. "Maybe it'd be good for you to get away for a spell. Smooth-talking voters have surely exhausted you. Leave town and clear your head. By the time you get back, you'll probably have all kinds of plans."

For every conniving Stanford in the world there were hundreds of loyal Harolds. "I'm grateful for your help. I won't worry about loose ends as long as you're here."

Because Nick had enough heartache to keep him distracted.

Anne didn't know what Nick was hiding, but she aimed to find out. A visit to the jailhouse was worse than finding weevils in your biscuits, but if you were hungry enough you'd bite anyway. Entering, her eyes were drawn to the corner where Finn's body had lain. She'd spent some time behind bars herself and couldn't enter a jail without a sense of foreboding, but unlike Finn, she'd been found innocent and released. Someday she'd have to tell Sammy what happened to his father. Hopefully by then the boy would be strong enough to make sense of it, if any sense could be found in the situation.

The back door opened. According to the badge on the man's suspender, he was the sheriff. He scraped his boots on the threshold and rinsed his hands in the basin by the door. "How can I help you, miss?"

"I'm looking for Deputy Puckett," who usually appeared wherever she didn't want him.

The sheriff approached, drying his hands with a cheesecloth towel. "I think I know you. You're tending the train robber's child. Well, Joel's getting ready for the journey tomorrow. I bet you'll be relieved to have that kid off your hands."

"The kid?" Anne felt the blood drain from her face. The flapping towel blurred and the cell bars tilted. She gripped the back of a chair. Tessa wanted Sammy? Not after she'd abandoned him. Not after she'd made Anne his mother. She couldn't undo that.

Anne wouldn't allow it.

Her first instinct was to snatch up her skirt and run, but she'd tried to flee once before without making preparation. Although she wasn't hiding from a monster like Jay this time, there was even more at stake. She had to save Sammy.

"Yes, he's a nuisance." Even if she'd eaten a plate of soda crackers, her mouth couldn't have been drier. "That's what I wanted to see Joel about. What time . . . ?"

"Eleven o'clock train. He wants to reach Atoka by Wednesday."

Atoka? Tessa had gone back to Indian Territory?

And Nick already knew.

"I'll get his duds together," she said. "Thanks for the information."

How could Nicholas hide this from her? How could he let them sneak up on her without warning? Once outside, her steps sped toward the Pucketts'. Nick wouldn't let them take Sammy, would he? He said he was preparing something. Getting them ready. He'd said that they were going together, so obviously Nick had made plans — plans that he didn't trust her to keep from Mrs. Puckett and Joel. Maybe he would try to reason with Tessa and whatever yokel she'd hitched her wagon to. Maybe he'd contest Tessa's rights legally. He had connections . . . well, until that vote on the bridge he had, but she knew the resourceful Mr. Lovelace wouldn't let her down.

She found Mrs. Puckett and Sammy in the back of the house doing the washing. At the wicker basket, Sammy bent, grasped the wet bed linens and strained to pull them free. The toothy determination on his face made her proud, and desperate. No matter what Nick's plans, she couldn't hide Sammy in the deputy's parents' house. In her opinion, they needed to be out of town by sunup.

"Nick didn't need me today," she said. "I hope you don't mind me being underfoot."

"Of course not. Sammy is certainly glad to see you." Mrs. Puckett pinned a sheet on the line. "God knew what He was doing when He brought you together."

Was God going to make up for all the wrongs He'd put her through? Were they finally going to get even?

Anne stopped a few feet from Sammy and knelt down. His eyebrows rose, and he squealed as she held out her arms to him. With his hands over his head he stumbled forward one step and then another. His next step carried him close enough that he leaned his chest out and fell into her arms with a low chuckle. Anne buried him against her, kissed the top of his head.

"Let's go inside," she said.

Tonight. Tonight she had to find Nick and

tell him outright that she knew. If he didn't come of his own volition, she'd sniff him out and demand to know his plans.

Fighting the urge to run, Anne carried Sammy to the house, but as soon as the door latched behind her she spun to peer out the window.

Mrs. Puckett still had two sheets to scrub and half a basket of linens to wring and hang. That gave Anne a good half hour to pack their bags. If they took Sammy on the lam, she'd have to think ahead. Fresh milk wouldn't be delivered to her door every morning if they were in hiding. There'd be no cows to supplement his baby formula. Still holding Sammy, as if she wouldn't let his feet touch the ground until they were safe, Anne barged into the kitchen in search of the Nestlé infant food to drop into her knapsack. She was reaching for the cabinet door before she realized that Mr. Puckett was sitting at the kitchen table.

He looked at her from over a pie tin, blinked once, and moved another forkful to his mouth. "You're in a hurry. Did you lose something?"

Straightening his arms, Sammy pushed against her. Only then did she realize how tightly she held the boy.

"No, sir. I didn't expect you home already."

"I missed dinner. Thought I'd stop by for a bite to stretch until supper."

"Oh." The porcelain cabinet pull was within reach, but she had to slow down. "I-I thought Sammy might be getting hungry, too. If we had some of that powder food, I thought I'd go ahead and use it up before he outgrows it."

Mr. Puckett grunted. "I thought he already had. He's been drinking cow's milk for a while now. Besides, isn't it about his naptime?"

Anne bounced the increasingly frustrated child on her hip. He leaned over her arm stretching for the floor and freedom. It wouldn't do to take the canister up to her room, and mixing it in the kitchen would only waste it. She'd have to get it later.

"You're right. Maybe that's why he's fussing." She transferred Sammy to her other arm. "We'll be upstairs."

As much as she'd like to find a quiet corner and drink in his every movement, she couldn't afford to waste time. Anne took the stairs, paying particular attention to the creaky spots, although she'd located each one the first week of her stay. Once in her room she released Sammy to the freedom

316

he sought and fished her knapsack out from under the high bed.

She threw her buckskins and trousers into the bag, leaving one pair out to wear. If they needed to skedaddle, she was ready. Her money and gear were in Pushmataha. She trusted Anoli to send them to her if she asked, but where? Nick might know the railroads, but that'd be the first place they searched. They'd have to rely on her skills. She could get Sammy somewhere safe.

Anne had no desire to return to Ohio. Her father had worked diligently to arrange her departure. Nothing, no one remained for her there, but that left the rest of the country. Going east toward Arkansas would provide more cover and a woodsy terrain like she'd grown up in. On the other hand, they were more likely to find work and anonymity if they went west. Maybe it wouldn't come to that. Hopefully, Nick would straighten out the mess, but the outcome was too important to leave up to chance.

The bag wasn't nearly full. She wouldn't take any of the dresses Mrs. Puckett had loaned her. She needed to travel light and fast. Checking to see that Sammy wasn't watching, Anne took the gun belt down from the high shelf in the wardrobe. As usual the barrel was loaded and not a leather loop on her belt was missing its bullet.

She returned it to the top of the wardrobe and then dug Sammy's gowns from a lower drawer, thankful for those she'd sewn and those she'd purchased with her own funds. He helped her empty it, strewing his gowns, long socks, and wool coat across the room. They took next to no room in the bag, so Anne crammed all the diapers she could fit on top and pulled tight the drawstring.

With winter coming on, she shouldn't head north for long. Not without shelter and warmer clothes for Sammy. Thankfully, she wasn't fleeing alone. For the first time in her life Anne had someone willing to sacrifice for her — someone who didn't view her as a nuisance or a possession. But as sweet as he was to get involved, Nick didn't know the first thing about traveling through the wilderness with a baby. Well, maybe his plans were more civilized. The least she could do was to give him a chance. After all they'd been through together, she owed him that much.

19

The attendees said that Nicholas had done well with his speech, but he couldn't remember it. Yes, he announced that the bridge project had passed — a crash of applause and hats thrown in the air weren't quickly forgotten — but he'd lost interest recounting his business success and construction experience. He grew impatient answering the same questions over and over. It was getting late. Time for him to leave. The encounter with Anne loomed larger than any election.

Had the wanton cook returned for Sammy, he could reasonably argue that Anne could provide a better future, but grandparents — a pastor, no less?

He wished he had a villain to blame, but with Joel administering the law and the grandparents seeing to their familial responsibilities, everyone doing as they ought. Would Anne?

His resources were at an end. Usually Nicholas stayed a couple of steps ahead of the game, and if something didn't work out, he wasn't troubled. Other opportunities would present themselves. Even with the painful loss of his business, he had hope. He'd find a substitute, another venue for his aspirations.

But losing Sammy had no upside. More exciting opportunities weren't opening. This tragedy would devastate someone he cared for — cared deeply for. It was a thick stone wall. He couldn't see any light through it; he couldn't see any good that would come of it. And if he couldn't find a way to help, he would lose her.

Nicholas walked the quiet street, trying to ignore the poster plastered to the wall of the pharmacy, blazoned with his name and tomorrow's date.

He didn't know what was ahead, but God did. He had to trust that He had good planned for Anne, and he'd pray that God would let him see that good. Without Sammy, there'd be no reason for Anne to stay in Garber. Not unless Nick gave her a reason. But he was afraid he wasn't enough.

Nick pulled on his ear. If the people back home knew he was keeping company with crazy Mrs. Tillerton, they would laugh.

Then again, they might know already. Molly had been quick to notice the attraction between the two of them, but in the past Molly had been the only one to see through the shell of toughness Anne had cultivated.

No lamplight glowed from the front of the Pucketts' house. Nicholas stuck his head around the corner, but everything was dark. Had Anne already retired for the evening? It was probably for the best. Hiding the truth from her hadn't been easy. He'd just have to make sure she had enough time in the morning to pack and catch the train.

He'd walked back to the street when he realized that ever since he'd approached the house, some bird had been sounding a distress call. Nick could barely identify a hoot owl's greeting, but this sounded peculiar even to his unqualified ears. Keeping his eyes trained on the giant magnolia tree, he stepped around Mrs. Puckett's flower bed to view the figure perched atop the sagging branch.

"Don't look at me," Joel whispered urgently. "I don't want her to see me."

"Why are you hiding?" Nick followed his gaze to the dark window that must have been Anne's room. "If you wanted to spy on her, why not go inside?"

"Anne knows. Sheriff Green told her."

Nick rubbed his neck, hating the ball of guilt knotting there. "I should've told her."

"Well, now I have to keep an eye on her, and Ma wouldn't want me watching a guest of hers like a cat at a fishbowl."

"Good to see you're honoring her wishes."

"*Shh.* Step back so she can't see us."

Anne lifted the shade on her bedroom window and studied the yard below. Dark and quiet, just as she'd hoped.

She tied off the leather drawstring at the neck of her billowing shirt and crammed her shirttails into her britches. She couldn't afford to waste any more time. As soon as Sammy began rubbing his eyes with his grimy fists, she'd given him his bath, hidden the infant formula in the towel, and gone upstairs. She had to find Nick first, but just in case, she was prepared to cover miles before daybreak.

On tiptoe she reached for her gun belt, careful not to wake Sammy until it was necessary. The leather rasped against the shelf and then swung free, the metal buckle clicking in the air. She fastened it just above her hips, a little high for a true gunslinger, but most gunslingers weren't shaped like she was. Out of habit she fitted the palm of her hand over the grip and loosened it from its holster. Not that she planned on using it, but one didn't carry a gun without the realization that someone might challenge them.

She looked around the room one last time. Of all the places she'd lived, this was the only home she'd known. Her father's cabin in the woods of Ohio had just been a place to get out of the rain. The farmhouse in Prairie Lea had been her prison. Sleeping outside with the buffalo hunters had given her space, but no sense of belonging. No one else had worked at cultivating a relationship like Mrs. Puckett had. Anne's time in Garber had grown her and softened her.

But now she was sensitive and she hurt. Whatever shield she'd lowered had to be taken up again to protect her son from those who would tear him away from her.

While here she'd learned to love, just as she'd learned to survive from her time in the woods. Now she'd need both lessons at her disposal to find her way.

Anne slung her knapsack over her shoulder and gathered Sammy in her arms. Nick might tell her to go home for another night, but she couldn't rest without understanding his strategy. As daunting as the journey before her was, at least she had help.

■ ■ ■

Nick thought he saw movement at the front door. Joel's whispered soliloquy halted as Anne stepped outside and skimmed to the edge of the porch, leaving the door open behind her. With one foot touching terra firma she froze. Her head cocked and she turned slowly to where Nick stood, even though he'd thought the darkness hid him.

As silent as a shadow she rushed toward him with Sammy in her arms. She let the knapsack tumble off her shoulder and land at his feet, looking relieved, as if she'd expected to find him standing in the yard at midnight, waiting on her. Her grip on the sleeping baby loosened.

"So you did know about this. I thought so from the way you were acting this morning, but you're right — probably better to wait until tonight when no one's watching. I knew you wouldn't let Tessa take Sammy, but I couldn't wait until morning to hear your plan. I was pacing that room like a rabid animal."

She watched him intently, her curly hair dancing unhindered in the breeze. The child sleeping against her breast created a perfect picture of motherly love. A picture he would see destroyed.

"Tessa has nothing to do with it. It's his grandparents — Finn's parents."

She shook her head. "Finn said he was an orphan."

"He lied. His parents live in Atoka — Reverend and Mrs. Holland. They heard about his death and now they want the baby."

Her lips tightened. "Not if we have anything to say about it. They raised Finn. They can't be good people."

Anne noticed the movement in the tree before Nick did. Joel swung down, stirring the dust with his landing.

"You might as well take the boy back to the house. We'll talk in the morning," the lawman said.

"I can't have a word in private with Mr. Lovelace? Last I checked citizens were free to converse without supervision."

"You can do what you want. I'll take the kid back inside while you and Nick chat." He held out his arms, but Anne was having none of it.

"I think I have the right to know what's happening tomorrow."

Joel couldn't look her in the eyes. "Tomorrow I'm taking Sammy to Atoka on the eleven o'clock train. His grandparents are expecting him."

The plains of her face sagged, pulled down by an invisible weight.

Nick placed his hand on her arm. "We're going, too. That'll give us more time." It wouldn't be enough. He knew that, but he was trying to give what he could.

She stared at him, as if trying to decipher some hidden message.

"You want me to go with you? With Deputy Puckett?" Her head tilted.

"I hope you will," Joel said. "Have his duds packed and ready when I come get y'all."

"Are you sure?" she asked Nick.

"We can talk tomorrow on the train," he said, and for some reason his answer seemed to comfort her.

Anne cradled Sammy against her chest with one arm and bent to pick up her knapsack. With one last meaningful look at Nick, she turned and trudged back to the house.

"I should've told her." Nick rubbed his forehead. "I hated hiding it from her."

"You can explain tomorrow, but now you'd better get some shut-eye. I can sleep on the train, but one of us needs to watch her at all times."

Nick's shoulders drooped. As if he could look away.

20

The line at the courthouse was short when Nick arrived thirty minutes before the polls opened. What was the point of secret ballots? No one had voted yet, but from the men's reaction to his presence he could gauge their opinion. And overall it was positive.

As the time for the opening of the polls approached, many walked up the line to shake his hand or wish him luck, but a few dropped their voices as he neared and murmured in a most disapproving fashion.

What had Ian Stanford accused him of? No way would Ian leave the election up to chance, and no way would he feel any compunction to tell the truth. Funny how quickly, how completely, a friendship could disappear. He thought of Ophelia and all the times she'd tried to engage him in small talk as if she genuinely cared about his opinion. He thought of Ian's flamboyant praise and predictions of his success, but when it came down to it, they were only there to see what they could get out of him. When he ceased to be useful, they wanted him buried six feet under.

He'd won the bridge vote, but there was much more to fight for. Nick couldn't leave the county in the hands of a crooked judge and a ruthless businessman. Anne's trouble devastated him, but he couldn't lose sight of his purpose. Just as she wanted to rescue Sammy, he was obligated to bring justice to the political process. The two didn't conflict, but one would have to wait until the other was settled.

The courthouse door cracked open, was shoved wide and propped open by a pollster. Up the steps went the line, and soon Nick was holding a ballot.

The blue ink smelled fresh. The orange county crest proudly denoted an up-and-coming community that could afford two-tone printing. He scanned the short list of sheriff, treasurer, and commissioner candidates until he saw his name: *Nicholas Lovelace — County Commissioner, District #5.*

He ran his finger over the print. His name. While inclusion on this list of who's who hadn't taken much effort, it had cost him everything. He'd volunteered to finish Richard Garrard's term only thinking of the prestige it'd bring, but staying true to his oath and his own conscience meant that he'd lost more than he'd imagined possible.

He hoped he'd never look back and regret what he'd done. With every hardship, he'd have to remember that obedience had led him to that consequence. As much as he enjoyed fine things, he'd have to learn to appreciate honest austerity over guilty luxury.

Nicholas lifted the pen from the inkpot and tapped the excess on the rim. With a quick flourish he circled his name, marked the other candidates he'd chosen, and dropped the ballot into the glass jar.

One vote. That was all he had to give today at the courthouse, but much more would be required at Anne's side. Was what he offered enough?

She followed Joel like a criminal to the gallows. Sammy rested on her hip, drawing attention with his grins and babbled greetings to everyone they passed. If she only had the grace to return the cheerful acknowledgments . . .

Courage. She needed courage, because this wasn't the end. Today was Election Day and Nick wouldn't miss it for a joyride to

Indian Territory. When she thought of all he'd given up to oppose the Stanfords, she knew he wouldn't hesitate to fight this injustice, as well. Nick was taking care of her. And Sammy. He wouldn't let Finn's family win.

But there was Joel. Anne couldn't imagine Nick openly opposing his deputy friend, which left two options. Either Nick planned to challenge the grandparents legally, or he would distract Joel to give her an escape. Most likely he'd try the first and save the latter for use only if the situation became desperate.

The cold air tingled on her cheeks. She tucked Sammy tighter against her duster. Mrs. Puckett had begged her to dress appropriately, thinking that a good impression might sway the family. Despite her pleas, Anne refused. She wouldn't rely on the kindness and judgment of strangers — or friends for that matter. All she could count on was the abundance of a forest to feed and conceal them if needed. And for that she couldn't be decked out in a cumbersome skirt.

Anne's steps slowed as they neared the train station. Joel turned quick as a cat, ready to snatch her if needed. He transferred her bag to his right hand and took her arm with his left.

"We're almost there," he said.

Barely two months ago Anne had arrived in Garber. Two months ago if Sammy's grandparents had claimed him, she would've thanked the Lord, handed him over, and trekked back to Pushmataha to resume her hunting. Now she was determined to keep him, no matter what the cost. But giving up buffalo hunting had been easy compared to walking away from the weeping Mrs. Puckett . . . her son notwithstanding.

"You don't need to drag me." Anne pulled away from him. "I'm right behind you."

"Do you want the porter to take that knapsack?"

"No. It has Sammy's food, diapers, and pins in it. I can't expect the porter to get it every time he's wet or hungry."

"At least put your guns with the luggage. We're going to be on the train for two days. You won't need them."

"Have you forgotten?" Nicholas joined them, his own satchel in hand. "Anne saved my life in a train holdup. If anyone has a right to be armed, it's her."

Warmth crept across Anne's chest in response to his thoughtfulness. Of course she needed to be armed. Finally she wasn't facing a battle alone.

"You voted already?" She tried to tuck a stray curl behind her ear, but her hat got in the way.

"I did. Harold and I went over any possible decisions he might need to make in my absence, and rebuttals in case the Stanfords choose to protest today's results. With that done, I'm at your service." His eyes didn't sparkle with their usual merriment but watched her intently, his thick lashes tipped in gold.

"I've already purchased the tickets." Joel handed Nick two slips of paper and took his satchel from him. "Maybe you want to carry the babe."

"I think Anne's quite capable." But he took her arm, which seemed to pacify Joel and bent to whisper, "He's behaving poorly because he caught you sneaking out of the house."

"The fact that he was sitting in a tree doesn't speak in his favor."

"Well, we'll do what we can to cooperate. No use making his job any more unpleasant than it is."

And no use raising his suspicions again. Nicholas was right. The more they pretended to go along with Joel's plan, the easier it would be to break away.

■ ■ ■ ■

She wasn't as upset as Nick had expected. Naturally, she bristled whenever Joel spoke to her, looked at her, or made his presence known in even the most innocuous fashion. Still, she hadn't transformed into the raving lunatic that he'd feared would appear.

The miles flew past them, at least twenty an hour from his estimation, and Sammy spent the majority of them alternating between banging on the window and sleeping on Anne's lap. Soon they'd stop in Pushmataha for supper, and then the bunks would be lowered and the railcars prepared for the night.

"It's been awhile since you've seen the other hunters in Pushmataha," Nick said.

"They'll be glad to see Sammy. Those who frequented the depot saw him often. Anoli in particular had a soft spot for him."

Nick caught Joel's eyes as they darted to Anne and then away. The deputy's index finger tapped against the wooden arm of the bench. He was thinking hard on something, and Nick could probably guess what had him troubled. Anne knew her way around Pushmataha better than anyone, and she had friends there — rough men who were a law unto themselves. If she was going to make a run for it, it would be there.

The train whistle blew as they approached the station. The clatter of the wheels slowed, and the brakes screeched as the brakemen on top of the cars did their jobs.

"I'll check in the kitchen to see if the crew is in town." Anne leaned forward, her face almost in the empty seat across from her as she fished out her knapsack. "You can ask there to find me."

Joel stood, blocking her way. "Do what you want, but leave the boy with me."

Anne adjusted her knapsack and straightened her shoulders. "They'll want to see Sammy. They knew both of his parents, and if I don't visit when we're in town, they'll take offense."

Joel's face was granite. He didn't move.

"I'll stay with Sammy." Nick stood. "We all have to get off the train to eat. If she wants to poke around town, I'll go, too."

Joel's shoulders relaxed a bit. Nick felt for his friend. As a young deputy Joel didn't want to fail at his assignment, but coming between a woman and the child she loved wasn't easy on him.

"All right, then," Joel said, "but first let's get some grub."

From the smile Anne flashed Nick, his offer pleased her. Maybe after thinking it over she'd decided Sammy would be better off with his grandparents. She'd definitely resisted when first given the responsibility of caring for the child.

Their meal of lamb chops and custard wasn't half-bad. The cook Anne had hired back in Garber was obviously working out splendidly. Sammy ate his custard with enthusiasm and smacked the end of a spoon before flinging it across the dining hall.

This stop would be the longest while they waited for the porters to prepare the cars for the night. Anne barely touched her food, instead making sure that Sammy ate his fill. She watched Nick's plate, too, and when he'd scraped the last spoonful of the tomato sauce she stood.

"Let's go."

Nick looked to Joel, who nodded and chewed his dinner roll thoughtfully as they departed.

Anne stuck her head into the kitchen. The cook recognized her immediately and unlatched the Dutch door to allow them entrance.

"Finally you're back. I didn't expect it to take you so long." She tickled Sammy under the chin, which he seemed to loathe.

"I've missed being here. Do you know if

Anoli and the other men are in town?" Anne asked.

The cook nodded. "They grabbed their meals from the back door and headed to the stable to eat. You'll find them right across the way. Does your baby want another roll?"

Sammy turned his head by way of rejection.

"I'll save it for later. It could be a long night." Anne tucked it into the deep pocket of her duster.

Nicholas followed her out the back door of the depot kitchen and into the street. Anne did a complete scan of their surroundings. Her eyes lingered on the depot window. She took Nick's arm and pulled him around the corner to the blind side of the wood-planked building.

"What's the plan?" Her gray eyes blinked up at him so trusting.

"I don't understand."

"I'm here, just as you requested. What do we do now?"

"Do?" But even as he spoke, his supper turned sour. "I don't have a plan."

Her lashes flickered down. She lugged Sammy higher on her hip before continuing. "Then I wish we could've talked earlier. We could've left Joel behind in Garber

337

instead of coming this far, but that's all right. I appreciate any help you can give. If you'd run back to the train and get your bag . . . but don't let Joel see you, of course. We'll have to hurry. He'll know we're missing —"

Nick's hand immediately rose between them. "I don't know what you're talking about, Anne. We are taking Sammy to his grandparents in Atoka."

Her eyes flashed. Her skin flushed. "You mean you consented to this? You're going to take my child?"

"It's not that I want to."

"I thought you understood. I thought you were on my side. This is Finn's family we're talking about — strangers to Sammy. I can't leave him." Her chest rose in quick hops. "How can you ask me to do this? How could you imagine I would?"

Nick reached for her, but she shied away.

"I wasn't trying to trick you. I thought you'd come to terms with giving up Sammy. We really have no choice."

Why did they have to discuss this? They should be bargaining for kisses. Flirting during moonlit walks. Now he was the man who was stealing her child. How much would God take from him in one week?

"That's it, then?" Anne held Sammy

tightly against her. "You came along to guard me. You wanted a hand in taking him from me?"

"I wanted you to have more time with him, and Joel wouldn't let you come without me. He would've taken Sammy away in Garber and made this trip alone if I hadn't volunteered. Isn't this better? Wouldn't you rather be with him?"

"It's not much consolation."

"There's still hope. Miracles do happen. The family could change their minds, or they could meet you and decide they want him to stay with you." From her short burst of air, he guessed she didn't think the chances were likely. Well, neither did he. "I know it's not much to go on, but what else can we do? How can I protest Ian Stanford's misuse of the law if I'm willing to break it, too? We can't ignore it when it doesn't suit us."

He watched her rock from side to side, her arms wrapped around Sammy. Her old boots emerged from beneath the loose cuffs of her trousers with every sway. She seemed to reach a decision.

"I'm taking Sammy to see the fellas. I suppose you'll want to come with us."

Nick trusted her. He trusted her to sacrifice everything she had to keep Sammy safe, but he did not trust her to bring the tot back to the train. He flipped his collar up against the cold wind and followed her to the stable.

Anoli's sharp black eyes were trained on the door, no doubt expecting Anne even before she walked around the corner. His black braids and the rifles reflected the weak light, but everything else was covered in dust. Fred cradled his bowl of veal, and Tracker dozed against the feed sacks, barely distinguishable from the burlap.

Had they always been this dirty? The first time Mrs. Puckett had washed her coat, Anne protested. Soap introduced scents that weren't familiar to the animals. Come in upwind of your game, and there'd be no game waiting on you. But once her duster had been cleaned, she hadn't thought about it again. Her clothes were laundered along with the rest of the household's. She couldn't help but steal a glance at Nick. After working in his office, she'd grown accustomed to the finery, but how filthy she must've been when he first saw her.

"It's good you're back." Anoli's strong brow didn't flinch. "You heard about Finn?"

Anne set Sammy down in the dirt. "Of course. Turns out he lied about his parents. They are alive and in Atoka."

Sammy took uncertain steps toward Tracker and crashed into him, waking the man. Tracker threw Nick a long look. "Who's your pal?"

Nobody. Not to her. Not anymore. Wouldn't take long for Nick's pretty suit to get spoiled in a tussle out here. One wrong move from him and she'd arrange it. "Just a railroad man who came with me to stretch his legs."

Anoli studied her like she was storm clouds blowing in. Anne knew she hadn't fooled the wise hunter.

"The boy's the spitting image of his pa," Fred said. "Should do well with the ladies."

Losing interest in Nick, Tracker lifted Sammy above his head, allowing him to soar. "He's grown into a fine boy, and now he's big enough to spoil." Sammy squealed and dropped a string of slobber on Tracker's shirt.

"Well, I won't be the one to do it." Anne dropped her hands into her pockets. "His grandparents want him."

"After you deliver the boy, you'll come back?" Fred asked. "We've missed our little Annie."

"We're shorthanded this winter." Anoli's eyes kept straying to Nick. "And the signs point to a mild one. We might be able to hunt throughout."

She didn't expect them to understand, but their lack of sympathy amazed her. What did they care about who raised the child? Yet, while they wouldn't understand her desire to keep him, neither would they feel obligated to help some unknown family in Atoka take possession. Their disinterest might work in her favor.

"The train is leaving soon, and I really can't make plans yet." She turned to Nicholas and instead of spitting in his face asked, "Would you mind taking him back?"

His back straightened. "To the train? Without you?"

"I don't want Joel to come looking for us. I'll catch up."

Fred ruffled Sammy's noggin before handing him to Nick. With a last questioning look, Nick left and she was free to speak.

She took off her hat and fanned her face. "We need to settle up, Anoli. How much can you give me?"

"I can look up your share, but I only have fifty dollars on me."

Fred whistled. "Don't let anyone know you carry around fifty dollars, Anoli. They'll be hunting your hide."

But the Indian was unruffled. "Fred has been using your horse. He won't want to give her up. Ask him top dollar."

"Hey! Whaddya tell her that for? I had plans for this money."

Anoli's cheek twitched. Fred got up and fished a wad of bills from the saddlebag hanging across the dividing wall. "That'll have to do until you come back. I do like the horse."

Anne crammed the bills into her pocket, the one without the bread roll, and waited for Anoli to untie his leather money bag and spill the correct amount of gold into her hand. "Whatever your plans are, this should help. Send word when you're settled, and I'll send you the rest."

"Subtract out the price of a knife, a canteen, and some matches, if you have any to spare."

Fred rummaged in his own bag without being told.

Anne took the items from him. "And I might need assistance on the train. Anyone in the mood for a short trip?"

Tracker rolled to his feet. "Headed to Atoka? I wouldn't mind hitting a real town for a change."

"Thank you." Anne tossed him a coin. "Buy your ticket and stay clear of me. If I need you, I'll let you know." She knelt and slid the remaining coins into her boot.

"That man — he going with you?" Anoli asked.

"No, and if he ever comes around, you mustn't tell him where I am. If we part, it'll be because he's turned against me."

Tracker grunted his disapproval.

"We won't tell him nothing," Fred said.

Anoli nodded. "You can trust us."

But she couldn't trust Nick. Not anymore.

21

Night had fallen but she couldn't sleep and neither could the two men determined to keep an eye on her. Anne drew small satisfaction from every one of Joel's gigantic yawns. Nicholas rested heavily on the bench next to her and seemed to lean closer to her with every mile.

"Sammy has been asleep for hours," Nick said. "You should put him down. Your arms must be tired."

Her mouth opened to protest, but then she thought again. She should rest while she could. "I have nowhere to lay him. If Deputy Puckett would leave, Sammy could lay on the bench across from me."

"Why don't you get a bunk?" Joel asked.

"I will when I'm tired," Anne said. "No reason to be stacked like firewood before I'm sleepy."

Nick's toe tapped Joel's foot. Anne pretended not to notice the look they exchanged.

"I'll stay with her," Nick said. "That's why I came, after all."

To keep an eye on her. To guarantee that she didn't save her child.

Joel's mouth grew taut as he fought against another yawn. "All right, then. Last night in the tree didn't do me any favors. I'll catch some shut-eye while I can."

He ambled off, leaving them as perhaps the only ones awake in the car. Nicholas took Sammy from her arms and held him while Anne spread her duster on the bench. Once he was arranged she wrapped the old coat around him, tucking it snugly beneath his sleeping form.

Anne fell back against her seat and shivered after losing Sammy's warmth. The cold crept in from the walls of the railcar and chilled the room.

Nick shrugged out of his coat. "Anne, I'm here for you, not for Joel. If there was any other way, you know I'd help."

She leaned forward so he could place his coat between her and the seat.

Would he help or had all his concern been a lie? Unbidden, the memory of their time in the kitchen returned — Nick holding her hands, easing her painful story from her. The threat to Sammy had so primed her anger that she'd forgotten his kindness over the last couple of months. Here he was on a train rolling through Indian Territory the night of the election. Shouldn't she give him another opportunity to prove himself?

"You should be in Garber, receiving your congratulations."

He reached around her and pulled his coat closed, nestling her in its warmth. "That can wait. You are more important to me than the election."

Anne felt his gaze and felt the blush creeping up her neck. "I'm surprised to hear you say that."

"It's true. Whether I win or lose, it doesn't compare with the honor of knowing you and calling you my friend." He found her hand inside the sleeve of his oversized coat and threaded her fingers through his. "You've been through a lot, Anne, and tomorrow might be the worst yet, but I want you to know that you aren't alone."

She closed her eyes. Tomorrow. Where would the dear little boy be sleeping tomorrow? Who would rock him? Who would fix his breakfast in the morning? Who would she have to love after he was gone?

Anne's fingers tightened on Nick's hand. She wanted so much out of life. The family, the home, the security, but it was always just out of reach. Did she have the courage to grab it before it disappeared, or had all of Nick's words been empty? "You said if there was any way —"

"Any *legal* way."

She nodded. Her throat squeezed tight. What was she willing to sacrifice for Sammy?

She scooted to the end of her chair and turned to face Nick.

"You said they might meet me and decide I'd make a good mother. I hope that's true, but wouldn't they want to know that Sammy has a father, as well? Couldn't we tell them that . . . that we're engaged? You are a respectable businessman. They would trust you."

His face was unreadable in the dim light. "I wouldn't lie to them, Anne. We couldn't say we were going to provide a home for him if we have no plans to do so."

She took a deep breath. "Then marry me. We could have Finn's father perform the ceremony. It'd be worth it to keep Sammy."

"Worth it?" His mouth quirked. "You're only willing to marry me if it means keeping Sammy? Goodness, Anne. It's no wonder they leave proposing to the men. Your offer isn't exactly flattering."

Didn't he understand that she was serious? Still holding his hand, she pulled herself closer, their knees bumping. "My offer is practical and you claim to be a practical person. You've worked and saved to impress a wife. I don't want to be cruel, but that's gone now. Your choices are more limited than ever."

"Now I'm not only unwanted by you but despised by the rest of the female sex, as well. My fragile ego is battered."

"You know I appreciate you. Maybe I haven't demonstrated it fully, but I feel more comfortable around you than anyone else I've known. We get along just fine when we aren't fighting."

The smile on his face gentled. He studied their hands linked together. "If we married, if you were my wife, would you be comfortable demonstrating your appreciation . . . fully?"

Anne's heart pounded. His question was valid. What kind of offer was she making? Even if this was a marriage of convenience, he had the right to the comforts of a wife.

Could she? The thought terrified her, but Nicholas wasn't Jay. He'd never been cruel or threatening. He was different.

She lifted her hand to his face, soaking up the vibrant warmth of his cheek. The day's growth of whiskers teased her palm as she tilted his head toward her. He waited — his blue eyes encouraging — for her to act. Anne leaned, pulling herself forward by his shirtsleeve. She stretched until their lips met.

She kissed him — her lips on his. Her hand trembled, and when he slid his arm beneath the coat to pull her closer, she had to school herself not to resist. She was cornered in an empty railcar. She should've been terrified, but that emotion lacked conviction beneath his leisurely perusal. And although Nicholas was in no hurry, he definitely wasn't timid. His mouth took hers again, and he savored it as he did every good thing in life — with no apology for his enjoyment and with no pressure that it must lead to anything more.

Her hand dropped to his shoulder as she allowed, no welcomed, the intimacy between them. She wanted to confront her terror from the safety of his arms, but no sooner had she lowered her defenses than a yearning was birthed and it alarmed her. A desire to be his, to share her heart and not just her hand in marriage. But that desire meant a loss of control. It meant putting herself in his power, and she wasn't willing after all.

Sensing her reluctance, Nicholas drew back. The questions in his eyes forced her to turn away. Pretending to check on Sammy she pushed out of his embrace.

"I guess he's still sleeping," she said.

"He is." Nick's breathing could be heard over the clacking of the wheels beneath them. Anne stretched the duster over Sammy and arranged it for the fourth time, afraid to settle her attention anywhere near the man sitting beside her.

Finally Nick leaned over the gap in the benches to place a hand on Sammy's cheek. "If you're worried about him, I'll find you room in the sleeper car. He's snug for now, but it would be warmer in a bunk."

"Crowded in a room full of strangers? No thank you. Besides, I can't sleep anyway." It would take days for her heart to slow. Weeks for her lips to forget the feel of his caresses. Months before she stopped reliving —

"If you'd rather stay with me, you'll hear no complaints." Nicholas kicked his feet up on the bench next to Sammy's legs and stretched his arm behind her along the back of the bench. "I'm afraid I'm too exhausted to be any company, but I'll offer my person to make this arrangement as cozy as possible." He wrapped his arm around her shoulders, pulled her to his chest, and snuggled his cheek against her head. At the conclusion of an enormous yawn his body sank against hers. "Ah, you make a lovely pillow, Mrs. Tillerton. And before I fall asleep I'd be remiss if I failed to mention something. I've never once told you how beautiful you are, although I've noticed on countless occasions."

Anne's insides quaked, still very aware of how strongly he'd affected her. How much she desired the security of a bond with him. "Just this once," she said. "No need to tell me again, because I won't ever forget."

Her cheek rubbed against his satin vest to the rhythm of the tracks flying beneath them. She tucked her hand up against his chest and felt his heartbeat — steady and strong. The heart of a man she'd like at her side always.

"Nick, you never answered my question." Her bravery would flee if she had to face him, so she kept her face buried against him. "Will you marry me so I can keep Sammy?"

His chest rose in a deep breath. His voice drawled through the haze of exhaustion. "What if the Hollands refuse to give us Sammy? What then?"

"Nothing happens." Anne brightened. "We leave Atoka and never mention it again. No one would even know that we'd discussed marriage."

She felt rather than heard his sigh. He wrapped his other arm around her and held her securely. "Then my answer has to be no."

"No?" Anne pushed against him, angry tears springing to her eyes. "No? You said you would do anything to help. Isn't it worth a try?" He didn't respond. Was he pretending to sleep? She punched his chest. "If you weren't going to marry me, you shouldn't have kissed me."

His hand slid up her arm. "Are you sorry for it?"

"Furiously! I'm sorry that you don't have the backbone to save Sammy. I'm sorry that our friendship now has the taint of a regretful familiarity. And I'm absolutely sorry that you enjoyed it so much."

"Ah, you could tell?" He peered at her through drowsy eyes, his smile satisfied. "I really shouldn't have any discussions when I'm this sleepy, but for the record I don't feel a taint on our friendship, and I don't regret the familiarity. Now, it should be obvious that you have me completely intoxicated and there's no telling the foolishness I'm likely to spout, but I will promise this, tomorrow I'll do my best to convince Finn's parents that you are a good mother. That's all I can promise. In good conscience I can't inform them of our plans to wed when such plans were only created to reach another goal. I'm sorry to disappoint you. Now, once again I offer you safe escort to a bunk or" — he squeezed her shoulders — "a guard for the night. Either way, the stress of the week's events is catching up with me. I won't be a fit companion . . ."

His didn't complete his sentence. His chest stretched with a long breath, and then his head dropped against hers again. Unbelievable. By morning he probably wouldn't remember a word of their conversation. At least she could hope. And as much as she'd counted on Nicholas to aid her, she had to accept that no help was coming from him.

She and Sammy were on their own, and the only help Nicholas would provide was the fact that he seemed to be a heavy sleeper.

The motion that had lulled him into dreamless sleep ceased. Nick opened his eyes, relieved to find Anne still in his arms. Before dozing off, he'd wrapped her tight and wedged himself across their aisle to block her path, but he'd still worried that she'd spirit away during the night.

"Good morning." He arched his back and released her. "Have you been awake long?"

She shrugged his coat off her shoulders. "Not too long. I need to get out, please."

He looked at the boy bundled up on the bench across from them. "Sammy slept well. At least, as far as I could tell. He didn't wake you, did he?"

Anne shook her head. "Please. I need to go to the washroom. I've been trapped here all night. I couldn't get around you." Her lips were pursed, her eyes cold.

Of course she was angry. They would be in Atoka in a matter of hours, and to make matters worse, he'd had to reject her desperate proposal.

"I apologize." Nick stepped out in the aisle and let Anne pass. She knelt and fished her knapsack and duster from beneath the bench.

"Why do you need your knapsack?" he asked.

She glared. "I'm going to the washroom to freshen up before the train starts moving again. Must I go into detail?"

Nick motioned her past and collapsed in his seat. He'd have to find a way to win her back. It wouldn't be easy if she returned to hunting, but he'd take the time to visit, woo her, let her know that he cherished her.

He looked at the sleeping child. Sammy had brought so much good to Anne. Nick hoped she'd be able to remember the joy. He hoped that she would realize how much she'd healed and not go back to her isolated existence in buckskins and an old duster.

Nick frowned. Last night her duster was wrapped around Sammy, but she'd carried it away just then. Whose coat was wrapped . . .

His hand shot to the bundle, but instead of meeting a warm little body he felt the coat collapse. Empty. He jumped up and shook it out. He'd never seen the coat before, but more importantly, where was Sammy?

Nick spun and ran toward the washroom, but before he could get half the length of the car a man blocked his path.

"Excuse me," Nick huffed.

"Slow down, there." The man halted him with a hand on his chest.

The whistle blew. The floor shifted as the train began to move.

"I must pass." Nick tried to squeeze by, but this time the man deliberately blocked him. Furious, Nick looked up and recognized him.

"You. You're one of the hunters. Where is she? Where did she take Sammy?"

The train rolled forward. A quick glance out the window told Nick his time was up.

"Don't worry about her. Let's have a seat and I'll tell you everything I know. I would like to get my coat back, though. It was chilly this morning."

Nick sized up the man. He could force his way through him, but he would lose valuable time. Besides, Anne wasn't in that washroom. Not anymore.

The car swayed. Nick spun around, grabbed his coat and hat, and then ran full speed in the opposite direction. He busted through the door and leapt over the connecting platforms, startling a porter.

"There's a deputy onboard by the name of Joel Puckett. Please find him." Air rushed past him as the train picked up speed. Nick stepped around the guardrail and hung free over the track as it moved beneath him. "Find him and tell him Nick has gone after Anne. We'll meet him in Atoka."

"Don't jump, sir. You might not clear . . ."

But his words faded as Nicholas shoved off.

He took the landing with bent knees and rolled backwards, propelling himself away from the deadly steel wheels as they picked up speed. Unable to regain his balance, he tucked and took the six-foot journey down the slope with as much grace as he could muster. When he stopped tumbling, all he could see of the train was the tops of the cars as they sped out of view, leaving him alone with the sound of birds singing their morning greetings.

Nick bellowed out his frustration, silencing the birds. Anne's reckless actions would destroy every step of progress she'd made. If she kidnapped Sammy, she'd have to spend the rest of her life hiding. She'd give up the friendships she'd made. She'd give up him.

He wouldn't let her. He loved her, and whether or not she ever loved him in return, he couldn't allow her to start down this destructive path. Perhaps the love for Sammy that compelled her was noble, but she needed an intercessor. What he would do, how he would change her mind, Nick didn't know, but he did believe God had given him this mission. Perhaps he'd faced his own sacrifice earlier to prepare him for this assignment.

Where had she gone? Nick scanned the woods that pressed in around the tracks. Dense timber packed this section of the Choctaw Reservation. In seconds Anne could have disappeared in any direction, and he didn't know what to look for. Footprints? Unlikely on ground covered with pine needles. He had a vague recollection of a scout at one of their lumber camps talking about broken twigs and bent grass, but Nick knew finding minute signs was beyond his ability.

What did he do when he needed help? He asked for it. It'd always worked before.

He raised his head to the sky and hollered loud and long. "Anne! Anne, where are you?"

His voice echoed off the hills. She didn't answer. But someone else did.

"What's wrong with you?"

For the first time Nick noticed a shed built at the forest's edge. An Indian man dressed in buckskins like Anne favored stepped out and eyed him suspiciously.

Nicholas stumbled forward. "My friend didn't make it back on the train. Have you seen anyone?"

The man scanned the forest in every direction, much as Nick had. He swung a smoothly polished walking stick against the moccasin that laced up his leg. "You are going to follow this friend into the forest?" His eyes showed clearly what he thought of Nick's chances.

Nick pulled on his coat. "It's going to be a complete disaster, but yes. Can you help me? I'll pay for a guide."

"You find your friend on your own. If he

doesn't want to be found, he's not your friend."

That's what most worried Nick. "Can you tell me anything to help? I'm pretty sure I'll never find my way out of here alive."

The man nodded toward the east, causing the turkey feather in his hat to bob. "When you get lost and abandon your journey, go to the valley and find the river. Follow the river downstream to the bridge. Follow the bridge's road west and it will bring you back here."

"Thank you. Which way should I start?"

He pointed the stick. "See the break in the trees? Follow that trail."

"Is that the easiest path?" Nick asked.

"No, but that's the path your friend took," he said. "The baby should slow him down for you."

Nick slapped his dusty dented hat on his head and scrambled across the rocky ground to the edge of the forest. Did he dare imagine what Joel must be thinking? Hopefully he'd at least believe that Nick hadn't orchestrated her flight, but he had to admit it looked suspicious when they'd both disappeared.

Once he'd found the trail, Nick broke into a jog. He had to find her before the trail forked. The fewer options available, the better his chances of success. At least she was on foot, and carrying a baby. If he hurried he'd catch up with her quickly.

Round stones covered the ground, pieces of boulders that had broken and rolled to the bottom. He had to watch his step lest his foot land on one of the obstacles, but when he looked down, the branches swatted at him, catching his clothes. One switched him across the face, stinging like a whip, but he pressed on, expecting to see her at every bend.

Should he holler for her or hope to catch her unaware? His advancement could hardly be called stealthy. She'd hear him before he came within a half mile of her.

Hurrying, he held up his arm to protect his face but took his eyes off the ground. That's when his polished Oxford shoe sank into a muddy depression and was sucked off his foot. Without thinking, Nicholas balanced himself with his sock in the mire. The cold, slimy moisture seeped through his sock. Nick groaned. A gentleman should never have mud between his toes.

Bracing himself on a tree trunk, he retrieved the shoe and hopped to a drier spot. There was no way he'd insert the sopping sock into his custom-fitted shoes. They might be dirty on the outside, but the inside should be dry.

Nicholas tugged off the offensive sock, cleaned his foot the best he could with dry leaves, and slipped on his shoe. Lacing it up tight, he resumed his pace, although slower now.

The path dipped and climbed. It narrowed when branches obstructed his view, and it widened in private sunlit clearings. The rising sun told him that he'd been trotting along for an hour. Plenty of time to catch a woman carrying a baby. Either she'd left the trail or there was a branch-off he'd missed. Nicholas hopped over a clear spring. He started to dip his sock in the stream when he remembered he had a clean handkerchief in his pocket. The scratches on his face stung when touched by the icy water. The air had a bite to it, too, colder than it'd been in Garber. How did Anne think she was going to survive here with a child? How would he?

But a rustling just ahead of him gave him hope. "Anne, is that you?" The branches thrashed, but they still hid her from his sight. "Please don't run again. We need to talk. I promise I won't force —"

A low grumble emitted from the undergrowth. Nick's hair stood on end. The leaves parted and a fat black bear ambled into the

362

clearing. Swatting at the ground, it erupted in hoots and snorts like a bull preparing to charge. Salivating, it watched him with beady eyes almost lost in a massive head the size of a bushel basket.

Bear attack. Nick had heard advice before. He remembered a logger from the northwest who'd survived a grizzly attack. Praying that he was doing the right thing but too afraid to try anything else, he fell to the ground and wrapped his arms around his head.

"Get up! Fight it!" Anne yelled at him. She was there? But he didn't have time to celebrate.

"Get Sammy out of here!" He raised his head to look for her, but ducked it again when the bear charged. "I'm playing dead!"

"You won't have to play if you don't get up."

Sammy's cries mixed with the roaring. The bear hit him and he rolled beneath it. Searing pain stabbed his shoulder, and he smelled the bear's putrid breath warming his neck. He needed a different plan.

Nick flopped over and stuffed his muddy sock into the bear's mouth with his left hand, barely moving in time to keep the razor-covered jaws from catching it. He swung with his right fist, but the bear's thick fur muffled his strike, only angering it. He shoved both hands beneath the animal's chin and forced its head high.

The crack of a gunshot exploded, the sound ricocheted off the mountain, and the bear stopped its struggle. Blood coursed through the thick fur and dribbled down its snout onto Nick. Digging his fists into the bear's chest, Nicholas heaved it off of him and rolled to safety.

He gasped, his face pressed against the cold ground. What would've happened had Anne not appeared? How long had she been following him?

"You took your time getting the shot off," he said, "but now you've saved my life twice. Is being in your company always this risky?"

When she didn't reply Nick lifted his head off the ground and found her pistol, if not pointed at him, still raised in his general direction. Sammy's face had creased into soft folds of worry, and tears filled his eyes. He clung to Anne's neck and, with a last shudder at the bear, hid his face against her shoulder.

"What are you doing here?" Fear tinged her question.

"I came to find you." His heart pounded, unsure if he was safe yet or not.

"Why?"

Nick raised himself on his elbows. If he'd expected to find the breathless woman who'd clung to him the night before, he would've been disappointed. He knew better. He'd anticipated this warrior's appearance since he'd first heard the news. "I'm here to convince you to give Sammy to his family."

Her grim expression softened enough to register hurt. Her chin lowered, but she didn't take her gray eyes off of him. "You still believe I'm not a fit mother?"

Lying on his belly, he spread his hands over the fine needle-strewn path. "You would be a wonderful mother under the right circumstances, but this . . . this is impossible. Hiding from the law, traveling from place to place without anyone helping you support him or raise him — no. Not only is it illegal, it's also unfair to the boy. I can't let you disappear with Sammy."

Her pistol wavered as she scanned the woods behind him, listening to sounds he couldn't hear. "What are you going to do — yank Sammy from my arms?"

It hurt that she thought him capable of force, but of course that was what she expected.

He raised himself slowly, knowing he was a much easier target than the bear. My, she was beautiful framed by the greenery of the cedars, the fair-haired child and her authoritative stance casting her as some Valkyrie, one who hopefully wouldn't shoot him.

Nick worked his shoulder, wincing from the injury. "I won't bully you. What would be the use of taking Sammy when you could snatch him from the Hollands as soon as we leave town? No, I'm here to persuade you to do what's right. I won't hide you. I won't help you escape, but I want to be with you. I want to help you find the truth through this."

"You aren't going to fight me, and you aren't going to help me? Sounds like a thankless job."

"Sometimes the most important ones are." His shoulder burned. Gingerly, he prodded through his ripped coat and touched the warmth of his own blood. He shuddered. "I've never been attacked by a bear on the streets of Garber."

"Should've stayed there." Anne holstered her pistol.

Nick could finally swallow. "Why would anyone think it was a good idea to lie still and take a bear attack?"

"It might work on a grizzly. They don't want any challengers in their territory. If you aren't a threat, they'll leave you alone.

Black bears are different. If they attack, it's because they're looking for dinner."

"And I was making her job easy for her?"

Anne shrugged. "You wouldn't live long out here." She pulled a knife from her belt.

Nick's eyes widened. "Exactly how angry are you about last night?"

"Put your eyeballs back in your noggin. We need breakfast and there's some fresh bear meat available. I'm hungry and so is Sammy."

Nicholas was, too, now that he thought about it. Eat or be eaten. Life out here boiled down to two possible outcomes.

She set Sammy down beside her and didn't seem to mind his tugging on the bear's shaggy pelage. Twisting, she pulled her canteen strap over her head. "Seeing how you probably want me to cook for you, would you mind filling this? The stream you just crossed is clean."

"Sounds like a fair trade."

"I'll make enough to get you back to the depot on a full stomach."

So she was handing out the orders now? The reversal of their situation amused him . . . would've amused him had there not been so much at stake.

The pinecones made good tinder. Anne

367

blew gently on the flame until it stretched up to embrace the sticks. In a few minutes the fire burned steady enough for her to balance the spit of bear meat over the center. Crouched by the fire, she listened for what the woods could tell her. Birdsong was plentiful, letting her know that no predators were detected in the area. The pine needles brushed high overhead. The wind was changing. Finding shelter for the night would be essential if it turned cold, and it sounded like it might.

Anne rotated the spit and then propped the brace arm with a fourth stone when it wobbled. Sammy played contentedly in the dirt, digging up handfuls and then dropping them from high and watching the clay bounce on the ground.

It'd be hard going for her and Sammy over the next few days. Once she got to McAlester she knew of a place where they could ride out the winter — a crew of trappers who'd let her stay in their bunkhouse, but that meant skirting past Atoka, where the fuming Deputy Puckett lurked. Surely he wouldn't expect her to head directly toward him. As long as she stayed away from town and left no tracks, hiding under his nose might be her best option. But what would she do with Nick?

The bear she was cooking didn't scare her nearly as much as the turmoil in her heart. She'd trusted Nick, followed his instructions, and he'd turned against her. All this time Anne had thought her insecurities were their biggest obstacle, but when she'd set them aside, she found that Nick didn't want her after all. Never again would he get the chance.

And even more important than his rejection, she couldn't let Nick slow her down. That's why he was there, wasn't it? To delay her progress until Joel could catch up with them. If that bear hadn't attacked him, she would've never come out of hiding. She wrinkled her brow. But what if she hadn't intervened? A city boy like him had no business trekking through the forest without a guide.

He was bound to get hurt . . . and maybe he deserved to. He'd kissed her. *Really* kissed her, and it wasn't just a friendly exchange or even a flirtation. He'd seemed sincere, but he'd seemed equally sincere when he told her he wouldn't marry her — a fact he should've mentioned before the kissing.

Anne threw another stick in the fire. Marrying Nick had seemed possible. He was easy to talk to, easy to work with — he was even easy to fight with — but the kissing showed her that he wouldn't be content with a shell of a wife. He would want someone less damaged, whole, healthy. He wouldn't want a woman like her.

She heard him approach before she saw him — you'd have to be deaf to miss the limbs snapping and the pinecones crunching as he fought his way between two evergreens. How could he navigate a dinner party yet not know to walk around a tree instead of through it? She watched the fire, ignoring him for as long as possible.

"Would you mind looking at this?" he asked.

Anne turned and wished she hadn't. Naked from the waist up, Nick stood before her with his shirt and coat in one hand. He shivered once, sending an uncomfortably defined ripple across his chest. The goose bumps on his arms had the blond hairs standing on end. Much as hers had when they'd kissed. She hopped up and away.

"I will not look at you, you conceited fop. Prancing around here half-dressed like a pale Indian —"

"The bear scratch, Anne. Look at the wound and tell me if it's clean."

How could he sound so reasonable? Anne's face burned. She was already addled over Sammy's situation. She didn't need him multiplying her confusion.

"Turn around." She bit her lip. His stocky shoulders were just as disconcerting as the front of him. "Bend down."

"Can I sit by the fire? I'm cold."

Evidently he took silence for approval. Patting Sammy's head as he passed, Nick sat by the fire and draped his arms over his bent legs. "It doesn't feel very deep, but I don't want to leave any hair or dirt in it."

She shoved her hands into her pockets and leaned as close as she could from five feet away. "It looks fine the best I can tell."

Nick twisted to peer at her from over his shoulder. "Could you tell any better from closer?"

Anne scrunched her nose. The three parallel gashes were deeper than he'd let on, but they probably wouldn't need stitching. He shivered again. So did she. Might as well get it over with so he'd cover up.

She pushed her duster back so she could hunch down behind him. Sure enough, a couple of coarse black hairs were visible along the cut skin, and dark flecks of dirt were stuck in the blood. Anne eased her hand on his shoulder to steady him . . . or herself . . . she wasn't sure which. His skin was cool and firm beneath her touch. But she wouldn't think of that. She'd concentrate on picking out the dirt.

She teased the hair out of the crease with her fingernail, pressed the pad of her finger into the cut, and lifted the hair out. She picked out the more stubborn flecks of dirt and winced at every contact.

"Touching dead meat doesn't bother me as much," she said.

He chuckled low. "We wouldn't want you to get bothered."

Only then did she realize how tightly she was holding on to his shoulder with her free hand.

He tensed beneath her grasp as she dug deep for the last piece of debris. Satisfied there was nothing remaining, she released him.

"I don't have a pot to boil water in, and I can't afford to give up any of Sammy's diapers."

"It's already starting to throb," Nick said. "But I have a feeling it might for days."

"You'll have to get it looked after when you get back to town."

Anne emptied her canteen over her fingers and scrubbed them before picking Sammy up. She hid behind the child, not daring to raise her eyes until Nick had finished buttoning his bloodstained shirt.

Her mouth watered at the meat's savory aroma. Anne held her knife in the flames to clean it, and then sawed into the hunk of meat to see if it was cooked through. Finding a flat stone, she set the meat on the rock and sawed off some shavings for Sammy. The greasy meat wouldn't be easy for Sammy to chew. What a pickle. She'd just learned to care for a child in town only to find that providing for one away from civilization required a whole other set of skills.

She'd chew it up for him. Mrs. Puckett wouldn't approve, but Anne couldn't let him choke.

Anne sawed the meat in two and handed Nicholas a chunk.

"It's definitely fresh." Nick made a face as she ground a piece between her molars and spit it into her hand.

"It's not as tender as I'd like for Sammy, but it'll do." She gave Sammy the mashed-up food, which he immediately popped into his mouth. Nick had bowed his head over his food. She took another bite. Since when had he taken his religion so seriously? Maybe that bear had delivered hellfire and brimstone better than a brush-arbor evangelist.

He lifted his head and scrutinized her over

his dinner. "I was thinking about something you said a few weeks ago. At church you said I only followed God because I'd never been tested. Well, you were right. Up to that point, doing the right thing had always been beneficial. If you hadn't identified my misled expectations, I might not have had the courage to oppose the Stanfords." Holding the meat between one finger and his thumb, he bit off a piece before continuing. "You saw right through to my weakness, and it makes me wonder . . . what's God telling you about this situation?"

Anne wiped her sleeve across her mouth. "I'm praying about it. He knows what I want."

"But will you do what He wants, no matter what that is?"

"Why do you want to know my plans? So you can help hunt me down?"

"You did a fine job of caring for Sammy in town, but you had Mrs. Puckett to help you. You had a safe home and meals ready when you came home every day. I have to wonder if you'll find it as easy to earn a living and watch him at the same time."

Her neck tightened at the unfairness of his appraisal. She'd done her best to find a father for Sammy, but no point in reminding him. "I have savings set by. After Jay

374

died I sold the farm and invested some of the money in my gear, horse, and tackle. I sold most of that back to Anoli. Living out here doesn't take much money, and I have enough to last for a spell."

"That's what you needed to talk to Anoli about? Money and getting that brute to hide Sammy and help you escape?"

"You're the one who needs help, not me. So go back home before I lose my patience." The bloodstain on his shirt hadn't dried yet, and here he was pretending to know what was best for her.

She gave Sammy a last bite of bear meat and noticed that his eyes were already drooping. She'd fashion a sling out of her spare set of clothes and tie him over her shoulder. Hopefully she could cover some ground before his afternoon nap was over and he grew restless again.

"I'm staying with you." Nick produced a handkerchief and cleaned his fingers.

"No."

"You have a gun. If you could dispatch the bear, you shouldn't have any trouble getting rid of me."

"So I'd have to shoot you to get you to leave me alone?" Anne ripped another mouthful of meat off the spit and took time to consider that option. "It's no good. I'd be wanted for murder, and with my history I'd be hanged sure enough. I guess you're free to travel wherever you'd like . . . just as I am. But if you hinder me —"

"Sounds fair."

The sight of Nick disheveled and bloody didn't fit with the rich voice she'd become so familiar with in the office. The wilderness wasn't his realm, and it unsettled her to see him there.

"Why does this matter so much to you?" She took another bite. "Sammy isn't your kin. You don't know his family. What's this got to do with you?"

"I'm not here for Sammy. I'm here for you. If you make this mistake, you'll be a wanted criminal. You'll be throwing away your future."

"What future? I'm alone. I'm unwanted. Sammy is the only chance I have for a family or for someone to love. I understand if you don't want to be involved, but don't begrudge me his company, too."

She stood and kicked dirt over the fire to smother the coals. Why couldn't he mind his own business? Just like on the train when he interjected for that prissy lady. No matter. Nick would tire of the game. Already injured, he wouldn't have the stamina to persist. By nightfall he'd be asking directions to the nearest inn, if he made it that long.

Anne looped her canteen over her neck.

"Is it empty again?" Nick carefully shrugged into his battered coat.

"There's another creek just ahead." She pulled her second shirt out of her knapsack and tied the arms together. She ducked her head through the circle and pulled it over one of her arms as well.

She turned to find Sammy. Her throat clutched when she saw him in Nick's arms, but he wasn't fleeing.

"I promised you." Nick held her gaze.

Anne swallowed down her protest. He handed her the boy, and she wrapped him tightly in his baby blanket, tucking the ends inside each other until he was as cozy as a papoose. Then she slid his cocoon into the torso of the shirt, leaving the narrow laced-up neck lowered so he couldn't slip out. Nestled against her, supported by her arm but with his weight distributed around her back, she was ready to travel. They were moving closer to Atoka, and she wouldn't rest until their trail shied away from the area.

With a last scan of the campsite — the fire and the bear both dead — she placed her feet on the overgrown path and followed it until it crested the next mountain.

22

Never in his life had Nicholas walked so long without seeing another human being — the only exception being the slight form in front of him and the child she juggled as she crossed mile after mile of wilderness.

Sammy whined and flailed against Anne's hold. After a healthy nap he'd fought to be released from his wraps. Anne had freed him from the sling and from his diaper. It didn't take long toddling half naked in the cold air for Sammy to relieve himself, then she bundled him back up, but he wasn't ready to relinquish his freedom. Every step since, Anne either wrestled to keep him from shoving out of her arms or held his hand, allowing him to take his slow and patient steps.

Nick choked back an offer for the hundredth time. Even with his wound, carrying the boy on his shoulders would be simple, but he wouldn't ease her way. If she chose this path she needed to understand how difficult it would be. Besides, with Sammy riding high on Nick's shoulders, the low-hanging tree limbs would probably scratch him. They'd already shredded Nick's nice coat into ribbons. Twigs and debris tangled in the broken threads. His eyes flickered over Anne's form. Nothing got to her through her duster and her buckskins. As impervious as a coat of armor.

The fresh pine lifted his spirits. Hard to believe back in Garber they were announcing the winner of the election. The newspaper would print the official tallies. People would either be looking for him to congratulate or wondering how he'd lost to a latecomer.

What were Ian and Ophelia doing? Were they toasting their success with Philip Walton, or were they gnashing their teeth and planning his overthrow? Somehow neither scenario seemed to bother him from his current location.

Nick estimated they had only an hour or two of daylight left. How she could keep going while carrying her bag, her guns, and Sammy, he didn't know. Must be pure determination propelling her onward.

Anne lost her footing and slid backwards a couple of feet. Nick placed his hand on her back to steady her.

"Thank you." She didn't turn around.

Sammy waved at him and pounded on her shoulder, his emphatic jabbering making it clear he expected Nick to rescue him.

"Sammy boy, you hang on tight. Miss Anne doesn't need you making her way more difficult."

"He calls me Momma." Anne grasped a branch to pull herself up a steep passage. "And there's no use in changing that."

Nick took the rise in two vertical steps. "Well, Momma, may I inquire what exactly you have in mind for you and your son?"

"There you go again. I'm not telling you anything."

Nick grasped her elbow as she took the next step, propelling her further up the mountain before he followed behind. "Be as vague as you'd like — no locations, no names. I suppose you have family to help you?"

Her dry chuckle possessed no humor. "None that I'd call on."

"But you must have a lot of friends in this area, people who'd help you."

"The buffalo don't like the forest. They tend to roam the prairie just to the west. I've been through here a few times . . ." Her eyes followed the trail down the mountain they'd just climbed. "Are you dropping bread crumbs, too?"

"If I had any I'd eat them."

"Well you're leaving a path so obvious that even Deputy Puckett could find us blind-folded."

Nick looked behind him but saw only trees and leaves. "I'm just walking, trying to keep up with you."

Anne removed her hat and buried her hand in her mass of curls. "I thought you could tag along, but you swath a path as big as your trains and are just as loud. This has got to stop. You can't go with us. There's no way I can hide with you."

She almost sounded regretful. Could she still think they had a chance together? Could she ever forgive him for the stand he had to take?

"I'm not ready to say good-bye." Nick squared his shoulders.

Anne looked across the hills. "Then I'll send word when I get somewhere safe, after I've had a chance to settle." She turned to him. "That's the best I can offer, but we have to part ways."

Not yet, Lord. Nick wasn't ready for this showdown. Didn't God understand what a struggle this was for her? Couldn't He give them more time before requiring this sacrifice of her? Of himself?

With a lump of coal in his throat, he spoke words he wasn't ready to say. "I haven't always been patient with you. I haven't been understanding at times, and I've been wrong. You've matured since you came to Garber, but I can't play a role in this. You love Sammy. I know that. But if you take this child from his family, you won't see me again. This will be our farewell." He swallowed. "I don't want it to be our farewell."

Not a muscle on her face moved. He waited for the outburst. He waited for the dismissal that would rend his heart, but it didn't come. Slowly her countenance fell from defiance to exhaustion. "I'm not ready to leave you, either," she whispered.

If only he could run with her. He would leave the mess in town, forget the Stanfords and their cronies, and start fresh — but with the law chasing after them . . .

"I know it's painful, but I want you to be brave and take the hard path."

Sammy flapped Anne's hat in her face. She pushed it away to look at the horizon. "It's almost dark. We have to stop tonight, anyway. I guess our decision can wait until morning."

He'd take any delay he could get. "I agree. Let's set up camp, eat, and maybe we can figure out our plans from there."

"Sounds good. All but the eating part."

Nick's jaw dropped. "I've been hiking through this forest all day, and now you're telling me there'll be nothing to eat?"

Anne unscrewed the lid to the canteen and tilted it to Sammy's mouth, spilling more than he drank.

"We're too close to Atoka for me to shoot something. The train's been there for hours now. Your deputy friend could already be out hunting us. No use giving him a direction for his search." The charming slant of her eyes tilted even more. "So go on and rustle up something for yourself. I have infant formula to mix for Sammy and a few biscuits to fill his tummy. Besides that, there's not much to forage out here in the winter."

Nick's stomach growled. The knowledge that he wouldn't eat until morning, and maybe not even then, made him drastically hungrier. "I should've eaten more bear."

"Maybe there's one following us even now." She braved a grin when he looked over his shoulder.

The wind whipped around them, flapping his jacket tails and inflating her duster where buttons were missing. She adjusted Sammy's coat and looked over the valley spread beneath them.

The sun rested low in the western sky. At first Nick thought the bare strip through the trees below them was a river, but it was too straight. Railroad. And the bright flashes of light reflecting from the east were the windows of Atoka.

"If you think that you're going to slip away tonight to get help, you should know I won't be here when you return."

"I told you, Anne, I want you to hand him over. Otherwise there's no guarantee you won't take him back."

Her head dropped a bit. "The wind won't be so strong on the other side of this hill. I'm settling in. Didn't sleep much on the train last night."

Nick followed her, his shoulder pulsating with each step. How he'd slept soundly was still a mystery. Anne's despair at the loss of her son and her offer of marriage had both made indelible impressions. He, too, was pained by the devastating news. He'd imagined that the little boy and his surrogate mother might someday live under his roof. If it weren't for his duty to the people of Blackstone County and his conviction to see this through . . .

Anne began her descent. The narrow shoulders before him bore such a heavy burden. He ached to hold her, to comfort her, but he couldn't. Men had toyed with her before. And while the memory of her lips warmed him from within, their encounter had proved once again that she was fragile. Maybe she could aim a gun, maybe she could trek over miles of wilderness carrying a baby, but her heart was as delicate as a robin's egg.

Honestly, if he thought his love could pull her through the ordeal ahead of her, he'd offer it without reserve, but he was no substitute. He wouldn't insult her by offering himself as a trade, and he wouldn't base their relationship on a dishonest ploy to trick Sammy's family. She needed more grace than he could offer, and he'd pray that she would turn to God and find it. Hopefully before his blistered feet got any sorer, hopefully before she made a life-changing mistake.

The temperature dropped with the sun. The night would be frosty, cool even inside the cave they'd found. Anne hunched over and scurried through the low, wide opening almost on her knees, the kindling digging into her chest through her thick clothing.

More than burning the chill out, she needed the light to make sure the den wasn't already spoken for. Nick was keeping Sammy safely away from the mouth of the cave until she flushed it out. The man did have his uses.

The match flared in the weak light. Smoke, then crackling as she blew life into the small pile. Anne sat back and stretched her arms. She was so tired. Her back ached. She couldn't completely straighten her elbows. Even her feet hurt.

She'd learned much from Mrs. Puckett, and she wouldn't have traded that time for anything, but she'd lost the hardiness she'd always taken for granted. Even riding all day would probably wear her out in her condition, much less skinning a half-ton buffalo and handling their hides.

Anne roasted a pine knot in the flames until it caught. The low ceiling prevented her from standing as she extended the torch around the damp room, searching for neighbors. Out of a black corner bats raced, swooping near her in their flurry to find their evening meal. She switched hands, the torch already shaking in her exhaustion. Anne crept forward twenty paces until the dark corridor narrowed. She extended the torch through the dripping rock walls once she'd gone as far as she could, but she saw nothing that posed a threat. The ceiling rose through the gap and would hopefully draw the smoke out of the room. If an animal was hiding in the tunnel it would have to be small to squeeze through the opening.

The light flashed around the room as she inspected it, looking for further hiding places, but she finally determined it was clear.

She dropped the stick into the fire and crawled outside.

"Come on in."

Sammy staggered toward her the second Nick set him down.

"He's been fighting me ever since he saw you crawl in there. He's afraid he's missing out on the fun."

Anne grabbed Sammy's chubby leg before he disappeared into the cave. He smelled. She'd planned to rinse out wet diapers and hope they dried overnight, but stinky messes . . . ? She wrinkled her nose.

"Yeah, you don't want to breathe that all night." Nick fanned the air.

"The Indians use rabbit skins lined with moss. They throw the moss out and wash the skin. Not sure bear skin would've worked so well, but I thought we'd reach the trading post by now —" She clamped her mouth closed, afraid to look at Nick. She'd been so careful not to share her plans.

Not to give any indication of her destination, but she'd made a mistake.

"I can't believe I'm saying this, but if the cave is warm enough, clean him up, and let him sleep *au naturel.*" Nick's mouth twitched to one side. "On the other hand, after the mess he made with the fern in my office I'd hate to see what he could do stark naked."

His smile reached through her concerns and tugged her to a lighter time. She'd felt so helpless when she'd stumbled into Nick's office looking for aid, but it reminded her that someday she might look back at their adventures and laugh at what they'd been through. Someday she and Nicholas would tell stories . . .

She hadn't meant to gaze at him. Did her eyes match the wistfulness in his? Anne shook her head, clearing the cobwebs. "We're not that desperate. I have a couple of spare cloths. Would you mind gathering more firewood while I change him? We'll need enough to keep the fire going all night."

"Be glad to. Anything to get me out of the area when you unleash the monster that's fouling his pants." He strode off into the forest, his whistling echoing through the trees. Even injured, hungry, and tired he

kept his good cheer. Was she really determined to send him on his way?

Anne had to catch Sammy to keep him
from following. She found a flat place to lay
him and cleaned him with corners of his
diaper that were untouched before pinning
a clean cloth on him. After a full day of being carried he resisted her efforts to wrestle
him into his stockings. Where did the boy
get so much energy? She was exhausted and
he was rearing to go.

Much like Nick.

She led him by the hand out of the camp
a safe distance and let him collapse repeatedly into a pile of leaves while she buried
his mess.

"If Deputy Puckett has bloodhounds,
they'll find this from five miles away," she
murmured to herself.

But Sammy didn't care. He stood, reached
his arms over his head, and fell stomach first
into the pile of leaves again. Flakes of leaves
stuck beneath his nose. The night air was
making it run. Time to get him inside.

Sammy crawled through the opening, bel-
lowing excitedly at the echo that answered
him. Anne followed him and parked herself
between him and the fire. She fished the
glass bottle out of her knapsack and the
canister of formula. At the sight of the bottle

Sammy bounced on his haunches until Anne had mixed the water from her canteen with the powder and secured the rubber nipple. His eager hands sought the bottle, and he turned his head to the ceiling, pulling long draws of milk.

Nick's voice came through the opening. Thick logs were thrust inside. Anne bent to pull them in the rest of the way and clear the path for Nick, dragging the last of them.

"Nicer than some hotels I've stayed in." He straightened and cracked his head against the low ceiling. "Oww!" His knees bent and his hand covered his head. "That'll raise a knot." Nick stumbled to the fire and lowered himself gingerly. "Low ceiling and dusty, but besides that —"

"That's not dust. It's guano. From the bats."

"Bats?" He looked up.

"Are you afraid?"

"No, just hungry."

Anne's eyes widened, until he laughed. He was fooling. Good thing. She didn't want to sleep with the odor of roasted bat in her nostrils.

Sleep. She needed some. Her trouble had worn on her for two days now. If she had any hope of slipping around Atoka without Deputy Puckett catching wind of it, she had to keep her wits.

Sammy had emptied his bottle. He waved it as he got to his feet.

Nick caught him as he passed, wrapped him in his arms, and growled, much to Sammy's delight. After securing the glass bottle, he let Sammy wiggle away, but the boy returned, his fingers shaped into tiny claws to growl at Nick before pouncing on him.

"Be careful," Anne said. "He'll claw your other shoulder."

But Nick didn't seem to mind, and Sammy enjoyed the roughhousing. Anne found herself wondering if Finn's father was young enough to play on the ground like Nick. Would he have the energy to keep up with the little fellow? She bit her lip. Of course he wouldn't. That's why she was keeping him.

Nick fell on his back, groaning and laughing as Sammy pummeled him. He caught Anne watching them and sighed. "I can hardly bear the thought of not seeing him again. I can't imagine what it's doing to you."

"I'm not dwelling on it. Instead, I'm preventing it."

Nick was silent. He rolled to his side and prodded the fire with a stick while Sammy climbed on his back. "Do you think you'll ever have children of your own, Anne?"

In the firelight the stubble on his jaw looked almost red. The room was getting warm. Suffocating. She removed her duster, wadded it up, and reclined against it, keeping the fire between them.

"When I married Jay, I wanted to have a little family, a house, a kitchen. I didn't know much, but I had a general idea of what a real family with a ma and pa should be like. Sometimes when Jay was mean, I thought that if I bore his children, he would appreciate me. I thought he'd be gentler if he was a father. My own pa was rough around the edges, but he didn't hurt us. He left us to fend for ourselves, so that's the worst I could imagine from Jay."

She pulled a stick from the fire and tapped at the burning logs from her side. "There was a baby once. He wasn't pleased and turned real nasty about it, always accusing me of . . . well, you can imagine." The fire blinded her to everything else in the room. She'd never shared this part of her story, and somehow telling it made it real again. But maybe it could be real with Nick. Maybe if she lived it again but this time with his fearlessness beside her, maybe it'd lose its power. "I was at least five months along.

The child moved, kicked. It was a joy. And no matter how mean he was, I could talk to my baby. I figured God had brought me someone who would love me back."

Now she was jabbing at the fire. Sparks rose, angrily bursting from the coals.

"But Jay noticed. When he realized I was happy, he figured out how to steal it. He beat me, beat me good. Threw me on the ground and kicked me until —"

The stick wavered. Her throat closed.

"That was evil," Nick said. "Pure evil that he did to you."

"He was a murderer, just the same as if he'd knifed the child in the chest. After that I didn't care. I felt like he'd killed me, too, because I was as good as dead. He took the baby outside, but I found his body and wrapped it up. When he came back to the house, there I sat, rocking it like I'd lost my mind. Maybe I had, but it made him furious, so it was worth it. Even worth the whipping, because it didn't hurt. Dead people don't feel pain. But I couldn't stay dead. I wished I could, but I couldn't help but wake up in the morning and wish for something more. That's when I tried to run away the first time."

"And a few months later you had to shoot him to protect Rosa?"

She could still see the red spreading on Jay's white shirtfront. The shock as he saw her holding the gun. The hatred when he realized what she'd done.

"He would've killed her just as he did my baby." Anne couldn't believe the hurt could return as raw as the first day when she realized that the child would never know her. That the child was gone forever. "I promised myself I wouldn't care that much again . . . not about anyone. And I kept my promise until I came to Garber."

Her chest felt banded. Nick watched her through the flames but gave her time to decide what she needed to say and what was best left unspoken.

"I've grown fond of Sammy, but it's not just Sammy I care about." She dropped the stick into the fire and hid her trembling hands. "Nick, you've been good for me. I've wanted to tell you before we part . . ." When Nick's eyes darted away, she stopped. Had she said too much? But Nick wasn't listening to her. He rolled to his back and looked behind him.

Anne sat up, expecting to see Sammy playing on the other side of Nick, but he was gone.

"Where did he go?" She scrambled to her feet, her heart in her throat.

Nick sprang up, grasped a firebrand, and swung it around the cave. "He didn't go outside. I would've seen him at the opening."

That left only one other possibility. Anne's stomach twisted as she ran for the back corner. In the shadows she searched the wall, sliding her hands over solid rock until she found the narrow crevice.

"Sammy!" She thrust her hand through the void and reached as far as she could. Frantically she swept her fingers over the floor of the passage but felt nothing.

Nick pulled her back and crowded the gap. Crouching he pushed a torch through the hole.

"Do you see him? Do you see him?" How could she have let him out of her sight? What kind of mother was she?

"Sammy!" Nick roared, his voice echoing against the unyielding rock walls. Anne touched her ears with shaking hands. "Sammy, can you hear me?"

She listened, but there was no reply. Scrambling and pushing against Nick, Anne knelt at the gap to look for herself, but the torchlight only exposed bare rock. He had to be close. The alternative was too horrendous to consider.

Nick stood. He paced the room, made a

complete circle around the fire, inspecting every bump and depression. "There's nowhere else he could've gone?"

Anne wiggled forward. Her head fit but her shoulders were too wide. She curved them toward each other and was able to inch a bit further, but the space narrowed even more before the passage opened. Her arms were already pinned to her side. There'd be no way . . .

With a tug at her waist, she was jerked backwards.

"You can't." His breath was ragged, his face sickly white even by torchlight. "If you get wedged in there Sammy won't be able to get out, and I'd lose both of you."

Anne swatted at his hands. "Maybe the rock will give if I push against it. The hole might break loose, and if we can get past the opening, the room widens."

He caught her hand. "No. Use your head, Anne. You can't chip at any of these walls with your bare hands. The only way we're going to break it open is with pickaxes. But there might be other ways. Someone might know of another opening. I don't know, but we can't do it on our own. We need help."

Anne turned again to the dark void in the wall. Was Sammy wandering further and further away from them? Was he crying in the darkness, tottering toward a pit or a deep lake? She clawed at the unforgiving stone and called his name. She had to reach him.

"Anne." Nick's voice reached her from a strange distance. "I can't stand by and let his chance of rescue slip away. I'm going to town . . . but I'd like your consent."

23

"Do you know what you're asking?" Her legs shook beneath her. She couldn't believe it had come to this. All she'd done for Sammy, the daily care she'd given him, the unexpected love that had grown for him, and now her plans to carry him away — was this the end? "They'll take him from me. If there's any other way —"

Nick dropped the torch and knelt beside her. "I love him, too, Anne." He took her face in both of his hands and forced her to look at him. His blue eyes searched hers for — what? Acceptance? Forgiveness? "If I could trade places with him, I would. The man from Allyton, Anne, I know how he felt when he plunged into the roiling river, desperate to get the doctor. If giving my life would bring Sammy back, I'd do it. But to save him I have to get help. Please tell me you understand. Give me some peace."

They had to find him. Even if they gave

him to the preacher all wasn't lost. Wouldn't she find an opportunity to steal him back? Unless Finn's parents intended to guard his nursery window, she'd have no trouble reversing the day's events. Their custody would be a temporary inconvenience.

"Go." Anne gripped his wrists. "I'll light a fire in front of the cave so your way back will be easier."

The fear didn't vanish from his face, but he kissed her on the forehead and scrambled out the low opening into the night.

Branches snapped as he barreled forward, and then the sound faded. The silence terrified her. Was she alone? Was Sammy already beyond their grasp? She rolled onto her stomach, sliding buckskin against the rock floor until she could once again feel the damp air from deeper in the cave's belly.

"Sammy! Can you hear me?"

Her heartbeat was the only answer. "Sammy, Momma's right out here. If you can hear me, please come this way."

Not a sound.

Anne dropped her head to the rock. Maybe someone from town could help. Maybe they'd rescue him and then . . . and then they'd give him to the reverend and his missus. She scratched at the rock barring the way ahead of her, willing it to turn into chalk and flake away, but her efforts were futile. Unless he happened back to their opening, she couldn't reach him. They needed a miracle.

A sinking realization settled on her. She was planning a kidnapping, designing lies for the Hollands while Sammy was still in danger. Wasn't this the time to bargain with God? Shouldn't she make some desperate plea with Him before she decided to steal a reverend's grandson?

"God, there's no reason this boy needs to die," Anne hollered into the crevice. "If you're doing this to teach me a lesson, then bring him back. I'll do what you want."

Had she expected an answer? Anne realized she was listening for one, but why? Why did she feel that God was right on the other side of the wall, waiting for her to figure something out?

"Isn't that what you're waiting for? For me to give him up? Fine, then. Just please keep him safe. Lead him back to me."

The second her voice dropped, the silence engulfed her. What if Sammy was trying to find his way out? What if he could barely hear her? She tried to keep the panic from her voice. She didn't want to scare him, but every second he could be wandering farther and farther from safety.

"Are you hungry, Sammy? Do you want a biscuit? Momma will get you something to eat. Or I could hold you. It's got to be cold in there." Her fingers dug into the damp floor. "I know you're getting cold, baby. Please come here." She dropped her head; her anger boiled at the thought of the child whimpering in the vast darkness.

"What's Sammy ever done to you?" she cried. "Why would you let him get lost? It's not his fault. Whatever bad I've done, it isn't right for you to punish him. I thought you were supposed to be just."

No longer did she wonder if God was there. He was. But He was withholding something from her. There was something just out of reach, but she couldn't grasp it without His consent. And she knew attaining what He offered meant the world.

"What do you want me to do? Grovel? If you are who they claim you are, you know that I'd say anything to get Sammy out of that cave. You know that, so why go through the motions?"

A noise sounded behind her. Anne shoved away from the hole and spun around, but it was only a log on the fire that fell through the burnt timbers beneath it.

She'd promised Nick a fire to guide him. Leaning into the gap once again, Anne called for Sammy and then rose to build the bonfire outside.

Grasping the unburned ends of the logs, she rolled them through the porthole before exiting herself. The presence followed her even outside the cave, but she had nothing else to offer. The greatest sacrifice she could make would be to hand Sammy over, and she'd already promised . . .

But she hadn't meant it.

An empty promise wouldn't suffice. He'd know after all. But could she give Sammy up? Was that the test?

She stacked the logs and ransacked the fallen leaves looking for more hidden beneath. Sammy had been wandering in the dark for over half an hour. He might be gone to her already. She heaved the fallen branches onto the pile. If it was truly between his dying alone in a cave or living with the Hollands, then of course she'd rather he be safe in their home.

Safe? The word hurt. She'd spent three days claiming he was in jeopardy with them. She'd thought she could protect him from everything, from everyone, but just that quickly he was out of her reach. Safety had eluded them after all.

She surveyed the slope of the mountain before her, but she could see nothing through the darkness. Why didn't Nick hurry? Without her duster she felt the wind cutting through her clothes, bringing sharp pinches on her skin.

Anne scurried into the cave and half ran, half fell to the hole in the shadows. Pushing herself into the gap, she called his name, but again no greeting was returned.

She had no pickax, but maybe she could smash the way open. She searched the cavern floor until she found a loose rock. The first blow crushed her fingernail. She adjusted her grip and hammered again. And again.

With Jay she hadn't bent. She hadn't bowed. She'd endured living with him, but she'd kept a part of herself back. He would not master her.

And while Nick deserved her appreciation and loyalty, she'd never consented to follow him. She might compromise with him over her clothing or aid him when he needed an employee, but she'd never put herself under his authority. She would be her own boss.

And now, here she was again. The law said that Sammy belonged to his family. Anne disagreed. She wouldn't acknowledge any power above her own. But she had no answer that would bring Sammy back to her. Maintaining her independence wouldn't help him. And if she made a pact with God, He wouldn't accept any portion less than total lordship. Complete surrender to His will. No arguing over what He wanted from her. No negotiating. If she agreed to follow Him, she was giving up her rights. She was giving up control of her life.

Flakes dropped from each strike, but most were from the stone in her hand, not the solid wall she pounded repeatedly. Her options were vanishing. She couldn't even know that Nick would find his way to town. What if he met with trouble? What else could she do for Sammy?

Only one option she hadn't tried — one that she should've offered long ago.

Anne felt like she was tearing away from something — ripping her soul out of a clawed paw. This would be no deathbed conversion. No empty bargain. If she promised God her life, she wouldn't go back, even though she knew now what sacrifice He required of her.

Finally the tears began to fall. What if God let her down? But she'd already crossed that river. He was her God and this was a commitment she'd longed to make for years. She would follow Him. She prayed He would save Sammy, but Sammy's future was His to decide. God alone had the right to determine what would happen to the boy. And she promised not to interfere with His plans.

"Sammy?" she whispered. Her tears dripped off her jaw onto the rock floor. "Sammy!" But her voice echoed back unanswered.

She wouldn't give up. With renewed purpose she grabbed the end of a glowing stick and thrust it through the opening. The darkness devoured the light in every crevice, revealing little of its secrets. She waited, listening for any noise that would assure her that the child was near.

The fire popped behind her. A green pine limb burst, its resin sizzling in the heat. Leaves rustled just outside the mouth of the cave. Was it Nick? The odd sniffing noise didn't sound human. She barely had time to stand before a dog scrambled through the cave opening. The hound's ears swung as he spotted her. He sat on his haunches, unsure of his mission.

Nick and the dog's owner must be close by. The bonfire needed to be lit.

The dog got to his feet as Anne did, but instead of exiting he skimmed his nose over the ground and circled the cave, inspecting the area where Nick had wrestled with Sammy. He must have followed Nick's scent to the cave, but now he'd reached the end of his trail. A sudden burst of inspiration had Anne grasping Sammy's blanket and thrusting it beneath the dog's nose.

"That's right. Fill your head with this." The dog's tail thumped, then he trotted off to sniff the room once more.

"Good boy. Go hunt." But the hound didn't need her encouragement. She clutched the blanket to her stomach as he plowed into the crevice. Would he find Sammy? Could he get him out? Anne held her breath until the dog's bawls broke the silence. His bass voice echoed in the cavern.

"You found him?" Her torch wavered, but nothing was visible. The dog continued barking, and then . . . then a baby's whimper.

"Sammy? Sammy! Come here."

The whimper turned into a full-blown cry. The dog barked again, and Sammy screeched.

"Sammy, this way." Once again Anne held the torch through the opening. "Come here. Come toward the light, sweetie." She gulped the damp air coming from the depths before her. Suddenly the torchlight reflected off two sleepy eyes. Streaked with dirt, Sammy crawled forward and then sat down just out of reach.

The dog danced between them. Sammy pushed away from the dog and turned to go deeper into the cave. Anne gasped. "Please, God," she cried, now more certain than ever that His presence was with them.

The hound barked again, trying to alert his master of his accomplishment. Sammy threw his head back and yawned, looking about him as if to find another comfortable place to lie down.

"Come here, Sammy." Her pleas bubbled with joy at the sight of him unharmed. "Are you hungry? Do you want a drink? Come this way."

With a last rueful look at the dog, Sammy lunged to his knees and crawled through the tunnel until she could brush him with her fingertips and drag him into her arms.

Anne pressed him against her, covering him in kisses. She ran her hands over his arms and legs, inspecting him for injuries, though the tot only wanted to find a quiet place to finish his nap undisturbed.

"Don't worry. We'll rest soon enough, and I won't make that mistake again. No, the next time . . ."

Her heart wrenched. She cradled Sammy to her chest. How long did she have? Only minutes before the men found them. Maybe she should run — not permanently, just far enough to give herself some room and time so she could decide what to do. She needed to make sure this was the best decision.

Anne pulled on her duster and snatched up her knapsack, Sammy, and a torch. She stooped out of the cave. She could leave. She could. Without Nicholas she could travel faster and leave less of a trail. No matter what he said, she'd write him. She couldn't bear the thought of his disapproval. Given time he'd forgive her, and they could be friends, at least, no matter the distance. He couldn't expect her to do something as heartbreaking as to give up her son.

Anne's knapsack dropped to the ground. Nick was different. He might understand, but he wouldn't approve. He wanted her to do better.

But could she?

The dog behind her barked. Men's voices could be heard in the valley below, drifting up in the chill night air. She couldn't stay, not on her own, but she wasn't on her own any longer. She'd made a promise to God. He'd delivered Sammy to her arms. She must take him the rest of the way.

Before her resolve vanished Anne sprang to the stack of logs and stabbed the brand into the dry wood. Down the hill she saw torches. Voices, the neighing of a horse, and

Nick's urgent coaxing reached her.

"It's further on. Hurry. I misled you."

"Up here." Holding Sammy in one arm, she threw dried leaves on the flames with the other. "We're up here. Just a bit further."

Four horses threaded between the trees as the fire roared. The men stopped at the bonfire, staring at her and the child. Nick slid down and wrapped them both in his arms.

"Thank God. I didn't know if we'd ever see him again."

"I didn't run," she said.

His inhaled and his eyes held hers. "No, you didn't, did you."

The leather of a saddle creaked as the men dismounted. The dog pranced about them, eager for his master's approval.

"Good boy!" a bearded man exclaimed.

Joel stood beside the fourth man. Anne stumbled to the deputy and laid a hand on his arm. "I'm sorry, Joel. I'm so sorry. Whatever you need to do with me, I understand."

He patted her on the back and nodded. "Let's get him out of the cold. That's enough for now."

"Thank you, Lord." It was all Nick could manage to say, so he repeated it over and over. The guilt he'd felt when Sammy disappeared had crushed him. The baby had been right there climbing on him. He should've realized that he was gone, but he'd been so absorbed in Anne's story that he'd forgotten about the child. He ran his hand through his hair. Sammy was safe, but was it only temporary? The horrible story of Anne's breakdown was still fresh. The image of Anne rocking her dead child would haunt him.

How would she survive what was to come?

But she hadn't run. That was as big a miracle as finding the boy. When the time came, would she be able to leave him, or would she steal away again? He prayed that she'd be strong.

Joel eyed her nervously. Obviously Nick wasn't the only one who remembered she carried a pistol. The dog handler was taking to his saddle again, shouting encouragement to the hound for his good work. The older man only watched, seemingly content to stay out of the way. Content to hide his identity from Anne for a bit longer.

"Look at him." Anne lifted Sammy so the firelight illuminated him. "He was probably asleep that whole time. He found a little niche and dozed off right around the corner."

Nick cupped his hand over Sammy's white hair. Sammy raised an eyebrow and stuck his thumb in his mouth. "It's a miracle he didn't go further."

Anne gazed at the boy proudly. "So energetic. He could've kept going half the night, but he just lay down and slept." She hummed a sweet tune, rocking him in her arms.

"It's time we head to town." Joel stood with arms crossed.

Nick's eyes lowered. Anne froze, her song ceased.

"I don't suppose there's any reason for me to sleep here," Anne said. "I'll come with you."

"That'll depend," Joel said. "If Sammy's grandparents want you arrested, I'll have to comply. Otherwise you're free to go. What will it be, Reverend?"

Nick opened his mouth to protest, but the badge shone in the firelight and reminded him that Joel was doing his job. Anne had kidnapped a baby and eluded capture. Joel owed her no favors.

Before he could speak, Anne turned toward the older gentleman. "Reverend Holland?"

Removing his gloves, Reverend Holland stepped forward. "Right here, my dear.

We've been eager to meet the lady who has taken such wonderful care of our lad."

Anne sputtered. "But I failed miserably. He could've been lost —"

"He's fine now, and my wife and I would be honored if you'd be our guest tonight at the parsonage. You could help us get acquainted with our grandson."

"Reverend Holland," Joel said, stepping forward, "as kind as your offer is, it might not be prudent. We'll find a place for her tonight."

"At the jail?" Mr. Holland shook his head. "How could I lock up the woman who kept my grandson safe after his own parents abandoned him? How could I earn Samuel's affections when the person he loves most is barred from visiting him? I'm in the business of grace, Deputy Puckett, and while I understand the trouble Mrs. Tillerton has made for you, I think it was a journey she had to travel to get to this point."

Tears welled in Anne's eyes. Either the reverend was dangerously optimistic, or God had been working.

She approached the reverend. Slurping on his thumb, Sammy was too sleepy to notice her brave smile as she passed him into the reverend's arms.

The man's breath caught. He cradled his grandson and stroked his head with gentle hands.

"He has Finn's white hair, doesn't he? Those eyes, they must be his mother's, but the hair is unmistakable. You never know when God's going to replace what you thought was gone forever. What a gift — a precious gift from God."

He blinked at Anne. "And so are you. I can't wait for you to meet Mrs. Holland. What do you say we all head back to town?" He motioned for Anne to precede him. She found her knapsack while they extinguished the fire. Joel held Sammy while Reverend Holland mounted, volunteering before Anne had an opportunity. She stood apart, her face unreadable. Nick untied the reins of the horse they'd loaned him and went to her.

"Are you going to take him up on his offer?"

The moonlight splayed across her cheeks and lips. "I'd much rather sleep at the parsonage than the accommodations Joel has arranged."

"You can't blame him, you know."

Her chin lowered. "I know. He let me come with you, and I broke his trust. I brought this on myself."

But was she going to break their trust again? Nick wanted to ask but was afraid to. If she was weighing her options, if she was trying to find the courage to let him go, Nick didn't want to push her.

"Do you want to ride with me?"

She wiped away a stray tear that had only now found its way down her cheek. "You know how to ride? I never dreamed . . ."

Nick rolled his eyes but was pleased. Her teasing was a good sign. He strapped her bag onto the horse, mounted, and then offered her a hand so she could climb on behind him.

Anne wrapped her arms around his waist. Her hands rode flat against his stomach as they descended, the last in the line of horses and men heading to Atoka. When Nick succeeded in tearing his gaze from the sight of her hands holding him, he couldn't help but appreciate the vastness of the untouched forest. A fortune of lumber covered the hills. This land belonged to the Choctaw tribe, but who was harvesting it? With the railroad running right through Atoka, transporting the timber to the eastern market would be simple.

Inside his shoe, Nicholas wiggled his sockless toes. Had he been out here only one day? Blisters on his feet, bear-mauling marks on his shoulder, a knot on his head — roughing it was . . . rough. But the mind was a funny thing. Keep it busy looking for bears, following a trail, watching your step, and it doesn't have time to worry about elections, reputations, and etiquette. Even his collapsed business felt like a minor setback. Maybe that's why Anne did so well out here but had little patience for city life. *So you voted yes on a bridge, Nicholas Lovelace? She came out of hiding to shoot a bear and save your life. Which took more courage?*

And still he dreaded going back to Garber. Nick sighed. If he was going to stay in Garber for the duration of his elected term, he'd have to land a new contract quickly. Combined, his hotel fees and office rent were expensive.

He felt Anne lay her head against his back. He covered her hands with one of his own. Today held enough trials. His troubles could wait until they arrived back in town.

"Reverend Holland seems very nice," Anne murmured against his back. "I'm sad for Finn, throwing away their love to raise Cain. People don't realize how good they have it."

"Does this mean you're content to leave Sammy with them?"

Her arms tightened around him. "No, but

I'm determined I will. He has no business being carried through the woods and living a life of secrecy. God gave me another chance to do what is right, and I'll do it. You might have to pry my hands off of him and drag me away . . ." Her voice faded.

Nicholas tried to swallow down the lump in his throat. "I'm proud of you, Anne. There's no shame in doing right through heartbreak. Actually, there's an honor to it. Not many have the strength."

"You can imagine how badly I wanted to leave once I had Sammy in my arms."

"You can imagine how strongly I feared you would."

The steep grade caused the horse to stumble. Anne's head knocked gently against his back, but she settled into her spot again.

Joel rode directly in front of him, his posture never so rigid as when he was on a difficult assignment. Nick knew Joel well enough to know this was tearing him apart, too, but he wouldn't let on. The sheriff counted on him to do his duty. Which was all any of them could do.

The streets of Atoka were dark. Bedtime had long since passed. With a wave, the tracker broke away from the line and headed to the north of town. Nick stayed behind

Joel and followed Reverend Holland to the only lit house on the block. It was a two-story frame house — tidy and neat with church pews along the front porch instead of chairs. Room for lots of visitors.

Mr. Holland turned his horse at the drive. Sammy was still sleeping soundly. "We don't have much room, but you gentlemen are welcome to sleep on the floor. Nothing will disturb you there."

Joel's saddle creaked. "No thank you, sir. I've already got a room rented for me. This is considered county business, so they're putting me up."

"How about you, young man?" He turned to Nick.

"I think the hotel will suit me just fine, but thank you for the offer. What time can we come by in the morning?"

"The train leaves at ten o'clock, so you'll want to leave here by nine. Mrs. Holland will have breakfast on by eight, and you're invited to join us."

"That sounds wonderful." Nick tapped Anne's hands, prompting her to release him so he could dismount. His first action was to lift her down, pretty awkwardly, considering she was sitting astride in her buckskins and didn't need his help, but it did him good to be able to take care of her for a change.

Anne went to Reverend Holland and held out her arms.

He passed the sleeping boy to her and then swung down from his horse. "I don't know how you carried him all day," he said. "He's as heavy as an anvil."

"He does feel heavy, now that you mention it." Anne brushed her lips across his sleeping brow. "I guess I grew accustomed to him."

The hotel didn't shine with the opulence of Garber's, but the bed looked inviting. Nick's bag had arrived, thanks to Joel, but his ripped clothes, stained with his blood and the bear's, would remain on him for a little longer. He wasn't ready to call it a night.

The moonlit streets directed him to the parsonage, where he stood gazing at the house and wondered how Anne was doing. He closed his eyes and imagined her hovering over the sleeping child, memorizing his features, breathing in his innocent scent. That's what he'd be doing, and his devotion paled next to Anne's.

The front door opened. Nick spun on his heel, embarrassed to be caught lurking about.

"Come on over. You're welcome to stop and visit." Mr. Holland wore a nightcap and striped robe, but he smiled bright enough that Nick couldn't imagine that he'd woken him.

"I hate to take any more of your time. The day's events must have taxed you."

"I'm not all that old, Mr. Lovelace. Finn was a child of our youth."

"My apologies. I'm attributing my exhaustion to you."

Reverend Holland walked to the edge of the porch. "Is the hotel unsuitable? Our offer still stands." When Nick didn't answer Mr. Holland took a seat on the bench and patted the space next to him. "You're exhausted but not sleeping. Let's talk."

Nick sat. The reverend opened his palm to reveal a small rubber ball. "I found this in Finn's old things the day I heard about Samuel. Of course that was the same day I learned that Finn had died. I'd hoped all these years that he'd come back. He didn't, but he left us the best gift he could've."

"Sammy's a delightful child."

"What exactly is your interest in the boy? Deputy Puckett said you were here to assist him, but I don't think he is your primary concern."

Nicholas caught the ball that was tossed

to him. He bounced it against the boards. "Anne is a friend of my family's. Her story . . . well, she's traveled a hard road but has grown past it, and caring for Sammy brought about much of the change."

"Change that affected more than just her?"

The ball bounced again. "She's a brave, strong woman — too brave and too strong for her own good sometimes. I had plans . . . I still do, but when she asked me to help, well, she asked me to marry her in hopes that you'd let us raise Sammy. I had to refuse. It seemed backward somehow."

The reverend tugged on the pointed end of his nightcap. "Our love for Samuel has nothing to do with whether his guardian was married or not, so don't trouble yourself on that account. But am I mistaken to assume you'd like to make an offer of your own?"

"I lost my business this week. I'm going home to serve on a county board while trying to get charges brought against the judge for corruption." He squeezed the ball in his fist. "I don't have much to offer."

Mr. Holland studied him through a sidelong glance. "You might not be much, young man, but you're all she has."

Nick nodded. "She'll need more than me tomorrow."

24

Anne had expected to stay up all night watching over Sammy, but to her surprise she slept soundly, waking after the morning light had already illuminated the angular attic room. She sat up slowly, getting her bearings. Her pallet had been hastily assembled from a mismatched assortment of bedding, but it was clean and warm. A pile of blankets at her feet changed shape. Her first response was the joy she felt every morning when Sammy woke and gifted her with his first dreamy smile of the day, but then she remembered where they were.

Anne pulled aside the blankets, kicking her legs until they were unencumbered. The day had already begun, their last day and she'd wasted a goodly portion of it sleeping. She pulled on her boots and laced them, her eyes never leaving the towheaded bundle stretching and scrunching like an inchworm.

The night before she'd offered to wake

423

Sammy to introduce him to Mrs. Holland, but because of the hour and in consideration of her feelings, Mrs. Holland insisted that they go on to bed. A true lady, Mrs. Holland would be patient and wait her turn, knowing that Anne would soon be gone and she'd have him all to herself.

Anne knew they wouldn't change their minds. Not after asking a deputy to bring him to them, not after Anne ran off with him and then lost him in a cave. No, Anne would have to abide by her resolve. She would tell him good-bye today and return to Garber without him.

Footsteps sounded on the steep staircase outside her door. Anne scooped Sammy up, blanket and all.

"Mrs. Tillerton? It's morning." Mrs. Holland's hesitancy slapped her with guilt.

"Yes, ma'am." Anne opened the door. "Do you want to take him downstairs? I'll fold up the blankets and clear the room."

"Don't worry about the room, dear." She turned and began descending the stairs. "Bring him on down and get yourself some breakfast. I can't have you leaving on an empty stomach."

Anne followed her, relishing the arm Sammy had wrapped around her neck as he cuddled into her shoulder. She entered the kitchen, causing a flurry of movement when Reverend Holland rose and Nicholas and Joel remembered their manners in time to imitate him.

"Here's your seat." Mrs. Holland tapped the back of a chair as she flew by, her apron strings floating behind her.

Nicholas pulled out the chair and helped her to be seated. He bent over her shoulder and kissed Sammy on the forehead.

"Good morning, little cowboy. You have no idea how badly you scared us last night, do you?"

Sammy brightened, his legs finding their usual restlessness as he bounced. He struggled against Anne, ready to explore this new location, but she wouldn't release him. Not yet.

Reverend Holland passed her a bowl of scrambled eggs, from which she was able to get two serving spoonfuls while wrestling Sammy, a task she would've bungled a few months earlier. She clicked her tongue against her teeth, getting his attention and maneuvered a bite of eggs into his opened mouth.

"He likes eggs, does he?" Reverend Holland beamed at the boy. "Our boy likes eggs, Ma."

Mrs. Holland managed a smile, but with a

sad glance at Anne she turned back to the stove. Sammy grunted for more eggs. Anne fed him, hoping that no one would notice she couldn't eat a bite. She held the glass of milk for him, smiling at the way he tried to take the glass from her. Already acting so grown up.

Joel cleared his throat. He wiped his mouth on the napkin then laid it on the table. The parlor clock chimed nine. Nine o'clock already? Anne's throat closed up as she prayed for strength.

On weak limbs she rose, Sammy in one arm and her knapsack in the other. She laid it on the kitchen cabinet in front of Mrs. Holland. Her hand fumbled through her own clothing, scattering it until she found Sammy's things.

"Here's his infant formula. He likes cow's milk and goat's milk more, but this packed well for the trip, and well, you saw him with the cup. I don't think he'll want the bottle for long, but I have no need for it, so you might as well take it."

The glass bottle, so familiar in the Pucketts' kitchen, looked strange and forlorn in the new place. She tore her eyes away and looked instead inside the bag. She fished out his wool coat and smoothed it over the counter. "Mrs. Puckett bought him this. She had a secondhand coat of Joel's but she wanted him to have a new one all his own. She would've been here if she could've. Be sure and tell him it's from her, when he's old enough to understand. And here . . . here are his shoes. They weren't the sturdiest available, but he wasn't walking much when I bought them. He'll need bigger ones before winter is over. I'm sorry I didn't prepare better, but I'll send some newer shoes with the post —"

"There's no need," Mrs. Holland said. "We consider it a privilege to buy for him."

"Yes, of course . . ." Anne paused, uncertain of what to do next. She turned to Nick, to Joel, to the reverend. Everyone waited on her.

Sammy batted at the shoes, then seeing her troubled face he put his hand to her cheek. "Momma." He grinned impishly, but Anne struggled to return his smile.

Yes, your momma loves you, Anne cried in her heart, but in deference to Mrs. Holland, she left the words unsaid.

She turned and presented him to Nicholas one last time. Nick's red-rimmed eyes were almost her undoing, but she'd see this through. She had to be brave for Sammy. No emotional demonstrations to upset him. One last ruffle of his hair and Nicholas stepped away, leaving her with the inevitable.

"I know," Mrs. Holland said. "I know what it's like to say good-bye to your child."

Anne nodded. She feared her voice would betray her.

The reverend came to her side. "You've taught him what real love is. Some people go their whole life without experiencing it."

Indeed.

They were all looking at her, waiting. Anne gazed into Sammy's cherub face that was blissfully unaware that this was good-bye and wondered how much it'd change. If he saw her on the street a year from now, would he know her? Maybe it was better he didn't.

"And I do love you," she whispered above his downy head, breathing a prayer, a blessing, any last benediction that would stay with him long after the provisions she'd brought had worn through. One last hug and she placed him in Mrs. Holland's arms.

That was all. Anne picked up her knapsack and hat and stumbled outside, leaving Joel and Nick to exchange the farewells. The tears began to flow, blurring her vision. She pulled her hat further over her brow and careened toward the street, but before she could reach it, Nick caught her, spun her by the arm, and crushed her into his chest.

She threw her arms around him and sobbed, crying for every milestone she would miss, every innocent kiss, every smile that would belong to others. She cried for her first son that had been stolen from her womb and for every lonely night, past and future, that she would spend with empty arms.

And she cried because, for all her pain, she knew it had been her choice. She had chosen the cup of suffering instead of rebellion, and although her grief was acute, it was different because of it. Her tears were not of anger and frustration. They were healing tears. Tears that washed a clean conscience. Tears that invited God to comfort her instead of tears that accused Him and the world for her pain. She would taste sorrow for a time yet, but she had a peace that God would watch out for Sammy — that He'd trusted Anne with the child for a season, and now it was time to put him in someone else's care.

"The train," Joel said.

"Do you think I care about a blasted train?" Nick growled.

Anne laced her fingers behind his back and enjoyed the sensation of being held. This loss she hadn't endured alone. She had someone safe to turn to, and she had God to sustain her. She would make it through.

She looked up at her friend. Evidently his bags had been waiting for him at the hotel, because he had a clean suit and a fresh shave, but the creases around his eyes evidenced his concern for her.

"Deputy Puckett is right, as usual," she said. "We might as well catch the train. I can cry on the way home."

Nick wrapped a strand of her curly hair around his finger. "If you need to, that'll be fine. I'll be there handing you handkerchiefs the whole way."

As they left the tidy parsonage Anne glanced one last time at the lace curtains hanging in the kitchen window. If the Hollands were watching them depart, they remained out of sight, but Anne preferred to imagine them on the floor playing blocks or reading a story together. That would be Sammy's home, and it was better than anything she could give him, because he was with his family — a word she was only now learning the true value of.

The train rolled through the forest. No problem coming up with lumber for this section of track. The vast pine fields flashed past Nick's window, leaving him breathless over the untapped resources available in the virgin land. Someone would make a fortune here, and he wouldn't mind volunteering for the job if it weren't for the duties he assumed were awaiting him in Blackstone County.

Anne also stared out the window, but he'd bet his last dollar she wasn't thinking of the trees.

He nudged her boot with his foot. "I liked them." And he loved that she didn't have to ask of whom he spoke.

"Reverend Holland seemed younger than I'd imagined, and Mrs. Holland was so careful not to offend. They'll do right by him." She tucked her chin and studied her hands folded in her lap. "I wonder if he's destroyed their home like he did your office —" She gasped. "Nick, I've been so worried about Sammy I haven't considered what awaits you. You must be frantic to hear about the election."

He leaned back against the bench. "I'm not as concerned about the election as what comes afterwards, but being out here brought my priorities into line. I needed the respite. Bringing Judge Calloway and the Stanfords to justice is important, but I have to look past that. Whether or not they're convicted, I'll have to move on. Sour grapes won't nourish me for the rest of my life."

"Move on to what?"

"I'm not sure." Nicholas stretched his legs. "Molly and Bailey don't need me back home, but lumber is what I know. Maybe I could get hired on at a local operation, or maybe the Pucketts will be willing to take in another charity case."

The smile she gave him was more out of pity than anything else. Well, he was pathetic. What would people think when they realized they'd elected an unemployed ne'er-do-well? And no matter what his financial situation, he had to be prepared to defend his reputation. Clearly the Stanfords wouldn't kick back and wait for him to make the first accusation. Nick hoped once he and Joel got back and were able to get into the courthouse records, they could find evidence of their manipulation. Exposing the Stanfords wouldn't help him financially, but he'd have the satisfaction of knowing that he wasn't leaving unscrupulous men in power.

"I never thought I'd be headed back to Garber without Sammy." Anne's lashes lowered. "I swore to myself that I wouldn't give him up."

"What changed your mind?"

"Trust. When I realized what a gift God

had given me in Sammy, that's when I started to love Him for opening up my world. But last night I realized that I had to love God even if He took Sammy away. Sammy was never mine. He's been God's all along."

Nick leaned forward, elbows resting on his knees. "That's precisely where I've been. God's given me all kinds of blessings. It was easy to believe and follow until this county mess showed me what I was really worshiping. Was I willing to follow God through deprivation, or would I keep chasing the benefits I expected out of life?"

"Is God to be loved apart from His gifts?" Anne asked.

"Is He to be obeyed despite the consequences?" Nick replied.

They sat, eyes locked, affirming the truth they'd found.

"He's worth it, Anne. You did good today."

"I have a friend who'd already set a fine example." Emotion filled her eyes along with a message that gave him hope.

He watched her hands — well formed, capable, empty — clasping the edges of her old green duster. Nothing more than she'd arrived with on her first train ride to Garber. He was the one who'd had a turn of fortune, but the more time he'd spent with

Anne the less he felt the loss.

But what of her feelings? The clear light delineated her fine profile as she turned to the window again. He couldn't look at her delicate neck and imagine that it'd once been bruised and swollen. She'd come so far. Was it too much to pray that she'd someday love fearlessly? How about him? Would he offer his love even if he was unsure that she would return it?

Yes, she was worth it, too.

25

The braided strap of Anne's knapsack dug into her shoulder. Had the road to the Pucketts' house always been this steep? Her legs wearied as she approached. Nick grasped her elbow. Without a word he slid the knapsack off her arm and threw it over his shoulder — and she let him. Taking her arm, he braced her for the final steps.

She'd rested poorly in the sleeping car the night before, finding herself reaching for Sammy on the narrow bed and then having to wrestle the heartbreak when she realized he wasn't there. Well, at least their first night apart had been covered in prayer, because the early hours found her beseeching God on Sammy's behalf.

She'd needed the time on the train, a haven to tend her wounds and adjust her armor for the difficulties ahead. Despite Nick's inquiries, she had no plans to share. Without Sammy she could return to Pushmataha and hunt, but doing so felt like defeat. Had God brought her all this way for her to return to the life she'd left?

But what else could she do? Nick had been clear that he didn't want to marry her, and that part she understood, but then exactly what was their relationship? Yes, they were close friends, but they were too close. How could Nick court another woman while she was around? How could she make any decisions for her life if he was going to claim first right to her company?

Anne stopped before the house. As much as she wished for the comforting arms of Mrs. Puckett, she dreaded entering. No doubt Sammy's blocks still filled the basket at the foot of the stairs, and his little tin cup rested on the cabinet. She'd watch around every corner expecting to find him in some mischief.

Nick held the gate open, and before she knew it she was standing at the front door, grateful for his supportive hand at her back.

Mr. and Mrs. Puckett were in the kitchen, but when they heard their approach, they both rushed into the parlor to meet them. Mrs. Puckett stopped a few feet away. She gaped at Anne's empty arms and wrung her dish towel. Mr. Puckett rested his hand on his wife's shoulder as her full cheeks began

436

to quiver.

"Oh, Anne." Mrs. Puckett ran to Anne and swallowed her in an embrace. "I tried to convince myself that he wouldn't be back, but I couldn't give up hope. I kept praying that God would be merciful. . . ."

Anne's chin dug into Mrs. Puckett's soft shoulder. "He was. He absolutely was. If you could've met the Hollands, you would've loved them. They'd prayed for years for the return of their son. . . . I wouldn't want to take this joy from them, too."

Mrs. Puckett wiped her eyes with her dish towel. "If you say so . . . and I guess I'd do anything to get my hands on my grandchild. Still, it would've been easier if you'd never met him. So much needless pain."

"Pain, yes —" Anne found an unexpected smile tugging at her lips — "but not needless. I've known hurts that had no benefit. Loving Sammy wasn't like that."

Mr. Puckett cleared his throat and wiped his nose on his sleeve. "Well, it's been a sorry business all the way round. A sorry business this baby snatching and the election, not to mention —"

"The election?" Nick stepped forward. "What happened?"

Mrs. Puckett's cheeks set to quivering

again. Mr. Puckett rubbed his forehead. "That's right. You just got back into town. I'm sorry to tell you, Nicholas, but Philip Walton won your seat. There was a big push for him right toward the end. Rumors flew about you being in some sort of trouble and fleeing the state."

"Oh no." Anne couldn't bear the look on his face — the awful shock of an unforeseen blow. "You shouldn't have come to Atoka with me."

"I can't believe it." Nick's arms hung limp. His Adam's apple jogged. "I knew we'd have rough track ahead, but I thought the election was assured. I assumed I'd be fighting the battle from my office in the county courthouse, but now . . ?" His head bowed. He tilted his foot as if studying it from different angles. "I can't believe people listened to them. Where did all my supporters go? How could people change their opinions so easily?"

"I don't understand, either." Mr. Puckett's chin jutted. "If there was any justice in the world, Ian Stanford would've ridden a rail out of town, but now that you're back, maybe you and Joel can expose him."

"Without Commissioner Garrard's records at the courthouse . . ." Nick shook his head. "Walton probably already figured out a way to dispose of them the moment he took office."

"And won't people think you're a sore loser if you accuse your former benefactor?" Mrs. Puckett asked. "Especially when you owe him so much?"

"Harriet!" Mr. Puckett said. "Surely you don't think you're helping?"

"She didn't mean any offense." Nick grasped Anne's arm and ran his hand the length of it, catching her fingers with a squeeze. "I'd better go." He dropped her knapsack on the sofa.

"Wait. I'll walk you out."

The evening air had cooled into another frosty night, but Anne shuddered more from tension than from the temperature. Two months ago her only worry was finding a cook for the Pushmataha depot. Now she feared for Nicholas's business and his reputation, and on top of that there was a little boy in Atoka who'd be spending another night in a strange house.

Nick grasped the chain hanging from the front-porch swing. Anne slid her hands into the pockets of her duster. "After all the work you put into this election, it doesn't seem fair. Maybe the votes were tampered with."

The swing creaked. Nick straightened. "Maybe so, but it doesn't matter. I'm standing here thinking about how I've let you down, how I wanted to offer you more, but in the end it's not about my accomplishments." A glint danced in his eyes. "So unless you were set on marrying a county commissioner, we might as well settle the critical issue first."

Anne's eyes opened so wide they burned. He'd lost his mind. The strain of defeat had snapped his good sense like a fresh string of beans. Ever since they'd left for Atoka, Nick had thrown himself into helping her. Now, with his own problems facing him, he was acting as if nothing mattered. With a cocky grin, he rocked the swing like a pendulum. Was he waiting for her to say something?

"Surely you could get a recount. Once they see that the judge and Ian Stanford were conspiring —"

"Tomorrow I'll see what can be done, but let's forget about it for tonight."

"We can't. If someone wronged you, they must be brought to justice."

He released the chain, and she tensed but managed not to flee as his hands slid beneath her open duster and around her waist. Her lungs swelled with a bubble ready to pop at the slightest bump. Nick kept her at arm's length, but it wasn't far enough to keep her heart from racing. Considering that he'd refused to marry her, his actions were pert near inexcusable.

His blond lashes lowered. "I'm aware that reminding a lady of an unpleasant event is impolite, so I beg your apology in advance. On the train to Atoka you made a tempting proposal, one I wanted to accept but didn't. Now it's unlikely you'll have another occasion to propose."

Her mouth dropped open. "You rejected me. You said —"

His thumbs drew circles on the waist of her cotton shirt. "If I would've agreed to marry you in Atoka, you would've been petrified. You would've spent the rest of your life wondering if I loved you or if I'd only done it for Sammy, so I said no. Under the laws of negotiation I have no obligation to further consider that offer. It is old business. Do you understand?"

Anne clutched at his arms to keep from swaying and nodded.

"This is new business." His hands tightened. He winced and whispered something disparaging about a bear.

Anne noticed a dark wet spot easing through the shoulder of his coat. "Have the doctor look at that."

"*Shh!* I'm about to make another speech, and I expect you to listen to this one." He cleared his throat. "Anne, I'd like to promise that I could exchange your buckskin and canvas wardrobe for silk and satin, but besides the fact that you'd never wear them, I can't afford it, which is fine, because my love for you isn't the love of roses and troubadours. Roses wither and troubadours get hoarse. It's the love of an oak tree that will grow stronger each year. It's the love of Adam finding his rib, the missing part of himself, packaged in a breathtaking woman —"

"Nick, stop!" Anne covered his mouth with her hand. "Mr. and Mrs. Puckett will hear you."

He took her wrist. "I don't wish to embarrass you, although I do want —" He drew her nearer as a smile teased his mouth. "Close your eyes."

She raised an eyebrow. "I'm not your employee anymore, and still you're bossing me around?"

"Insubordination," he said. "We'll nip that in the bed."

"What?!"

His eyes widened and he chuckled. "Bud. I meant bud. Have some compassion. This is my first proposal. I'm nervous." Although his smile brimmed with confidence. No longer was he careful of her fears, but he didn't need to be. They had vanished.

Anne could tease him, argue with him, and would put her life in his hands. She already loved him. All that was left was to show him. And as he lowered his head toward hers she realized that she wanted to very, very much.

She stepped into his embrace, hungry for the feel of his body against hers, wanting him to understand she would hold nothing back from him. She was not a child. She was not an innocent girl being taken advantage of. She was a woman who wanted to share a healthy, God-approved relationship with the man she loved.

His arms were warm and welcoming, his lips sure and challenging. Was he testing her? This time she wasn't afraid. Despite her spinning head, despite her fluttering heart, she didn't flee, but instead reveled in the gift they were sharing and the promise of more to come.

Maybe having the Pucketts within earshot was a good idea after all.

Nick smoothed her curls away from her face and whispered into her ear. "Never did I imagine I'd enjoy kissing someone . . . in trousers."

Anne chuckled. "What the neighbors must think."

The curtains inside moved. Anne and Nick stepped apart and shared a grin at their sudden awareness. Nick took a seat on the porch swing, leaving room for her, but Anne couldn't sit. Not all stirred up like she was.

"How much work do I have to do?" He removed his hat to fan his face. "You are my friend — you will always be my friend — but I love you. I want more."

Anne wrapped her palm around the chain. "You're more than a friend, Nicholas. I think I've known that for a while but was afraid to admit it."

He lowered his hat. "You never need to fear me, Anne. I promise that."

She leaned her weight against the chain, causing it to swing catawampus. "Remember when we stopped in Pushmataha on the way to Atoka? I didn't tell you what Anoli said to me after you left the livery with Sammy."

Nick tilted his head up, the evening sky reflecting in his eyes. "I'm afraid to ask."

"He said for me to be careful. He didn't know if I loved you yet, but he could tell that I trusted you, and for me that was even more rare."

"You didn't trust me. Not when I kissed you on the train."

Anne's cheeks burned. "Even then I trusted you. . . . I just didn't trust myself."

26

Never before had Nick so appreciated a bath and a shave. He sloshed his straight razor around in the soapy water and then patted his face dry. Traipsing through Indian Territory was tough, but his return to civilization didn't bring the relief he'd expected.

Garber looked smaller, more crowded than he'd remembered. Before, he'd never noticed the constant noise around him — the creak of wheels, the rattle of chains, the boisterous voices urging their teams through town. Even inside, muffled voices oozed through the thin walls, hard-heeled shoes thudded down the hall, and the piano in the parlor was rarely silent.

The buildings trapped the day's dust — nowhere for it to escape. Same for the other odors that resulted from a mass of people and animals living in close proximity. Nothing like that on the mountain with Anne.

Except for Sammy's diaper.

Nick dipped his comb in the pitcher of clean water and ran it through his hair. How was Anne doing this morning? He could hardly believe he was engaged, but it settled his heart. Of all the unknowns, his relationship with Anne provided a spot of peace. It was right.

And he hoped the assurance of his love gave her some peace, too — particularly where the loss of Sammy was concerned. She'd think of the child every day of her life. She'd never forget him, but Nick hoped the memories wouldn't block her joy for the other gifts God had in store for her . . . for them.

Nicholas slid his arms into his coat on his way downstairs. He'd thought he'd risen early, but Joel was already waiting for him in the lobby, a doughnut in hand.

"You aren't going to believe this," Joel said.

"Ian Stanford's been arrested?"

Joel stopped chewing. "I wish . . . but he's coming in for questioning today. That's a first step."

"Seriously? That's more than I'd hoped for." Nick lifted the glass dome and took a sugar-dusted doughnut for himself. "Did Sheriff Green find something?"

"Appears so. Evidently he and Harold got to the late Commissioner Garrard's records before they were destroyed. They're trying to gather up Stanford's records, too. He's not cooperating, but all signs point to him bribing officials. Did you know Philip Walton's wife is now on the Stanfords' payroll as a maid — probably the best paid help in the nation?"

"Mrs. Walton's a maid? Didn't you suspect that Ian's interest in her was more than political?"

"That's the rumor. And I'm surprised Ophelia lets a woman that beautiful anywhere near her home — especially with Stanford's roving eye."

Nick shook his head. "You know, for all of Ophelia's faults, I do pity her. No matter how much money she has, she'd probably rather have her husband's devotion."

"I hope she doesn't try to earn it now. There'll be consequences if she's caught impeding the investigation," Joel said.

"Jail?"

Joel shrugged. "Depends on how much she was involved and how much she cooperates."

"I wonder if it's too late to talk some sense into her — convince her to come clean." Nick studied the shiny toes of his shoes.

"Speaking of women in trouble with the law, thanks again for your patience with Anne. She put you in a tough spot, and you were gracious to her. But just so you don't think she's getting away with her bad behavior, I'm making her marry me. Giving her a life sentence."

"That's rather harsh, isn't it? And without a thought for my druthers." Joel's brow lowered in mock agitation. "Now Ma's going to be all over me about being the last bachelor in town who hasn't found a woman and settled down. Nice going, pal."

Nick guffawed. "If it's helpful, I'll keep Mrs. Puckett informed of any single young ladies who are on the market."

"I'd really appreciate it." Joel's beard stretched over smiling cheeks. "And while I hope y'all are happy, if you're not, please let Ma know. It'd help my case considerably."

"I'll report every fight and disagreement — and there's sure to be several."

"Naturally. You need to be put in your place every now and then, and I'm grateful to Mrs. Tillerton for taking that duty on herself."

The empty cot pressed up against the foot of her bed. Anne smoothed the seersucker coverlet, letting her hand drift over it as she had so many times before when it covered the small, warm body that had lain near her. She wished Nick would come back, wished she had something to do besides fight the dangerous impulses that called her to throw away everything and go after the boy. Like an unruly dog she swatted down the temptation, only for it to bound up again and again.

Sammy is crying at this very moment, wondering why you left him. Nick would understand. He loves you. He'd come find you wherever you end up, but you can't leave your child with strangers.

She took a deep breath and pushed away the rebellious thoughts. She couldn't break Nick's trust. That night at the cave she'd been filled with peace, but now all she had left were empty arms and a terror that she'd made a horrible mistake. How had she convinced herself that leaving Sammy with the Hollands was best?

She startled at the knock on her door.

"May I come in?" Mrs. Puckett asked.

Anne stood and clutched her hands behind her back. "Sure."

Mrs. Puckett strode directly to the cot and dropped onto it. She gathered the blanket to her face and inhaled. "It still smells like his talcum powder."

Could she confide in Mrs. Puckett? Anne sighed. If she couldn't, then she hadn't learned a blessed thing. "What if I made a mistake?" Anne backed against the wall, then slowly slid down it until she rested on her haunches. "What if they aren't treating him well and he's miserable?"

Mrs. Puckett clutched the blanket to her chest. "You liked them when you were there, didn't you? What were you thinking when you left Atoka?"

"That I was doing the right thing. My heart was being pulled out of my body and trampled, but I thought they'd be best for him." Anne brushed her knee, even though her buckskin britches were clean. "It just seems like I should do something to stop the hurting. Why just sit here and take it?"

"I wish I could stop the hurting for you, dear girl, but missing Sammy is going to sting, no way around it. The only remedy for it is to offer your suffering up to God. The hurt is part and parcel of the sacrifice you've made."

"I know they don't want me up there hovering over him, but I wish I knew if he was doing well. I still feel that he's my responsibility."

"Go on and write to them." Mrs. Puckett lowered the blanket. "Ask them how he's doing. If I judge them correctly, they'll want to ease your fears."

Anne brightened. "I could, couldn't I? I'd like to hear how he's eating, if he's mastered handling a cup on his own yet . . ." She stood. "You don't think they'd mind, do you?"

Mrs. Puckett rose and hugged Anne to her side. "I have stationery downstairs. They'd be delighted to hear from you."

Was he doing the right thing? Nick prayed he had noble motives, prayed he was trying to help Ophelia, not gloat over her fall. A word of caution. That's all he had to say. A reminder that she could easily be caught up in this crime and be found a coconspirator.

Clouds obscured the noonday sun. Leaves chased along the street gutters, racing to tangle in the shrubs. A man paused from harnessing his team inside his carriage house to watch Nick stroll by. What had Ian said about him? What had transpired while he was gone?

People would believe what they wanted to believe. Once Ian and Judge Calloway were arrested, Nick's name should be cleared, but that wasn't his primary concern. His first duty was to see that the citizens of Blackstone County had an honest government committed to meeting their needs and that ruthless men were held accountable.

Nick stepped up the brick walkway to the Stanfords' mansion. How proud he'd been to receive his first invitation to their home. How important he'd felt doing business in Ian's oak-lined study. He never thought he'd come to the house under these circumstances.

The electric buzzer sounded when he pushed the button, an angry clamor that reflected the welcome he expected to receive. The door swung open. Theo, the butler, appeared. His eyes narrowed as he sneered.

"You have no business here."

"I have no business anywhere thanks to your boss, but I'd like a word with her just the same."

Theo's chest puffed out even rounder than it did the night Anne attacked him. "That's impossible. Of all the gall—"

"Who is it, Theo?" Ophelia descended the staircase, her lime dress flouncing as if she floated on sea foam. She squinted at the open door and seeing Nicholas, her face went white.

"How dare you!" But instead of retreating she barged toward him, pushing through Theo to present her hurt, reproachful expression at close quarters. "Is that how you show your gratitude for our help over the years? By sharing all your nasty suspicions with the sheriff? Without us you'd have nothing. You'd be nothing. And instead of helping, you try to ruin us." A vein protruded from her temple, angry blue even beneath her rice powder.

"I've haven't tried to ruin you." How different she looked now, as if years had passed since he'd last seen her. "This isn't about revenge. I'm here to talk some reason into you. You might find leniency if you'll cooperate. And we both know you're fully capable of directing this railroad. If you can stay out of trouble, you'll keep it running."

Ophelia righted herself. She tugged her sleeves down to her wrists. "Are you saying that you had nothing to do with these charges?" Her green eyes narrowed. Her sharp brows made dark gashes across her forehead.

"I'll answer the questions they ask me." Nick leaned against the fancy end table. He tapped his hat against his leg. "And I'm asking you to do the same."

A cabinet door slammed in Ian's office. Ophelia turned her head toward it, a wrinkle of annoyance puckering her brow before she could hide it from him.

Nick moved toward the office. "Is Ian here? I thought he was in town."

"Maybe you're right." Ophelia's voice echoed in the spacious foyer. "We should cooperate more fully with the investigation. We have nothing to fear . . . nothing to hide. And I should know. Ian doesn't spend a dime of NTT's money without my knowledge."

Nick's chin dropped. He should've known Ophelia would rather go to jail than give up her share of the credit for the railroad's success.

She turned to face the giant gilt-framed mirror in the entryway. The glass caught her reflection perfectly, her hair highlighted by the electric chandelier, the slight sag to her jaw nearly disguised by the high collar. And then there was Nick's own reflection peering over her shoulder, looking much younger than he felt.

"I was with him every step of the way." She gazed, mesmerized by her image. "If it had been left up to him, he'd have stayed in his office, chewing cigars. It was I who brought the right people to our dining room, got us invited to parties where we could meet investors. I even studied the journals, and managed to go to every contractors' meeting so I could make informed decisions."

She turned to Nick, all traces of her anger carefully vanquished. "I thought getting you the position with the county would help you. If I would've known you were going to object, I would've never put you in that position. I meant it as a boon, but Ian used it to ruin you."

So she was only looking out for his good? Was that why she treated Anne so poorly? Was that why she paraded Philip Walton around at a soiree meant to honor him? But this wasn't about him. This was about showing mercy while there was still time.

The door to Ian's office opened. The new commissioner's wife stepped out, clad in a stylish traveling coat and carrying a crate brimming with ledgers. Seeing him, she stood as motionless as the marble statues that graced the foyer. Only her expressive eyes moved as they darted from Nick to Ophelia.

"Come." Ophelia took his arm. "Let's let the housekeeper finish tidying up. We can visit in my office."

Tidying up? Nick's shoulders tensed. "That's a heavy load you're carrying, Mrs. Walton. Lots of thick ledgers. How about I take that for you?" He couldn't let Ian's records disappear before his eyes, but could he wrestle them away from the ladies? How he wished Anne was with him. She wouldn't hesitate.

Another tug on his arm. "She's doing her job. Let her be. I want to hear more about your plans —"

"But she's not dressed for cleaning houses," Nick said. "She's going somewhere. Look at her nice traveling coat, Ophelia. And her —" And then he saw it dangling from her velvet cuff. He pointed. "Isn't that . . . ?" Before he could cover his gaffe, Ophelia's keen eyes lighted on it.

An ornately beaded red handbag swung from her housekeeper's wrist. Ophelia released Nick. Her hand covered her finely wrinkled throat, and her chin went up. Her voice dripped with syrupy curiosity.

"That's a beautiful bag, Mary. Where did you get it?"

Mrs. Walton tried to shrink behind the crate she held. "I got it from . . . it was a gift."

Ophelia came closer. "A gift? Who would give you such an expensive gift?"

Mrs. Walton's chin trembled. "I'd rather not say, ma'am."

Ophelia narrowed her eyes. "I demand you tell me."

Nick stepped forward, ready to intervene

if necessary.

Mrs. Walton pressed her well-formed lips together and shook her head. "I can't," she muttered and dropped the crate to the floor.

The burn creeping across Ophelia's face in splotches was a disturbing sight. Her nostrils flared. Nick caught her around the waist as she lunged for the younger woman.

"How dare you carry my bag into my house! Did you think I'd just step aside?" she screeched. "You just wait. Where will you be when Ian and your husband are in jail? Did you think of that?"

But all Mrs. Walton was thinking about was getting out of reach. Throwing an arm across her face, Mrs. Walton hugged the elaborate bag to her side and sped past them, out the door.

Ophelia pulled out of Nick's grasp but stopped at the threshold. She fumed at the door, her stays creaking with each angry breath. Turning, she stalked back to the gilt-framed mirror only long enough to catch sight of her terrifying expression. Then in a fury she swept the Chinese vase off the table before her. Lilies, water, and glass exploded on the marble floor and embedded in the thick silk runner. Delicate flowers lay mixed with the sharp edges of glass.

"Theo!" Her voice rang off the vaulted

ceiling. "Theo, have my carriage brought around." She turned on Nick. "I think I'll take your advice after all and do what I can to help the investigation." Her coils of hair hung slightly awry. "You wouldn't mind getting those ledgers to the sheriff's office, would you? I'm in a rush to get there myself. I have a story to tell, and it can't wait."

She stood before the door. Theo jumped when he realized she was waiting for him to open it.

Ophelia stopped on the threshold and jabbed her finger toward Nick. "After I give my testimony I'll be looking for you, so don't go anywhere. I'll need your help more than ever once we get rolling again. Ian Stanford doesn't own the monopoly on success in this household. The NTT Railroad won't miss a stop."

She barged outside with her boiler at maximum temperature. Theo scrambled to keep up, juggling her parasol and hat that she'd forgotten in her haste. The door closed and the house seemed to sigh in relief.

Nick shuddered. How exciting her words would've been to him a few weeks ago. He would've jumped at the opportunity to help Ophelia manage the railroad, but his blinders had been removed.

Bending, Nick picked up a lily. He snapped the stalk, brushed the shards of glass off its tender petals, and pushed it through his buttonhole. No longer was he blinded to the bait and snares they'd laid before him. In order to open his eyes God had taken away his success, but he could finally say he was grateful.

One last look at the marble floors, the soaring arched ceiling, and all the symbols of power and wealth that had once so impressed him. One last look, for he'd never enter again.

The basket dangled from her arm as Anne wandered in the general direction of the market. Her rough boots scraped the hard-packed road. Her tear-stained letter to the Hollands rode securely in the pocket of her duster, but she hadn't had the nerve to post it. Would they think she was meddling? Would they resent her inquiries after Sammy? What if she mailed it and they never answered? What if they closed the door on her? She wouldn't be able to bear it.

The wind slapped her hair ribbon against her neck. It was a feeble gesture, but she'd thought an attempt at beauty might raise her spirits. Ridiculous to think a red ribbon at the nape of her neck would make an impression against her faded coat and battered hat. It definitely hadn't assuaged her anxiety.

She reached the bins of vegetables at the storefront. Potatoes, corn, and a bag of flour — that's all Mrs. Puckett had requested. Probably only an excuse to get Anne out of the house. She lifted the lid to the bin and grasped a rough, cold potato. Its weight satisfied. Solid. Something to hold on to. She was still holding it when Nick stepped up next to her.

"Hello, beautiful." He bristled with excitement.

Anne dropped her head, dropped the potato in the basket, and hoped he wouldn't notice her melancholy.

"What's wrong?" He frowned. "Did something happen?"

"Tell me your news. You're about to split at the seam."

"Well, if you're worried about me, don't be. Ophelia has decided to give testimony against her husband."

"Ophelia?" Anne raised her eyes. "Did she have a change of heart?"

Nick shrugged. "A revelation you might say. When she saw Mrs. Walton carrying a beautiful red beaded purse, she erupted."

"Mrs. Walton got the purse Ophelia wanted?"

"Yes, and she refused to tell Ophelia who bought it for her."

"It had to be Stanford." Anne whistled. "I bet she's hot. But if the judge and Ian are both convicted, what will happen to your contracts and NTT?"

"I don't know. Ophelia offered to honor my contract, but that's out of the question. I can't yoke my future to a corrupt operation. Even if the courts can't pin anything on Ophelia, she's benefited from her husband's unsavory activities for years." Nick scratched his neck. "Protecting the people from the Stanfords and Judge Calloway was my first priority. At least we've accomplished that much."

A lanky man with a handlebar moustache caught sight of Nick, skidded to a stop, and changed course to join them.

"You know this fellow?" Anne asked. Ever since returning, Anne had been feeling more and more protective. After the election and Stanford's lies she was watching diligently for Nick's enemies.

Nick turned just as the taller gentleman stepped up behind him. Anne grasped the metal rim of the potato barrel, ready to intervene if necessary.

"David." Nick nodded to Anne. "Anne, this is David Anderson, the commissioner from precinct three. David, my fiancée, Mrs. Anne Tillerton."

His smile seemed genuine. "Congratulations!" When he shook her hand instead of bowing, Anne knew she'd found a friend.

"Nick, I've been right anxious to talk to you. I guess you heard . . ."

His concern was touching, but Nick hurried to put him at ease. "Listen, the election is behind me. My goal now is to see they can't interfere again."

"But that's not all. The election results have been thrown out. They can't stand, not when Ian and Judge Calloway are guilty of tampering. They'll have another election."

Nick's face lifted. The potato in Anne's basket doubled in weight.

"Another election? It only makes sense."

"And you're a shoo-in," Commissioner Anderson said. "Once the story is out people will be falling over themselves to elect the right man."

"After Garrard and Walton we need someone new, but I'm not sure I have another charge in me."

Still, his eyes sparkled at the thought.

Anne felt Commissioner Anderson's gaze on her. She straightened her shoulders and lifted her chin. "I need to go. Mrs. Puckett is waiting on her groceries."

Nick caught the basket handle. "You have to pay for them first."

Of course. She selected some more potatoes and shuffled inside, but not before she heard Nick ask, "When will candidates be able to apply?"

Anne lifted her basket onto the countertop inside and let the clerk unload the potatoes to the scale while she selected some ears of corn from a bushel nearby. For a woman newly engaged to the man she adored, she was dragging. Another election? As his fiancée how many dinners would she have to attend? And if he won, how many functions would she preside over? Anne placed the corn on the counter and watched the needle of the scale bounce before settling. When Nick proposed he'd already lost the election. She'd never considered that he might have another chance. Anne pointed to a bag of flour. The clerk scratched some numbers on a pad and did some quick math.

Was the heart of her trouble Nick's political ambitions or the loss of Sammy? As much as she loved Nick, as much as she enjoyed being loved by him, she still sifted through a heavy fog of sorrow. What she'd had a week ago, what she'd been forced to give up, felt tangibly more real than whatever vague future they'd have together. Maybe this commissioner race was a first step. They needed something to look forward to. Their plans needed one solid hope.

Nick waited for her at the door. He took the basket. "Where are you headed now?"

She shrugged, not looking up.

He didn't move. His soft leather shoes didn't budge.

"Excuse me." The woman carried a child at her hip. Its gown rode up, exposing perfectly plump limbs above high-laced booties.

"I beg your pardon." Nick took Anne's arm and escorted her out of the doorway.

Over her shoulder she got a last glance before the child disappeared into the store. She couldn't go back to the Pucketts'. Not yet. Not when every corner still rang with his laughter and every room still echoed with his footsteps. Instead, she took the street to the edge of town where the river swooped near. She needed space, and Nick wasn't giving her much.

"You're not excited about the prospect of my running for office again." Nick strolled at her side.

Anne looked ahead. The river brought a nice touch of green to the otherwise barren town. Soon a bridge would span it and the people of Allyton —

"Anne, I'm speaking to you. We have some big decisions to make, so I'd like your opinion. I might not be able to honor it, but I want to know, just the same."

She walked past him to the trees, yearning to stand beneath something that had survived much longer than she had. "Why, if it makes no matter?"

"It matters. It's not *all* that matters, but it matters." He set the basket at the foot of a tree and crossed his arms. "Were you disappointed when I lost the election?"

"I was sad. It meant so much to you. . . ." And maybe it still did. She sighed. "I'm not being fair. Don't pay me any mind. I just feel like something's missing."

"Something? You mean someone?"

She didn't answer. Nick gently took her hand. "It's been a difficult day for you. All my plotting and planning hasn't lessened your burden."

The wind caught a rebellious lock of Nicholas's hair untamed by his morning's grooming. Anne licked her finger and smoothed it. "I've never been in the Pucketts' house without him. I keep thinking he's upstairs asleep. I keep expecting him to come around the corner . . ."

"Do you blame me?"

"Not at all. It has to be this way, I know. And with time it won't hurt as bad — but it's not that time yet."

He drew her close and pressed his chin against the top of her hat, or maybe it was a kiss, she couldn't tell.

"Truthfully, I came back to Garber for one reason — to clear up this mess. I was obligated to serve if elected, but I don't need Garber to succeed." He stepped back, his eyes following the path of the river. "When I first got started I didn't care what I was successful at, just as long as I achieved. This time I'm going to be more particular. I like being the boss — no surprise to you. I like dealing with crews, lumber, shipping. I know the railroad business, but that's not the only game in town."

"Town? So are we staying in Garber?"

"No. I have some ideas, but none of them involve us living here. I'd rather start somewhere new. Somewhere fresh for both of us. Truthfully, I can't stop thinking about that dense forest around Atoka."

Anne's throat closed. "Atoka? We could move there?"

His smile was wide. "I hope you will, because that's where I'm headed, and a giant saw won't keep me company."

She didn't know what to say, what to do, but he seemed to enjoy her floundering. "We would . . . we could see Sammy?"

"Before we left, Reverend Holland invited us back anytime. He even mentioned a place for lease by the river where one could start a lumber mill. It's not in town, mind you —"

"But they wouldn't care if we visited Sammy?" Her fingers dug into his hand.

"They encouraged it."

Anne wasted no more time and threw herself at him. She clutched the back of his head, knocking his hat off. She kissed him, laughed, and kissed him again. "I would've gone anywhere with you. You didn't have to do this."

"My life here is closed, and I can think of no place I'd rather start anew, but it's not too late. If you'd rather stay —"

Anne didn't allow him to complete the thought before sealing his lips with yet another kiss.

27

The sight of her husband in his Sunday-go-to-meeting clothes always gave Anne's heart a turn. More time in the mill yard that spring had heightened the gold in his hair and bronzed his skin. Had he much use for his suit coats, she would've let them out, but wearing them only once a week, he claimed not to mind the way they strained across his shoulders.

"They should be here any moment. How do I look?" Nick held his hands apart.

Anne wiped the side of the brimming gravy boat. "As if you didn't look in the mirror already."

"I enjoy my wife's praise more than my own reflection."

"In that case, you are one handsome devil, and it's fortunate that I have you out here in the woods to myself, else I'd be getting into scrapes with all the girls."

He smiled and turned to the window to admire the stacks of pine boards lining the mill yard. "I don't miss the view from my office one bit."

"Or the rickety staircase?" Anne set the gravy boat on the table and opened the box of silverware — a wedding gift from Weston and Rosa Garner.

"Harold says the new staircase is holding up just fine, which is a blessing. I wouldn't want something to happen to Garber's favorite county commissioner."

"It could've been you," she said. "Are you sorry you left?"

"Not for a moment." Nick eased the silverware box away from her. Just as well. He had a better idea of how a place setting should look. Anne went on to slice the ham instead.

Outside their dog barked.

"Quiet down, Rex," Anne called out the window to the puppy. The Hollands must be arriving. She scanned her kitchen one last time. Orderly. Simple. Their good china graced the table. The food filled the house with delicious aromas. The only extravagance in their temporary home was the Glenwood Grand stove that they would move to their new house when it was finished.

"You look beautiful." Nick wrapped his arms around her and untied the apron strings behind her back. She ducked as he lifted the neck strap over her head, trying not to let it snag on the gold brooch pinned to her lace collar. Nick handled her carefully, probably more because of the fancy French twist she'd forced her curly hair into than for her delicate condition.

Merry voices flooded through the open windows.

"Sammy, there's Rex," Reverend Holland boomed. "That little mutt loves you."

Mrs. Holland *tsk*ed. "Don't let it jump up on you, Sammy. You're all clean."

Anne waited patiently by the stove for her favorite moment. Every time Sammy came to visit, he always looked to that spot first. He expected Anne to be there, and she didn't want to disappoint him.

The door burst open. Sammy shoved off his hat, tossed it to the floor, and headed straight to her. No more toddling now, he ran to Anne and collapsed against her knees.

"Auntie! Auntie!"

She knelt, kissing him on both cheeks. "Hello, Sammy. How's Aunt Annie's big boy?"

"I want the dog." He pointed behind him and grinned. "Can the dog come in?"

"No." Mrs. Holland pulled the door shut behind her. "The dog stays outside. I don't want it to steal any of Aunt Annie's delicious food."

"Your ma is right." Anne picked him up, lifted the pump handle, and swished a bar of soap over his grasping fingers. My, how he'd grown. "Rex gets enough scraps, as it is."

"I don't have to preach today, do I, Nicholas?" Reverend Holland shook Nick's hand. "You being all spiffed up has got me confused."

Nicholas waited for Anne to deposit Sammy into his chair and for their guests to be seated before he took his place at the head of the table. "Today is a special occasion," he said.

Anne's face warmed as she arranged her skirts, even though she had nothing to be embarrassed about.

"A special occasion?" Mrs. Holland tied a bib around Sammy's neck. "Do tell. I love surprises."

What was Nicholas waiting for? Oh. His hand was outstretched above the china, waiting for hers before continuing. She hesitated and then met his grasp. Her other hand touched the gold brooch, a gift from Nick's parents. By next week they'd get the letter, and then everyone in Prairie Lea would know. Maybe Molly and Mrs. Puckett would come up to be with her when the time came.

Nick cleared his throat. "As the only family we have in the area, we wanted you here to celebrate our joyful announcement."

But he never got to make it, because judging from the Hollands' pleased cries, they'd guessed it already.

"How marvelous," Mrs. Holland cried. "When?"

"I hope it's a boy," Reverend Holland said. "What fun Sammy and he will have together."

Amid the happy questions, Sammy tugged on Mrs. Holland's sleeve and asked why no one was serving the food set before him.

How different his life would've been had Anne run away with him. She didn't like to think about it, knowing how close she'd come to denying him this family.

How close she'd come to losing it herself.

Anne looked around the little room filled with the people she loved. Not everyone she loved was there, but she enjoyed the thought that they had happy rooms of their own. All over the world there were families deciding to care about one another and encourage one another along the paths God had given them. She'd always wanted to be included in one of those circles, and although she'd never thought she would have this much, it now looked like God might give her even more.

ABOUT THE AUTHOR

Regina Jennings is a graduate of Oklahoma Baptist University with a degree in English and a history minor. She has worked at *The Mustang News* and First Baptist Church of Mustang, along with time at the Oklahoma National Stockyards and various livestock shows. She now lives outside Oklahoma City with her husband and four children.